Second Place
SISTER

SUE HORNER

Second Place Sister

ISBN 978-0-9912177-0-0

Library of Congress Control Number: 2014910209

Published by: ROSU Publishing
Roswell, GA USA

Acknowledgments

I am grateful to many people for their support and guidance, including Christina Ranallo: An inspirational professional story coach. She is creative director of Penpaperwrite. When Christina formed WriteGroup consisting of Mary Helen Witten, Kerith Stull, Karen McGoldrick, and Anthony Gilmore she invited me to join. We met faithfully for a year reading each others' works and offering constructive and gentle comments.

Mary Helen Witten: When the WriteGroup disbanded, Mary Helen took the lead and formed another group including Kerith and me. We welcomed brilliant Jason van Gumster. I'm grateful to Mary Helen for always "getting" my sense of humor and encouraging me to continue my goal of finishing the manuscript.

Wayne South Smith: He is a gifted writing coach, content editor, speaker, and writer.

Linda Hines: She is an outstanding writing coach who contributed significantly. I'm grateful for her patience and wit.

Debbie Gsell: She found time in her packed schedule to read the manuscript several times, and spent countless hours on the phone offering helpful and perceptive critiques.

Margee Chesson: Along with Debbie, Margee read my first chapters. She encouraged and supported me. Margee has countless friends because she knows how to be a friend.

Pat Armgard: She read one of the early drafts and made observant notes. Pat is a member of the real Book Babes.

Jill Horner Weisenberger, my younger sister: The only similarity between my character Janelle Jennings and Jill is that both were prom queens. My sister sets the standard for a loving sibling. Thank you, Jill, for reading my manuscript while we enjoyed the beach on Sanibel Island, Florida.

I owe immense gratitude to my dear husband who took me seriously when I said, "Please don't bother me, I'm writing." He read several drafts, always offering keen observations. I love you, Roland.

Chapter 1

Willoughby, GA – Daphne Bailer Dwyer, 89, passed away yesterday surrounded by her loving family, which included an assortment of rescued greyhounds and crippled cats. She asked to be buried wearing her beloved Atlanta Braves cap while clutching her secret lemon meringue pie recipe. "I'm taking my recipe to the grave," was a frequent comment by Mrs. Dwyer.

Ali Lawrence's friends and family thought her daily habit of reading the obituaries in the *Willoughby News & Record* was quirky. Ali disagreed. She believed citizens of a town were obliged to read about their residents, known or unknown. Sometimes the only public recognition a person received in his or her lifetime was the obituary.

"Did you read the one about Mrs. Dwyer?" Ali's best friend Ellen asked. "You could have written a better one."

"Ah, well, I did write that one."

Ali often discovered that a person who led an unassuming life had been a decorated wartime hero or an advocate for homeless families. The local obituary revealed much about the virtues and character

1

of a town's citizens, according to Ali. "If more people would read obituaries, maybe they would be motivated to live better lives," she often opined.

Years ago, when Ali applied for an internship with a public relations firm, she was asked to write her own obit. "Tell me your goals and make me laugh," the instructions informed her. She thought for a few moments and then wrote:

> *Willoughby, GA – Alicia Maureen Withrow McCormick Puterbagh Wilkerson, 95, died while typing her 100th novel. Investigators found her frail arthritic body hunched over an IBM Selectric while she sat at her kitchen table. The coroner estimated that Mrs. Wilkerson died two days before the discovery of her body. Mrs. Wilkerson's housekeeper of fifty years, Ella Mae Browning, said she didn't notice anything unusual even though rigor mortis had set in. "Mrs. Wilkerson always slumped over that machine."*

Ali was hired.

***

The cell phone buzzed in the pocket of Ali's jogging shorts. She held the phone at arm's length so she could read the caller ID. *Why ruin a lovely spring morning with a call from the famous Janelle Jennings, even if she is my only sibling.* She let the call go to voice mail.

The white wicker rocker on 2323 Plum Court's wraparound porch beckoned, but seemed miles away. Even Roxie, the family's miniature schnauzer, was dragging. Without husband Matt's prodding, Ali would have stayed in bed for another hour. She breathed a sigh of relief as she approached her porch. Her legs ached from walking the two miles to Willoughby Park and back, and she regretted not bringing a water bottle. When she plopped down in the rocker, she noticed paint peeling on the columns that rose to the ceiling. She meant to begin scraping the mess. Now the chore languished at number twenty-nine on her to-do list. Ali shed her ancient walking shoes, pulled off her socks, and rubbed her aching feet. She tossed her red and navy blue Braves cap on an adjacent chair, slid the scrunchie from her ponytail, and shook her mass of curly frizz, which was as red as the brim of her cap.

Ali surveyed yellow and white daffodil sentries in her front yard and that of her neighbor's across the street. The green-and-white-striped hostas her mother, Virginia Withrow, had planted for her last year were showing signs of emerging. Regal royal-blue irises, another of her mother's additions, bloomed in the side yard adding a fruity aroma to the spring air. Roxie found a sunny spot on the front lawn to take a snooze, but a scampering gray squirrel interrupted her nap time.

Ali loved their modest three-bedroom 1950s-era house. Twenty years ago, as newlyweds, she and Matt had often walked the side streets of Willoughby Lane, admiring the charm and architecture of the neighborhood. "Some day we'll live in one of these houses," Matt said, smiling down at her.

"That's the one I want." Ali pointed to 2323 Plum Court. When the house became available three years after they were married, they pounced on it even though the mortgage payments stretched their paychecks. They had followed a strict budget that precluded dining out and eliminated vacations. The new homeowners agreed that the small sacrifices were sensible in order to have their dream home.

Ali especially enjoyed sitting on the front porch admiring her garden. Well, not exactly *her* garden. Her mother presided over the planting and caring of the palette of vibrant flowers. At least once a week, Virginia would arrive to observe, trim, or critique her daughter's ability to maintain the garden. She wouldn't want her friends in the Willoughby Garden Club to think her daughter didn't know a weed from a sunflower.

"You're falling down on the job, Alicia," her mother commented last week. "You need to weed and water, weed and water, especially when summer gets here." Virginia's expertise produced blooming flowers all year long: copper chrysanthemums in the fall, white camellias in winter, golden daffodils in spring, and butterfly bushes in the summer.

Blazes of dazzling purple and pink azaleas propelled Willoughby out of brown winter doldrums. Ali savored this weather because humidity would soon hit Willoughby like a tsunami.

Ali watched Matt as he returned from his run and jogged up the sidewalk to their house. They had left together this morning, but Ali's pace slowed Matt. The couple had met when mutual friends introduced them at a 10K run. They spent their first dates running at the park or along the Willoughby River. They ran together until Ali's troubled pregnancy with their daughter Kayla. Over the years, Ali regressed from running to jogging and now fast walking. Maybe not so fast, but definitely walking.

That morning they parted ways at Willoughby Park. Matt's Peachtree Road Race T-shirt he bought at the Goodwill store, after he had dropped off their year-end donations, was drenched in sweat and his face was as red as the cardinals perched on the nearby feeder. Ali assessed her husband's body as he slowed his pace to a walk and joined her on the porch. Despite complaining about his forty-five-year-old knees, Matt continued to run in an attempt to ward off middle-age spread. The jelly-like flab around his stomach needed to go, but Ali had no right to criticize her husband's waistline.

Ali went to the kitchen, returned with a glistening pitcher of ice water filled with sliced lemons and limes, and placed it on a table near the chairs on the porch. Carolina Chickadees serenaded the neighborhood while competing with the early morning tick, tick, ticking of sprinklers and the sound of shared greetings to neighbors picking up their newspapers or walking their dogs.

Ali handed Matt a towel to dry the sweat from his body. He took off his Maui Jims and rubbed the towel through his hair. Although graying on the sides, he still had a thick head of hair the color of brown sugar.

"Cheers. I need it today." He gulped the water, wiped his body, and then placed the towel on the rocker before he sat. Ali handed him the Metro section of the newspaper. He turned to the obituaries—a routine he had learned from Ali.

"I don't know how you two can read those awful dead notices every day. Sick," Kayla said as she opened the screen door, let it bang shut, and joined her parents on the porch. A pink dog leash dangled from her hand.

"*Death* notices or obituaries. Not 'dead' notices, princess," Matt corrected. "There's a smoothie for you in the refrigerator."

"Thanks, Dad. I don't want to hurt your feelings, but some of that stuff makes me gag."

"You'll like this one. Lots of fruit and yogurt."

"We should write our obituaries," Ali said to Matt.

"Not much to put in mine."

"That's the point. We should start writing now and then try to accomplish whatever we put in it."

"Too maudlin. Not for me." Matt returned to the newspaper.

At the sound of Kayla twirling the leash, Roxie scurried from her resting spot. Kayla leaned over to hook the faux-leather leash onto the diva dog's faux-diamond-studded collar. She hugged Roxie and air kissed her damp black nose.

"I bet Aunt Janie will have an awesome dead notice—I mean, obituary—when she dies. A big photo, too. See you later." She bounded down the walkway like a friendly black Lab. She stopped at the sidewalk and hollered to her dad, "I'll try the smoothie later. Promise."

"I wonder what my legacy will be," Ali muttered.

Ali and Matt married in their mid-twenties, and it was five years before they were able to conceive. Fifteen-year-old Kayla considered her forty-five-year old parents "elderly" compared with her friends' parents—a fact she often mentioned. When Kayla reached the age of five, she invented an imaginary sister who lived in the master bedroom of her Barbie condo. These days, Roxie took on the role of sibling.

Once when Ali attended middle school, she asked Janelle if she could wear her favorite designer jeans to Ellen's boy–girl party. "If you think you can squeeze those big old thighs of yours into them, go ahead." Janelle stood back and watched Ali as she struggled and wiggled to pull the jeans over her hips. "Told you so." Janelle left Ali staring at the pants, wondering why she attempted such a stunt.

"Too short," Ali called out to Kayla. "I think her clothes are shrinking by the minute." She assessed Kayla's frayed denim shorts and tie-dyed tank top, as skimpy as the shorts. "Kayla claims the stores don't sell anything longer, and I'm forbidden to shop with her."

"Why the sudden interest in taking Roxie for walks so early on a school holiday? Shouldn't she sleep till noon like most teenagers?" Matt asked as he turned to the business section of the newspaper.

"Logan is the incentive. He's her new mixed doubles partner on the tennis team and lately they walk their dogs together. He and his dad live around the corner on Shamwood. Don't know about the mother."

"I hope they're just friends. Fifteen is too young for the steady boyfriend thing."

"You don't like admitting our little girl is growing up because that means we're getting older."

Matt cleared his throat before returning to the paper.

"I don't think a walk in the park with their dogs is anything to worry about." Ali watched as Logan and his two dogs joined Kayla and Roxie. Logan towered over Kayla and hunched down to talk to her. "The older Kayla gets the more she resembles Janelle. Her hair. So straight." Ali twisted a piece of errant frizz around a finger and made a mental note to drop by the beauty school for a trim of her split ends.

"I like your hair. So many luscious ruby curls to run my fingers through. Stop complaining about it, babe. Speaking of Janelle, isn't it time for a visit? Usually she comes to town before a book tour."

"I'm in no rush to see her."

Matt placed the newspaper on the wicker table between them. "Better get ready for work."

When the phone rang, Ali followed him into the kitchen. "Well, it's my favorite sister-in-law. We were just talking about you."

"Hope it was good."

"Of course," Matt said. He often bragged about Janelle's celebrity status to their friends and neighbors—out of Ali's hearing distance. "Sure. I'll put her on."

Ali stood by the kitchen table, wildly shaking her head. She mouthed, "No, no." She waved her hands back and forth like a railroad crossing.

Today was not Ali's scheduled day off from Kitchen Bliss. Ellen, the owner of the gourmet store where Ali worked part-time, insisted. Last minute details for the Willoughby Book Awards Banquet, about two weeks away, filled Ali's schedule. Ali had agreed, in a weak moment, to chair the event. Although time consuming, she had to admit she enjoyed the responsibility.

"Sorry. Guess she's not here. Must have gone to work. I'll tell her you called."

"Is your welcome mat ready?"

"You're welcome anytime. Kayla constantly talks about you. She's waiting for that trip to Italy you promised."

"Soon. Soon. Later, Matty." She hung up.

"Why did you say I was at work? She'll call Kitchen Bliss, find out I'm not working today, and then she'll know you were covering for me. Oh, sugar. Give me the phone."

At arm's length, Matt handed the phone to Ali. "Don't kill the messenger." He shaped his fingers like a gun pointed to his head. Matt found Janelle entertaining, but dreaded Ali's 180-degree personality change when his sister-in-law was within five hundred miles of Georgia. Even a phone call from Janelle rattled Ali.

"Did she say when's she coming? Or why?" Ali's voice rose an octave higher than usual.

"Call her back and find out." Matt left the room.

Janelle answered at the first ring.

"Hello. Sorry I missed your call." Ali winced at her big fat lie.

"I think it's time for a visit. I'll come in the next week or so. Call the folks," Janelle ordered her younger sister.

"Any particular reason you're coming?"

"Didn't think I needed a reason to visit family."

"I didn't mean that, Janelle. Forget it. See you when?"

Without answering Ali's question, Janelle asked, "By the way, have you seen Phoebe Patterson lately?"

"She spoke at the library last week. Why?"

"No reason."

"Why don't you ask Mother?"

"Even though they're friends, Phoebe's a touchy subject. Mother still hasn't forgiven me for dedicating my first book to Phoebe and not her. I assumed when I dedicated the second book to her she would get off that runaway train."

Ali was all too familiar with the role of runner up. She had a recurring dream. Virginia and Janelle were walking hand in hand on

Willoughby Lane engaged in a lively conversation. Ali was running as fast as she could to match their pace. They entered a store, but when she followed them, they disappeared. Ali had been trying to catch up to her sister for years.

"Have to run. Call the folks and let them know I'm coming. I'll stay with you. Don't want to disappoint Kayla. Bye, Li'l Sis."

"You'll hurt Mother's feelings if you don't—" Too late, Janelle was already gone.

Ali sat down at the kitchen table and put her head on top of her folded arms. "Too bad we have longevity genes in the family. Guess I'll have to endure Janelle for her lifetime," she moaned. When Ali lifted her head, she gazed out the window at nothing in particular. *At least she only comes to town every two years. If I were a rational human being, wouldn't these visits become easier rather than more difficult?* Ali reached for the Tums bottle decorating the kitchen table behind the napkin holder, and poured three of them into her hand.

Matt stuck his head into the kitchen. A dark green terry-cloth towel was wrapped around his waist and water dripped from his hair. "What could I do? Tell her we moved?" He entered the kitchen, stood behind Ali, and put his hands on her hunched shoulders. "Don't let your sister get to you. She'll come for a few days then leave."

"Why can't I erase our history and start over?"

"Someone has to take the first step. Since you're the bigger person, guess that's your job."

Withstanding the short visit was one small hurdle, but the residual effect of her sister's visit would resound for months. "I guess you're right." Ali stood and faced Matt. She raised her right hand. "I hereby promise to make sure this visit with my sister is sweet, pleasant, loving." She paused. "Maybe there's a tooth fairy, too."

Chapter 2

Later that evening, Kayla was cleaning up the kitchen. Matt was in the den reading automotive magazines, and Ali was at her "desk" at the kitchen table with her laptop.

The phone in the kitchen rang. "I'll get it," Kayla said. "For you, Mom. Mrs. Jenkins."

"Hello, Carla. How's your mother?" Carla's mother was under the care of Willoughby Hospice Center.

"She's dead."

"Well, it's about time. Ah—I mean, there's never a good time. She did linger. Must have been the excellent care you gave her. I'm so sorry, Carla. What can I do?"

"I need an obituary. Something wonderful, glowing, and false. Shirley Sweeney told me you wrote one for her mother. You turned the old battle-axe into a saint. Will you do it for my mother?"

"Carla. What I wrote for Shirley was, oh—I don't know—somewhat of a stretch. Besides, I don't know anything about your mother."

"Please say yes. The funeral home needs something ASAP. Can I come over?"

Ali eyed the to-do list for the upcoming book banquet on her overloaded bulletin board. "Will you promise not to tell anyone? Promise?"

Carla disconnected the phone without answering Ali's request.

"What are you committing to now, Ali?" Matt shouted from the den.

"Remember the obit I wrote for Shirley Sweeney's mother? Carla wants the same for hers."

"I warned that you would regret doing that for Shirley. If Carla knows, the whole town will know. They'll be lining up at our door."

"I only agreed to help Shirley and now Carla because their mothers were mean old biddies. Imagine writing an obituary for someone—" An image of Janelle flashed before her.

The doorbell rang. Carla must have been in the driveway when she called. Ali opened the door. Carla brushed past her and headed straight for the kitchen table. No hello. No how are you. Carla, a perpetual dieter, was at the high side of the yo-yo arc at this point. Her black stretch pants expanded to the limit while her long purple top clung to ample breasts like plastic wrap. Her eyes were bloodshot and their lids drooped. "Tea, please," Carla demanded. "No sugar. I'm on a diet."

Matt heard Carla and entered the kitchen. "I'll get the tea."

Carla acknowledged him with a flip of her hand as she ran her fingers through salt-and-pepper hair, which needed a brush or a comb.

Ali retrieved a notebook and pencil from a drawer and put on her reading glasses. "We'll begin with the basics. Date and place of birth, names of parents, husband, and children. Other relatives, alive or deceased. That takes up a good bit of space."

Carla answered Ali's questions without hesitation.

"Where'd she go to church?" Ali asked.

"Church? She was an atheist."

"Any hobbies?"

"She smoked three packs a day, drank her bourbon straight, and had a framed photo of Jerry Springer on her dresser. She used a BB gun to shoot at the neighborhood dogs and cats if they came near her property. Probably shot at a couple of kids, too." Carla took a sip of tea. "Mother was obsessively protective of her backyard, so I think there were some suspicious plants in her alleged garden. I never saw one tomato or cucumber."

"Any specialty in the cooking department?"

"Hot dogs. Canned pork and beans. The only things she never burned." Carla narrowed her eyes. "I take that back. Hot dogs—sometimes she burned them."

"Can you remember one thing about your mother that's noteworthy?"

Carla put her head in her hands. Tears cascaded down her cheeks. She wiped her nose on her sleeve. "Maybe if I had been more patient with Mother. Maybe if I had spent more time with her or brought the grandkids around more. This is the one last thing I can do for her. I don't want the entire town to remember what a witch she was."

Ali reached across the table and patted Carla on her shoulder. "Okay. Let's recap. Disliked animals and kids, didn't believe in God, watched trashy TV, smoked like a chimney, and drank like a fish." Ali suppressed a smile.

Carla howled again, grabbing the handful of tissues Ali offered. She pushed away from the table, stood, and paced up and down, wringing her hands.

Ali inhaled deeply and exhaled slowly before typing on her laptop. After about five minutes, she read what she wrote. She typed some more then hit the print button. "Follow me, Carla."

The two women moved to the den that served as Matt's office. Not quite a man cave but masculine, decorated in greens and browns. Photos of antique cars covered one wall and a flat-screen

TV hung on another wall. Ali took the white paper from the printer and handed it to a sniffling Carla.

"I want people to know the Lucy Willis she might have been. Thank you." Carla gave Ali a bear-like hug.

"Aren't you going to read it?" Ali asked.

"No. I trust you."

"You can't tell anyone about this."

They hugged again and Carla moved toward the front door. "You'll come to the funeral home for the service? Sure would appreciate it. I don't think many people will be there."

Maybe after they read what I wrote they will.

Chapter 3

"**G**reat morning for a run. Sure you won't join me?" Matt asked Ali who was sitting on the front porch. "Not today. Kitchen duty calls."

"Cheer up, babe," he said as he laced his running shoes. "Your sister won't stay long. She never does." He kissed Ali goodbye and left for the park.

The ringing telephone in the kitchen interrupted Ali's pity party.

"Heard some bad news. Phoebe's in the hospital. Prognosis not favorable," Ellen said.

"At 95, not unexpected. Still sad. I suppose her grandson Brad will come to town. He was devoted to Phoebe."

"Brad's already been sighted. All the single women in town will try to comfort him. They'll line up at the door bearing chicken casseroles with their phone numbers taped to the bottom."

"Let's ask Brad to accept the award we had planned to give her, you know, in case she . . . uh . . . doesn't survive. Liven up the banquet with some eye candy."

"What about the programs? We've printed over two hundred," Ellen said.

"An insert will work."

The two women had been friends since childhood. In recent years, Ali worked at the store Ellen had inherited from her parents. Ellen relied on Ali to manage the front of the store while she took care of the bookkeeping, inventory, and other administrative duties.

"I have more bad news," Ali sighed. "Janelle's coming to town in a couple of weeks."

"Oh no, call Dr. Phil. Order buckets of Prozac. Hide sharp instruments. You're dangerously nutty when B.S.—I mean, Big Sis comes to town."

"That bad?"

"Trust me. What can I do to help? Make sure she has a roundtrip ticket from wherever she's coming?"

"She'll have a field day critiquing me. My clothes are out of date, my hair's its usual mess, my house is old-fashioned. Everything is wrong with me." Ali pulled her scrunchie off, shook her head, and then put cinnamon curls back into the ponytail, all while cradling the phone on her shoulder.

"Don't you think that everything is okay with you especially compared with Janelle? She has no adoring husband, no terrific kid. More importantly, she doesn't have me for a friend. All she has is money and fame. I hate her."

Ali smiled. "I appreciate your trying to cheer me up, El, but it's not working."

"Then we need a plan."

"You have enough going on."

"No, I don't. You manage the store for me. I don't even know why I hold onto it. Would rather take a world cruise on a yacht with a brawny captain at the helm and a couple of hard-body deckhands."

"I'll get Matt and Kayla to help me. When I need someone to listen to me whine and complain, you'll be the one."

"You wouldn't know how to complain if your life depended on it."

"Matt might disagree. He says I'm too hard on my sister."

"I think you're too hard on yourself. Okay, I need to open the store. Call me later if you want to talk."

Ellen was the sister Ali wished Janelle had been. They were confidants, partners in crime, and supportive of each other.

Ali surveyed her kitchen. The wallpaper with a beige background and tiny baskets of faded strawberries showed signs of coming apart at the seams. For as long as the wallpaper hung, well-meaning friends presented her with towels, cookie jars, switch plate covers, rugs, and spoon rests decorated with the red fruit. A cabinet contained another collection of the fruit-themed items. Ali rotated these in and out of their storage spot so she wouldn't hurt anyone's feelings.

Ali had a major task in front of her: cucumbers waiting to be peeled, cream cheese warming to room temperature, and phyllo resting under damp towels. She and other members of Book Babes, Ali's cadre of friends, were hosting a bridal shower for Nancy Jorgensen's daughter Rebecca. Since this was marriage-challenged Rebecca's third try, Nancy decided low-key was appropriate. Ali had agreed to make fifty cucumber sandwiches, fifty mushroom tarts, and fifty mini cheesecakes, which was not Ali's definition of *low-key*.

When the phone rang, Ali let the machine answer. She listened to Kayla's recording. "We can't come to the phone right now. Please leave a message. If this call is for Kayla, try her cell." The postscript was new.

"I committed to make fifty chicken satays, but this awful pollen has affected me," a breathless Lisa May said with a scratchy voice. "Will you make them? Please, Ali."

Ali picked up the phone and hit the speaker button. "Who else did you ask?"

"Oh, you're there. Thanks for answering. You're the girl who can't say no," Lisa pleaded.

"Why don't you send your husband to Maria's to buy them?" Ali lifted the damp strawberry tea towel to ensure that the phyllo hadn't dried out.

"And be the only one who doesn't fulfill her commitment?"

"'Commitment' doesn't mean homemade."

"Please. This time will be different. Hold on for a sec."

Ali could hear coughing and sneezing—sounded believable. Maybe this time Lisa's allergy attack wasn't a charade.

"I won't pretend I made them. I'll give you all the credit."

"Ah, gee. Why do you always do this to me, Lisa?" Ali peeked at the phyllo. "Okay. I guess."

"I knew I could count on St. Ali. Thank you."

"Bye for now," Ali said, eliminating the possibility of Lisa enumerating the details of her runny nose and itchy eyes. She had tightened her shoulders and bit her upper lip when Lisa called her "St. Ali." Sainthood was never a career choice for Ali. But, she had never imagined living in Willoughby for the rest of her life making cucumber sandwiches and mushroom tarts for countless showers and parties. Sometimes Ali regretted resigning from her job at the small public relations firm where her boss had told her she had a great future. Both Matt and Ali thought Kayla would benefit with a stay-at-home mom. With careful budgeting, they decided Matt's paycheck would suffice. Recently, Ali was rethinking that decision.

Ali washed her hands and began brushing melted butter on the phyllo layers. The phone rang again.

"I have great news, Alicia." Virginia Withrow, Ali's mother, sounded uncharacteristically happy. Maybe this would turn into an uncharacteristically pleasant conversation. "Your cholesterol's down? I knew you'd do it, Mother." Ali hit the speaker button and continued coating the phyllo.

"More exciting. Guess who's coming to Willoughby?"

"George Clooney?"

"Alicia. Behave yourself. Janelle's coming to Willoughby—and take me off that awful speaker thing."

"Yes, I know. She called me." Whoops. Ali regretted the words the second she uttered them.

"What? She called you first? Before her very own mother?"

"Your line was probably busy."

"Maybe your father was on the phone. He doesn't know how to work call waiting."

Ali wanted to ask her mother how being second choice felt but she refrained. It would be futile. Virginia was oblivious to the way she had treated Ali and continued to treat her.

"Why did you think she was coming before you knew for sure she was coming?" Ali asked.

"The bridge club's telephone tree was activated. She died."

"What? Mother, what are you talking about? Who died?"

"Phoebe. She died." Virginia sounded less than morose over the news that her longtime bridge partner and sometimes friend had passed away. Usually Virginia's and Phoebe's disagreements centered on their weekly bridge games. Each one claimed superior knowledge of the rules. Despite their disputes, they were regular partners, and often the top scorers at the duplicate bridge tournaments at the Willoughby Senior Enrichment Center.

"I assume Janelle will come for the memorial service."

"Why?" Ali asked.

"Phoebe and Janelle had stayed in touch, according to Phoebe. I never understood why. Don't forget, your sister dedicated her first book to Phoebe. That created quite a stir in my bridge club. The girls all assumed Janelle would dedicate her book to me, her very own mother. Of course, everyone sided with me without letting on to Phoebe. She boasted about that until Janelle dedicated her second book to me."

"At least Janelle did that, Mother."

"I suppose. But, second—not first? Janelle didn't understand that blood is thicker than water." Virginia's cup runneth over with clichés and wasn't shy about using them.

Ali was unaware that Phoebe and Janelle had kept in touch. Even though Ali saw Phoebe casually at many library-related functions, Phoebe never mentioned Janelle. Nor did Janelle ever reveal to Ali a relationship with Phoebe.

While continuing the conversation with her mother, Ali walked to the kitchen counter, picked up the strawberry-shaped timer, and set it for thirty seconds. She held it close to the phone. Virginia was the Energizer Bunny once she began her "Janelle didn't dedicate her first book to me" lament. "Actions speak louder than words, my dear," Virginia opined.

Ali was inclined to say, "Some people can't see the forest for the trees."

When Ali was young, she complained to her mother that Janelle was her favorite. "You take Janelle shopping. Why don't you take me shopping? Is it because I'm not as pretty as she is?"

"Honey, now quit that. I do take you shopping," Virginia said while snipping the tips of her hydrangea blossom stems over the kitchen sink. "We go antiquing together all the time, right?"

Ali poked her lips out and wrinkled her forehead refusing to answer.

"Alicia, you're overreacting. Why last week we attended the estate sale in Decatur where you found that lovely Blue Willow plate. Remember?"

"I don't care. You still think Janelle's prettier."

Virginia stopped mid-snip and set her scissors on the counter. "Janelle may be pretty, Alicia, but beauty is in the eye of the beholder. Besides, you're the smart one."

"My cookies are calling from the oven," Ali lied as the strawberry beeped into the phone. "We'll talk later. Why don't you and Dad come over for dinner tonight?" Ali immediately regretted that invitation. If Virginia accepted, she'd have to bake the darn cookies.

"Not tonight. Bridge, you know."

"Mother, by the way, how are you coming with the phone calls I asked you to—?" Too late. Virginia hung up. She insisted on some role in the book banquet preparations, but when Ali assigned her an easy task, she reneged on her duties. If Janelle asked her mother to scrub her toilet, Virginia would run to her aid, overburdened with cleaning tools. Virginia wasn't interested in helping Ali or the banquet committee. She wanted her friends to notice her name in the program under the heading: *Many Thanks to Our Dedicated Volunteers.*

"Come to think of it, cookies weren't such a bad idea," Ali said aloud as she opened a bag of dark chocolate chips from the pantry, tossed a handful into her mouth, and then another. *Ahh.* Creamy morsels of comforting chocolate. Dark chocolate every day was beneficial for the heart, according to her husband, the diet guru of the family. Did he mean a little bag or a little bit or a little bite? He was becoming a nutritional expert after losing ten pounds. Ali expected him to install a lock on the pantry. Instead, he posted a sign that did not amuse Ali: "Stop. Think. Don't Eat."

She was tempted to make a batch of cookies and eat every single one. Eating the bag of chocolate morsels would comfort her more than devouring two dozen cookies and much easier. Beanpole Janelle's upcoming visit was enough motivation to return the tempting treats to the pantry. Ali guessed that not a single piece of chocolate had touched Janelle's enhanced lips in years.

Ali dismissed the cookies from her mind, but a comment Virginia made about Janelle's book dedication resonated. Another person deserved the dedication in Janelle's book—a person who helped Janelle write book reports and award-winning stories for their high school newspaper. This person gave Janelle the idea for her first best seller. This was a person who adored and admired Janelle and often said, "I want to be like my big sister when I grow up."

Janelle should have dedicated her first book to me.

Chapter 4

Janelle Jennings paced back and forth in the Jeffersonian Suite of the Lafayette Grand Hotel in New York City like a caged leopard. She considered champagne more effective at calming her nerves than the Xanax in her purse. She selected a bottle of sparkling wine from the mini-fridge and inspected the label with disdain. Not French, but sufficient, she decided. She removed the gold foil and untwisted the wire cage that secured the cork. She placed a white linen napkin on top of the cork and then slowly twisted the bottle until the cork released, making a refined burp. Janelle selected a crystal flute from the bar, and filled the glass as she watched the bubbles form on the bottom and propel to the brim.

Janelle gazed into the mirror-backed bar, gave a toothy grin, and wiped smeared red lipstick off her alabaster teeth with one of the pristine napkins.

Glass in hand, she moved to the floor-to-ceiling window to observe the masses below. People packed the streets as they hurried to the subway, waited for buses, or hailed cabs. Grateful for mild weather, bike messengers navigated between cars and pedestrians.

Everyone seems to have a destination, a purpose, a goal.

Janelle moved to an end table and picked up her phone. *Should I call or not?* E-mails and occasional visits were acceptable, but both parties had decided no phone calls. *To hell with it.* She scrolled the contact list and selected the number to Phoebe Patterson's home in Willoughby, Georgia.

A male voice answered. Phoebe's husband had passed away several years ago so the voice didn't belong to him. "May I please speak with Phoebe? This is Janelle Jennings."

"Janelle. Hmm. This is Brad, Phoebe's grandson. Remember me, from high school? I'm the one you backed over in your family's driveway."

Janelle remembered him all right. He followed her around Willoughby High like the geek he was. He shouldn't have been in the driveway in the first place. His broken leg healed, didn't it? So what if he missed a few football games. He wasn't the quarterback.

"Yes, of course, Brad, how are you?" Janelle strained to find her sweet and sympathetic voice—the voice of her character Angelica Austin in *Love Secrets of Luxemburg.*

"Under the circumstances, okay. Sad. Mimi was the only mother I ever knew."

"What do you mean? Is there something wrong with Mimi—I mean, Phoebe—rather, Mrs. Patterson?"

Brad was silent.

"Is she in the hospital? I must visit her. Where is she?"

"She's where she always wanted to go."

Janelle tried to recall the places Phoebe wanted to visit. "Machu Picchu, Tibet, Buenos Aires?"

"No, somewhere better, according to Mimi."

Janelle didn't want to play the "Where in the World is Phoebe Patterson?" game.

"My grandmother died following an accident. I still can't believe she's—"

"No, no, no!" Janelle shouted. The champagne flute slipped from her hand spilling the pale yellow fizzling contents on the Oriental carpet.

"Janelle, what's the matter?"

"Nothing. Housekeeping tossed some of my mail. What happened? What accident? When's the funeral?" She was mouthing every four-letter word in her vocabulary of the profane. Every time she uttered an obscene word she stomped her foot like a spoiled three-year-old denied an ice cream cone before dinner.

"She had left a Zumba class at the library, carrying an armload of books, and tripped in the parking lot. Probably a concussion. We have to wait for the arrival of relatives from the west coast, so I scheduled the memorial service for next week. She stipulated cremation in her will."

"I'll be there." She disconnected and screamed loud enough to reach the Empire State Building. Janelle slapped her forehead with the palm of her hand. What would Brad think of her rudeness? She must avoid antagonizing him. She redialed Phoebe's number. "I was so shocked, Brad, I forgot my manners," she said when he answered. "I'm sorry for your loss." Janelle returned to the window and stared below.

"Hell, his loss, what about my loss? What did Amber Knightly do in *The Secret of High Mountain Love* when she was distressed?" Janelle mumbled to herself. She picked up the phone and ordered from room service. "French champagne. This California stuff is undrinkable."

Chapter 5

The soft morning sunlight filtered through the bedroom window casting crooked lines on Ali's plaid chintz bedspread awakening her from a restless sleep. She could hear the whirring of the blender in the kitchen. Matt was becoming a smoothie expert, claiming fiber consumption helped kick-start his day. Ali preferred high-octane caffeine and waited patiently for her wake-up java.

Matt appeared in the bedroom doorway holding an oversized ceramic mug. He was an early riser who never hit the snooze button but sprung out of bed invigorated. The aroma of hazelnut, Ali's favorite, lured her to face the world. "Here, you might need this. You tossed and turned all night as if you were on the Titanic. Thinking about your sister?"

Ali sat up with her back against the headboard and shrugged her shoulders. She was reluctant to admit the bitterness she felt for her sister. She sipped coffee from the mug noting the not so subtle phrase printed on the side: "Stop Unnecessary Volunteering." Ali thanked him for the coffee and glanced at the clock, noting his departure for the dealership was later than usual.

He left the room but returned to stand in the doorway. "Can I give you some advice?"

"Shoot."

"Accept your sister for the narcissistic nut case she is. She's not going to change. *You* have to change *your* attitude."

Ali agreed with Matt. She had been obsessing about Janelle's arrival. Last night she awakened around midnight, tiptoed into the living room, and watched reruns of *Toddlers & Tiaras*. When she tired of listening to screeching mothers, she turned to *The Real Housewives* of somewhere and then watched *The Real Housewives* of somewhere else. Around two a.m., she crept into bed still unable to find the refuge of sleep. Matt slept peacefully eliciting Ali's desire to slug him with a pillow.

Ali finished drinking her coffee, gathered baggy shorts and a T-shirt the color of putty from a nearby chair, and plodded into the bathroom to brush her teeth. She ran her fingers through her mop of hair and pulled it into her usual ponytail. She made a furtive glance at the dreaded scale but decided to weigh in tomorrow. The elastic waistband on her pants was looser than last week, allowing Ali to breathe comfortably. Maybe her lame exercise regime was working. *Why did I sabotage my diet with those chocolate chips yesterday?*

When Ali entered the kitchen Matt was drinking a blueberry, kale, flax seed oil, blender concoction. "Phoebe's obit's in the paper this morning."

"Read it to me, please," Ali asked while she refilled her coffee mug.

"'Phoebe Downey Bullard Patterson, Willoughby, GA, resident and former mayor, passed away unexpectedly.'" He raised his eyebrows slightly and said, "'Unexpectedly?' She was 95."

"Keep reading," Ali said.

"We called her Mrs. Pee Pee, you know. Phoebe Patterson. Get it?"

"Don't make fun of the dead. She was nice to me."

"I never understood why you and your sister were enamored with that old grouch of an English teacher."

"She wasn't grouchy to Janelle and me. She liked us because we read the assigned books and wrote intelligible reports about them." Ali snatched the paper from Matt, took her red reading glasses from their resting spot on her head, and read aloud, "Phoebe Patterson was born in Frostproof, GA, to the late Edna Louise and Duncan Bullard. Her husband of fifty years, Joseph Johnson Patterson, predeceased her."

"We called him Jammin' Joe." Matt took a sip of his new smoothie recipe and wrinkled his nose. "J.J. Get it?"

Ali glared at him over the top of the paper. "Quiet, please." She skimmed the list of Phoebe's achievements in education and local government of Willoughby. At the age of seventy-five, Phoebe ran successfully for the position of mayor and served one term. She remained on the city council for ten additional years, the paper stated.

"Poor Brad. He's lost his parents and now both his grandparents," Ali said.

"I'll give him a call," Matt said. "Maybe there's some way I can help." Although Matt and Brad, high school friends, took different life paths, they had stayed in touch through social media.

"I'll take food Brad can put in the freezer," Ali said.

"Love you, babe." He tilted her chin upward and kissed her lips.

"Me too." She grabbed a baseball cap on the kitchen counter and a sugar-laden so-called energy bar. She glanced at the green and gold wrapper in her hand, replaced it on the counter, and reached for a banana instead. Ali patted herself on the back and headed out the door with Roxie in the lead.

An overnight shower had washed away the annoying yellow pollen that powdered its signature on cars, streets, and outdoor furniture in early spring. Forsythia glistened like gold coins on bushes. This was a frustrating time of year for allergy sufferers. The dreaded pollen was the price the town paid for the colorful canvas of flowers soon to emerge.

Ali chose her favorite route along Willoughby Lane, watching the merchants open their doors, clean windows, and position easels announcing specials. The Lane had experienced ups and downs over the years but now business was flourishing. New shops and restaurants were in abundance. Flowering trees lined the red brick sidewalks. The Lane was "postcard pretty," residents and visitors often remarked. Charming replicas of Victorian streetlights added to the attractiveness of the area. Alfresco dining was so popular restaurants extended sidewalks and increased the number of tables and chairs to accommodate customers. During the winter, heat lamps enticed diners to brave the cold and bundle up with blankets provided by the restaurants.

As Roxie and Ali passed Kitchen Bliss, she waved to Ellen. She was brewing a special coffee of the day, her only cooking ability, for customers to enjoy while shopping for anything and all items kitchen related. Ellen hated to cook and rarely entered the kitchen in her home. She had promised her deceased parents that she would keep Kitchen Bliss in the family. Her only sibling, Winston, rarely visited Willoughby and had no interest in the store. Since Ellen had no children, she decided to keep it open for a year or two with the goal of selling it. That was fifteen years ago. After a contentious divorce, Ellen kept the store as an investment, and for something to keep her occupied.

Roxie gained speed as they neared Sally Barker's Dogwood Barkery in anticipation of a dog biscuit Sally would toss to Ali's grateful companion as they passed by. Ali acknowledged Sally with a wave, picked up the dog biscuit, and put it in her pocket. Roxie knew the routine. She would have to wait until they returned home before begging for the treat.

Diane Richardson was hanging a poster in the window of The Books in the Nook advertising the Willoughby Book Banquet when

Ali and Roxie passed by. She let the poster fall to the ground and signaled frantically with both hands.

Ali approached the bookstore, taking advantage of the excuse to rest. "Why? What?"

"Janelle called to ask if we needed a replacement speaker for the book banquet since Phoebe died."

"Hmm. She's never expressed interest in attending the event let alone speaking. What did you tell her?"

"I told her that Phoebe wasn't the speaker. She was our lifetime achievement award recipient." Diane tapped her finger on the side of her face and gave Ali a puzzled look. "Of course, I explained that Laurel Atwood was our speaker this year. Janelle mumbled something about Laurel, but I couldn't understand what she said."

"What else did she say?"

"That was it. She ended the conversation rather abruptly. Do you think she's coming to town?"

"I don't know her plans." Ali waved goodbye and continued for a few steps. She turned to face Diane. "If you hear from her again, will you tell me?"

Diane nodded and returned to hanging the poster.

Ali had asked Janelle for years to speak at the banquet. Since Ali chaired the event this year, she hoped Janelle would acquiesce out of family loyalty. What a laugh. Janelle had offered some lame excuse. Ali vowed never to ask her sister again, no matter what. She was tired of groveling at the feet of Aphrodite.

Ali increased her pace to compensate for the time lost speaking with Diane. The lights in the Tea Cozy Shoppe were out, which was unusual. Ali didn't want to interrupt her exercise again but concern for the owner, Maggie Stratford, caused her to pause. Tomorrow she would take a route without the interruptions from well-meaning friends. Typically, Maggie Stratford was the first merchant to open her doors to her welcoming and popular bakery and teashop.

When Ali tried the door, it opened. "Hey there? Where are you? Everything okay?"

"Problems with delivery of the cranberry scones, that's all. What's up, dear?"

Eighty-year-old Maggie had been experiencing shortness of breath and dizzy spells. Widowed and with no relatives close by, Maggie relied on Ali to check in on her. Perched on the shelves of the walls of the shop was an extensive collection of garden-themed bone china and porcelain teapots. Red, coral, and pink roses, butterflies, and bumblebees decorated her precious assortment. Walls painted lemon yellow complemented the cheerful atmosphere. Overstuffed club chairs covered in floral fabric waited for customers to sit and sip fragrant tea while enjoying intimate conversations. Behind a clear glass case, scones, muffins, and sweet breads enticed hungry clientele.

"Diane told me something odd. Janelle called her—"

Maggie interrupted Ali. "Diane told me about the call. Word travels fast on Willoughby Lane."

"Janelle knows I'm the chair of the banquet. Why didn't she ask me?"

Maggie shook her head and poured hot water into a bright blue teapot. She encased the teapot in a quilted Red Hat Society cozy as she began the morning ritual of readying the store.

If the Cabbage Patch kids needed a grandmother, Maggie was the perfect choice. Her doughy round face begged for a loving squeeze. Her cheeks wore two perfect circles of rosy rouge. Pale blue eyes peered from wire-rimmed glasses. "Don't let your sister get to you, Ali. She did enough of that in high school. You're a better person, Alicia Maureen Lawrence. You were then and you are now."

"Have you been talking to Matt? He says the same thing. See, I didn't even finish my walk. Instead, I'm sitting here with you, complaining about my sister."

"Thanks a lot," Maggie said with a smile. "Is this so awful sitting here with your old friend?"

"Sorry, Maggie."

"Maybe next year you'll publish a book and you'll be our speaker. How's the latest one coming along?"

Only a handful of people knew Ali had tried to write a novel. "About the same. Another author always beats me to the punch with one of my ideas. Guess I'm not original."

"Don't give up. I never envisioned that I would own a small business at my age, and look at me. Someone once said, 'No telling how many miles you will have to go while chasing a dream.' Put on your running shoes, darlin'."

Ali hugged Maggie and left for home with Roxie without finishing the tea. She needed more than chamomile to calm her.

During the walk home, Ali processed Maggie's remarks. She didn't want to wait until she was eighty-years-old to accomplish her goal. Did she want to write and publish a novel—a novel most people would compare with Janelle's popular romance books? Competition was not in her genes. She didn't even like to compete in a game of Scrabble or on the tennis court. No, it wasn't the competition that was holding her back. It was something else. Something Ali was unable to identify.

Maybe baking those cookies wasn't such a bad idea, Ali decided when she and Roxie returned home. Ali opened the refrigerator door with the intention of removing ingredients for the cookies. She knew that even Motivated Matt wouldn't resist a homemade cookie. She stared at the butter and eggs, had second thoughts, and closed the door. No reason to deprive her patient companion. Ali tossed the treat from the Bark-ery to Roxie.

Chapter 6

Ali was sitting on the rocker on the front porch to remove her shoes and socks when she heard the phone ring in the kitchen. She walked inside barefooted.

"Hi, Ali. Just me again."

When am I going to learn not to answer the phone? "What's up, Janelle?"

"My plans have changed."

Ali did a happy dance. A delay in Janelle's arrival was like winning the MegaMillions—almost.

"How so?"

"I'm coming sooner."

Phone in hand, Ali returned to the rocker on the porch, bracing for bad news. "Great. When?" She willed enthusiasm into her voice. She hoped she had a Costco-sized supply of antacids on hand. Ali accelerated the rocker, faster and faster. She closed her eyes while waiting for the answer.

"I'll be there tomorrow. Gotta go. I'll rent a car at the airport. Can't wait. Call the folks for me."

"She hung up on me," Ali shouted to the brown-headed nuthatches hunting for seeds at the feeder on the side of the front garden. The startled birds scattered. She held the receiver in her hand before disconnecting. Ali wanted to morph into a bird and fly away. Janelle always chose an inconvenient time to visit. Was there a convenient time for a visit from a diva?

Last time Janelle visited, the family formed a pool guessing how many pieces of luggage she'd bring. Ali won when Janelle showed up with a whopping twelve pieces of Louis Vuitton suitcases including rolling, soft-and hard-sided, a carry on, and multiple totes. Ali had no idea there were so many different styles of luggage. She still owned the two-piece baby-blue set her parents gave her for college graduation. The only time she used the gift was for trips to Florida or South Carolina beaches.

Ali returned to the kitchen. This was a four-Tums-day and at least two aspirins in anticipation of the big headache about to arrive. She called her mother to report the *good news*.

Virginia was ecstatic. Her firstborn, famous daughter was about to make an appearance in Willoughby.

"She'll have to stay with you for now. I'll need time to prepare her room."

"Mother. About those phone calls I asked you to make for the book banquet."

Virginia hung up. No goodbye, no thanks for calling, only a click.

The phone rang again. "Why is she coming? Did she say? Is she coming for Phoebe's memorial service?" Virginia asked.

"Mother, I know as much as you do. We'll find out when she arrives."

With a click, Virginia ended the conversation with her second favorite daughter.

Ali glanced at her baggy shorts and sighed. Janelle would not approve of Ali's daily uniform. Or her frizzy hair. Or home décor. Or anything else Janelle would pinpoint.

"Knock, knock. Anyone home?" Ellen didn't wait for an answer and opened the screen door.

"Why aren't you at the store? Is something wrong?" Ali asked.

"Bailey's in charge. I wanted to give you the latest budget figures for the committee meeting." She placed a green folder on the countertop. Ellen was a math whiz who served as treasurer for the book banquet. "We're going to come up short based on Delaney's projected food expenses." She bent down to pet Roxie, who gave her a playful welcome.

"Something else to worry about," Ali said.

"What's the matter, Al? You look awful."

"Janelle's coming sooner. Tomorrow."

"Whenever you want me to come over to mess up Janelle's hair, call me. Seriously, what can I do?"

"Nothing, now. I'll call when I need you. Thanks for the budget figures."

"Take time off, if you need to," Ellen said.

"Don't want to take advantage of our friendship."

"After Janelle arrives, triple your hours. Would give you an excuse to avoid her. By the way, I suppose you are responsible for Lucy Willis's obit in the paper this morning?"

"Whatever do you mean?"

"No one's going to believe that stuff about rehabilitating abandoned baby birds. Don't you think you defied believability this time?"

"Well, I—I mean, she…" Ali shot Ellen a smile.

"Forget it. Back to work," Ellen said. They hugged goodbye and promised to keep in close contact during this perilous time.

Ali was grateful to have Ellen's friendship, especially since Ellen knew the sisters' history. She had served in many capacities in Ali's life: childhood playmate, high school friend, college sorority sister, maid of honor, godmother to Kayla, and employer. When Ali was planning her wedding, her mother encouraged, cajoled, and pleaded with her to choose Janelle as matron of honor. Virginia couldn't imagine what people would say or think when Ali chose Ellen instead of her only sibling. Ali relented as she had been doing all her life. To the dismay of Virginia, Janelle declined, saying she had too many commitments. In fact, she said she was unable to attend the wedding, devastating Virginia. Surprise, surprise. Janelle showed up and was the star attraction.

"I swear I wanted to stay away. I knew I would detract from Ali's big night but Mother wanted me there," Janelle had claimed.

Ali had wanted to remodel the kitchen for at least a year. No time for that. Besides, her to-do list summoned: take Dad to the eye doctor, help him pay monthly bills, meet with the book banquet committee, take Roxie to the groomer, cook a meal for a sick friend, write the library's newsletter, spend more time with Matt and Kayla. Well, the last item wasn't on the list, but Ali recognized her deficiency in that category.

As soon as the book banquet was finished, she'd spend more time with her husband and daughter. During Kayla's summer break, they would head for the beach. Matt would have to take time off from work. No excuses this year.

The Willoughby Book Awards Banquet was two weeks away. Compared with other book events in the country, Willoughby's needed upgrading. Ali and the committee had plans to raise enough money to improve the event. For now, they were satisfied with a guest speaker and a student writing contest. Next year they would add a modest scholarship for budding authors. She still had work to complete: committee meeting agendas, a program insert to write, a budget to review. Now Hurricane Janelle was about to hit land.

Ali called Kayla on her cell and told her to come home from the park immediately. "I need your help."

"What's happening, Mom? Is someone sick?"

"Worse. Your aunt's coming tomorrow. I need you. Now."
Ali held the phone at arm's length to protect her eardrums from
Kayla's shriek.

"Awesome sauce! I'm running home right this minute."

Ali semi-jogged into the bathroom fogged with steam. She yelled
at her naked husband. "Hurry up. Get out of there. Meet me in the
kitchen."

"What the...?" he shouted. "Has someone died?"

As she left the bathroom, she took a nanosecond to look over her
shoulder to admire his wet, lathered body through the glass shower
door. *Ahh, so little time.* In a frenzy, she slipped on a bathroom rug
and nearly flopped on her back. She caught herself by bracing both
hands against the countertop. She hoped she avoided a sprain.

Died? Oh, jeez. Phoebe. Ali completely forgot about her and her
grandson Brad. She must go see them. No, not them. Brad. Too late
to see Phoebe. She decided to wait for Janelle's arrival. They could go
together. Right now, there was too much to do.

Ali retrieved paper and pencils from a drawer in the kitchen and
sat down to prepare a to-do list. She was focused on the list when
Matt walked into the kitchen, dressed for work wearing neatly
pressed, by him, not his wife, khakis and a black polo shirt with the
Graham Automotive logo on the pocket. His hair was damp and he
had a spot of shaving gel resembling a white mole on his chin.

"Okay. What's the big deal?" he asked as Kayla and Roxie arrived
home. Logan and his Chihuahuas, Jake and Elwood, accompa-
nied them.

"Janelle's coming! Tomorrow!"

"Here goes the fire drill. Lawrence household in panic mode,"
Matt said.

"Mom, chill. You sounded crazy on the phone." Kayla leaned
toward Ali, with her back to Logan, and whispered in her ear, "Don't

embarrass me, Mom. I really like him." She knitted her eyebrows together and glared at Ali.

"Sit down, everyone." Ali didn't mean Logan and his teeny-weeny dogs, but all three obeyed and sat. The Chihuahuas and Roxie huddled together in a small circle, staring at Ali, and occasionally sniffing each other.

"You don't have to stay, Logan," Ali said.

"Wouldn't miss this, Mrs. Lawrence. Sounds sweet. My house is boring. Don't have any famous relatives. This gonna take long? I'm sure hungry." He took the hem of his shirt to wipe his forehead. The pimpled-faced interloper resembled a basketball player more than a tennis player, and wore his baseball cap backward. Ali thought she glimpsed a tattoo on his inside wrist.

"We need assignment sheets," Ali barked as she distributed paper and pencils to everyone including Logan. Ali needed all the help she could get. "No time for eating," she added. Ali told Kayla to drive to Wal-Mart to buy sheets and towels for the guest bedroom. She spewed out a litany of items the sophisticated guest would approve.

"Slow down, Mom. I can't write that fast. Anyhow, I'm too young to drive with only a learner's permit and no adult in the car. Another year." She winked at Logan and repeated one more year. He gave her a high five.

"Of course you can't drive. Not according to the State of Georgia. I give you permission. Permission granted by Mom for today only. Drive slowly."

"Ali! No way is she going to drive," Matt warned.

"Damn it! This is an emergency."

"You shouldn't cuss in front of me and Kayla, Mrs. Lawrence," Logan, the arbiter of etiquette, said.

"'Damn' isn't cussing; it's not polite," Kayla said. "You shouldn't correct adults. Even if they're wrong. And, you should say 'Kayla and me' and not 'me and Kayla.'"

"Okay, enough about our vocabularies. Kayla, call Gramps and tell him to get over here pronto. He can take you and Logan shopping. Tell him to leave your grandmother at home. She's too high strung."

Six sets of eyes, dogs included, focused on Ali when she said "high strung."

"Now wait one minute, Ali. You are out of control." Matt spoke each word deliberately as though he were talking to a toddler. "Calm down." Matt rose from his chair and moved behind Ali. He put his hands on her shoulders and massaged her tight muscles. "Take deep breaths, babe," he said.

"Dad's right, Mom."

Ali glared at Kayla.

"Back to this guest bedroom thing," Matt said, still massaging Ali's stiff shoulder muscles. "What guest bedroom? Not in this house. You have all those stacks of platters and plates from your previous catering business. Not to mention the unsold scrapbooking supplies and who knows what else from your former hobbies."

She ignored him. They weren't hobbies to Ali.

"Flowers, too, Mom. Aunt Janelle says fresh flowers in a house make it a home."

Ali had never heard Janelle make that comment, but it sounded like a character from one of her books.

"Not Wal-Mart. Macy's," Ali shouted.

"Does Wal-Mart sell flowers?" Kayla asked.

"No, the sheets and towels. Better go to Macy's. Janelle's a label checker. "Now, about the guest bedroom, Matt. Let's move all that stuff somewhere else," Ali said.

"Where do you suggest?" he asked.

"You can figure that out. Maybe the garage. We'll clear out the guest bedroom. Kayla, will you do a fast decorating job? I think there's a bed underneath all those boxes."

"Sweet. Now I can say I decorated a bedroom for a famous person."

Logan opened his mouth to say something, but Ali cut him off with the evil eye only a mother can deliver. Instead of speaking, he curled his upper lip so it sat at his gum line.

"I knew I should have redecorated the guest bedroom," Ali said as she eyed the paint samples and fabric swatches pinned to the crowded bulletin board. "Back to business. Here's the modified plan. Gramps will drive Kayla and Logan to the mall. Guess Matt will go to work for a few hours—"

"One second, Ali. Here's the modification of the modified plan. I'm going to work. Gramps, Kayla, and Logan will do the shopping today. Tomorrow I'll do some reorganizing in the garage to make room for the boxes we can all take downstairs tomorrow. No cooking tonight. I'll get takeout on the way home from work." He stood, approached Ali, and said, "Stop this insanity and calm down. See you tonight, babe." He kissed the top of her head.

Matt makes everything sound so easy, Ali thought. She still had food to purchase, bathrooms to clean, windows to wash, floors to vacuum. She gave herself another assignment—make a 9-1-1 call to Nate Berkus.

Do I have another choice? Book a flight to Bali?

Chapter 7

A knock on the door interrupted Janelle's self-pity. She stepped over the champagne flute and the puddle on the carpet then squinted through the peephole. An attractive Hispanic man wearing a starched white shirt and black waiter's jacket stood at the door with a room service cart.

"It's about time, young man," she said as she opened the door. His name badge read "Rafael."

"So sorry, señorita." He wheeled the cart into the living room. He saw the flute on the floor and picked it up. He also noticed an opened bottle of champagne on an end table and a dead one in the wastebasket.

"Why don't you sit for a while? I've received some devastating news and I need someone to talk to."

"So sorry, señora. Please sign here. I have more carts to deliver. Food will get cold. Busy time."

The switch from "señorita" to "señora" was not lost on Janelle.

She snatched the bill from him, scribbled her name, slammed her hand on his chest, and pushed him into a nearby green and red striped wingback chair.

Rafael eyed the door, assessed Janelle, and eyed the door again. Beads of perspiration formed on his tan forehead. Usually wealthy guests occupied this suite. He couldn't risk missing a generous tip.

While Janelle filled two glasses with champagne, the bewildered Rafael reconsidered. A drunken woman could make all kinds of accusations. He observed Janelle, glanced at the door, and bolted out of his chair leaving the cart behind.

"Damn." She hurled a red patent-leather four-inch Jimmy Choo platform sandal at the confused young man but missed, hitting the door instead.

"Ay Dios mio," Rafael said to a fellow worker as they passed in the hallway.

Janelle settled where Rafael had sat and gulped champagne. While contemplating her next move, she heard the doorbell ring again. Perhaps Rafael reconsidered. Janelle looked through the peephole. A well-groomed, middle-aged man in a gray pinstripe suit and a white carnation pinned to his lapel stood at the door.

"Oh, no. Not him." She opened the door wide enough to face him, but didn't invite the visitor in. "What may I do for you, Mr. Fiedler?"

"Rafael reported that you seemed upset when he delivered your meal. The staff of the Lafayette Grand wants to ensure every moment you spend with us is pleasant. On a personal note, my wife is a big fan of your books."

Maybe this pesky man wasn't so bad, she thought, discreetly unbuttoning the top button on her blouse revealing a plunging neckline. "Thank you for your concern, Mr. Fiedler. Please come in." She gazed into his eyes giving him an inviting smile. Janelle walked to the bar, poured a glass of champagne, and offered it to him.

"I'm on duty. Perhaps another time."

"Please sit." She gestured toward the same wingback chair where she had confined Rafael. She took the chair opposite him.

"I've been so upset with my latest divorce I don't know when I can finish my next novel," she said.

"We have a lovely spa on this property, Miss Jennings. Perhaps a massage is what you need. A Swedish massage with hot stones is what I recommend. May I send a masseuse or a masseur up here? Then, in the morning, when you are more relaxed, we can talk about the length of your stay."

He's placating me because he wants me out of here.

The doorbell rang for a third time.

"May I?"

"No more guests. Whoever it is will have to wait until tomorrow," she instructed Mr. Fiedler.

Whoever was there was anxious for the door to open. The bell rang again. Mr. Fiedler walked to the door, opened it, and said, "Whom may I say is here for Miss Jennings?"

A short, balding man whose body was too big for his navy blue blazer faced Mr. Fiedler.

"Is your cell phone turned off?" the visitor asked as he pushed the door open, squeezed by the hotel manager, and nudged the abandoned room service cart out of the way. A red rose in a bud vase tumbled to the floor leaving another puddle. He ignored the mess he created and stepped over it.

"Are you avoiding my calls, Janelle?" He walked toward Janelle and took Mr. Fiedler's chair.

"Who's this?" the intruder asked, pointing a finger at Mr. Fiedler who was gathering the vase and flower.

The hotel manager presented his card. "Charles Fielder at your service. Welcome to the Lafayette Grand Hotel." He sounded like a recorded message.

"Have tried to contact Miss Jennings for days." He fumbled in his pocket for a card. "Kenneth. Kenneth Luzi. Janelle's agent and babysitter."

"You and your client must have much to discuss," Mr. Fiedler said, as he read the card.

Janelle's cell phone rang. "Hold on. I'll be right with you." She dismissed the hotel manager with a wave of her manicured hand.

Before Mr. Fiedler left, he placed the food from the cart, along with the fallen bud vase and flower, on the mahogany dining room table. An ice bucket and a bottle of white wine were on the cart. He moved the items to the lower shelf of the cart covering them with a linen napkin. He pulled a small red notebook and pen from his inside jacket pocket, and jotted a reminder to deduct the cost of the wine from Janelle's bill.

Since Janelle was having a spirited phone conversation with her back to him, Mr. Fiedler took the opportunity to move toward the agent. "You might encourage her to eat," he said, as he left with the cart and the broken champagne flute.

"I'm catching a flight to Georgia . . . Have to attend a memorial service . . . I'll call you when I get there . . . Yes, more important than the damn—" She disconnected.

"What's going on, Janelle? I want to help you but you don't make it easy. Is there anything stronger in the bar than that stuff you bubbleheads drink?" He withdrew a white handkerchief from a pants pocket, and wiped his shiny forehead.

Janelle waved her hand toward the bar. "Be my guest."

"So, what's your plan, Janelle? You have to bring me into the loop. I have a plane to catch in two hours. I have bills to pay, too. Haven't been able to reach you or your assistant either."

"I fired Bobby. Too temperamental."

"Hell you say. He's been with you forever. He did everything for you."

"Guess I'll have to learn self-sufficiency." Janelle plunked down on the four-cushioned floral-covered sofa and put her now shoeless feet on the glass-topped coffee table.

"My sister has it right, Ken. A quiet, sedate life in boring Willoughby. No one bugging me. No problems. Parents who adore me. A niece who reveres me. My only sibling. Well, I don't know what Ali thinks about me, but I could make her like me again. I'll get my business out of the way in Willoughby, finish the book, and take a staycation. Surely, there's a spa in Willoughby. Willoughby, Georgia."

Chapter 8

Ali unplugged the vacuum cleaner in the living room and dragged it upstairs. She had only a few more hours before Janelle's arrival. Ali doubted whether Janelle knew how to operate a vacuum cleaner. When they were young, Janelle bribed Ali to do her chores around the house. "This one time. Please, Ali. All you have to do is clean our bathroom, dust our bedroom, and hang up all my clothes in the pile on the floor. That's not much. After all, we share the bedroom and bathroom, so half the mess is yours."

"But, Janelle, I have my own chores," Ali protested.

"How much is it worth to you? I'll pay you."

"You owe me from the last time."

"Okay. Here's the deal. You can come to the movies with my friends and me."

"Agreed."

The sisters shook hands.

The vacuum cleaner seemed heavier than when Ali began her chaotic cleaning. Kayla and Logan charged down the staircase carrying boxes and nearly collided with her and the fifteen-pound monster halfway. "Be careful. Slow down," Ali warned as the two-some squeezed by her.

Ali reached the top of the stairs where she met her dad, Ed Withrow, in the box crew.

"I didn't know you were here, Dad. Thanks for helping."

"You were so intent on vacuuming I didn't want to scare you. Why are you so uptight every time your sister comes to visit? Your mother's equally as nutty. Relax," he said.

"Don't carry too much, Dad."

Ed Withrow's height belied his Herculean strength. A dislocated shoulder precluded a collegiate wrestling scholarship. He had retired from Willoughby High where he taught shop and woodworking and coached the wrestling team. "Everybody's giving me orders. I came over here to escape your mother. I'll do the hell what I want," he said. "Relax," he repeated.

"You should relax, too, Dad," Ali said.

"Being away from your mother when she is preparing for your sister is all the relaxation this guy needs." He zipped down the stairs with the alacrity of a much younger man.

"You don't have to vacuum up there, Mom," Kayla shouted from the bottom step. "I did it two weeks ago. Aunt Janie won't care. She sent me a text and said not to make any special arrangements for her."

"We're not doing anything we wouldn't do for any visitor to our home," Ali lied.

"I heartily dispute that statement," Matt said as he trailed his three assistants down the stairs.

"Texting? How long have Kayla and her aunt been texting?" *Something else to learn. I can barely use my cell phone.*

Matt deposited the boxes and rejoined Ali upstairs. "No more room in the garage. Decide what to do with all that stuff."

"For now, leave the rest in the guestroom. Janelle will have to live with it."

"What happened to that garage sale you were going to have?" Matt asked. "Would be nice to have room to park two cars in a two-car garage."

"I promise. One of these days."

Each box or container in the garage reminded Ali of a failed attempt at home-based entrepreneurship. She tried selling scrap-booking supplies and household cleaning products, but ended up buying more of the items than she could sell.

After Kayla and Logan emptied the guestroom of the boxes and stored them in the garage, they dashed upstairs carrying items they purchased at the mall. After about an hour, Kayla announced it was time for the unveiling.

Ali entered the guest bedroom/storeroom to inspect Kayla's hasty decorating not knowing what to expect. Kayla was partial to retro colors of bright orange and sunny yellow and used those colors in her room. A visitor needed sunglasses when entering her private sanctuary.

Kayla had selected a seashore theme in recognition of Janelle's love of the beach. The coverlets on the twin beds were solid sea foam green with matching bed skirts in stripes of varying shades of greens and blues. Throw pillows in terra cotta in a variety of shapes sat against two pillow shams. Boxes filled the rest of the room. Kayla made great progress on a room Ali should have finished months ago.

"The walls need painting, Mom. You have to get rid of all those boxes. I tried to make Aunt Janie feel welcome. Didn't spend a whole bunch of money either."

Please don't make her feel too welcome.

A lit candle adorned with seashells sat on the nightstand between the beds adding an exotic aroma of sandalwood and jasmine. Ali extinguished the flame. Some of the leftover boxes were crammed into the closet leaving no room for the soon-to-arrive luggage.

Kayla had placed childhood photos of herself and her aunt on the dresser. She filled a glass container with her precious seashell collection and set it next to the photos. Missing were pictures of Kayla's parents or grandparents. A piece of driftwood Kayla had found during the last family trip to Sanibel and a big conch shell added a beachy touch to the whitewashed antique desk.

Kayla had continued the seashore theme in the adjoining bathroom with fluffy bath towels in soft greens contrasted with hand towels in terra cotta to match the pillows in the bedroom. A throw rug in a seashell pattern was on the floor. A mango scented candle was glowing. Ali blew this one out, too.

Ali stashed the vacuum cleaner in a closet, returned downstairs to the kitchen, and took a butter knife out of a drawer. She tapped the knife against a water glass and called—"Attention, attention." Matt, Kayla, Logan, Ed, and the three dogs answered her clink.

"Please, sit down," Ali said as her crew gathered around the table. Even the dogs obeyed. She thanked her captive audience for their help preparing for Janelle's arrival and complimented Kayla on her decorating skills.

"If you would get rid of all your stuff, Mom, I will make a truly wonderful room for Aunt Janie. Logan helped, too."

"We have a lot more awesome ideas," Logan said as he flipped his blond bangs out of his eyes.

Ali acknowledged Logan with a half-smile.

"Let's go out to dinner tonight, Ali. You must be exhausted," Matt offered.

Kayla fiddled with her phone. "Her plane landed. She sent me a text."

The banging of the screen door announced a visitor. Lavender scented perfume arrived before Virginia Withrow, the matriarch of the family. "Did I hear 'restaurant'? We're coming to my house to-night. No restaurant. We'll have a welcome home dinner for my firstborn daughter," she said. Virginia's knees creak but her hearing was keen.

Virginia was decked out in a billowy amethyst skirt and matching blouse. The flattering color complimented her dark hair and sky blue eyes. Red flats said lunch with the Red Hat Society had been on the schedule. Virginia's hair was dark for her age with no telltale gray wisps. Clairol was her best friend. Her lifetime habit of wearing sunscreen before dermatologists warned of skin cancer paid off because she had few wrinkles and even fewer sunspots. She retained the posture of the youthful ballerina she had dreamed to become.

Matt and Ed stood and each offered Virginia a seat.

Matt waved his hand at Logan. "Stand up, young man." He tapped his head telling Logan to remove his baseball cap.

"Sorry, dude—I mean, Mr. Lawrence."

"Kayla, aren't you going to introduce your grandmother to Logan?" Matt asked.

"Logan, this is my grandmother. Nana this is Logan."

"Nice to meet you, ma'am." Logan looked at Matt who nodded approval.

"You, too, young man," Virginia said as she joined the clan at the table. "She should be here by now."

If anyone else arrived, Ali would need a bigger table.

"I wonder what's keeping her," Virginia said. "I'm so excited. I can't wait. A watched pot never boils."

"She'll text me when she gets a rental car," Kayla reported as she checked her phone.

Everyone was ready and waiting. However, the level of excitement varied from person to person. Ali wondered whether Virginia would be as excited if her younger daughter was about to arrive after a two-year absence?

Forty-five minutes later, a blaring car horn interrupted the discussion of what's keeping the honored guest. Everyone rose from the table and gathered around the bay window to observe a tiny banana colored car. Someone was wailing away on the horn. Couldn't be Janelle. No way would she drive a toy car the color of fruit.

Virginia, Ed, Matt, Kayla, Logan, Roxie, and the enchiladas dashed outside. Ali chose to watch the welcoming committee from her post at the window. She observed five-foot, eight-inch Janelle as she attempted to exit from a clown car made for little people by opening the driver's side door. No doubt, Janelle threw a hissy fit when the car rental agent gave her keys to this car instead of a Mercedes.

"Aunt Janie! Aunt Janie! You're here! You're here!" Kayla shouted as she dashed toward the driveway. Janelle extricated one long, white pants leg and then slowly another from the driver's side. She was able to liberate her slender legs but the fastened seat belt held the rest of her body captive. She swung her hips too hard, leaving her butt suspended in the air. Whoops. Her phone and a gargantuan purse fell to the ground, emptying its contents including clothes and shoes— enough for an around-the-world cruise.

The family rushed to Janelle's aid. Roxie was welcoming, too, but after a few sniffs at Janelle's feet, joined Ali who had moseyed to the front porch. Smart dog with impeccable taste. One by one, the group hugged and kissed the returning celebrity.

Ali stood back from the crowd and watched Janelle. Her beauty always struck Ali as stunning. Her glossy straight black hair with bangs framed flawless skin, despite summers at the beach. A black, shawl collar jacket hung loosely over a lustrous, ochre silk blouse. Ali recalled snowy egrets that populated Sanibel Island. The fall from the car disheveled her hair and smeared her lipstick. *No one's perfect.* Even as a forty-nine-year-old former prom queen, she looked terrific. Ali examined the sloppy clothes she was wearing. *Surely, I could have found something better to wear. Janelle would have so much to criticize during this visit.* Ali was overdue for a clothes-shopping trip to Wal-Mart.

The group parted to make way for Ali and Janelle. Did they expect fireworks? Ali loved her sister but didn't like her much. To preserve family harmony, Ali promised to swallow years of humiliation and try a dose of civility.

"Welcome, Big Sis," Ali said while she hugged Janelle. Ali felt as though she had been inflated with air in preparation for flying at the Macy's Thanksgiving Day Parade compared with svelte Janelle.

"Let's go into the house," Virginia said.

"What's with this car?" Ed asked.

"My people screwed up when they reserved the car, but it's better for the environment. Don't you think so, Kayla?"

Kayla beamed at her aunt.

"Where are your other bags?" Ali was amazed that Janelle was traveling light with only a large tote and one rolling bag.

"This was all I could fit into this pea-sized car. We can send Matty back to the airport for the rest of it."

No other family member referred to Matt using his childhood nickname. He didn't seem to mind or at least he never corrected Janelle. The group walked into the house and moved toward the living room.

"Here, Mom. Take a picture of Aunt Janie and Logan and me. I'll post it on Facebook tonight. And Instagram, too," Kayla said.

Ali glared at the phone. "I suppose all your friends' mothers know about this stuff?" she said to Kayla who shrugged her shoulders.

Logan came to Ali's aid and took the phone from her. "I'll do it, Mrs. Lawrence. It's a selfie."

Ali was determined to take a class at the community center to teach her the technology that Kayla was so adept at using.

Virginia took Janelle's hand and led her to a sofa. Mother and daughter were mirror images, minus thirty years—porcelain skin, glossy black hair. They shared the same Paul Newman eye color. Like a press conference, a poised and rehearsed Janelle answered many questions about book tours past and future. After fifteen minutes, the visiting celebrity said, "I need to take a bath. Traveling is so grueling."

"Yes, that's a long flight from NYC to ATL," Ed said. "What is it? About two hours?"

"It's taxing if you booked your flight so late you were stuffed in coach," Janelle said. "Bathroom in the same place?"

"Yes. We even have hot water," Ali said.

After Janelle left the room, Ed spoke to Virginia. "That was a royal brush off. I don't blame Janelle for her rudeness; it's your fault. Always praising, and—"

"She's not rude. She's tired," Virginia said. "Let's go."

Ali assumed her dad loved both his daughters equally, but she knew he liked her more. Perhaps he was compensating for the inordinate amount of attention Virginia threw Janelle's way. Ali recalled conversations with her dad. "It's not so odd that one parent pays more attention to one child," Ali's father often told her. "Sometimes a parent has more in common with one than the other. Your mother was into fashion and beauty and superficial things. You weren't."

"Maybe I could have been. As it turned out, I became the opposite. Instead of fashion-forward, I went fashion-backward. I tried hard to emulate whatever Janelle liked, thinking it would bring me closer to Mother. Didn't work."

"Doesn't mean she loves Janelle more, Gingersnap," Ed had said.

"Wait." Matt motioned to Kayla who nudged Ed and Logan. They lined up in a straight row.

Matt addressed Ali. "May we be dismissed, sir—, er ma'am?"

Ali laughed. "Dismissed," she said while saluting her loyal troop.

Virginia shook her head and offered a weak smile at her goofy family.

"Ali, tell your sister we'll have dinner at our house tomorrow night instead."

"Sounds fine. Will give you more time to prepare. Don't overdo it, Mother," Ali said.

"Bring some of your mushroom tarts, dear. Oh, and don't forget. You promised to put my name in the program for the book banquet."

"But—you haven't—Sure, Mom. I won't forget," Ali said.

Kayla sent Logan on his way telling him she needed "family time." She jogged upstairs to ensure her aunt was comfy.

"Now that wasn't so bad was it?" Matt asked Ali before he headed to his computer in the den.

"I guess not." Whenever Janelle came to Willoughby, Ali compared her lifestyle with her sister's. How different would her life had been if she had followed Janelle's lead and ventured out of Willoughby to begin a career in journalism or publishing or anything else? Lately, she'd been questioning her lifestyle choices and the lack of a career. But, she wondered if Janelle knew real happiness living a nomad's life, no children, no husband, and no dog.

The house was calm and quiet. Ali's neck ached and she craved to sleep for a week. She had to keep positive. Maybe this visit with Janelle would prove better than previous visits. Virginia and Kayla would keep Janelle occupied and out of the way. Maybe now the sisters could accept each other's flaws and applaud each other's accomplishments.

Maybe there's an Easter Bunny, too.

"What do you think about your room?" Kayla asked her aunt. "Logan and I did all the decorating."

"Lovely. Absolutely lovely. You know how much I love the beach, even though I don't go there anymore. My skin, you know. Thank you, Kayla. But when my luggage arrives I don't know where we'll put it."

"We'll figure it out. Anything I can get you, Aunt Janie?"

"Let's catch up later. I'm going to take a bath now." Janelle gave Kayla a kiss on top of her head. "I need some alone time," she said, behind the closed bathroom door.

A solemn Kayla lumbered downstairs.

"Aren't you two pals going to hang out together, honey?" Ali asked.

"She said to leave her alone. She's probably tired. I better take Roxie for a walk."

Another royal rejection.

Ali understood how disappointed Kayla must feel to receive the brush off from the aunt she adored. "Kayla, let me tell you something about your aunt. She treats you the same way she treated me when we were young. One day you'll be best friends then the next day she'll ignore you. That's the way she is."

"She's probably sick," Kayla snapped. "Anyway, we have a different relationship than you did. We're more alike."

Ali's recent tact with Kayla was to agree with anything she said as long as it didn't involve a gun or a high-speed auto chase. Janelle had only been in the house a few hours and already Kayla was acting like an apprentice prima donna. Unfortunately, despite Ali's attempts to protect her daughter, Kayla would learn what the authentic version of Janelle resembled.

Chapter 9

The next morning, Kayla entered the kitchen out of breath. "Mom, where's the tray with the kittens on it you use when I'm sick and you bring me food in bed?"

"Shouldn't you be getting ready for school?" Ali asked.

"I want to bring Aunt Janie breakfast in bed. Don't you think she'd love that? So where's the tray?"

"Your aunt can make her own breakfast, Kayla. Logan's dad will be here any minute."

"Mom," Kayla said petulantly. She stretched it out to one long syllable: Mommmmm.

"Your aunt isn't awake yet. I'll bring her something, if that will make you happy. Is that a horn?"

"Make sure it looks nice. A flower, too. She'll love that. Tell her it was my idea."

"Yes, ma'am."

Ali's legs felt as though she had run a marathon—not that Ali knew what running 26.2 miles felt like, but she could guess. A dull ache gnawed at her lower back. More important, she was annoyed at herself for stressing out about Janelle's arrival. Her reaction made her appear jealous and weak. She was determined to paint a false face and pretend everything was hunky dory. Her sister would have to take Ali "as is." Attempting to impress Janelle or even trying to make her comfortable was impossible. Ali made choices a long time ago and should feel contentment with them and not second-guess herself. *Good advice, Dr. Ali. Now follow it.*

She went to the freezer in the garage to choose an item to take to Phoebe's that afternoon. The house would soon overflow with out-of-town relatives too tired to think about preparing meals. After choosing a pan of vegetable lasagna, Ali kept the freezer door open and stuck her head inside for a few minutes. *Ahhhhh. I'll have to remember this technique to de-stress.*

"Oh, here you are," Janelle said. "Why do you have your head in the freezer?"

"Ow!" Janelle's appearance in the doorway to the garage startled Ali into hitting her head on the freezer door.

"Sorry."

"Thanks for your sympathy. Let's go inside. I need ice."

After opening several cabinets, Janelle found a tumbler and filled it with ice and water. "Will this help?" she said as she handed the glass to her sister.

"It's my head," Ali said pointing to her skull. "Forget it." She went to the freezer and removed ice cubes to put in a plastic bag.

"Tell me more about Phoebe."

"She was active up until the end. Tripped leaving the library after a Zumba class, was taken to the hospital, and passed away. I don't know the actual cause of death."

"Where's the obit? I read it online, but can I see it again? Where is it?" Janelle asked. She was twirling a piece of her black glossy hair around her finger, a childhood habit she shared with her sister.

"Why the interest?"

"We sort of kept in touch. I haven't heard from her in a while." Janelle's face softened like a disappointed parent of her child's losing team.

"I didn't realize you were close."

"As I said, we sort of stayed in contact."

"Odd that you dedicated your first book to her. What was that all about? Mother still hasn't recovered."

"Mom was supportive of my beauty pageants, but she didn't know anything about creative writing. Phoebe helped me win the Willoughby New Talent writers award," Janelle said.

Ali felt her stomach tighten. "That she did." *And, who helped you write and edit the story?*

Roxie approached Janelle, nipping at her toes.

"Go away," Janelle said to Roxie. "I'm not a dog person."

"I don't think Roxie's a Janelle person."

Janelle shook her finger at Roxie. "Bad dog. Go away." She took a seat at the kitchen table.

Roxie replied by barking, then growling at Janelle.

"Damn that dog of yours. Get her out of here. She's vicious."

"Watch your language. Not a good example for Kayla," Ali said. "Come here, Roxie. What's the matter?" Roxie dashed to Ali's side.

"Aren't you going to apologize for your dog's behavior?" Janelle returned to reading Phoebe's obituary Ali left on the table.

"I think you make Roxie nervous," Ali said. *This dog needs a treat for outstanding behavior.*

"There's that phone again. It's been ringing nonstop since I arrived."

"I get phone calls about the book banquet." She took the plastic bag of ice to the sink and let the answering machine pick up. "I won't ask again, Janelle, but I'm curious. Why is it that when I asked you to speak this year, you declined? When you heard that we might need a speaker, you called Diane. Why not me?"

"Well, I was busy when you asked. My schedule changed. When I heard about Phoebe, I didn't want to bother you, so I called Diane. She said you already had a speaker this year. Laurel Atwood. She's a big competitor of mine. I don't mind friendly competition. Showing her age, though."

Ali sat at the kitchen table across from Janelle. The sisters were face to face. Even as an aging prom queen, Janelle looked good. More than good. Gorgeous. A piece of green jewelry dangled from a thick silver chain around Janelle's neck. Ali was gem-challenged so she couldn't identify it, but it spoke expensive. The pearls Matt had given her twenty years ago, as a wedding present, were her only big-girl jewelry. Not only did Ali's faded mommy jeans and white T-shirt stained with tomato sauce need an update but also her hair and her body.

"You look amazing, Janie."

"A few nips and tucks. I know this talented plastic surgeon in Beverly Hills I could recommend. Not that you don't look perfectly fine, Li'l Sis. Healthy. You look healthy."

Was the "healthy" a reference to Ali's waistline? *Why did I eat all those nasty chocolate chips?*

"Matt and I are trying to get fit and lose weight," Ali said. "We didn't think Kayla deserved losing both parents because we lacked the discipline to forego second helpings of mashed potatoes overloaded with butter." *Or triple chocolate fudge brownies.*

"Don't worry. I would take care of Kayla. Mother and I."

Ali shuddered at the idea of Virginia Withrow and Janelle Jennings parenting Kayla. They would mold Kayla into a Janelle-like clone.

"What's that pan of food on the counter? Are you planning to take some kind of a chicken casserole or something to Brad? Isn't that what you people do around here?"

"Yes, 'you people' usually take food. Don't think it's strictly a Willoughby custom."

"What can I bring? Flowers? Do you have any in your garden? Do I need to buy some? Where's the florist shop? Does Jill Porter still have that flower store?"

"You seem awfully interested in Phoebe and Brad." Ali shook her head and told Janelle she wanted to change her clothes before they went to Phoebe's. "By the way, you'll note in Phoebe's obituary—no flowers. She didn't know the difference between a dandelion and a daffodil. I think she was colorblind, too. I won't take long. Then, you and I can have a chat."

"Do something with your hair while you're at it, Ali."

Ali couldn't remember if she had combed her hair that morning. If Ali's hair were as obliging as her sister's, perhaps she'd take more interest. The short end of the stick again.

When the sisters were young, their mother continually praised Janelle for her choice of clothing and beautiful hair. Virginia could coax Janelle's hair into a variety of styles. She braided it, put it in pigtails, or made one long glorious ponytail that swayed like a thoroughbred's when Janelle walked. She wore a flip, or big hair, whatever was in style. In contrast, Ali's hair was out-of-control frizzy and Carrot Top-like.

When Ali was about to enter high school, Janelle decided her sister's hair needed straightening. Janelle set up the ironing board and iron when the coast was clear, meaning the parents were out of the house. Janelle put the iron on its hottest setting. She positioned Ali on a chair with her back to the ironing board. When the iron was sizzling hot, Janelle commenced the makeover of her sister's hair. Weeks passed before the smell of burning hair left Ali's nostrils.

Virginia defended Janelle saying she only tried to improve her sister's appearance. Ali knew the real reason. Janelle didn't want anyone to know that the freckled-faced girl with the Bozo hair was her sister.

The burned hair was Ali's fault, Virginia said, as they marched to the beauty salon to have her hair whacked off to barely below her ears. "Why did you ask Janelle to do such an outlandish thing?" Virginia demanded. "What will our friends and neighbors think?"

Ali had no answer that would satisfy her mother.

Janelle didn't seem bothered. "Ali begged me, Mommy. Honest."

Ali went to her bedroom and chose a denim skirt and one of her many white T-shirts—one sans coffee stains. She clipped on a pair of small, gold hoop earrings. She moved to the bathroom and found a mauve shade of lipstick in a seldom-used cosmetic bag. A straw hat covered her wild hair, and brown worn clogs completed her outfit. Ali made another mental note to buy new clothes. Her three sets of drab-colored sweat suits and faded jeans needed to join their friends in the Goodwill bag.

As Janelle and Ali were driving the short distance to Phoebe's house, Ali questioned her sister regarding the length of her stay. "I'm glad to see you but it is unexpected." A short stay would work; a long stay would require commitment to a mental health institution or multiple visits to a psychiatrist.

"I didn't think I needed to give my family notice." She pulled down the visor. "I should have known this old pickup wouldn't have a mirror."

"This truck may be old in years but she was in pristine condition when Matt appraised her at the dealership. She still looks good and I'll never give her up."

"Well, I guess that figures since you like old things—your kitchen and your disgusting walking shoes."

Why defend myself. It's a losing battle. "You're right. I like old things. I'm nostalgic and sentimental."

Janelle reached for the rearview mirror to check for non-existent lipstick smears on her sparkling teeth.

Ali repositioned the mirror. "With the upcoming book banquet, I can't promise much catch-up time for you," Ali said.

"No problem. I have lots to keep me occupied."

"Like what?"

"Business things. The business of being an author. And, want to spend time with Kayla. Don't you love the pictures she posts on Facebook? That Logan is adorable."

"Facebook? Sounds like Kayla and I are the ones who need to play catch up." Ali renewed her vow to sign up for classes to learn about social media.

They approached Phoebe's home, which was in need of a paint job. Yellow pansies lined both sides of the pathway to the house like welcoming Munchkins. Nailed to a majestic oak were several brightly painted, wooden bird feeders, the creative work of the deceased Joe Patterson. Some birdhouses swung from low hanging branches on various trees. Azaleas in vivid pinks and purples were beginning to pop.

"Look at all the cars. The casserole brigade is in high gear," Ali said.

"Isn't it curious why she never bought a fancier house by now?" Janelle asked.

"She probably lived on a teacher's pension and social security. Her husband never succeeded financially. They were always able to afford interesting trips around the world, though." Ali held the lasagna pan in both hands as she stood at the front door waiting for Janelle to ring the bell. "I need some help. Your lipstick is fine. Put the mirror away and please ring the darn—"

Brad opened the door. He gave them a wide welcoming grin. He wore black jeans and a snug black T-shirt. He had a towering presence, wide-set brown eyes, and eyelashes any woman would covet.

"I'm so sorry about your grandmother," Ali said.

He ushered the sisters into the house.

"Thanks, Ali. The noise will lead you to the kitchen." He stepped aside. "Here's the famous author," Brad said. "Mimi spoke about you frequently. I'll catch up with you in a minute." He admired Janelle's figure as she wiggled her way to the kitchen.

Brad's comment puzzled Ali. Why would Phoebe speak about Janelle *frequently*?

Ali followed enticing aromas that led to the kitchen where many of Phoebe's friends milled about. Platters of cookies, funeral cakes, several sweet potato pies, and mile-high layer cakes with thick chocolate frosting crowded the harvest gold countertop. Ali crammed the lasagna pan, labeled with date and contents, into the already full harvest gold refrigerator. Sweet iced tea in clear glass pitchers shimmered on the avocado green Formica-topped table in the breakfast nook.

Janelle said, "Look at that toaster. Must be as old as Phoebe. I'm going to find Brad."

"Was that your sister who came in with you?" Evelyn Sheldon asked Ali. Her eyesight, despite thick glasses perched on a generous nose, was sharp. "Is she coming to the book banquet? Did she come for Phoebe's memorial service?"

Ali gave a non-committal nod but wished for the impertinence to say, "Ask her and let me know her answer."

Janelle didn't waste any time cozying up to Brad. Her intense interest in Phoebe was curious. She never mentioned to Ali that she had kept in contact except for visits to Willoughby every few years when she would make a point to see Phoebe. Ali assumed that was out of respect because her former English teacher encouraged Janelle's creative writing.

Ali watched Janelle and Brad move into the den off the dining room where Phoebe kept her old typewriter and piles of books. The books were everywhere—on the shelves, on the floor, and on the several occasional tables scattered around the room. A computer was in the middle of the desk.

Janelle closed the French doors. Her back faced the guests. She made sweeping gestures of the room with her right arm as she moved over to the desk and sat down facing the glass doors. Brad, smiling at Janelle, stood in the corner of the room with his arms folded across his body.

In the kitchen, Ali approached the popular dessert table and waited in vain for an opportunity to spear a piece of chocolate cake and stuff it in her mouth. Instead, she decided to vacate from temptation. She spied Janelle and Brad in the den and opened the doors. "Time to leave, Janie."

"I invited poor Brad to Mother's for dinner tonight, but he declined." She avoided looking at Ali while scanning the top of the desk.

"Another time," Ali said. "You'll be here for how long, Janelle?"

Janelle didn't fall for the trap, but merely shrugged her shoulders. "No longer than necessary," she said. "You have a mound of paperwork on your dear grandmother's desk. I have outstanding organizational skills. Perhaps I could drop by tomorrow after the memorial service and help."

"I'm going to gather it all up and give it to Mimi's attorney," Brad said. "Never know what might be hiding in that heap of paper." He winked at Janelle.

"Oh, no," Janelle said. Like a rocket, she stood and faced Brad. "It's no bother. We'll talk tomorrow." She struggled to gain her composure.

Brad gave Ali a brotherly hug and a light kiss on her cheek. He shook Janelle's hand. She grabbed onto his hand with both of hers and pulled him close to her in a tight grip. She wrapped her arms around his waist and whispered into his ear.

"I wish you had grabbed me like that when we were in high school," he said.

Ali took Janelle by the hand and led her to the front door. "What was that about? Molesting him in front of Phoebe's friends?"

"Relax. A friendly hug, that's all."

"Why did you invite 'poor Brad' for dinner?" Ali asked Janelle as they walked to the car.

"When we were in Phoebe's office, he said she might have left something for me, but he wouldn't say what."

"You'll have plenty of time to catch up with Brad. How long are you staying?"

"There you go again, Li'l Sis. Enjoy me while I'm here."

Guess it's time to make that appointment with a shrink.

Ali practically tripped over a mountain of luggage as she entered her home with Janelle trailing behind.

"Oh, goody," Janelle said. She grabbed a small tote bag and wobbled up the steps in her high heels.

"Don't fall on Aunt Janie's suitcases, Mom. You wouldn't want to damage them," Kayla yelled from the top of the stairs.

"You are so right, Kayla. Wouldn't want to hurt the luggage but no problem if your mother breaks her neck."

Oblivious to Ali's comment, Kayla bounded down the stairs. She and her aunt met halfway and air kissed each other.

"Don't forget. Dinner at Mother and Dad's tonight," Ali called out.

Janelle waved her hand at Ali and continued sashaying up the stairs.

"Aunt Janie promised to buy me luggage like this when we go to Italy," Kayla said, when she came downstairs and retrieved another bag before joining her aunt.

"How did all this get here?" Ali asked Matt.

"Janelle asked if she could borrow my car to return to the airport since her car was too small. Didn't like that idea. I decided to go alone. Then Kayla asked if she could come."

Ali knew that Matt chose the better of two options, but she resented Janelle for taking Matt's time away from work and Kayla's focus off her schoolwork. Ali ran a finger over the soft saddle-colored leather trim of a large tote waiting for delivery upstairs. She imagined all the places in the world this luggage traveled with her sister, places Ali would never visit except on the Travel Channel. "One of these days…" she said.

"Let's get the kitchen renovated and Kayla educated and then we'll travel," Matt said. He lifted two more pieces of Janelle's belongings and trekked up the stairs like a bellman at the Ritz Carlton. "This is the last trip up those stairs I'm going to make."

When Matt returned downstairs, he found Ali in the kitchen. "Why do you think she's staying with us?" During Janelle's previous visits, she had stayed with her parents or at the Willoughby Inn. For Janelle, staying with her sister's family would be quite different from staying in a hotel.

"Who knows? Hard to figure her out," Ali said. "She's in for a shock when she finds out we make our own beds in this house and no one has ever put chocolate on my pillows. Well, except when I might have dropped brownie crumbs while eating in bed."

"You might have determination on your side, but one of you will have to change her habits, Ali, and I doubt that Janelle is the one."

Chapter 10

Ali arose early and slogged to the kitchen. Matt and Kayla had left without waking her, and the prom queen was still asleep. While Ali waited for coffee to brew, she read the obituaries, noting particularly well written ones that she would put in her archives.

Ali pushed the paper aside and surveyed the to-do list for the food she was making for another shower, this time a wedding shower for Chrissie's daughter Emma: peel cucumbers, bring cream cheese to room temp, place defrosted phyllo under damp towels. "Wasn't this the same menu for Rebecca's shower?" she asked Roxie who angled her head and replied in schnauzer talk. The phone rang. Ali inhaled, *1-2-3-4.* She held her breath and let the answering machine do its thing. *Damn breathing exercises are useless.* She turned off the ringer.

The doorbell rang. Ali walked to the front door and jerked it open.

"Whoops. Bad time? You look awful," Ellen said.

"Come on in. I need some diversion."

Ellen followed Ali into the kitchen.

"Looks more like you could use a personal chef. Throwing a party? Not inviting me?"

"I promised Chrissie to help with the food for her daughter's wedding shower. Plus, the book banquet meeting, which you *claim* you can't attend, and I promised Dad I'd take him to the eye doctor because Mother's playing bridge. What's on your agenda this fine day, Miss Ellen?"

"You mean after my appointment at the spa?"

Ali chuckled at her friend's humor.

"Not funny. Look at these nails. Nothing humorous here."

Ali moved to the kitchen table where she sat and put her face on top of her folded arms. "Help me," she said.

"You have to clean it up. You created this mess."

"I should hire a cleaning crew. What's the going rate?" Ali asked as she lifted her head.

"I don't mean this mess of a kitchen. I mean the mess of your life. Just say no."

"I don't do drugs."

"You're going to need drugs if you don't learn to say no. Try to say no to the next three people who ask you for something."

"Can't."

"Can't or won't? Call Chrissie and tell her you can't help with the food. She has enough money. Let her buy the stuff."

Ali twirled a piece of her loose hair into a tight knot. She undid her ponytail, shook her hair, and put the scrunchie back on.

Ellen picked up the phone and handed it to Ali. "Here. Call her."

Ali bit her upper lip. "Awfully short notice."

"Damn it. Call her."

Chrissie answered on the first ring.

"Change in plans. I apologize but I can't bear to make another cuke sandwich or a mushroom tart."

Chrissie was silent. "Anything you want to make is fine," she said softly. "I only asked you to make those items because everyone raves about them."

"Actually..."

Ellen leaned toward Ali inches from her nose. She made a *wrap it up* gesture with a finger.

"Actually," Ali repeated, "I don't want to make anything."

"Excuse me? You can't cancel at the last minute. What am I supposed to do?"

"Go to Costco. You'll find wonderful food: cheesecake, chicken salad, pimento cheese. Call Vanessa and ask for her help. She owes me."

Ali hung up before she changed her mind and returned to the kitchen table.

"Congratulations."

"How come I feel awful?"

"Your life doesn't depend on whether you make thousands of cucumber sandwiches for a dumb shower. I'm proud of you. Pour yourself a glass of wine and take a bath."

"It's nine o'clock in the morning! Life is simple for you but not for me. I should call Chrissie back and apologize." Ali stood and headed for the phone.

Ellen motioned for her to sit. "You need to reexamine your life. What about your husband and your daughter? They need you, too."

"I don't think so. Unfortunately. We all go in our personalized circles, hoping to converge now and then. Matt is distracted lately and Kayla has succumbed to Janelle's spell. Did you know Kayla keeps a journal of 'interesting' things Janelle says?"

"I've said my piece. You are one stubborn lady. No need for me to attend the banquet meeting. You have the budget figures. See you later."

Ali hoped she might feel better lightening her schedule, but she didn't. Guilt crept over her like kudzu climbing a telephone pole.

She returned the phyllo to its box and placed it in the freezer; she put the cucumbers and the cream cheese in the refrigerator. *Wait until Chrissie tells the entire town that I reneged on a promise. I should call her back.* She looked toward the phone, hesitated, and then went to the bathroom to dress for the meeting.

***

Later in the morning, Ali gathered the materials she needed and tossed them in her Land's End canvas tote with her initials embroidered in red. She checked Roxie's water bowl before she left for the short walk to the Tea Cozy Shoppe. A lingering veil of saffron-colored pollen covered cars, streets, and pedestrians. When Ali entered the store, Maggie's glass case, filled with luscious pastries and muffins, accosted her. *Keep walking. This place is beating me up. Bad choice for a meeting.*

One by one, the committee arrived and sat at a round table in the rear marked "reserved" until all members were present except Ellen. After they shared pleasant greetings, Maggie poured a citrus flavored hot tea into cups decorated with yellow roses. A glass tiered platter of freshly baked lemon scones and blueberry muffins beckoned in the middle of the table. Ali tried to avoid even a glimpse of the super-sized muffin that shouted her name.

Ali called the meeting to order and distributed agendas. "Short story contest?"

"Winners chosen. Teachers informed," Ethyl said.

Ali moved through the reports of committees.

Lisa presented the publicity report: "Photographer and reporter confirmed."

Vanessa described the decorations. "We chose pastel colors to match the cover of Laurel's latest book."

"Any news on the menu?" Ali asked.

"Won't be fancy, but we'll make sure it looks pretty," Delaney said. "Don't want to embarrass Janelle."

"*Or* our keynote speaker," Maggie said while glaring at Delaney.

"I have an idea," Lisa offered. "Since Janelle's in town maybe we could ask her for a donation. At the least, we must give her a spot on the program."

Ethyl added, "Let's ask Janelle to join this committee. We have one more meeting scheduled. No telling what wonderful ideas she'll have."

Ali squirmed, twisted a piece of her hair, and remained silent. The committee directed their focus at her anticipating a response like, "Great idea. I'll ask her." A sip of tea gave her time to form a reply. Ali wished that Ellen had joined the meeting because she would know what to say and had the courage to say it. As it stood, three con-Janellers—Ali, Maggie, and Jill—and four pro-Janellers—Ethyl, Lisa, Vanessa, and Delaney—were at the table.

Maggie came to Ali's rescue. "We have to ensure Janelle doesn't upstage Laurel Atwood. Remember, Laurel's not charging us a speaking fee as a favor to her cousin, the mayor. You know how much attention Janelle attracts when she's here."

"But this would make the banquet more exciting," Vanessa said. "Two famous authors."

Maggie looked at Ali and mouthed, "I tried."

"What about flowers for the buffet table?" Ali asked.

"Won't be lavish but I'll donate what I can," Jill said.

Ethyl distributed copies of the program. Ali flipped to the back page with the heading: "Gratitude to our Volunteers" and was relieved to see her mother's name listed, even though Virginia's contribution was as beneficial as a turtle's.

"Looks great," Ali said. "I don't anticipate any problems. Thanks to everyone. You are a wonderful group. We'll meet in a week."

"Don't forget to bring Janelle," Lisa reminded.

During the walk home, Ali recalled her parting words to the group: "Don't anticipate any problems." *With my sister in town, who knew what unpredictable events might occur.*

To: kbellen
Fm: flowersbyJill
Re: Banquet committee meeting today

You'll never guess who might join the committee. Our very own prom queen.

Chapter 11

Around dinnertime, Ali stood at the bottom of the stairs, called out to Janelle and Kayla, and told them to hurry up. "We're late for dinner at Mom and Dad's."

Matt called earlier to say he would meet them at his in-laws' house. Years of practice gave Matt the knack for diffusing tension between the sisters, so she hoped he wouldn't be late. Ali collected a few items from the fridge—plump green and black olives, ruby red grapes, and a round of creamy brie. She went to Matt's wine collection and chose a few bottles, one for Matt, and two for Janelle. She changed her mind and replaced the bottles. She didn't want to waste Matt's favorite wines on Janelle. Ali selected a few bottles from the pantry for the basket. Her dad would stick to drinking manhattans and her mother's drink of choice was a gimlet. Ali packed the items in a wicker basket even though she sensed the evening with Janelle wasn't going to turn out to be a picnic. But, she could hope. Ali glanced around the kitchen. She was forgetting something.

Aunt and niece were quiet upstairs—no water running, no footsteps, and no response to Ali's call for departure. She dashed up the stairs and knocked on Kayla's bedroom where the two were ensconced. Still, no response. Ali gingerly opened the door and found two escapees from a spa side by side in the twin beds. Plastered on their faces was green gunk and circles of cucumbers sat on their eyelids. A sudden craving for guacamole and a margarita overcame Ali.

Janelle and Kayla were wearing matching plush white terry-cloth bathrobes with large gold curlicues on each pocket and around the collars. Kayla, plugged into her earbuds, was rolling her head back and forth like a metronome. On her back in the adjacent bed, Janelle made noises through her nose like a male seal on the prowl.

"Wake up, you two. Nana and Gramps are expecting us. Five minutes ago."

When Ali shook Kayla's foot, she noticed neon green polish on her toenails. Kayla never showed interest in painting her nails prior to Janelle's recent arrival. Kayla sat up and both cucumber slices fell to her lap. The tender approach didn't work with Janelle, so Ali leaned into her ear and said, not so lightly, "Time to get up, Queenie."

Janelle sat upright with such a shock she rolled off the bed and tumbled to the floor face down into the carpet with arms outstretched.

"Aunt Janie, are you hurt?" Kayla cried out.

"I think I broke my wrists and maybe my nose!" Janelle shrieked.

Roxie, who had followed Ali upstairs, joined in, barked wildly, and jumped up on Kayla's bed.

"Oh no, I'll never get that green stuff off the carpet!" Ali screamed. She charged downstairs to retrieve carpet cleaner and paper towels and returned to find Kayla consoling Janelle. Roxie, who shared Ali's love of guacamole, was licking avocado off Janelle's cheek.

"Get that damn dog off me."

Ali's neck began to warm, foreshadowing a rash of stress-induced tiny bumps. Ali wasn't sure whether she was more irritated with the disaster on the carpet, the concern Kayla offered her aunt, or Janelle's screaming at Roxie. If she had to choose, she'd take all three.

"We've kept Mother and Dad waiting long enough and now I have this mess to deal with. Care to help, either of you?" Ali asked as she attempted to shove paper towels into their hands.

"You stay where you are, Aunt Janie. I'll clean it up. Do you need an aspirin after that fall?"

Janelle uttered something incomprehensible and stomped to the bathroom. "I spent a lot of money on this nose. If it's broken, Ali, it's your fault. You didn't have to scare the hell out of me."

Kayla gawked at the green imprint of Janelle's face on the floor and turned pale. She loved her new carpet, spending many hours deciding on whether white was the right choice.

"It wasn't her fault, Mom. You scared her."

"I should have scared her so much she'd pack her bags and leave. You should have been downstairs anyway." Sometimes Ali didn't recognize her own voice. When did she begin growling at Kayla?

"I don't get you, Mom. She didn't do this on purpose."

"You'd defend your aunt even if she was a serial killer, wouldn't you?"

Kayla shot her mother a look of defiance. "Mooother. Why are you so mean?" Without another word, she helped her mother wipe up as much of the avocado glop as they could and then soaked the area with carpet cleaner.

Janelle offered no apology for possibly staining the carpet nor did Ali apologize for causing a potential nose flattening to her.

Here I am again, Ali thought, *cleaning up after Janelle.* When they were young, Ali kept both sides of their shared bedroom neat. Every morning she made their beds. She gathered Janelle's clothes from the floor and hung them in the closet. Frequently, she tossed empty potato chip bags and other garbage. Ali took a secret oath, instigated by Guess Who, that she would keep her mouth shut and never tell their parents of Janelle's devious and lazy ways. As an incentive to keep the secret, Janelle offered her sister rewards. The bribes might consist of a couple of dollars or the opportunity to hang out with Janelle's friends. Ali didn't care about the rewards. She wanted to please her sister.

Ali glanced at the stained carpet before returning downstairs to sit on the porch. With the wicker basket in her lap she felt like Red Riding Hood trying to escape the Big Bad Wolf named Janelle. While sitting in the rocker she tried to enjoy the warm spring breeze and the calming effect of the back and forth motion. She snatched a ladybug from the white chair and threw it in the air homeward bound. Ali wished she could jump on the ladybug's back and leave town. The sphere of an orange-red sun descended behind the trees, out of sight, and announced dusk. She still had the feeling she was forgetting something.

Ali called her parents from her cell to tell them they were running late. Ed answered the phone. "Covering for Janelle as always, I suppose."

"Something like that."

Ed knew Janelle better than anyone else in the family, especially better than Virginia.

"Hurry on over. Your mother's driving me crazy getting things ready for her royal highness. Her feelings were hurt that Janelle didn't make a beeline over here as soon as she arrived in Willoughby."

"I've been meaning to talk to you, Dad. Do you think you and I could conspire to move Janelle out of my house and into yours?"

"I think we can accomplish that. Let me think about it. We'll talk later. You'll owe me, of course."

Good old Dad to the rescue.

Chapter 12

For the moment, the brief conversation with her dad had calmed Ali. She continued to rock on the porch, admiring the white-tipped hostas in her shade garden. She made a mental note to pull the weeds before Virginia, Master Gardener, made a visit.

In record time, about twenty minutes, Janelle appeared, transformed from an ad for a Mexican restaurant to an urban sophisticate. Janelle's hair was styled and neat. Her impeccably made up face was void of traces of green. She was wearing a girly plum colored sleeveless blouse with a cowl collar. Ali didn't know much about clothes, but it was silk-like compared with Ali's polyester wardrobe. If Janelle had a wrinkle on her neck or face, one would need a hunting license to find it. Her slim cropped jeans revealed no waistline bulges or evidence of eating too many tortilla chips. She wore strappy platform sandals about ten inches high—well, maybe only five inches, but she strolled to the car as poised as a runway model.

Ali didn't recognize Kayla's outfit: tight and revealing mini shorts similar to underwear. A bright pink halter-top was unfamiliar, too.

"Are those clothes new?"

"Aunt Janie chose this outfit for me from her suitcase. We're the same size. Isn't that cool, Mom?"

"The shorts are too skimpy. I don't want your dad or your grandparents to see you dressed like that. Please, Kayla."

"Oh, Ali, you're such a tight ass," Janelle said.

"Please don't use that language in front of Kayla."

"Oh, Mom, lighten up. I've heard worse."

"Kayla, you cannot go to your grandparents' home dressed like a hoochie momma or whatever the term is."

"How could you say that about me? You know I'm not a slut. You never let me do anything I want. You're jealous of Aunt Janie because you couldn't squeeze even one leg into these shorts."

She hit the bull's eye with that one. A smart-mouthed teenage daughter can put her dumpy mom in her place anytime.

"Besides, Aunt Janie would never drive an awful truck like yours. Her yellow car is only temporary."

"Upstairs. And watch your mouth. We'll talk later about respecting your mother. Make it snappy," Ali growled.

After taking her time, Kayla returned wearing a short flouncy skirt in a crazy pattern of light blues and pale greens over ivory leggings.

"Much better. You look adorable," Ali said.

"I don't want to look 'adorable.' I want to look like Aunt Janie."

Janelle had the sense to stay out of this one.

"Your aunt is older. All I ask is that you dress appropriately for your age. Subject closed for now."

"Guess we'll have to squeeze into your jalopy," Janelle said.

Ali slid into the driver's side, Kayla in the middle, and Janelle on the passenger side. They drove in silence. Evidently, Janelle realized she had gone too far today. Kayla didn't say a word, but when Ali caught her daughter's attention, she detected a slight smirk. Ali wanted Kayla to have a loving relationship with her aunt. What the mom said should count for something. Ali felt relief when she saw Matt's car in the driveway when they arrived at her parents' house.

As the threesome exited the car, the front door flew open. Virginia stood with outstretched arms and hugged them one by one, as they entered the house.

"Why are you crying, Nana?" Kayla asked.

"Because I'm so happy. These are tears of joy, dear. Both my girls and my granddaughter. All together." She took a handkerchief from her apron pocket and dabbed at her eyes.

"Ed, where are you?" Virginia called out. "Kayla, go find your father and your grandfather and tell them to meet us in the kitchen. That grandfather of yours thinks I don't know about his pipe smoking."

When Ed and Matt joined them more hugging and kissing ensued. Ali thought they made a wonderful picture of family unity—parents, granddaughter, daughters, son-in-law—all sharing joy in each other's company. All they needed was a dog. A dog! Ali forgot Roxie. She should have left Janelle at home instead.

Virginia Withrow and Phoebe Patterson shared the same style of kitchen—both in need of renovation. Virginia would never part with her avocado green appliances. She often told the family that if she discarded the old kitchen table and chairs, memories of happy family gatherings might vanish as well.

The sweet aroma of cinnamon and apples conflicted with the smell of burned toast. Since Ali assumed toast wasn't on the menu, her guess was that Virginia overcooked one of her "surprise" casseroles. As kids, Janelle and Ali withstood dinners of tuna casserole topped with mushy potato chips or leathery roast beef drowning in cream of mushroom soup because they anticipated a luscious lemon meringue pie or a multi-layered coconut cake for dessert. Virginia's baking skills more than compensated for other cooking deficiencies.

Ali unpacked the picnic basket and put the items on the counter.

"Do you need to warm the mushroom tarts?" Virginia asked.

"The what? Oh, gee, I'm sorry, Mother. I forgot."

"No matter," an ebullient Virginia said. Nothing could dampen her spirit with Janelle in the house.

Ed and Matt joined the family in the kitchen. Ed made a gimlet for his wife and a manhattan for himself. Matt uncorked the bottle of zinfandel Ali brought from home.

Ali watched as Janelle glimpsed into the still-gleaming chrome, 1950s-era toaster on the countertop checking her makeup. "Maybe you should wear a mirror around your neck."

If Janelle heard Ali's comment, she ignored her.

"I've made my family's favorite appetizer," Virginia said as she removed a tray from the refrigerator. "Let's move where we'll be more comfortable."

The family followed Virginia into the living room that displayed her skill at eclectic decorating. Several types of chairs purchased at estate sales filled the room: wingback, tub, and armless. The fabrics varied from formal brocade to comfortable chintz, yet she pulled it all together. Virginia served celery stuffed with pimento cheese on a glass plate. The plate sat on a silver plated tray with a chalkboard embedded. On it, she had written *Welcome, Janelle.*

"Love this pimento cheese," Ed said before he crunched a piece of celery.

Trying to find distraction from the fattening cheese, Ali focused on the bookshelf and noticed some new framed photos of Janelle. One was a publicity head shot and another was the jacket cover of one of Janelle's books. Shoved behind a pewter vase were pictures of Ali.

"Please take the tray to the kitchen, dear, and refill it," Virginia asked Ali. While in the kitchen, Ali *accidentally* smudged Janelle's name on the tray.

After the appetizers were finished, Virginia excused herself. "Ali can help me. Everyone else stay and entertain our special guest?"

"Guest? What guest?" Ed said.

"That's where you get your sarcasm from—your father," Virginia said to Ali.

Ali put the food on the table and Virginia announced that dinner was ready.

Mismatched fine china and sparkling crystal goblets in various shapes adorned the rectangular table in the dining room. Ivory taper candles stood like guardian angels at either end of the table protecting the meal and the family's stomachs.

When Janelle and Ali were young, a popular women's magazine extolled the use of mixing and matching china patterns. Their parents' budget didn't allow the purchase of a matching service for eight or six or even four, so this article caught Virginia's attention. She clipped the story and hung it on the refrigerator to dispel the notion that she was eccentric. That may or may not have worked—the eccentric part.

From then on Virginia was on a mission. She would explore yard sales, auctions, and thrift stores in search of attractive china and glassware. Many times, Ali would tag along. Janelle never joined them on these excursions much to the disappointment of Virginia. Sometimes Virginia would allow Ali to choose a plate or a glass for purchase. Most of the items found a home in Virginia's revenue-producing booth at Queen of Hearts.

Growing up, Ali loved the joy of sitting down to a special dinner to discover which plate Virginia would set before her. The Blue Willow pattern was her favorite because she discovered it during one of her treasure hunts with her mother.

Janelle was embarrassed when her friends came for dinner. Bad enough that Virginia's cooking was less than perfect, but they ate on unmatched plates, opined the older sister to anyone who would listen. If Janelle hurt Virginia's feelings, she didn't seem to mind.

"Let's sit down and eat," Ed said. "I hate cold food." He moved to one end of the table and Matt to the opposite end, their usual places. Virginia positioned herself on one side of Janelle and Kayla sat on the other side. Ali sat alone across from Janelle, eyeball to eyeball. *Alicia Lawrence, 140 pounds, in one corner wearing the white shirt; Janelle Jennings, 102 pounds in the black, in the other corner. Shake hands, ladies, and come out fighting.*

Immediately, Ali noticed the Blue Willow plate in front of Janelle.

"I see you gave *my* Blue Willow plate to Janelle, Mother."

Matt cleared his throat and ran a hand through his hair. He rubbed his forefinger across his lips hoping Ali would get the hint to shut up.

"Oh, did I? Not the plate thing again." Virginia took her napkin from her lap, tossed it on the table, stood, and marched over to Janelle. "Hand it over," she said to Janelle.

Virginia took the coveted plate and approached Ali. "Hand yours over, missy."

Oh no, the dreaded "missy." Ali was in trouble now. Over forty years old and the word "missy" still stabbed Ali in the heart. She tried to exchange the Blue Willow plate with the plate her mother had assigned her but it didn't work. Both plates slipped from their hands and landed on the carpet. One plate survived but the Blue Willow plate hit the edge of the table as it flew toward its death. Ali picked up the two shards. Did this mean banishment to the kitchen to eat alone after this blunder? *Not a bad idea.*

"Accidents happen, Alicia." Virginia moved to the sideboard where she kept her plates and selected one. With purpose, she held the plate up for all to see before she placed it in front of Ali. The plate had a Christmas motif that read "Naughty or Nice?"

"Funny, Mother," Ali said.

Everyone laughed.

"What about Aunt Janie? She needs a special plate, too," Kayla said.

Virginia selected another plate and held it up. It pictured a brown cow and a Dutch dairy maid. The young girl was pondering a pail of spilled milk. "You know what they say—"

"Don't cry over spilled milk," the family said in unison, anticipating one of Virginia's clichés.

More laughs.

"Virginia, sometimes you surprise me," Ed said.

"You think I don't have a sense of humor. I don't have a *sarcastic* sense of humor like some people in this family." She directed her comment to Ed and Ali.

"The sooner we eat and get it over with the sooner we can hit the Alka-Seltzer," Matt whispered across the table to Ali.

Ed lifted his cocktail and announced a toast. "Welcome home, Janelle."

They clinked glasses and cheered Janelle. Some cheered more enthusiastically than others.

"What about a blessing? Don't you people say a blessing?" Janelle asked.

"Kayla does the honors," Ed said.

"Aunt Janie. You say something. I know you will choose the perfect words."

Janelle told the family to bow their heads and close their eyes. She took a swig of wine when she was sure no one was looking.

"This ought to be good," Ed said quietly.

"God, the Father, the Holy Ghost, and the angels in heaven . . . in heaven . . . and in other places, wherever angels go and do not fear to tread . . . watch over this family today and forever and forever bless us and keep us forever and forever and—"

"That's enough. Let's eat," Ed said, interrupting Janelle's holy and sacred blessing. "Time for a toast. Welcome home, Janelle."

"We know Janelle is welcomed, Ed. You've already said that," Virginia noted.

As Ali predicted, the evening continued with everyone reveling in Janelle's stories of her fabulous life, her fabulous friends, the fabulous places she had visited, and her fabulous books. Gee, she's fabulous. Every now and then Matt would give his wife a double wink, his code for "lighten up." Ali would force a smile and make a flattering comment about Janelle's success. She was determined to get along with her sister. Even Matt would insert a laudatory remark when he could get a word in edgewise between Virginia's non-stop interrogation of Janelle.

Ed sipped his manhattan and observed. Kayla listened to every word her aunt uttered and watched her in an adoring trance. Every so often, Janelle would put her arm around Kayla, give her a tight hug, and kiss her cheek.

"You must save time for me, Janelle," Virginia said. "My friends always ask about you. We can go to my garden club, my church circle—all kinds of things. I want you to move in with us for as long as you want, dear. Remember a rolling stone gathers no moss. Unfortunately, your father has filled your old room with his junk. He promised to clear it out now that you are here." She pointed a finger at Ed.

"Not junk," Ed said. "Inventions."

Ali rose to his defense and reminded everyone that his inventions were important to him. She hoped no one brought up the fact that she too had a garage and a guestroom filled with stuff. A genetic trait?

Virginia changed the subject. "I haven't seen you recently on any of the morning talk shows, dear. Tell us about that pretty girl on TV who interviewed you last year. The one who was sick. She's a doll. So glad she's back on TV. I prayed for her, you know." Virginia and

Janelle chatted back and forth. Virginia seemed to know more about Janelle's schedule than Janelle did.

"Isn't it about time for your latest book to come out? Seems like you've been working on it a while. Every time I see your mother's friends they ask," Ed said.

"Soon. Need to make a few final edits."

Janelle spent the next hour talking about her previous book tours and all the famous people she had met, her TV appearances, book signings, her adoring fans.

"Traveling is so hard. I'm off to a new city every day. Frankly, I tire of always being on. I do have a devoted fan base, and I can't disappoint my readers with a dreary face," Janelle said.

"Absolutely not. Don't want to disappoint your fans," Ali said quietly.

Matt gave her another double wink.

"Something in your eye?" Janelle asked Matt.

Ed spoke up again. "It's great to see you, Janelle. But, why *are* you here?"

"Like I said, Dad, the manuscript needs a few edits. In fact, I need to spend time alone so I can complete some details. You might not see me for a few days. That's the life of a writer. So solitary."

"Why not finish the book and then come for a visit?" Ed persisted. He was tenacious, that's for sure. Go Daddy Go. If anyone wanted to know, it was Ali.

Not waiting for Janelle to respond to Ed's question, Virginia changed the subject again. "The Barrington Hall Guild asked me to give a presentation on china and silver patterns of the 1850s. Please come. I would love to show you off to my friends," Virginia pleaded.

"That would be wonderful sometime, Mother," Janelle said.

Virginia beamed. She either did not hear or ignored the "sometime."

"For Pete's sake. Doesn't anyone listen to me? What made you decide to come now? Usually you come after your book is published," Ed said.

"Mother's right, Dad. Time for a visit, that's all. No reason." Janelle tapped a finger on the rim of her glass and Matt refilled it.

Ali compared her short stubby fingers and ragged cuticles with Janelle's long and slender fingers. She swallowed another forkful of cheeseburger pie or whatever it was. The food wasn't too bad, Ali observed, taking a sip of wine.

"By the way, Alicia, don't forget the estate sale this week. Should be worthwhile because the site says the house belonged to a former New York City socialite. That provenance adds to the value."

"Yes, Mother. I won't forget this time."

Janelle changed the subject. Must be another genetic trait. "So sad about Phoebe Patterson, Mother. You played bridge together, didn't you?"

"Every week."

Janelle reached to the middle of the table toward the wine. Her shaking hand missed. Red wine splattered over Virginia's pristine white tablecloth that had belonged to her mother.

Virginia gasped. She stood, put her hand under the tablecloth, and placed her napkin on the stain. She took the pewter saltshaker shaped like a bird and poured the contents of his head on the wounded tablecloth. "Not to worry. Accidents happen. Heloise says salt will do the trick," Virginia said while wrinkling her forehead. "What do they say, don't cry over spilled wine?"

This time no one laughed at Virginia's attempt to make a joke.

Another accident. First, it was the guacamole and now the wine. This was beginning to become a food-related-accident-prone family.

Matt went to the kitchen and returned with another bottle of wine. He refilled Janelle's empty glass.

Janelle made no apology for spilling the wine. She sat there with her eyebrows together as though deep in meditation. She was overdue for a Botox fix.

"How's the casserole?" Virginia asked, defusing an awkward situation.

The family made individual and various comments and noises.

"Mmm."

"Like always."

"Never changes."

Virginia interpreted their responses as compliments and thanked everyone.

"Seconds?" she asked.

"Oh, no, Nana. We have to save room for your award-winning apple pie," Kayla said.

"Every old lady needs an adoring and loving granddaughter," Virginia said.

"You're not old, Nana," Kayla said to a smiling Virginia.

"Mother, I know what I'm going to give you for Christmas. One of Ina Garten's cookbooks. I hear they are wonderful," Janelle offered.

Since Janelle's arrival, this was the second time that she had insulted her mother. Sure, the family mocked their mother's cooking, but in a way, it was endearing that Virginia strived so hard to please them.

Virginia made a nervous giggle. "That would be a considerate gift, dear."

Considerate, hell. If she cared, she'd hire a personal chef for Mother, Ali thought.

"Let's have coffee and dessert in the living room," Virginia said as she gaped at the wine stain.

"No, let's stay here at the table. Like when the girls were young," Ed said. Finally, someone was listening to him. Everyone obeyed.

Virginia went to the kitchen and returned with her magnificent apple pie that won first place last year in the Annual Willoughby County Apple Pie Contest.

"How many calories in that? Guess I can have a tiny piece but no whipped cream. I can't eat the crust. The way you people eat is alarming," Janelle said.

That was the third time that Janelle used the phrase "you people." But, who was counting?

When they finished dessert, Janelle proclaimed it was time to leave.

"Not until we do the dishes," Ali said.

"Leave everything on the table. Dad and I will clean up in the morning," Virginia said.

Ali ignored her mother's remark and collected plates to carry to the kitchen. Matt and Kayla helped with the glasses and silverware.

Virginia scooped up her cherished tablecloth the minute the table was cleared and dashed straight for the washing machine where she dunked it in soapy water and hoped for the best.

"I'll wash, Kayla will dry, and Ali will put away," Matt instructed. This was the routine when they visited Virginia and Ed. The dishwasher in the Withrow home functioned as a storage container filled with a seldom-used slow cooker, various skillets, and pots.

Ali peeked around the corner and caught Janelle watching the trio cleaning up.

Kayla asked if she could quit kitchen duty and join her aunt and grandparents in the living room. "Permission granted, princess," Matt said. "By the way, you look nice tonight."

"Thanks. I guess," she answered. "Did Mom tell you to say that?"

"I don't need any help telling my daughter how pretty she looks."

When Kayla left the kitchen, Matt said, "She adores her aunt."

"Eventually, Janelle will let her down. If I warn Kayla, she'll think I'm jealous."

"Maybe you are? A little?"

Ali shrugged her shoulders.

Everyone said their goodbyes to Virginia and Ed with hugs and kisses. When they reached the driveway, Janelle claimed the passenger side of Matt's car. Kayla hopped into the seat behind her. Ali observed Janelle pat Matt on his shoulder. She stood next to her pickup and watched the taillights on Matt's car fade. As Ali drove home, she recalled Matt's comment.

Jealous? Just a little? Maybe more than a little.

Chapter 13

The following day, Ali and Janelle entered All Saints Church together. They stood in line to sign the guest book.

Steve Watterman, the funeral director, caught Ali's attention. "Great job on the Lucy Willis obit," he said when he was sure no one could hear.

Ali put a finger to her lips.

"You have quite the creative touch. You should write, like your sister."

"A few obituaries don't compare with Janelle's talent. But thank you, Steve."

"Who are all these people?" Janelle asked Ali as they found an empty pew in the back of the church.

"Lots of folks in this town were influenced by Phoebe—especially her students."

Outside the church, behind a large glass window facing the congregation, stood an imposing wooden cross. This seemed, at first, an unusual place to position a cross but striking and hard to ignore.

Janelle crossed her left leg over her right. She uncrossed her leg and then shifted the right leg over her left. Then she bounced her right leg up and down. She circled her foot, clockwise, then counterclockwise. She reached for a hymnal from the holder in front of her. Then she thumbed through it as though she were looking for a misplaced boarding pass minutes before a flight departure. As she put it back into the holder, it slipped from her moist hands. She picked it up and then took a white envelope from the holder and examined it.

"What's this? An offering? Will they take up a collection? I don't have cash."

Ali shook her head. "Not at a memorial service."

Janelle opened her cavernous Louis Vuitton tote and pawed through it: cosmetic bag, smartphone, Robert Cavelli sunglasses, coconut water, bottles of prescription medicine, Fendi wallet, small can of hairspray, and six black Sharpies held together with a rubber band. Janelle set the contents next to her and put each item back into the purse, one by one, like a bank teller counting money.

"Most people find churches relaxing and calming," Ali said.

"Hard to relax with that behemoth of a cross in front of us."

"Guilty perhaps?"

"I'm nervous around death. Don't like anything connected with death. Have I had one dead person in any of my books? No funeral homes. No caskets. No embalming fluid. No cremation. Nothing dead. Except a cheating husband or lover. I've had a few of those. And once a dead camel."

Janelle's phone started playing, "Time to Say Goodbye."

The sisters shared a look. "Really?" Ali said.

"Don't get your hopes up."

Fortunately, the organ prelude muffled the sound of Janelle's phone. She found it in the bottom of her purse, removed it, but it slipped out of her hand while continuing to play the song. Ali wanted to send her to the crying room.

When Virginia and Ed entered the church, Ali motioned to them. They joined their daughters in the pew. Matt was close behind.

Virginia climbed over Ali so she could sit in between both her daughters. "You look lovely," Virginia said to Janelle. Recognizing the slight to Ali, she turned and said, "You look nice, dear. Now don't forget to sit up straight like your sister."

"Mother. What am I? Five?"

Janelle bent forward and spoke to Ali. "What's with all the bright colors? I thought people wore black to events like this."

Ali observed the sea of silver-haired ladies dressed in bright colors, many wearing hats decorated with ribbons and artificial flowers.

"Phoebe often said she thought wearing somber colors to a funeral was maudlin," Virginia said.

"Message received," Janelle said. "Looks like Easter Sunday." Loud enough for Ali to hear, she added, "I wonder who sent that absolutely gorgeous flower arrangement on the altar?"

"Someone who didn't know Phoebe. Remember? Her obituary said no flowers."

"Girls. Be quiet."

The minister came forward and asked the mourners to stand and sing "Amazing Grace" before she conducted the service.

"I don't know the words," Janelle said.

"Look in the program, dear," Virginia said softly.

Then it was time for the family to speak about their departed loved one. Brad approached the lectern with slightly lowered shoulders, but when he took his place before the congregation, he stood to his full 6' plus height. He wore a slim-fit black suit with narrow lapels and a black and white striped tie. His white shirt was heavily starched and his pocket square was bright red in deference to Phoebe's favorite color. He pulled a piece of paper from his inside jacket pocket, turned to the photo of his grandmother on a stand to his left, and then turned back to the congregation.

"This is difficult. Not difficult to write a glowing recap of my grandmother's rich and full life. Hard to read it though. First, thank you for coming. The outpouring of kindness you have shown me is overwhelming. Since I'm an only child, I could have felt isolated, but I didn't, thanks to you. You have lifted me up like the words to Mimi's favorite song." He paused to remove a white handkerchief from his pants pocket and turned his back to the congregation for a moment. When he regained composure, he recited the accomplishments of his grandmother and gave a beautiful tribute without referring to his notes. He talked about his grandparents adopting him as a newborn after the death of his parents in a car accident. He told touching anecdotes about growing up with a "mother" who physically resembled a grandmother but acted like an energetic teenager. "As I went through Mimi's desk, I came across many notes and emails from former students. There was a universal theme in these touching messages that quoted her: 'Find your purpose in life and pursue it.'"

Brad returned to his spot in the pew with his relatives. Many of the congregants were dabbing their eyes with tissue or handkerchiefs.

A soloist sang: "Then sings my soul, my Savior God, to Thee, How great Thou art. How great Thou art." The minister continued with the service.

After the congregation finished singing the concluding song, "On Eagle's Wings," Janelle leaned behind Virginia and said to Ali, "Now what? Do we go back to the house?"

"The ladies of the church have prepared light refreshments in the Fellowship Hall. Then family and close friends will go to Phoebe's."

"So no one's at Phoebe's house?"

"Not yet. Why?"

"I'm not feeling well. I'll use your truck."

"You hate my pickup."

"Give me your keys. Now. I can manage. I'll meet you at Phoebe's."

Despite Ali's reluctance, she handed the keys to her sister who was hopping from one foot to the other as though she needed to visit the ladies' room. "If you don't feel well, maybe you should go home." Ali's comment was unheard.

"Whew," Janelle said aloud, as she started the engine on Ali's truck. She plodded along, ignoring a red light, and was nearly T-boned by a school bus.

Upon arriving at Phoebe's, Janelle surveyed the neighborhood to ensure she could enter undetected. She tried the door, but it wouldn't budge. Janelle took a guess. She lifted the *Welcome* doormat and found the hidden key. She entered the living room, established her bearings, and tiptoed into the den. She rifled through the top of the desk.

The safe. I bet that's where she put it. Wasn't much of a safe, Janelle observed as she lifted a lightweight container from the bookshelf. She tried stuffing it into her Grand Canyon purse but no luck. Janelle checked her Rolex.

"Hello? Anyone home?"

Oh, no. Busted. Can't hide; that jalopy of Ali's is in the driveway. That was stupid. I'm a writer. I'll figure something out. What did Kimberly Rockwell do when she was caught red-handed going through her husband's mistress's lingerie drawer in my book Burning with Desire?

Evelyn Sheldon, Phoebe's neighbor, greeted Janelle. "Oh, how thoughtful of you to come. I suppose you're getting things in order for the family. Virginia's girls are so considerate. Where's Ali? Her pickup's in the driveway."

"Anything I can do for poor Brad, no matter how small. I was looking for platters for food. To make it easier for Brad."

"You won't find them in here. I'll show you."

"Damn," Janelle said.

"What was that, dear?"

"Nothing. Broke a fingernail."

Janelle followed the visitor into the kitchen. She had to devise a way to get rid of her. A smidgen of brandy into the nosy old lady's coffee would make her sleepy. No, time is running out. She's so frail. A light tap on her head with Janelle's purse might work. Too chancy. Bad enough being stuck in Willoughby but worse would be imprisonment in the county jail.

"You've been a great help. Why don't you leave and go back to church? I can handle everything." Janelle put her hands on Evelyn's bony shoulders and turned her around so her back was facing Janelle.

"You can't push me out. She was my BFF."

"Your BFF is gone now. I can handle everything. Brad would want it that way."

"But would Phoebe? Relax, Janelle. Pour yourself a glass of wine that your characters in your books love so much."

She reads my books. Hmm.

"I'm going to go into Phoebe's computer and check my e-mail. Might have something important from my editor, you know."

"Make sure it's the computer and nothing else. Don't you dare touch the IBM Selectric. Phoebe was particular about that old thing." She stood in the doorway observing Janelle. "Let me know if you find anything interesting."

"You'll be the last one to know," Janelle said quietly. She might have been Phoebe's BFF, but she was also a big freakin' gossip, as Janelle recalled.

Janelle checked her watch again. *Where? Where?* She searched through every file on Phoebe's desk. She opened the desk drawer. Nothing. Must be the safe. She took a brass letter opener off the scratched and well-worn mahogany desk and pried the cheap lock. Success! Janelle lifted the lid. Empty. Nothing in there.

Janelle stopped to recall what one of her characters had done in a similar situation. *Think Janelle. If I were going to hide something, where would I put it? Safe deposit box? Breaking into a cheap plastic safe is one thing, but I can't get into her safe deposit box unless I could cozy up to Brad or maybe Phoebe's lawyer. Or maybe I could bribe a bank employee who is a fan of my books. No, too drastic and illegal. More potential jail time. What would Egyptologist Brooks Barrington do when she was searching for a letter from her lover, which would exonerate her from murdering her philandering husband?* Nothing came to mind.

Janelle tiptoed into Phoebe's bedroom, hoping to be undetected. She could hear the coffee pot perking and water running. Phoebe's bedroom was a vision of flowers. More like a nightmare. Flowers everywhere—bedspread, rug, and window treatments. For someone who didn't want flowers at her funeral, she certainly decorated with them. Janelle crouched down on her knees to look under the bed.

"Janelle. Now what are you doing?"

"Thought I lost an earring. Guess not. Still have two." Janelle put her hands on her ear lobes and jangled gold earrings the size of hula-hoops.

Evelyn stood in the doorway with her hands akimbo giving Janelle that crabby-old-school-teacher stare.

Saved by the doorbell. The visitors from the church were arriving. Janelle could lose herself in the crowd. Janelle saw Evelyn whispering in the ear of one of her geriatric friends probably spilling the beans about Janelle's behavior. Janelle acknowledged, with a syrupy comment, all the elderly people she hadn't seen since her last visit. Although she couldn't remember any of their names, they knew hers. Everyone in Willoughby knew Janelle Jennings.

Janelle vowed not to leave until she found what she needed.

To: Book Babes
Fm: bookmaven43
Re: Janelle sighting

I saw Janelle at Phoebe's memorial service today. Is she here for the book banquet? We already have a speaker. I can't believe this is true. We have to rally around Ali because you know how she gets when Janelle is in town. What can we do? Please note I deleted Ali from the distribution list. Are you paying attention, You Know Who? Remember how many times you've ruined surprises with reply all.

Chapter 14

Ali entered the kitchen looking for Matt. He was dressed for work and typing on his laptop. The morning sun glared like a spotlight into her half-opened eyes. She closed the shutters to block the bright light. Usually Matt delivered morning coffee to her while she stayed in bed.

"How'd you sleep?" he asked without waiting for an answer. "Is she still asleep?"

"She doesn't roll out of bed until later. What're you doing?"

"Detective work. Look here." He turned the laptop around to face a yawning and stretching Ali. She pushed her tangled hair off her forehead.

"A list of Janelle's books?" she asked.

"I checked her website: janellejenningsromancequeen. But look—no book tours, no speaking engagements. Nothing but a hint about her next book: *publication date TBA.*"

The coffeemaker beeped its ready signal. Virginia gave Matt a fancy espresso/latte/cappuccino maker one Christmas, an estate sale bargain. Matt took great delight in making a cup at a time to suit his preferences and that of their guests. He measured the coffee and water with the accuracy of a chemist. Ali found the multiple bells and whistles on the machine complicated. She preferred their old Mr. Coffee.

"I'll get our coffee," Ali said as she went to the cabinet, took out two mugs, and filled them.

"'No events scheduled. Please check back soon,'" Matt quoted from Janelle's website. "This means she lied to us. She said she needed rest before the book tour."

"She told me it was editing."

Ali and Matt thought the absence of speaking gigs was curious. According to Janelle, a big hunk of her income came from personal appearances, keynote speeches, and the books she sold at these events and publishing conventions. In addition, she sold bookmarks, calendars, pens, and magnets, all kinds of things with her logo, photo, and website address.

"She could be burned out. She churns those books out as fast as she spends the money they generate. Remember, last night she said she was tired of always being 'on,'" Ali said.

"Maybe she has enough money to quit writing," Matt said.

Something didn't ring true to Ali, but she couldn't identify what was off with Janelle. "I don't think she's so financially secure that she can give up writing novels," Ali said. "She complains about all the alimony she pays. She's still paying one of her husbands, maybe Phillip, even though he moved to Aruba with a pole dancer."

"At least her behavior was impeccable last night, for Janelle anyway," Matt said. "She only drank one bottle of wine and spilled another. Her language was clean and repeatable even to church ladies."

Matt rose from the table and refilled their mugs. He turned around to face Ali. She admired his wrinkle-free gabardine slacks and his lightly starched pale yellow Oxford cloth shirt opened at the collar. He was working hard to get back into shape and to lose the extra weight around his waist. That should be enough incentive for

Ali to emulate him. She wondered how a cute, almost-fit husband felt about having an overweight, dumpy wife.

Ali reached for her reading glasses to peruse the town's obituaries in the newspaper.

"Which old timers checked into Motel Deep Six?" Matt asked.

"'Beatrice Franklin, 99, died in her sleep surrounded by her loving family.'"

"Everyone in town knows Beatrice was a selfish old sourpuss," Matt said. "Sounds like your work."

"Some," Ali said. "Death alters perceptions and memory. I heard she had bought Coca-Cola stock ages ago and never sold. At least that's what Mother's bridge group thinks. Money unearths previously no-where-to-be-found 'loving' relatives." She scanned the page.

"Ah, here's one of interest," Ali said. "Famous author and former local resident died under mysterious circumstances while visiting her family in Willoughby."

"What?" Matt asked.

"Only kidding. I don't wish death for Janelle. Why can't she leave? She depresses me."

"How many times do I have to tell you not to let your sister bother you? Compare your life with your sister's and figure out who's the winner."

Lately, Ali did the comparison and she always came in second place, never first. Regardless, Ali still admired Janelle. Writing a novel takes tenacity, concentration, and creativity. Janelle excelled in all three departments as evidenced by her eighteen best-selling books.

"She gave me some of her books to read," Matt said

"Mrs. Franklin? What books?" Ali asked.

"No. Janelle. Her books. The books she's written."

"When did she do that?"

"Write the books or give them to me?" Matt asked.

"You know what I mean. Haven't you read all her books?"

"I cheated a bit. She interrogated me about her book set in Africa and I obviously hadn't read it." Matt hesitated and took a sip of coffee. "I couldn't sleep last night. Tried not to wake you. Drank too much of that strong Ethiopian coffee your dad served at dinner. I woke up around two a.m. and found Janelle in the living room working on her laptop. Said she was checking her e-mail and Ed's coffee kept her awake," Matt said. "She found the Africa book in the den and told me to read it."

Ali didn't recall her sister drinking coffee last night. Janelle maintained caffeine wrinkled her skin.

"Did she say why she's here?"

"She repeated the story about resting before her big book tour. Misses her sis, I guess," he chuckled. "Maybe we'll never know the reason she's here." He shut down the laptop. "Let's deal with her."

"You mean *you* deal with her. Everyone else seems to worship her," Ali said.

"Kayla and your mother certainly do. Your dad's neutral."

Roxie left her bed underneath the bay window, stretched, and came to Ali's side reminiscent of the sisters' childhood brown and white cocker spaniel. Ali couldn't remember Janelle connecting with anything or anyone the way she loved that dog. The sisters were supposed to share Lady, but Janelle took most of the responsibility. She groomed her and walked her in the park. That changed during Janelle's teenage years. Then Lady was Ali's dog. Janelle treated her many boyfriends like dogs. Or, they acted like dogs, following her around, panting, and drooling.

"Do you think she's sick?" Ali asked. "Her hands shake quite a bit."

"She seems healthy to me. On the thin side, though," Matt said as he stood.

A voice behind them said, "Thanks for the compliment."

Matt and Ali gasped at the sound of Janelle's voice.

Chapter 15

Ali jumped out of her chair, startled by Janelle's unusual appearance in the kitchen at 7:30 in the morning. She wore a sapphire colored tunic over white leggings. Her feet were bare.

Ali and Matt weren't the only ones jolted by Janelle's appearance. Roxie barked and nipped at Janelle's toes.

Ali picked up Roxie and said, "Extra treats for you today."

"Very funny. I'll win her over yet. You'll see."

Matt lifted Roxie to take her to the backyard. Her yapping continued as Matt took her away.

Janelle appeared confused. She expected everyone to love her. "What's wrong with your dog?"

"She doesn't like you. Seems the obvious conclusion," Ali said.

"Let's get back to the discussion about my being too thin." She pulled out a chair and sat facing Ali. "I don't think I'm too thin. I've been a size two for years. Remember, when we were teenagers, we could never share clothes. Guess that's why we got along so well."

"I question your statement about getting along so well, but you had a few sweaters I admired. You would never let me wear them until they had snags or holes. Remember the cigarette burn? You told Mother and Dad that you burned it in chemistry class."

"We should write a memoir, Ali. You remember all the negative things while I remember all the happy events and the delight of having a sister."

Ali scrunched her face as though a dentist was preparing to numb her gum.

When Matt returned sans dog, he asked Janelle, "Cappuccino, latte, espresso? What appeals to our famous visitor this lovely spring morning?"

"Surprise me, Matty."

There's that Matty thing again. Why is he so accommodating to her? Ali thought.

Matty placed a mug of cappuccino on the table in front of Janelle.

"I have an announcement," Janelle said. "I'm so sorry I've neglected my family for the past several years. Oh, I know, I've sent fabulous gifts at Christmas and birthdays, but nothing beats starting a busy day with breakfast with my family. It's lonely on the road and in a hotel for days on end. You'll see more of me, I promise."

"You are generous, Janelle. However, as you can probably tell, I haven't been a size four since sixth grade."

Matt cleared his throat. "We appreciate your gifts, Janelle."

Janelle leaned across the table and patted Ali on top of her head. "A leave-in conditioner would help the frizz. Might want to get the split ends trimmed, too."

"You might want to cut back on the perfume," Ali said as she rubbed her nose and stifled a gag at the jasmine scent.

"Off to work. You two have a great day." Matt winked at Ali.

"So, what's on the agenda?" Janelle asked after Matt had left.

Ali's agenda consisted of distancing herself far away from Janelle—preferably in another state. "Matt's on his way to work, Kayla's off to school, and I'm on my way to—" She didn't want

Janelle to know her plans. She regretted not taking more hours at Kitchen Bliss, as Ellen had suggested.

"Don't worry about me. I have plenty to keep me busy. I'll work on my book today. Deadline approaching, you know. My editor wants a major rewrite. First time he's ever done that." Janelle's shoulders sagged. "I don't agree, but what can I do? I also have some phone calls to make and e-mails to send."

"You said you wanted to rest before the book tour," Ali said. "Don't you have to finish writing it first?"

"Yes, yes." Janelle dismissed Ali with a wave of her hand.

Now was the perfect time to ask Janelle about the absence of events listed on her website. She hesitated. Maybe something unspeakable was happening. For the sake of the family, she decided to show sympathy for her sister. A Virginia-ism came to Ali's mind: Better to bend than to break. It would be curious to see who would bend and who would break.

"I can change my plans. Would you like to spend the day together, Janelle?" *Is this a lunatic talking or me?*

Janelle hesitated. "I should work on the rewrite. But, okay, anything for you, especially if it will make you happy, Li'l Sis."

The ringing telephone interrupted Janelle's desire to please her sister.

"Where are you, Alicia? You should have been here thirty minutes ago," Virginia said.

"What are you talking about, Mother?"

"Estate sale. Pickup truck. Mrs. Baldwin's estate. Ring a bell?"

"Oh, crap."

"Please, Alicia. You know I hate that vulgar talk. If we leave now, we might get there before the vultures."

Ali didn't know which was worse—disappointing her mother for being late or spending the day with Janelle. "Sorry, Janelle. Have to help Mother."

"Are you going dressed like that?" Janelle asked.

Ali evaluated her baggy denim shorts and an old T-shirt of Matt's she threw on earlier. "Too late now." She grabbed a straw hat hanging on a hook behind the door and stuck her hair underneath it. "How's this?" she asked her sister. "Better?"

"You'll be mistaken for a farmer driving that disgusting green thing," Janelle said. "All you need is a piece of straw between your teeth."

Maybe I should take a new tack with my sister's criticism. "Janelle, you are so funny." With those parting words, she grabbed the keys to the pickup, her purse, and left.

Ali dreaded facing her mother. Since Janelle's arrival, Ali couldn't focus on anything other than getting rid of her sister. Ali listened to Virginia's continuous praising of Janelle while they drove the short distance to Sandy Springs.

"Can't you drive faster, Alicia? I don't want to miss out on the desirable items."

"I'm going ten miles over the speed limit, Mother. You should have Dad use my pickup to take you to the auctions and estate sales. He's got a lead foot."

"I don't trust him driving this thing of yours."

"Well, *this thing* comes in handy when you buy furniture."

As Virginia predicted, by the time they arrived at the sale, all the best items wore "sold" tags.

"Waste of a morning," Virginia said.

They drove home in silence. Ali dropped her mother off and returned to 2323 Plum Court.

"You weren't gone long," Janelle said when Ali arrived home.

Ali joined Janelle on the porch. "Arrived too late. Mother was not happy." The fan whirred softly and the birds sang a chorus of song celebrating the springtime beauty of Georgia. Ali noticed Janelle's closed laptop on the table next to the chair. "Working on your book?"

"Some. Let's take a walk," Janelle said. "I could use some exercise."

"What about shoes?" Ali asked, pointing to Janelle's bare feet.

"I was in such a hurry to leave the hotel—I mean, the condo. I didn't bring any walking shoes. Come to think of it, I don't own any. Perhaps you have a pair I could borrow. No, yours will be too big. I'll find a pair in Kayla's closet. She has a petite foot like mine."

Janelle reappeared, her big toe and heel extending off either end of a pair of purple flip-flops.

"Can you walk in those, Janelle? Too small, I think."

"My feet are slightly swollen, that's all."

The early afternoon sun shone through the trees along Willoughby Lane. A fresh breeze flowed through the air, a breeze that Ali wished would turn into a tornado and blow Janelle up and away.

"Here, hold this for me. No pocket. Never know when a fan might appear." Janelle shoved a Sharpie into Ali's hand.

"I know you're popular here, but I doubt if any of your fans are walking around with one of your books." Ali shook her head and accepted the pen from Janelle's trembling hand.

"I've noticed your hands shake quite a bit. What's that about?"

"Too much caffeine. Don't be so worried about me, Li'l Sis."

They continued their walk interrupted now and then by the merchants of Willoughby Lane who shouted friendly greetings to Ali along the way. A slow and steady stream of cars went up and down the street. Several cyclists flew by with a "get out of my way" attitude.

Janelle was uncharacteristically quiet. Perhaps she was disappointed because no fan recognized her or the paparazzi didn't jump out from behind a street lamp. When they were near Jill Porter's florist shop, Janelle jaywalked causing the driver of a delivery van to screech to a halt. He had a few colorful words for Janelle.

"Pedestrians have the right of way, you S-O-B!" Janelle shouted. She accelerated her pace and without saying anything to Ali, blustered into Shear Beauty Hair Salon displaying a "Walk-Ins Welcome" sign in the window.

Ali followed Janelle, feeling like a lady-in-waiting following the queen. She forgot to look both ways and barely avoided a collision with a speeding cyclist. "So sorry," Ali shouted.

"I need a trim and blow dry and look at her awful split ends," Janelle said to an attractive purple-haired young woman at the front desk. Janelle grabbed a handful of Ali's hair and shook it in front of the woman like a cheerleader's pom-pom. The woman gave Ali a sympathetic look. "My treat," Janelle added as an afterthought.

The Purple Hair Girl said there was one opening and the second would be about a thirty-minute wait. Janelle said no problem and Ali agreed despite her packed to-do list.

Naturally, Janelle took the first appointment. Ali overheard her giving detailed, lengthy instructions to the soon-to-be frustrated stylist named Robert. She showed him something on her phone. "This is how I want my hair trimmed. Watch this video and maybe you'll learn something from my stylist who is an artiste."

"I'll do my best, miss," he said.

"I realize this isn't New York City but surely you have had extensive training in hair cutting."

"Yes, Miss Jennings."

Meanwhile, the Purple Hair Girl offered Ali chai tea or Prosecco. Ali accepted the bubbly wine in a plastic flute. When her cell phone buzzed, she turned it off.

Ali inspected the array of products in colorful bottles and jars neatly placed on glass shelves. They promised to tame unruly hair, volumize thin hair, protect color-treated hair, or moisturize dry hair. Twenty, thirty dollars for a bottle of shampoo shocked Ali. She bought shampoo at the dollar store.

"Open the bottle. Take a whiff," Purple Hair said. "Raspberry Rapture is one of our most popular items."

"Sounds like the title of one of my sister's books."

"Excuse me?" the young woman asked.

Ali opened the bottle and inhaled the sweet fragrance. "I could buy the shampoo for the aroma alone," Ali said.

"Buy one, fifty percent off the second."

"I'll think about it. Thank you." Ali sunk into an oversized black leather chair. She closed her eyes while listening to the sounds of the busy hair salon: the buzzing dryers, swooshing water in the basins, crunching foil for hair lightening, the snip, snip, snip of scissors cutting and texturizing, and the constant binging of hair stylists' cells. The conversations between stylist and client were hushed as they shared secrets and dispensed advice.

After about forty-five minutes, it was Ali's turn. Janelle left Robert at the shampoo bowl and marched over to give strict instructions to Ali's stylist Sophia. "Eliminate those awful split ends and trim the bangs." Then she whispered something into Sophia's ear. All Ali heard was "Brazilian."

"Oh no, I came for a trim, not that Brazillian wax thingy."

"Relax, Ali. Not that," Janelle said. "Brazillian Blowout for that awful hair of yours."

"Don't we have enough blowouts," Ali grumbled.

Janelle returned to the shampoo bowl where Robert was waiting. "Are you here on business or pleasure?" he asked affably.

"I'm here for a trim and styling. And quiet time. No talking."

Robert caught the attention of another stylist and then raised his hands in amazement.

Ali asked for an explanation from Sophia regarding the services she planned for her miscreant hair. "The entire process takes about two hours. When I'm finished, your husband won't recognize you. Better buy some new lingerie."

Ali explained she didn't want anything special, only a trim like the one she gets at the beauty school. "No need for a blow dry. No fuss."

Sophia draped a gold cape around Ali and then massaged her shoulders. "Listen to your friend. Relax."

"She's not my friend; she's my sister," Ali corrected.

Sophia looked puzzled.

"As a welcome to our salon, all first-time customers receive a complimentary hand massage with warm cream," a young woman with green and pink streaks in her blond hair said to Ali. She took Ali's right hand, squeezed a dollop of almond-scented lotion into her palm, and massaged Ali's fingers, one at a time.

So, this is a glimpse into the life of Janelle Jennings. Ali could get used to this paradise that was within walking distance of her house.

The stylist led Ali to the shampoo bowl where she massaged Ali's scalp. "Close your eyes and relax." Then they moved back to Sophia's station were the disobedient split ends fell to the floor after meticulous snipping. Ali's hair was divided into sections and the miracle commenced.

Meanwhile over at Robert's station, Ali heard Janelle's diva voice turned up an octave. "I told you to use the large round brush. The biggest brush you have. I want big hair. This is the South, isn't it?"

"I think that brush is too big, but whatever you say, miss."

"If it doesn't come out right, you'll have to start all over."

When Robert had finished, Janelle stood in front of the mirror. She pulled a piece of hair on both sides to measure. "See. This one's longer."

"I followed the instructions on your phone."

"Obviously, not. My hair looks horrid." Janelle marched back to the shampoo bowl. Then, he and Janelle returned to his station where he trimmed the offending strand of hair. Following her instructions, he used a jumbo round brush to blow dry her hair.

"Not acceptable," she said to him.

"Lady, I don't know what you want. I've got clients waiting."

Janelle ripped the Velcro opening on the cape and threw it at Robert's face. She flew by Ali and Sophia. "Make sure there's no charge for this dreadful service. The beauty school would have done a better job. I'll see you at home."

After two hours, Ali's stylist asked, "What do you think?" She spun the chair around so that Ali was facing the mirror.

"Amazing." Ali took the hand mirror and studied the back of her head. She put the mirror down and stroked her hair. "Different. But, I think I like it. Yes. I like it." She shook her head and watched her hair cascade down her shoulders.

"Buy some of the maintenance products and I'll see you in about ten weeks or so," Sophia said.

Visions of repeated trips to this oasis halted when the young woman at the counter presented Ali with the bill. Her eyes widened and she took a deep breath when she saw the total, which was more than she had spent on her hair in her lifetime. Reluctantly, she handed over her credit card. "I'll pay for my sister." She hesitated before she signed the receipt adding gratuities for Sophia and Robert.

When Ali arrived home, she said to Janelle, "Your hair looks terrific. Identical to your latest publicity shot. What else could you want?"

"Ha. I hope we weren't charged for mine."

"I paid for it. I have to live in this town," Ali said.

Chapter 16

When Matt arrived at his father-in-law's house he found Ed puttering in the front yard with his Princess rose bushes. Ed was wearing a gardener's hat with a broad brim to shield his balding head and freckled forehead from the afternoon sun.

Matt had the habit of visiting Ed once a week, usually on the way home from a run. Today he brought Roxie along so Ed could visit with his granddog.

"Left work early?" Ed asked.

"Yeah."

"Glad you're here. Want to look at my latest invention?" He bent down and patted Roxie on her head. "Good to see you, little one." Roxie wagged her tail and ran around him in circles yapping for an anticipated treat. They walked to the workshop in Ed's backyard where he made his prototypes. His unsuccessful patent applications covered the walls. "I think this one has *Shark Tank* potential and then QVC. Everyone has stinky feet, every age, every size, and every nationality. This thing could go international."

Ed always assumed his inventions had "potential." He had shown Matt the universal shoe sanitizer several weeks ago. Matt pretended it was new to him.

"Tell me what you think, Matt? The truth now, son."

"I could be mistaken but I think I saw something similar at the 'As Seen on TV' store at the mall. Wasn't as compact as yours though."

"No kidding, you say? I better go to the mall and take a look." He hung his head and muttered something.

"Don't be discouraged, Ed. Keep trying." Matt patted Ed on his shoulder then pointed to a sign hanging above Ed's workbench: "If you can conceive it and believe it, you will achieve it."

Ed spent many hours in his well-equipped hideaway. He had every tool that Home Depot and Lowe's stocked including a variety of hammers, wrenches, vises, and saws. His workshop was his refuge from Virginia's smoke-free, dirt-free, dust-free, animal-free house.

"Guess these days you'd call my workshop a man cave?" Ed said.

"All that's missing is a sixty-five inch plasma TV and a cooler filled with Corona," Matt said. "Don't get down on yourself, Ed. One of these days."

"Yeah. Maybe. Only problem is my days are numbered."

"Why do you say that?"

"Not getting any younger. Let's take Roxie for a walk."

Ed lit his pipe with the Zippo lighter he carried in his pocket and then the two buddies and Roxie walked along Mimosa Lane. They stopped at the white picket fence surrounding Primrose Cottage, the event facility where Matt and Ali had their wedding reception.

"That was quite the memorable wedding," Ed reminisced.

"Glad we have lots of photos. I was so nervous, I don't remember much."

"Your sister-in-law did her best to upstage Ali. Ellen stepped in and directed Janelle toward the eligible men. That kept her busy."

Roxie sighted a small lizard basking in the sun and took off. Ed tugged on her leash and brought her back to the sidewalk.

"You're sure attached to Roxie, Ed. I don't remember a dog in your house when Ali and I were dating."

"When the girls were small they convinced Virginia they needed a dog. Virginia agreed, with my encouragement, to their pleas but after Ali left for college, she found another home for Lady. You know Virginia. No dogs, no feet on the coffee table, no eating in front of TV, no smoking my pipe even outside. That last one, I sneak that one in." Ed gave a playful poke to Matt in the ribs. "I borrow Roxie sometimes and take her for a stroll so I can smoke my pipe. I think some of the neighbors have seen me but they won't snitch. Except for that nosy Evelyn Sheldon."

"Speaking about being nosy. Tell me about this feud between Janelle and Ali?"

"I don't know that 'feud' is quite accurate."

"What's the source? Ali won't share."

"Sibling rivalry. This is the way it goes. Janelle makes a grand appearance, lords her success over Ali, Ali feels inept. After Janelle leaves, Ali meets me in my workshop and vents. Wish there was something I could do. She always puts up a good front, being the girl she is. Guess a father can't protect his children from each other."

"What started it?" Matt asked.

"The diary episode didn't help their relationship. Ali's never complained too much to me until this visit of Janelle's."

Matt couldn't recall Ali mentioning a diary. "Seems like she would confide in her husband before her father? No disrespect, Ed."

"Ali doesn't want to burden you or anyone for that matter. She wants to keep peace in the family."

"Ali's personality changes when Janelle is here," Matt said.

"I'm trusting you now, son; Virginia didn't want a second child. After Janelle was born, she made that clear. If the vasectomy had been popular then, she would have driven me to the doc's pronto. She probably considered taking me to the vet's. Her idea of birth control was separate bedrooms. No separate bedrooms for this guy."

They walked to the dead-end, then turned around and walked back toward Primrose Cottage. Ed took a puff on his pipe and then said, "Let's sit on your dad's bench." A plaque on the wrought iron bench read, "In memory of Matthew G. Lawrence."

"Your tobacco reminds me of my dad," Matt said. "He smoked that one, too. Smells like wood. I miss him."

"We often compared notes about tobacco. I miss him, too."

The two men sat in silence. They watched the smoke circles Ed blew into the air as they drifted away looking like powdered sugar doughnuts.

"Here comes that witch Evelyn Sheldon," Ed said, as he put the pipe behind his back hoping she wouldn't cross the street to speak to them. Evelyn kept walking without glancing at them.

"How would you describe your marriage, Ed?"

"That's coming out of left field."

"Curious, that's all," Matt said.

"I go along to get along. I haven't been unhappy. Virginia's interests keep her busy. To quote Virginia, "'Why rock the boat?'"

Ed had suspected that Virginia married him on the rebound. He was on the wrestling team in high school where he developed a muscular physique the girls were attracted to. After they were married and Ed was teaching high school, Virginia urged him to return to school to earn a Ph.D. She wanted to impress her friends by having a *doctor* in the house. Ed said he enjoyed working with high school kids and couldn't see himself hobnobbing with academia. After that decision, Virginia started her antique business at Queen of Hearts to earn what she called "pin money." Over the years, she became a popular speaker at women's groups, sharing her knowledge of antiques and what to look for at garage sales.

"This might be rude of me to ask, but why don't you ever stand up to Virginia?"

"The answer is easy. How did a frog like me end up with a princess?"

While Matt jogged home with Roxie at his side, he reflected on the insight Ed gave him about the relationship between Ali and Janelle. He planned to think of something to cheer Ali up after Janelle left. "Anybody home?" he hollered as he entered the house. Ali wasn't at her usual spot in the kitchen. When he entered their bedroom, Ali was standing in front of the mirror with her back to him.

"What the—?"

Ali spun around to face him. "What do you think?"

"I have to be careful here. I can't seem too enthusiastic because you'll say I didn't like you the way you were before." He approached her and touched her hair. "So silky."

"I guess Sophia was right. She said you wouldn't be able to keep your hands off me."

Chapter 17

Ali sat on the step of her front porch examining her prehistoric athletic shoes. On the left shoe, she had stuck a piece of orange duct tape where her little toe struggled for freedom. "Might get one more day out of these," she said to Roxie who was exploring the flower garden. Ali gazed at the clear, robin's egg blue sky and wished for monsoon rains or a tornado to avoid exercising with Ellen who promised Ali a "leisurely" nature walk. Ali knew "leisurely" to Ellen meant exhausting to Ali.

Ali heard the cuckoo clock chiming in the kitchen. Ellen was late. *Maybe she won't show. Maybe the weather report is wrong. Maybe my shoes will disintegrate.* For motivation, Ali imagined that an annoying mosquito landed on her shoulder and buzzed into her ear, "Get up off your lazy butt." Even though Ali couldn't match Ellen's pace, even for five minutes, she needed a sounding board and mental health therapist.

Meanwhile, Ali's cell phone chirped. The caller ID said Logan was calling. Ali's first thought was Kayla. "Everything okay?" she asked quickly.

"I have to talk fast. Not supposed to make calls during school hours," he said out of breath.

"Is there a problem?"

"Kayla's changed."

"Hmm. Tell me more." Ali's breathing returned to normal.

"She never has time for me. She's missed some tennis practices and she never wants to study with me anymore. Do you think it's something I've done?"

"She hasn't mentioned anything negative about you. When did this start?"

"After her aunt arrived. Just between us, ma'am, and I don't mean to sound rude, but I don't think that woman is a good influence on Kayla."

Ali bit her lip and tried not to laugh at his description of Janelle. "Quite observant, young man. I agree. Now don't you go missing tennis practices or forgetting about your studies. One juvenile delinquent is enough."

"I don't want to get her in trouble and you can't tell her I called."

"Don't worry. In another week or so when her aunt leaves we'll be back to normal."

"Thanks, ma'am, I feel better. My mom's been dead for five years and I still miss her."

"I didn't know that about your mother, Logan. I'm glad you called. Call anytime."

Ali's thoughts after the phone conversation were interrupted when neighbor Mr. Potthast sauntered by with his noisy beagles named Carmel and Romo. Roxie echoed their barks but a gray squirrel distracted her as it darted through the flower garden and up a massive magnolia tree. "Come here, girl," Ali yelled to Roxie. She didn't want her dog to trample the purple hydrangeas that were showing signs of blooming. Virginia would not be happy.

Ali moaned as she saw Ellen jog up the walkway. *No reprieve for me.* Ellen wore itsy bitsy black running shorts and a form-fitting iridescent green midriff-revealing top. She could be mistaken for a track and field competitor at the summer Olympics. A water bottle belt fit snugly around her waist. A baseball cap topped her blond hair.

"Looks like you were in a hurry and forgot half your clothes. Your belly button's showing."

"Perfectly appropriate. How old are those shoes?" Ellen asked, pointing to Ali's feet.

"I can't part with these old things. Matt keeps buying replacements and I keep stacking the boxes in my closet." Ali took off her wide-brimmed straw hat and shook her hair.

"Holy sugar! Your hair. What the heck happened?" Ellen walked around Ali, front to back, to form an appraisal from various angles.

"That bad?"

"Um...not bad. Different. Your sister's idea?"

"When I'm around Janelle, I become brain dead, idiotic."

"Your sister had a thing about your hair. Remember when we were kids and she tried to straighten it with a hot iron?"

"My hair embarrassed Janelle."

"Forget about your sister for once. If you want my opinion and I'm sure you do—your hair looks great."

"Matt likes it, too." Ali felt her face warming.

"Hmm. You don't say," Ellen said with a grin.

Ali attached Roxie's leash to her collar and the threesome took off. After a few blocks, Ellen said, "Remember when Janelle would practice putting makeup on both of us following the instructions in one of her teen magazines? When she was finished we resembled Ronald McDonald. And, then there was the time she wanted to dye my blond hair black. For once, you won an argument with her and talked her out of that one."

Ali said, "At least those misadventures didn't cost anything. Yesterday, when we went to Shear Beauty, she tricked me into this Brazilian hair thing and then stuck me with the bill—hers and mine."

"No treat by the famous author?"

"I stood there like the spineless coward I am with my credit card in hand."

Ellen shook her head. "You are hopeless. Do you think she's having money problems?"

"Has occurred to me. Doesn't seem possible. She leads an exorbitant lifestyle. I often wondered how different my life would be if Janelle hadn't stolen her first story idea from me," Ali said.

"You have to get over that. It wasn't such a great idea anyway. Something about a ski resort in Utah?"

"Colorado."

"Anyway, she pursued the idea. You were afraid to take a chance. You took the easy way. Married, house, child, dog."

"My life hasn't been easy."

"No, but you chose the safe way and Janelle took a risk."

Ali shrugged her shoulders. "Whose side are you on?"

"Not a matter of sides. Only the facts."

Ali poked Ellen on the arm. "You don't always have to be so truthful."

The two friends and Roxie walked in silence on Riverside Drive along Willoughby River. The water was thick with brick red Georgia mud after an overnight shower. Young mothers pushed three-wheeled jogging strollers as they zipped by the trio. "I wish I had their energy," Ali observed as she jumped a rain puddle.

"Anytime you want to stop, say so."

Ali shook her head and they forged on. She hoped for a sighting of something to distract nature lover Ellen—anything, even a dead snake.

"You know your house isn't big enough for both you and Janelle," Ellen said. "In fact, Willoughby isn't big enough for you two."

Ali trusted Ellen's perspective on the sisters' relationship.

"Why can't the romance queen live with your parents?" Ellen asked. "Or, stay at the Willoughby Inn as she's done in the past?"

"Janelle refused to stay at Mother and Dad's. Mother pretended it was her idea that Janelle stay with us, and used Dad's clutter as an excuse. Seems rude to send a relative to a hotel."

"I can name hundreds of times Janelle demonstrated her rudeness toward you," Ellen said.

"The Georgia prison wardrobe doesn't suit my color palette so murder is not a viable option," Ali panted. She slowed down and put her hands on her hips. "Time for a rest. I may keel over for lack of oxygen."

A breeze was absent this early spring morning and the humidity claimed Ali's energy. Her skin was damp and sweaty. She touched her hair and amazingly, it felt as straight as when she left Shear Beauty.

Ellen pointed to an empty bench. The two friends sat with Roxie at Ali's feet. Ellen took out binoculars from the pocket in her waist pack. She hoped to see a red-winged blackbird native to the area, a river otter, or a blue heron.

"I don't know what's wrong with me, Ellen. I can't shake the resentment I have for my sister."

"It's more than resentment. You struggle too hard to please your mother and your sister. You may as well give up."

"*Please* them?"

"Sure. You'll always be the runner up to them."

Ali recalled a conversation she had with Ellen when they were about ten years old. "You were probably an accident. Or maybe an afterthought. That's what I was," Ellen said.

"What?"

According to youthful sage Ellen, all parents loved the firstborn more than they loved the second child based on a conversation she overheard between her mother and her Aunt Debbie.

Both Ellen's and Ali's siblings were successful. Ellen's brother was an award-winning architect in New York. The two friends shared this bond.

"Are you awake?" Ellen asked Ali.

"Sorry. I drifted off. If I knew why she was here and for how long, I could deal with Janelle. Any suggestions?"

"How about her website?"

"Matt checked. Nothing scheduled," Ali said.

"Call her assistant. What's his name? Bob?"

"She fired Bobby."

"Who's babysitting her?"

"She's on her own," Ali said. "Why don't you ask her? Then, if we get the answer we want, I can relax."

"That means I have to actually speak to her."

"Anything for a friend? Right?"

They stood and continued their walk.

Ali's cell phone in her pocket vibrated followed by a melody. "What a shame. No, I understand. Not your fault." Shaking her head, Ali turned to face Ellen. "We'll figure it out. Yes, next year. I hope she recovers quickly." Ali glared at the phone before she disconnected. "Laurel Atwood canceled. Our keynote speaker broke both her arms. Nine days before the event."

"That's a lousy excuse. They make casts."

Ali glared at her friend. "No empathy?"

"We've publicized Laurel, banquet tickets are sold out, and people will demand a refund. Plus, we don't have any money in the budget for another speaker. We're screwed," Ellen moaned.

"Or maybe not. We both know a hometown girl who might be a bigger draw. She'll balk at speaking for free though," Ali said.

"Does the word *blackmail*, mean anything to you?"

"What are you talking about?" Ali said.

"We know lots of dirt about Janelle that she wouldn't like leaked to the media."

"Hmm. I don't think anyone knows about her latest divorce. Her ex, Gerald maybe, left her for a stripper. A male stripper. I can't, I can't!"

"Maybe not, but *I* can."

Chapter 18

Ali was in the storeroom of Kitchen Bliss checking inventory for a sampling of new olive oils and vinegars. When she heard a text message alert on her phone, she pushed several buttons to no avail. "Why don't people just call?"

"Need some help, Mrs. Lawrence?" Bailey, a part-time employee, asked Ali.

"I think this is a text, but I don't know how to read it or answer it."

Bailey gave Ali a mini texting tutorial. "It's from your husband: 'dinr 2nite @ 7?' Do you want to answer him?"

"No. Thanks, Bailey. I'll do it later."

"Once you get the hang of it you'll love it. Saves lots of time."

Ali returned her husband's call the old-fashioned way. "You called?" she asked Matt.

"I assumed you'd text me back."

"One of these days you can teach me. What's up?"

Matt said his boss invited them to dinner. In the past, a monthly dinner with Ellis and Genevieve Graham was routine but that came to a halt several months ago.

"We haven't been out with the Grahams in a long time, Al. I can't say no to the boss and it won't cost us anything."

"I shouldn't leave Janelle. She's been alone all day while I'm at work."

"Sure you can. Kayla's nuts about your wacky sister. Besides, maybe Kayla could use the extra attention Janelle gives her."

"I don't know."

"Listen. You'll have a lifetime to spend with Janelle, if she decides to stay in Willoughby."

"Please. Don't even think that." Ali rubbed her temple.

"Your sister's been truant for the last two years. She can manage one more night without you. The reservation is at seven p.m. at Mosaics, if you change your mind."

Ali returned to the front of the store and greeted the elderly widowed Grover twins, Adele and Aileen, who did everything together, even their recent hip replacements. Despite their ages, everyone referred to them as the Grover Girls. They were in search of wedding presents for their grandniece, they told Ali. She ushered them to chairs near the front door next to a small table reserved for bored husbands. "No need to walk around the store, ladies," Ali said. "I'll pick out some things and bring them to you along with the bridal registry."

"Thanks, dear. We're still not used to the canes," Aileen said.

"Speak for yourself," Adele said. The corners of her mouth turned so low they almost hit her chin.

Ali returned with a square lacquered tray with the image of two chickadees perched on a tree limb. "This is our most popular tray," Ali said. "We have matching placemats and coasters."

"Our niece loves to watch the birds in her backyard. The colors are so cheerful. This is perfect," Aileen said.

"How much? Looks expensive," Adele grumbled. "I was thinking along the lines of a chip and dip set."

The bell jingled over the front door announcing a customer. Without looking up, Ali said, "Welcome to Kitchen Bliss."

"Thought I'd check up on you, Li'l Sis," Janelle said.

"Aren't you supposed to be working on your book?" Ali said when she left the twins and approached Janelle.

The Grover Girls recognized Janelle and spoke to each other in soft voices.

"Why are you here?" Ali asked.

"Wanted to see exactly what you do." She walked toward the gadget aisle, picked up a lemon zester, turned it around in her hands, and replaced it. "I smell coffee." She walked to the back of the store.

Ali followed her. "I'm alone so please don't bother me."

"Maybe I can help," Janelle said.

"You can help by not causing any trouble."

"Is that you, Janelle? Over here," one of the twins said while waving her cane in the air. Janelle joined the sisters and kissed them both on their cheeks.

"You run along, Ali; I'll help the girls."

Both the *girls* beamed at Janelle.

Two more customers walked in the door. "Welcome to Kitchen Bliss," Ali said. "Behave yourself," she said to Janelle.

"I think a potato peeler and a whisk are suitable, if you don't like the chip and dip idea," Adele said after Ali had left. "You spend your money and I'll spend mine."

"We don't want to look cheap."

"Harrumph," Adele said. "Well, if we *have* to spend more money, maybe a martini pitcher and glasses."

"So appropriate for a young couple," Janelle said. She pulled the third chair around so she sat in between her customers.

Back and forth, the Grover Girls bantered and disagreed. Janelle encouraged them to tour the store. She pointed out the most expensive items she could find: espresso machines, copper cookware, knife sets.

"My sister and I try to find a common ground, a compromise." Janelle glanced around the store to make sure Ali didn't hear. "Perhaps you should select one gift from both of you."

"What do you suggest?" Adele asked.

"Easy," Janelle said.

After they made their choice of a ten-piece stainless steel cookware set, one of the most expensive items in the store, Janelle said, "Ali will be glad to wrap this excellent selection for you. May we deliver it, too?"

Before they left, Adele and Aileen gushed over Janelle and thanked her for helping them choose the gift.

"Janelle, we don't deliver. The niece lives way out in the country."

"What? No thanks for making a big sale?"

Ali shook her head. "Young people don't cook anymore. This will be the first item they return."

"We'll see. I'm off. This was fun. Maybe I'll come back tomorrow."

Later in the day, Ali sauntered home from work, weaving in and out of the many pedestrians and shoppers on Willoughby Lane while she processed Matt's words during their earlier phone conversation.

"Am I ignoring you, Kayla?" Ali asked when she arrived home and found her daughter in the kitchen.

"What do you mean, Mom?"

"Am I giving you enough attention; am I interested in your life?"

"The least you know the better."

"What does that mean?"

"Just kidding, Mom. With Aunt Janie here I don't need anyone else giving me attention."

"What are you looking for?" Ali asked Kayla who stood in front of the open refrigerator.

"Aunt Janie wants a glass of wine."

"Let me get it." Ali retrieved a bottle of white wine from the refrigerator, set it on the countertop, and took the corkscrew from a drawer.

"She wants red."

"You should tell your aunt we don't do room service."

"Mom. She wants red."

"F-Y-I, we don't put red in the refrigerator." Ali selected a bottle of red wine from the pantry, not from Matt's wine cabinet, and unscrewed the top. "I'm thinking about going out with your dad and Mr. and Mrs. Graham tonight. I told him that I didn't want to leave you and Janelle. Do you want to stay here with your aunt?"

"Awesome."

"Depending on what type of diet Janie's on these days, there's a chicken enchilada casserole in the freezer," Ali said. "Or, you could go to a restaurant. Your aunt would like that."

"Let me cook dinner, Mom. Please?"

"Tonight? You'll cook tonight?"

"Yes. I'll make something Italian. Might remind Aunt Janie about that trip she promised me. Please, Mom."

Ali wished that Janelle would quit dangling an Italian trip in front of Kayla.

Based on experience, Kayla might have an ulterior motive but Ali didn't care. *Please, Mom, can I go to the beach without a chaperone? Please Mom can I stay out till two a.m.?* Countless *Please Moms* to which Ali always replied no.

"Isn't it great having her here? She makes me so happy. I'll have her all to myself tonight." Kayla went to the china cabinet in the dining room and came back with a glass.

"I almost forgot. Mrs. Jenkins left a message for you on the answering machine."

Now I'm in trouble. I bet she's calling to complain about the obit I wrote for her mother. I told her to read it.

"Let me pour the wine and please use another glass. That's one of my Waterfords. A set of six."

"You are so uptight. I'm not going to drink it. I'm not going to break your precious glass. I'm not a kid." Kayla ignored her mother's requests, poured the wine into the crystal glass, and cautiously walked up the stairs.

"Don't spill the wine," Ali yelled. "Remember the Alamo. I mean, remember the guacamole."

Ali regretted declining Matt's invitation. Lately, they never seemed to connect. He complained that she spent too much time caring about other people while ignoring her own family. Maybe she did. The phone rang before Ali had a chance to call Matt and tell him she would meet him for dinner. Jill had a banquet question. "I'll call you tomorrow," Ali said. *A baby step but one in the right direction.* Ali complimented herself for saying no even though she didn't actually say no—she merely postponed.

Ali went to the answering machine to listen to Carla's message.

"Ali, Carla here. You won't believe this. The Willoughby Wildlife Club sent me a letter of gratitude. They had no idea that Mother did so much for birds. They were grateful that we suggested donations to the organization and the checks are pouring in. This is our secret, right?"

Ali erased the message. Matt warned her to stop embellishing obituaries. Ali did more than embellish with Lucy—she lied. Ali wondered if falsifying an obituary was a crime. A misdemeanor rather than a felony, she hoped.

Kayla went upstairs and knocked on the bathroom door.

"Come on in," Janelle said.

Kayla set the wineglass on the edge of the bathtub. "Here's your wine, Aunt Janie. In a special glass for a special person." She carried her journal under her arm.

Hot water from the bathtub fogged the mirror. Pink bubbles covered Janelle up to her neck. She wore a plastic shower cap the same color as the bubbles. Missing was a Mary Kay Cadillac in the garage. A lit mango-scented candle sent its tropical scent throughout the room. The soothing sound of Enya played softly.

Kayla put the toilet lid down and sat with her journal in her lap. "I'm keeping track of all the interesting things you say." She pulled a pencil from behind her ear.

Meanwhile, downstairs Ali dressed in a hurry, grabbed the pickup keys, and started upstairs to say goodbye to the two soul mates. She hesitated at the bottom of the stairs when she heard Kayla and Janelle giggling and laughing. She envied their relationship, a relationship with Janelle she yearned for when she was Kayla's age. She even longed for a bond now but it was too late. Too much water under the bridge, as Virginia would say.

She hollered upstairs. "I'm leaving. Don't stay up late, Kayla."

"Sure," Kayla said and then looked at her aunt. "I love having you around."

"Even though I drive your mother nuts?"

"Mom's busy with all her projects. She'll barely notice you're here. Wait. You'll see."

"Don't count on it. Besides, I may have to move in with your grandparents in a few days."

"Not if I can help it."

"I'm amazed your mother hasn't packed my bags by now."

"I'm supposed to tell you that Mom is meeting Dad for dinner. Just the two of us tonight and I'm cooking you the best dinner. Come down when you feel like it. We'll have a PJ party like when I was a kid."

"Whew! With your mother gone, I can relax. She makes me nervous. By the way, Kayla, I invited Brad Patterson over tonight, but he hasn't returned my phone call. You don't mind if he joins us, do you, sweetie?"

"But I . . ." Kayla's smile disappeared. "Okay." Her head downcast, Kayla descended the stairs. She tossed her journal on the bottom step and went to the kitchen to begin preparations for dinner.

"Oh, sh—shoot. Help."

"Aunt Janelle? What's wrong?" Kayla turned around and galloped up the stairs heeding the braying sound coming from the bathroom. She opened the door to the sight of pieces of glistening shattered glass that covered the tile floor like pieces of diamonds. "What happened? Are you hurt?"

"My hand was wet when I reached for the glass and it slipped."

The pieces of shimmering glass looked like boulders to the wide-eyed horrified Kayla. She could hear her mother in her ear, "Please don't use that glass. It was a wedding present. One of six."

"Mom warned me. She'll tell me I'm not responsible or something like that."

"We won't tell her. Our secret," Janelle said. "That's it for a relaxing bath. Better clean this up." She attempted to stand but her feet lost their grip on the soapy bathtub bottom. She grabbed a towel hanging on a brass rack above her head. Janelle captured the towel but the rack came along for the ride clunking her in the head. Janelle slid underwater on her back with her toes sticking out of the water and her head submerged. Splattered water drenched the bathroom. Janelle spluttered as she emerged, spitting out pink soap bubbles and gasping for air.

"My head is spinning. I think I might faint!" Janelle examined her hands covered in drywall dust.

"Please don't pass out!" Kayla shouted.

"I don't care what your mother says about my language. DAMN, DAMN, DAMN."

Kayla picked up the towel rack from the tub. "We'll have to keep Mom out of here until Gramps can fix the towel rack." She looked despondently at the hole in the wall. "At least I hope so."

"The towel rack, hell. What about me? If I have a concussion, can he repair me, too? Am I bleeding? I need water."

Kayla handed her aunt a small paper cup filled with water. "Don't be mad at me, Aunt Janie."

Roxie stood in the doorway of the bathroom and growled at Janelle.

Janelle stood in the bathtub, gargled with the water, and spit it out. "I'll never get that taste out of my mouth."

With Kayla's help, Janelle tried to stand for the second time. So far so good. When she put her leg over the tub, she stepped on a shard of glass. "Ow, holy sh…" Janelle plopped her naked bottom on the toilet. "I'm a mess, a failure; no wonder your mother wants to get rid of me."

"Don't be so hard on yourself, Aunt Janie. Accidents happen. If we fix it all up, Mom won't be mad at you."

"It will take more than that to repair our relationship," Janelle said.

Chapter 19

Ali scanned the main dining room of the busy restaurant but didn't find Matt. She checked with the friendly hostess who told her the Graham party was in the cocktail lounge. The stylish and sophisticated suburban restaurant could rival any upscale establishment downtown. Lots of shiny chrome and contemporary artwork decorated the walls. Since they started dieting, she and Matt usually dined at home. This was a treat.

When she entered the bar, she immediately regretted not taking more time choosing her outfit. Ali hoped her black pants and green sweater didn't look too much like a happy homemaker compared with this hip martini-drinking crowd. Ali sighted Matt sitting at the bar with his back to her. She tapped him on the shoulder.

"Buy a girl a drink?"

He turned around to face her. "Oh. You're here." He jumped off the barstool.

"I changed my mind," she said.

"I'm glad you came." He greeted her with a kiss on the lips. "You look great, by the way. I'm getting used to your new hair. I like it."

Ali blushed. Compliments embarrassed Ali, even from her husband.

"Where are the Grahams?"

"Ellis canceled. Sent me a text a few minutes ago. Something about Genevieve not feeling well. He said to enjoy ourselves and he'll pick up the tab." Matt helped Ali up on the only stool left at the packed and noisy bar. "I had already ordered my drink when I read the text—in case you're wondering why I didn't leave. I was disappointed you turned me down."

"Kayla was delighted to have her nutty aunt all to herself tonight. How much trouble could Janelle cause in a few hours?"

"You never know with that one," Matt said.

"When did you develop a taste for martinis?" Ali observed a glass with three olives in front of him.

"When I need courage to talk to you about things I would rather not talk to you about."

Ali's heart skipped a beat. According to Ellen, when a husband began a conversation with the *need to talk to you* phrase, adversity loomed. Janelle used that phrase often in her books. The "something" could be another woman, or a health problem like an inoperable tumor. Rarely was the "something" happy news like winning the Publisher's Clearing House sweepstakes. All signs pointed to danger.

"Sales are down again?"

"Yes. Plus some reorganization. Don't worry. My job's not in jeopardy. Might get a different assignment. Hopefully no pay cut."

Ali recalled that recently Matt seemed obsessed with watching Fox Business News and checking stocks on the Internet.

Matt's collar and tie were loose. Ali rubbed her hand on his forearm. "You look tired, sweetheart."

Matt signaled to the attractive female bartender. "Another one, Matt? And for the lady?" she asked.

"Yes, Dana. Pinot grigio for my wife." Did he emphasize the "wife" or was that Ali's imagination?

"First name basis with the bartender?"

"I come in here sometimes for lunch." Matt cleared his throat.

Unless Matt scheduled a business appointment, he ate his lunch at his desk not in a bar. At least that's what Ali assumed.

Matt worked for Ellis Graham after school when he was a teenager and during summer breaks while attending college. After graduating with a business degree, Ellis offered him a fulltime position. He worked himself up the ladder, attaining the position of general manager of one of Graham Motor Company's mega dealerships. Ellis hinted about giving Matt the opportunity to buy one of his stores. When Joey Graham, the son of Ellis's brother, joined the company two years ago, those hints ceased.

Ali was aware of Matt's career ambitions. He wanted to work for himself, be his own boss. He and Ali had many late night discussions about his dreams and aspirations. Lately, he seemed resigned to work for Graham Motor Company for the remainder of his career. "We should have left Willoughby a long time ago," he said.

"We couldn't. Your parents were both sick. Then Kayla came along. Mother and Dad were so attached to Kayla we couldn't leave. That's what happens in life. I have no regrets," Ali said. She wasn't telling the entire truth. Generally, Ali was satisfied living in Willoughby. However, when she compared her lifestyle with her sister's, the places Janelle traveled, the money she earned, it was then that Ali would daydream about a different kind of life.

"Don't worry, Matt. Remember, I have a job."

They both laughed. Ali could classify her part-time job at Kitchen Bliss as volunteer work. She made enough to pay for Kayla's tennis expenses. She named her own hours and enjoyed the contact with the residents of Willoughby who shunned the big box stores to shop along Willoughby Lane. Kitchen Bliss was close enough to home that Ali could walk to work.

The hostess found Ali and Matt and said their table was ready. As they left, Ali noticed Matt's generous cash tip for the bartender.

Ali's mouth watered as she read the enticing menu. Every item she coveted was not on her low fat, no carbs, no flavor, no fun diet. *To heck with it.* She ordered lobster ravioli in cream sauce, then changed her mind, and settled for grilled fish and vegetables. "No butter, please," she said.

Matt ordered appetizers and a porterhouse, medium rare. "And another round of drinks, please," he said to the server. "May as well live it up. Let's toast Graham Motor Company."

During their meal, they talked about options for Matt's job situation. "I don't want to worry you, Ali, but I'm getting bad vibes at work."

"How so?"

"Yesterday Ellis excluded me from an important meeting with BMW. He rarely asks my opinion. Joey has taken my place."

"I hate to see you unhappy at work, but if what you say is true, this may be our last meal on Ellis." She raised her glass.

"I've been thinking of something we could do together. Willoughby Lane is lively with activity. More art galleries and boutiques are opening and restaurants are relocating here. Timing might be right," Matt said.

"What do you have in mind?" Ali asked.

"Ellen's unhappy owning Kitchen Bliss. She promised her parents she would keep the store in the family. Her brother has no interest, and Ellen considers us family."

"This is a lot to think about, Matt. How would we finance the purchase? Ellen's our friend but she won't give it away. We have to think about Kayla's education."

"I've had a few discussions with Brad to pick his brain. He knows the restaurant and retail industries. He encouraged me."

"You talked with Brad before me?"

"I didn't want to get your hopes up."

Working together, living together?

"You can continue to manage the front of the store. I'll expand the coffee and tea section, update the bookkeeping, payroll, and inventory computer programs. Install a bridal registry. Create a website and maybe even a catalog."

"I guess I'm not much of a risk taker. Didn't think you were either, Matt," Ali said. "Thirty years with the same company. Unheard of these days."

"Let's at least think about it. Promise?" He put his hand on top of hers.

She nodded. "Quite a bit to think about."

"Maybe it's time to liven up our lives."

"Okay. I promise you I'll think about it," Ali reiterated.

"A toast to possibilities," Matt said as they clinked glasses.

Their discussion was over when their server appeared to take dessert orders.

"Anything chocolate," Ali said. "I do my best thinking with chocolate."

Chapter 20

"I faint at the sight of blood." Janelle shielded her eyes with her hands to avoid looking at the smear of crimson on the seashell-themed bathmat. "I'm dizzy. Seeing stars."

"Hold still. Might hurt," Kayla said as she plucked a piece of glass out of Janelle's big toe.

"You're damn right it hurt," Janelle barked, as she grabbed a wad of toilet paper and wrapped it around her wound.

"I better put the bathmat in the washing machine. You won't faint while I'm gone?"

"I'm fine. Don't worry about your mother's damn glass. I'll buy a replacement. I'm sorry I snapped at you."

"That's okay. You were scared." Kayla took the bathmat downstairs to the laundry room and returned with a broom and a dustpan to sweep away the telltale evidence of broken glass and drywall dust.

"Keep this door closed, Aunt Janie, so Mom doesn't see the disaster. Gramps comes every Friday. He can fix anything. He'll cover for us."

Janelle didn't hear Kayla. She was engrossed staring at her injury. "Everyone always compliments me on my beautiful toes. Hope I don't scar."

Roxie made an appearance and snarled at Janelle. "What do you want? Get out of here." The dog ignored Janelle and peed on the damaged toe.

"Damn that dog. This is a bathroom for humans not annoying animals. Get out of here."

Kayla made no apology for Roxie's impolite behavior. "Gee, Aunt Janie, don't pick on Roxie." The twosome left their houseguest sitting on the toilet, still half-naked, with a pink shower cap askew on her head. Kayla closed the bathroom door and shouted, "Bandages in the cabinet. Come on down when you're ready. We better leave Aunt Janie alone, Roxie, she sure is grumpy."

Janelle recovered from the accident and dressed for a date night but with a bandage on her toe. She wore tight black pants and a low-cut clingy yellow top the same color as her rental car. Her predictable well-coifed hair and makeup completed the package.

When Janelle passed the dining room on the way to the kitchen, she recognized the exquisite lace tablecloth from Greece that she gave Ali for a wedding gift. Ali's china and crystal adorned the table. Ivory tapers glowed. A white camellia floated in a glass bowl in the center of the table. She set her phone on the table, then joined Kayla in the kitchen. Andrea Bocelli was singing on the CD player. Kayla was wearing a green Kitchen Bliss apron over a black pleated skirt and a rose-colored shirt. Onions and garlic sizzled on the stovetop and a big pot of water bubbled. The pungent aroma of oregano and the sweet smell of basil wafted throughout the kitchen.

"Who taught you how to set a beautiful table? Not your mother?" Janelle asked as she joined Kayla in the kitchen.

"Nana loves a pretty table, even with all her old things. She taught me."

"Lovely," Janelle said. "I'm impressed. Thank you for doing this for me, sweetie."

"I went to a food website and typed in 'Italian dinners.' We didn't have time for a grocery store run so I used what I could find in the fridge and the pantry. We're having Italian meatloaf, Italian green salad, Italian green beans, and Italian pasta salad. Wait until you taste the dessert. You're not on any kind of diet are you?"

"Sounds, well, shall we say Italiano? Don't forget to add another place setting for Mr. Brad." She went back into the dining room and returned two wine glasses to the china cabinet. "I'm putting the glasses back. Can't afford another mishap."

Kayla brought three everyday wine glasses to the table.

"Do your parents allow you to drink wine?"

"Sometimes they let me have a tiny bit with dinner, for special occasions."

"This is a special occasion. You, Mr. Brad, and me. One small glassful. When we go to Italy you'll have wine with every meal."

"Even breakfast?"

"Not breakfast." She paused, examining Kayla's outfit. "Is that my Tory Burch shirt?"

"You said I could wear anything in your closet."

"Be careful. I don't want any red stains on it. Expensive you know. By the way, please excuse my behavior upstairs. I'm not used to animals." She glared daggers as sharp as stalactites at Roxie.

Janelle's phone chimed. "That's Brad now. It's about time," she said as she read a text message. "He's probably running late." She reread the message. "Damn. He could have called me instead of sending a da—a darn text."

"Bad news?"

"Just the two of us tonight."

"Do you like him?"

"We were high school friends...sort of," Janelle said with a dismissive wave.

"Did you date him?"

"Well, maybe we weren't close friends. We were neighbors but never spoke much. Then there was the time I backed over him. Oh, well, he shouldn't have been lurking behind my car anyway."

Janelle moseyed over to Matt's wine cabinet, selected a bottle, and scrutinized the label. She returned to the kitchen, opened the bottle, and took it to the dining room table.

Kayla hustled to and fro from the kitchen bringing the food to the table. Janelle stayed glued to her chair, sipping wine. When Kayla joined her for the meal, Janelle picked up her fork but replaced it quickly.

"You seem sad, Aunt Janie. Is it because Mr. Brad didn't come tonight?"

"I'm sorry. My agent says I'm never sorry, but I sure have broken the record in this house."

"That's okay. I think I understand. Probably Mom has something to do with it."

Janelle was unresponsive. "You say grace, Kayla. I muffed it at Gramps and Nana's. Out of practice."

Kayla bowed her head, thanked God for the food they were about to eat, for her parents, grandparents, and "especially for giving me an awesome aunt." She raised her head and smiled at Janelle. Kayla dug in while Janelle pushed her food around with a fork.

"Nice, Kayla. Molto buono. I truly am sorry for being so b—I mean, witchy."

"No problem," Kayla said. "You can cuss when Mom's not around."

They continued their meal while Janelle talked about her success. "You know I received an award last year from the National Book Lovers Association. And, I've been invited to something or other in Charleston." After every other bite, she complimented Kayla on the flavor of the meal even though she tried to hide bits of the meatloaf under the pasta salad.

"What a shame Brad couldn't join us tonight," Janelle said. "Not a nice way to welcome me."

"I'm glad he didn't come. I have you all to myself," Kayla admitted. "While we're alone, Aunt Janie, I have a question to ask you. As one friend to another. You are my friend, aren't you? Not only an aunt?"

"What's on your mind?"

"Why does Mom act so crazy when you're around? Even Roxie notices."

"She wants to create a perfect environment for me since I lead such a stressful life. Even when we were young, she tried to please me. She followed me around like Roxie follows you. When she disappoints me, she's displeased with herself."

"Dad calls her 'St. Alicia of Willoughby.'"

"No one's a saint. Not even your mother."

"What's it like to have a sister?"

"We had lots of fun together. Ask your grandparents to look at some of the old photo albums." Janelle paused. "When I started kindergarten she tugged and pulled on my dress pleading me not to leave."

"So you loved each other then?"

Janelle put her hands together and inspected her cuticles. "I was born first so it was different for me." She took a sip of wine before she continued. "Maybe I was slightly resentful of having to share my parents' affection and attention. Maybe I tried too hard to become the favorite child. And, it was a strain to live up to Mother's expectations, expectations she didn't have for your mother."

"I don't understand," Kayla said.

"Now, I don't want to criticize your mother because I know you love her. But...well, she was different from me. She wasn't interested in makeup, clothes, boys. Her hobbies were reading and scribbling in her diary. Your grandmother and I were more alike."

"Why don't you have kids?"

Janelle hesitated. "I suppose my books are my children."

"You'd make a great mother," Kayla said.

"Me? Well, I'm glad you feel that way, but that does it, no more wine for you, young lady. Your mother would murder me if she finds out. You had better go on upstairs and do your homework."

"Can't. She told me not to make a mess in the kitchen. But look at it."

"You go on. I'll clean up. I insist."

Kayla assessed the kitchen sink overflowing with pots and pans. "Really? Thank you, Aunt Janie. I love you so much."

"Don't tell your mom I swore. Okay?"

"You can always trust me with our secrets."

The two hugged. Half way up the stairs Kayla shouted, "I almost forgot. What about dessert?"

"I couldn't eat another bite."

Roxie entered the kitchen sniffing the floor hoping to find a morsel of dropped food.

"You don't like me, little one. We're going to change that."

Roxie bared her teeth and growled.

Janelle took a piece of meatloaf from her plate and offered it to Roxie from her hand. When Roxie gobbled it, Janelle put her entire plate of uneaten food in front of the dog. When the plate was empty, she added food from the pots and pans on the stove. Roxie was in doggy gourmet heaven. "This might be the beginning of a beautiful friendship, Roxie Moxie," Janelle said. Roxie cocked her head before she licked the plate clean.

Why in the hell did I offer to clean up? I don't know where to begin. She removed the plates, silverware, and glasses from the table, and stashed them in the dishwasher haphazardly. She put the crystal on the bottom and laid the china on the top. She fumbled around underneath the sink, removed a plastic bottle, and squirted its contents into the dishwasher bypassing the dispenser.

"Easy peasy," she said to a whimpering Roxie. "No more food, honey. I put it all in the garbage disposal."

In her haste to tidy up and exit the foreign territory of a kitchen, Janelle didn't notice a fork that slipped into the disposal. When she flipped the switch, she heard a loud grinding noise. "What the hell is going on?" she said. She tried to pull the fork out before turning it off, but the disposal tried to swallow her hand. She flipped the switch off, removed the fork, and examined its distorted tines. The fork now resembled a mangled arthritic hand. She opened one kitchen drawer after another hoping to find something to straighten the fork. Perhaps a hammer had potential. She placed the silver fork on the countertop, held it with one hand, and whacked it while holding the hammer in her other hand. BANG! All she accomplished was a big dent in the countertop. *Oh, well, Ali needs a new countertop anyway.*

Janelle gathered the dirty pots and pans then searched the kitchen for a spot to stash them. *Ali has nothing to do all day. She can wash them tomorrow.* She opened the oven door and stuffed them inside.

Although the kitchen was not up to Martha Stewart's standards, it was reasonably tidy after Janelle's cleaning. However, a panic attack hit her like a kick in the stomach. She recounted the evening's disasters: twisted fork, dented countertop, shattered wine glass, bathroom wall with a gaping hole minus a towel rack, and the blood-covered bath mat. Whenever Janelle confronted a problem, she relied on the characters in her books to offer solutions. *What would Savannah Strong in Deadly Dangerous do if she faced a similar dilemma?* Assuming the persona of Savannah, Janelle headed to the wine cabinet. She selected a bottle of cab sav without regard for its country of origin and went into the dining room. She was careful not to choose a crystal glass. She sat while sipping wine and contemplating a course of action. She needed to rectify or hide the various accidents that happened during the evening.

Janelle's new best friend Roxie trotted to her and sat at Janelle's bandaged foot. Roxie made a grumbling noise, coughed a few times, and then deposited her Italian dinner onto Janelle's feet with molto gusto.

"Damn you! You ugly rat! All over my feet! Kayla!" Janelle shrieked as the contents of her wine glass splattered on the tablecloth.

Kayla heard her aunt's screams of anguish and rushed downstairs holding a textbook.

"Are you okay?" Kayla asked.

"Roxie threw up all over me. Get something to wash my feet."

"Oh, my gosh. Red wine on Mom's tablecloth."

"Yeah, I know. I should switch to white. Not as hazardous."

"I should have known better. This is her best tablecloth. She only uses it for Thanksgiving and Christmas. All my fault."

"If she doesn't use it much, she'll never know. I'll take it to the cleaner's tomorrow. Hide it in the bathroom for now."

Kayla hesitated. "What's the matter with Roxie?" The dog was on the kitchen floor with her head between her paws making a sound like a human moaning.

"I gave her a few leftovers. Guess they didn't agree with her."

"We never feed Roxie from the table. Poor thing." Kayla filled Roxie's water bowl and encouraged her to drink. Then she went to the garage to retrieve cleaning supplies. She was getting lots of practice cleaning up after her aunt. First the green glob on the white carpeting, then the Waterford glass, and the hole in the bathroom wall. Now red wine on the tablecloth and a vomiting Roxie.

Janelle did not attempt to help Kayla who was on her hands and knees trying to clean up Roxie's leftovers from the carpet.

"We're in big trouble, Aunt Janie. Mom is going to have a fit. She didn't know I planned to use her fancy things for dinner tonight. And then the bathroom!"

"Don't worry. I'll think of something. If I don't, may as well pack my bags because I'm doomed for eviction from the Lawrence household after tonight's fiascos."

Kayla offered no sympathy. She climbed the stairs, one at a time at the pace of an elderly lady. Her aunt wasn't the only one doomed. "Don't forget to turn the dishwasher on," Kayla hollered. In a lowered voice, she added, "Maybe you can do something right."

Janelle was glad for the reminder from Kayla. She went into the kitchen and hit the start button on the dishwasher before she went to bed.

Ali and Matt returned home and entered the kitchen from the garage. A strong lemon scent overwhelmed them. A sea of bubbles had flowed out of the dishwasher and onto the floor.

"What the...?" Matt said.

"What did that loony sister of mine do? This has Janelle written all over it."

"Now what?" Kayla called from upstairs. After hearing her parents' screeches, she joined them in the kitchen.

"Who put the soap in the dishwasher?" Ali asked

"Aunt Janie was in charge of clean up."

Ali shook her head. "As I guessed."

"She must have used dish soap instead of dish*washer* soap," Matt said. "I committed that felony once."

Matt and Kayla hustled into the garage to gather armloads of old terry-cloth towels to soak up the flood. Ali joined them to check the recycle and garbage cans for empty wine bottles but found no evidence.

"I'm really sorry, Mom. Really." Kayla lowered her head and stared at her feet.

"Not your fault. A wet floor will dry. Could be a lot worse. Where is my sister? Getting her beauty rest?"

Kayla bit her lip when her mother said, "*Could* be a lot worse."

"Go to bed. I should not have left you alone with Janelle." Ali spoke in the voice that resurrected when Janelle was in town. Kayla left the kitchen with Roxie behind her.

"Remember, Ali, teenagers are attracted to rule breakers," Matt said.

"Kayla hasn't yet. I never did."

"If you say so."

Ali wondered what he meant by that comment. After the floor was dry, she continued her search for contraband in the kitchen cabinets and underneath the sink but found no proof of Janelle drinking. Maybe she was on her best behavior tonight, Ali hoped. When she began to clean the countertop, she said to Matt, "How in the world did this happen?"

Matt came to her side and they both gaped at the dent in the mint green Formica countertop.

"We had planned to remodel the kitchen anyway," he said.

"Maybe she did us a favor," Ali said. "An expensive favor."

Ali gathered the wet towels and took them to the laundry room off the garage. She lifted the lid of the washing machine and saw three empty wine bottles. She decided to wait until tomorrow to tell Matt.

When she returned to the kitchen, Matt embraced her in a warm and affectionate hold. He kissed Ali's neck and murmured in her ear. "Finish this in the morning. We've other things on the agenda tonight." He ran his hands through her now-silky hair.

"You know I can't leave a messy kitchen."

He turned her around, held her by her shoulders, and gave her a long, hungry kiss. "How about now? Is that enough encouragement?"

"Mmm. Do that again."

Matt complied as he put his hands inside her sweater until he found her bra.

"Let's finish this in the—" Ali said.

"We're only beginning." He took her by the hand and led her into the bedroom. For now, Ali forgot about the messy kitchen, the dented countertop, and Janelle. She had more pleasant activities to pursue.

Chapter 21

The next morning, Ali opened the shutters in her bedroom to assess the day's weather. Bright morning sun greeted her. Cumulus clouds smeared the Mediterranean blue sky. She opened the window and inhaled the sweet fragrance of the hyacinth blooming in the garden. An overcast rainy day would have matched Ali's mood better than the sunshine.

Ali dreaded facing her sister about the empty wine bottles. Confrontation was difficult for Ali, especially when her opponent was a pit bull disguised as a poodle. Ali never won an argument with Janelle. When they were young, Janelle chose the TV shows they watched, the games they played, and successfully persuaded their mother to buy the snacks Janelle preferred. Nothing white. Nothing orange. She ate the outside of a Twinkie, not the white filling, which she saved for Ali.

The wet floor was not worth an argument but the wine bottles were. A mother's resolve to protect her daughter would prevail and instill courage, she hoped.

The enticing aroma of hazelnut coffee made by her considerate barista led Ali to the kitchen. She filled a mug and sat down at the table to read the paper while inhaling the pleasant bouquet. *Wish I had one of Maggie's double chocolate orange scones.* She turned to the obituary section, her daily habit. Roxie sat at her feet still lethargic after the previous night's bacchanal.

"Morning, Li'l Sis," Janelle said when she appeared at the kitchen door. She was wearing large black sunglasses and a black and gold visor. She was dressed in black leggings and an oversized T-shirt that seemed familiar to Ali. Even at this early morning hour, Janelle's signature jasmine scent overpowered the room.

"You're up early," Ali said. "Coffee?"

Janelle nodded. Roxie whimpered but went to Janelle's side.

Ali stood and walked to the cupboard. She selected a mug with the words, "The Queen Has Arrived. All Bow." She filled it and returned to the kitchen table.

"Where is everyone?" Janelle asked.

"Matt's at work. Kayla's at school. Hope she doesn't fall asleep during her Spanish test, thanks to you."

Janelle ignored Ali's glare. "Heard you come home and then lots of muted noise. Luckily, I had my earplugs and eyeshade. Miss my white noise machine though."

"We have some things to discuss, Janelle. Sit down." She lifted two plastic containers that she had placed under the kitchen table. She put them in front of Janelle. "Dish*washer* soap. *Dish* soap. See the difference? When you put dish soap in a dishwasher, it's like putting bubble bath soap in a whirlpool tub. I should have dragged you out of bed last night and made you clean up the mess."

"Don't blame Kayla. I told her to study and that I'd take care of the kitchen."

"I didn't say it was Kayla's fault."

Janelle flicked a fingernail on both containers. "They both clean. I wasn't far off. Household cleaning isn't as easy for me as for you."

"Well, maybe if you hadn't paid me to do your chores when we were kids, it wouldn't be so hard now." Ali stood with hands akimbo staring down her sister.

"If that's the way you remember our childhood, whatever. I have no recollection of you doing my chores."

"Another thing, Janelle. This is more important than the wet floor. I found three empty wine bottles in the washing machine. For a writer, not a clever hiding spot."

"No lectures, Ali. For your information, Kayla's recipes called for wine. You should give serious consideration to sending her to Le Cordon Bleu."

"Don't you think Kayla's too young for culinary or sommelier training?"

"She only had one little sip."

"But three bottles? Who drank all that wine?"

"I spilled a tiny bit. Here and there. Trust me, I did not, nor did Kayla, drink three bottles of wine."

"If I knew that you let my teenage daughter consume alcohol, more than a sip, I would pack your bags now and send you to Mother's. Sister or no sister. And, for your information, Matt's wine collection is sacrosanct to him. If you want wine, go into the pantry."

"No problem. I'll buy my own wine, if that will make you happy. Besides, Kayla said—"

Janelle thought better of telling Ali that Kayla said she sometimes drank wine with her parents.

"Kayla said what?"

"Nothing."

"Another thing. What about the crater-size dent in the counter-top. That your doing, too?"

"I guess."

"Breakfast?" Ali snipped ending the discussion of the previous night's disasters.

"No food. Please, no food. I'm not a morning person." Janelle removed her sunglasses, revealing bloodshot eyes. "Too bright," she said. She turned her chair so her back faced the sun streaming through the window.

Ali went to the toaster and dropped in both halves of a bagel.

"You might consider cutting back on the carbs, Ali. I'm trying a gluten-free diet. Maybe you should, too."

While Ali waited for the bagel to toast, she took cream cheese from the refrigerator thinking she'd like to slather the bagel with it and smash it into Janelle's face. She returned to the table with her plate load of carbs and assessed her sister's physical appearance, which had deteriorated since her arrival in Willoughby. The prom queen was looking more like a bedraggled bag lady. Janelle's trembling hands and the dark circles under her dull eyes told Ali there was something wrong. A tiny part, but only a tiny part, of Ali wanted to reach out to her sister and offer help and support, if that's what Janelle needed. The memory of a lifetime of insults and criticisms quelled those thoughts.

The two sisters sat in silence. Ali ate her breakfast, Janelle sipped coffee, and they both read the newspaper.

Ali told herself that Janelle was a big girl. She was worldly, sophisticated, and rich. If she had a problem, let her resolve it or turn it over to one of her "people." What possible help could Ali offer?

Janelle stood and went to the coffeemaker. "More?" she asked Ali. She brought the carafe to the table and filled her sister's mug.

"Thank you."

"Before you leave for work, there's something I need to talk to you about," Janelle said.

"Let's talk now and get it over with."

"I don't know where to start."

"Try the beginning," Ali said as the phone rang. She considered letting the answering machine pick up but was expecting a call from Diane about the banquet.

Janelle left the room and returned upstairs. When Ali finished the phone conversation, she hollered upstairs. "I'm ready whenever you are."

"Changing my clothes," Janelle hollered back.

Ali reached for the bottle of Tums on the table before she went into her bedroom. When she returned to the kitchen, she called out to Janelle again. No answer. "Janelle. Come on down." She started for the stairs when she heard the shower running.

"She'll be up there for hours, Roxie. Let's take a walk." When Ali and Roxie returned Janelle's banana car was gone.

Now what is she up to?

Chapter 22

Ali sat at the kitchen table preparing remarks for the banquet on her laptop. She heard the screen on the front door open and close. Roxie hurried to greet the visitor.

"Anybody home?"

"Hey, Dad." Ali turned her head to look at the wall calendar. Rain or sleet, Ed came on Fridays. He called the weekly visit his "Friday Fixer" day when he would hunt for a leaky faucet or a squeaky door. He missed his days at Willoughby High teaching shop and woodworking.

Ed kissed Ali's cheek and then put his well-used traveling tool bag on the floor. He pulled a treat from his pocket and tossed it to Roxie who gobbled it and then returned to her comfy bed underneath the bay window.

"Help yourself to coffee, Dad. Can't think of anything that's broken."

"So, what's up, Gingersnap?" His thick glasses gave him a slightly nerdy look. White spots of paint splattered his rumpled work jeans. His blue Willoughby High T-shirt matched his eyes. He stood with his back up against the kitchen counter and removed his Braves baseball cap.

"I received a frantic call from your sister. Something about repairs to the bathroom. She said not to tell you under any circumstances, but I don't like secrets. Janelle has given all her characters secrets and how has that worked out for them? Disgraced, in jail, embarrassed. She can sure think up some doozies."

"But her characters all end up winners," Ali said. "What's wrong with the bathroom?"

"Let's find out," he said as he hoisted his tool bag. "Where is she anyway?"

"Don't know. She left while I took Roxie for a walk."

"She makes my blood pressure rise," Ed said.

"Don't let her. She won't be here for long. I hope."

Ali followed her father half way up the stairs when the telephone in the kitchen rang. She let the answering machine pick up. Then she heard Janelle's cell phone ringing a piercing sound. Ali retreated down the steps and followed the sound into the sunroom where she found the phone wedged between two cushions continuing its annoying ring. Ali wrenched the phone out of the cushions. Her phone was uncomplicated—green for on, red for off. Mystified, she stared at a picture of Ken Luzi, Janelle's agent. Tentatively, she hit the answer button.

"Yes?" Ali said, trying to imitate Janelle's curt voice seasoned with a touch of annoyance.

"Finally, you answered your phone. What the hell's the matter with you, Janelle? You promised your manuscript to your editor three weeks ago and now he's breathing down my neck."

"Sorry."

"Jeez. Now I know something's wrong with you. Hell, I've never heard that word 'sorry' out of your mouth in all the years I've been your agent. Janelle Jennings is never sorry. You will be this time if you don't finish the damn manuscript. Is something wrong?" The irate agent didn't wait for an answer. "That's it. You're at your sister's. I've tried everywhere else. I'm coming to Georgia."

Ali struggled to keep pace with this fast-talking, hell-spewing agent. Manuscript? Editor? Coming to Georgia? A million scenarios flashed before her. She tried to think as fast as Ken talked.

When Janelle and Ali were teenagers, they enjoyed confusing their friends and even their parents because their voices sounded alike. That was where the similarities ended.

"Give me Ali's address."

Ali closed her eyes and blurted out "2323 Plum Court." She'd better end this conversation before he detected the imposter.

"She's your emergency contact and this is sure as hell an emergency. I'm worried as hell. See you tomorrow come hell or high water." He hung up.

"Oh my gosh. That's the problem. Janelle hasn't finished her book," Ali said aloud. "No wonder she's a mess."

Ed came downstairs and found Ali in the sunroom. He put his hands on his hips. "What the blazes? Looks like a war zone up there."

"What do you mean?"

"The towel bar's been ripped out of the wall. I don't have enough tools or supplies. Need paint. I've a key, if you have to leave." He was muttering to himself and shaking his head as he left. "Don't imagine you have any paint to match?" he asked when he reached the front door.

Ali shook her head. Painting the bathroom was number thirty on her to-do list. Ali sprinted up the stairs and entered the bathroom. Ed would need more than his tool bag to patch up this mess. The bathroom resembled an abandoned DIY project. Ali sat on her heels, gathered pieces of drywall, and flung them into the wastebasket. Chunks missed their target adding to the mess. This was typical of the sisters' fractured relationship—Ali always picking up the pieces. More troubling to Ali than the trashed bathroom was that Kayla was probably an accomplice in Janelle's duplicity. Ali didn't doubt for a minute that the disaster was Janelle's responsibility. Using her proficient manipulative tricks, Janelle probably swore Kayla to secrecy.

Ali decided Janelle had to go. Living with her sister in the same state, the same county, the same town, was bad enough. Living together under the same roof threatened Ali's sanity. She vowed to confront the subject of saying adiós as soon as Janelle returned. Surely, Virginia could make room for her favorite daughter.

Ali sat on the toilet with the lid down and scrutinized the mess. When Ed returned they worked together without speaking. She collected more pieces of plaster and tossed them into the wastebasket.

"Ah, come on, Gingersnap. You can do better than that. Aren't you mad as hell at Janelle?" Ed teased, giving her encouragement.

Ali grinned. She emptied the wastebasket and one by one threw the pieces back in with fury. "Take that, and that. . .you—" Ali stopped short of calling her sister the "B" word in front of her father.

"Remember when you helped me with projects when you were a kid?" Ed asked.

"Some of my favorite memories, Dad. I think many of those projects were bogus. You wanted to keep me busy while Mother and Janelle left for the mall."

"What's wrong with a father who wanted to spend some quality time with his youngest daughter?"

"I love you, Dad."

The unfinished manuscript was the key to Ali's get-rid-of-the-evil-sister dilemma. If Ali had to tie Janelle to a chair, she would finish the book, Ali swore. *And, I know the person to help me.* "Dad, I have another project for you."

Chapter 23

J anelle parked the banana car around the corner from her destination, ignoring several empty places in front of Classy Consignments on Willoughby Lane. She lifted two rollerboards from the car and walked toward the store, struggling to pull both. She hoped Ali hadn't seen her loading her loot in the car when she left the house earlier.

Meanwhile, Jackie Glassen, owner of the consignment shop, heard a bing on her phone indicating a text: "Prom Queen approaching." Jackie looked out the front window of the store and waved to her across-the-street merchant friend who sent the heads-up message.

The bell above the door tinkled, announcing a customer.

Janelle kept her oversized sunglasses on when she entered. She wore one of Ali's straw hats, black Capri pants, a black T-shirt, and glittery flip-flops—her incognito outfit.

Jackie stood behind the glass counter with her arms folded as she watched Janelle maneuvering the luggage into the store.

"Some help, please," Janelle said.

"I think you're doing fine by yourself," Jackie said, planted behind the counter.

Janelle put down the luggage and closed the door.

"May I help you?"

"Isn't it obvious? I have high-end designer items to sell. Not enough room in my closet."

"For example?"

"Armani, Versace, Kate Spade. You might not have heard of these lines," Janelle said.

Jackie motioned Janelle to follow her. "You mean like these?"

Janelle was astonished at the range of designer handbags and shoes displayed on shelves.

"You look familiar," Jackie said.

"Well, I should."

"Is that you, the former Miss Willoughby County?" Jackie asked.

"I try to keep a low profile when I'm in Willoughby. Surely you understand."

The two women glared at each other.

"You don't remember me, do you? I was the runner up in the contest for Miss Willoughby County—Jackie Brevard. Glassen now."

"Of course, I remember you," Janelle lied.

"No you don't. I've gained fifty pounds and lost most of my hair."

What was I thinking? Janelle realized. *This is going horribly wrong. I should do this out of town.*

"Everyone said you stole the title from me—with help from your interfering mother. You excelled at stealing, especially everyone's boyfriends. At least I've been able to hold on to my husband." She pointed to a photo on the wall. "What number husband are you on now? Five?"

"I absolutely, honestly remember you, Jackie. How could anyone forget your beautiful eyes?" Another lie. "F-Y-I, I've only been married—ah, three times."

"Save the fiction for your books."

"Who cares about some extra weight? You look healthy. And look at this, your own business." Janelle turned to scrutinize the neatly arranged rows of women's accessories and jewelry. "You have children and a husband. Look at those beautiful kids and their handsome dad," Janelle said as she pointed to the picture hanging on the wall of two chubby teenagers and an equally as "healthy" man.

"Ah, thank you. Yes, they are adorable, aren't they?" She patted the photo and blew a kiss toward their chipmunk cheeks. "So, why are you here?" Jackie pointed to the luggage.

"I'm downsizing. Have too much of everything."

"Let's take a look."

"As you might imagine, I don't have any experience with consignments. How does it work?"

"We agree on a price. When I sell, we'll split the profit—sixty for me and forty for you."

"How long will it take?"

"Might take days or weeks. The luggage might go quickly since summer vacations and graduations are approaching."

Jackie's statement shocked Janelle—*days or weeks?*

"What do you have in the suitcases?" Jackie asked again. She walked toward the rollerboards and opened one. "O-M-G. Red soles. I might buy a pair of these myself, if it's my size." She took her shoe off, revealing calloused feet in need of an emergency pedicure.

Janelle snatched the shoe out of Jackie's hand. "I've changed my mind," she said, picturing Jackie's puffball feet stuffed into a precious Louboutin. "I think my niece might want some of these items for our trip to Italy. Nice to see you, Jackie." In a flash, Janelle closed the suitcase.

"But what about the shoes?"

No answer came from Janelle who managed to open the door by herself and flip-flopped off pulling the luggage behind her.

Standing at the front counter, Jackie opened her laptop and began typing.

To: Book Babes
Fm: classyjackie@classyconsignments
Re: Surprise visitor

Guess who trotted into my store on her high horse, er flip-flops. You'll never guess. Prom Queen. She didn't recognize me. Suppose 50# will do that. She wanted money ASAP for luggage and shoes. She changed her mind and left with the items she brought. Don't tell Ali. If the Prom Queen is selling luggage not a good sign…she may stay forever.

Chapter 24

"Ali. Please call me. It's Jill."

When Ali returned the call, Jill said, "I'm so embarrassed. Janelle ordered an extravagant floral arrangement for Phoebe's memorial service. She demanded. Excuse me. She requested a certain type of orchid and other flowers that aren't accessible. I convinced her low key was more sensible, but still it was the most elaborate arrangement my shop has ever assembled. I hope everyone at the memorial service knew I made it. Well, I digress." Jill gasped for air between sentences.

Ali recalled the standing spray of lavender roses, purple chrysanthemums, and blue irises adorned with a huge gold metallic ribbon that read "Our Phoebe." Jill should have second thoughts about having everyone know it was from her shop.

"The credit card company," Jill continued, "denied the purchase. I put it through twice. Money's tight and I can't afford to eat this. Could you talk to her? She probably has another credit card or maybe cash."

"I'm so sorry. Did you try calling her? I'll give you her cell number."

"I called several times. She doesn't answer."

"Don't worry. Probably a mistake on the credit card company's end. I'll see you tomorrow and take care of it." Ali tried to mask the embarrassment coupled with anger she felt toward her sister.

"I promise I won't tell anyone. Janelle has sold so many books. I bet she's rolling in the dough."

"No doubt. I'll see you soon." Ali quickly ended the conversation. She felt the Janelle-induced recurring pain in her stomach and reached for her friend—the bottle of antacid.

Ali wondered how Janelle could possibly have cash flow problems. If her personal finances were in turmoil, that was one thing, but Ali did not appreciate her sister jeopardizing friendships and relationships.

"I received a disturbing call from Jill Porter today," Ali said to Matt as he walked in the door that evening.

"Is her husband okay? I heard at Lions Club that he had pneumonia."

"She didn't say anything about Walt. Janelle ordered an expensive floral arrangement for Phoebe's memorial service, but the credit card company declined the purchase. Janelle won't return Jill's calls."

"That immense solitary floral arrangement on a stand at the church was from Janelle? I should have guessed. The flowers resembled something at the funeral of Marco Sleeps with Fishes." He went to the refrigerator and took out a beer. He opened it, tossed the cap into the garbage can, and leaned his back against the kitchen counter facing Ali. "Have you asked Janelle about it?"

"Why don't *you*, Matt. Our conversations always end up argumentative. She respects you."

"Wouldn't it be easier if we paid the bill? Then Janelle owes us and not Jill," Matt suggested.

"What? $300? I told Janelle not to send flowers. That was against Phoebe's wishes."

"When do you suggest *I* ask her for the money?"

"Anytime when I'm not around."

"When your sister's involved, life is complicated. I'll pay the bill tomorrow. The first chance I get, I'll ask Janelle for the money."

If Matt confronts Janelle, this would be the shock of the century.

Chapter 25

Ali was in the upstairs bathroom picking up towels when her vibrating cell phone startled her. "Holy sugar!" she said. "What're you doing, babe?" Matt asked.

"Recovering from a heart attack. What did you do to my phone? I thought I was being electrocuted."

"So what are you *actually* doing?" he asked.

"Maid duties in the royal suite." Ali kicked a towel into the corner of the bathroom Kayla and Janelle shared. "I'm still picking up after her. Wet towels all over the bathroom floor."

"Isn't that something your sister should be doing or Kayla for that matter?"

"It needs to be done. What's up?" With the phone cradled on her shoulder, she put the top back on the toothpaste tube and threw used cotton balls into the wastebasket.

"Let's meet for lunch today. I have some free time."

"What's the occasion?"

"Do I need a reason to have lunch with my wife? We never have time for lunch."

"We just had dinner out."

"Don't sound so enthusiastic."

"I've such a busy day. . ."

"Oh, come on. Don't be like that."

"Sorry. Give me time to change. Where to?"

"Fickle Pickle. See you in fifteen." He hung up without giving Ali the chance to change her mind.

Matt was right about two things. Kayla hadn't been doing her share of chores since Janelle's arrival. Janelle continued to act as if she were a guest in one of the five-star hotels she frequented.

"Do you want me to take the sheets off or leave them on? Where are the clean towels?" Janelle asked after one night in the Lawrence home.

"Janelle, you've slept on the sheets once. We usually sleep on ours for at least a month."

"What?"

"Kidding, of course. But, you should make your own bed. If you're still here in a week, we'll talk."

Ali hurried downstairs to the kitchen where she scribbled a note for Kayla: "Laundry. Upstairs." She reread it, ripped it, and rewrote: "Kayla, please wash the towels and sheets on your bathroom floor. Love, Mom."

It had been a while since Ali and Matt had met for lunch, something they did often when they were newlyweds. "Try to get away at noon," she had said. "I'll have a great lunch packed. Meet at our usual place—the bench on Riverside. The young lovers would leave their jobs at the dealership and the public relations firm and meet along the Willoughby River. They sat on "their" bench with arms entwined and watched the water drift by. They spent more time enjoying the feel of each other's skin than they did eating the lunch Ali had prepared. They fed each other, one nibble at a time. "Guess we can call this our appetizer before the main meal," Matt teased. That was pre-Kayla and before life interfered with their private time. Ali didn't want to take time out for lunch since she was counting calories. Eating fruit and cottage cheese while standing over the kitchen sink is what she had planned today. Matt's invitation was thoughtful and he chose one of her favorite restaurants, which was within walking distance of their house. She guessed she could use the exercise.

Ali went to her bedroom to change from baggy shorts into an ankle-length khaki skirt and cotton Mexican embroidered shirt she had bought at a consignment shop. She pulled her hair into a ponytail and topped it off with a wide-brimmed hat with a sunflower to shield her freckled skin from the sun.

Ali walked toward the standing mirror. She didn't need a mirror to know she was a nonchalant dresser. Mustard stains on the front of the shirt. A wrinkled skirt. "Hmm. Can't I do better than this?" *Maybe Janelle is right. I am dowdy, like that dowdy Alicia character in her book Dowager of Denmark.* She took off her hat, tore the sunflower from the brim, and threw both items in the wastebasket. She shook her head and let her hair spill over her shoulders. She kicked off her brown, worn clogs, and replaced them with a pair of open-toed sandals.

Ali walked out of the bedroom and hesitated in front of the mirror in the hallway. *Not good enough.* If Janelle saw her dressed like this, she would criticize her from the top of her now straightened hair to the bottom of her unpolished toes. She returned to her closet and pleaded, "Help me out here, please." She rummaged in the back, taking a second to glance at her watch. She found three stacks of boxes. One contained her unfinished manuscripts. *I should toss all those silly half-written stories.* Another stack held the unused walking shoes Matt continued to give Ali. The third group contained presents of never worn clothing from Janelle. She put the gifts on her bed and one by one pulled out each item, tried them on, and chose a sweater with a boxy fit, which wasn't a size two. Janelle had given Ali the sapphire blue Italian knit sweater years ago for a Christmas present. Ali was uncomfortable with the low cut neckline and had never worn the expensive gift still wearing its price tag, a favorite Janelle detail. She went to the bathroom, found a cuticle scissors, and clipped off the tag. Whoops! She might have made a tiny hole in the beautiful garment. A pair of black pants, shoes with a tiny heel, and a brush through her hair improved the reflection. The pants were tight, but the sweater was long enough to cover her love handles. She grabbed her purse and left.

Willoughby Lane was active with business people arriving for lunch and ladies browsing in boutiques and art galleries along the street. Shoppers carried the distinctive black and white bag from the Chandlery, a popular destination in historic Willoughby. Customers at the outdoor café sat underneath colorful umbrellas enjoying pleasant, breezy weather while sipping margaritas or glasses of craft beer. Ali approached the white Victorian cottage restored, renovated, and now a popular restaurant named the Fickle Pickle.

Matt was waiting for her at the entrance. He greeted her with a kiss on the lips, slightly smearing her lipstick. "Mmm, yummy." He used his thumb to make the stain disappear. "You look different."

"How so?"

"I don't know. Haven't seen this sweater before. Is it new? Those pants look great, too." He took her hand and twirled her around as if they were a couple competing for the mirrored ball trophy on *Dancing with the Stars*. He lifted her off the ground.

"Matt. Stop it." She grinned. "Are the pants too tight? Sweater showing too much?"

"Not too tight for me."

Ali was glad she decided at the last minute to change her clothes. If Matt had seen her try to squeeze her size twelve body into size ten pants, even with three percent Spandex, he might not have thought she was attractive. The boxy sweater camouflaged her fleshy muffin top—the result of too much guacamole and chips over the years.

They went to the counter where Matt ordered two of their favorite sandwiches, one order of fried pickles, and two peach teas.

"What about my diet?" Ali asked.

"Protein is an antidote for stress."

"You made that up."

They found a place in the cheerful main room. "This is a wonderful, unexpected idea. We don't seem to spend much time together. I love you," Ali said.

"Right back at you, Al," Matt said.

Oil and water color paintings by local artists decorated pale yellow walls. Ali and Matt sat beneath a bucolic scene of cows and goats. A brightly colored oil painting on the opposite wall from where they were sitting caught Ali's attention. When she glanced down the wall, she saw her sister sitting below the painting with some members of the Willoughby Book Banquet committee: Ellen, Ethyl, Lisa, Vanessa, and Delaney.

"Oh no. There's Ali with Matt," Ellen said to Janelle. "We're busted."

"Act normal."

"I have to acknowledge them." Ellen left her napkin at the table and moved toward Ali and Matt. "Do you two want to join us or is this a romantic rendezvous?"

"What's going on?" Ali asked. "You're meeting with the banquet committee without me?"

"Trust me. Nothing sneaky."

"What's the purpose of the meeting?"

"Can't say."

"Please leave. Go back to your friend Janelle." When Ali raised her voice, several diners turned to look at her.

"Trust me. Awkward but nothing for you to worry about."

Ali dismissed Ellen with a flip of her hand. She didn't know whether to make a fast retreat, break into tears, or dump her glass of peach tea over Janelle's perfectly coifed hair and plaster of Paris makeup. Janelle had finally worn Ali down as she whittled at Ali's self-esteem and confidence. The base of Ali's neck reddened. The color rose like mercury in a thermometer impaled in a turkey roasting in the oven. Someone was about to be cooked, if Ali had anything to say about it. She stood, staring at Janelle.

"Sit down. Please. Everyone's looking at you," Matt pleaded. He stood and pulled her arm trying to position her in the chair. He may as well have been trying to restrain a wild mustang.

Ali's lips twitched. She put her hand to her throat and pulled the clammy skin on her neck. She felt the cords of her neck pulsating.

Janelle continued to hold court without looking toward Ali and Matt.

"What should I do?" Ali asked Matt.

"Don't do a damn thing. Forget about her and enjoy our time together. Ignoring her is what irritates Janelle the most. You're over-reacting, big time."

A smiling young server carrying a tray of food approached their table. "Hi, Mr. and Mrs. Lawrence. Here's your favorite." Hannah was Kayla's former babysitter. She set the plates on the table.

"Sorry, Hannah. I was daydreaming. How are you?" Ali quickly took her seat.

Hannah and the couple exchanged pleasantries. Ali stared at her favorite Fickle Pickle sandwich, roast beef with horseradish mayo, blue cheese, and arugula on sourdough then turned her head toward Janelle.

"Anything wrong, Mrs. Lawrence?"

"No, no, Hannah, everything's fine. Thank you."

"Ali. Ali," Matt said, trying to get her attention. "I can think of several reasons why Janelle is meeting with those folks without you."

"Name one."

"They didn't want to burden you with another meeting. They know how much you hate meetings."

Ali took a bite of her sandwich.

Matt nibbled on his order of fried pickles. "Boy, these are great," he said hoping to distract her.

Ali studied the pickles. She leaned across the table, took a fried pickle, and hurled it like a discus in Janelle's direction. She picked up another and another and threw them in rapid succession like gunfire. One. Two. Three. They flew over Delaney's and Ethyl's heads and landed on the table between Janelle's and Ellen's plates. Vanessa and Lisa surveyed the room for the guilty party. Ellen tried to muffle a laugh.

Janelle sat as still as a block of cement without blinking her thick, black false eyelashes. She held a pickle, examined it as though it were a precious gem, and then popped it in her mouth. She fumbled in her purse searching for something. Then she spoke to Ellen who handed her phone to her.

Ali's phone vibrated. She glared at Matt. "It's a text. You read it."

The message was from Janelle: "Nice sweater."

"Ali. What in the hell is the matter with you?" Matt demanded. "Don't let your sister hassle you. She was probably looking for an audience of adoring admirers and sycophants. Look who's there. Everyone except Ellen is a Janelle fan."

"Why would she invite Ellen? She knows Ellen's my best friend." Ali spread her hands, palms up. "I don't understand."

"You don't know that Janelle arranged the lunch. Maybe one of the others did. Probably Vanessa."

"If they did, they are betraying me."

"Don't you think *betraying* is too strong a word for your little book banquet?"

A little book banquet. She had hoped Matt was her biggest supporter. Maybe working at Kitchen Bliss or with the book banquet weren't as income producing as his job, but she threw an inordinate amount of energy and enthusiasm into it. More importantly, it mattered to her. She reached across the table for another pickle and hurled it at Matt.

He watched as the pickle landed on his chest and then bounced onto the table. "Good thing we're out of pickles. What will you throw next? The silverware?" Wrinkles creased his forehead and he put both his hands in the air. "What gives? What did I do?"

"Why do you belittle everything I do?"

"Aren't I a supportive husband? I rarely complain about all those boxes of unsold stuff in the garage. I could name a few other things that drive me nuts."

"You've chosen a great time to pick on me—when I need your support more than ever."

"Ali, I give up. I should know better than to give you advice about your sister. You must take control of this relationship."

Ali motioned to Hannah.

"Could I please have a box? I need to leave."

"One or two?"

She held up a forefinger. She wanted to point a different finger toward her sister and at Matt, too.

"Please, don't do this," Matt said.

"Go back to work. Please leave me alone. I'm sorry. She makes me crazy."

As Ali left the restaurant, the bright sun momentarily blinded her. She wished she had worn the sunflower hat that was now in the wastebasket. She wove in and out of pedestrians and accidentally pushed a woman into the street. "So sorry," she said as the woman gave her a dirty look. Ali stopped at a trashcan. She felt nauseated but had nothing in her stomach to deposit into the large green receptacle. She wanted to vomit the vile feelings she had for her sister.

Ali's head throbbed with a super-sized Janelle-induced headache. Her head screamed for an aspirin. She increased her pace. When she arrived home, she put the white sandwich box in the refrigerator. Ali vowed one way or another to get rid of her sister, without using violence or arsenic, of course.

Chapter 26

J anelle smiled as she left the Fickle Pickle, assessing the results of the meeting she had arranged. The banquet committee agreed to give Ali special recognition, but Janelle would take credit and perhaps lessen the animosity building between the two sisters. *Too bad she and Matt had to show up. Throwing those pickles was so silly. Ellen is sure to tell Ali why we met.*

Janelle drove toward Phoebe's house. She parked her car in the bank's parking lot at the corner of Plum and Willoughby Lane within sight of her objective, but not too obvious. Janelle didn't want to take the chance that someone would see her. Her yellow car stood out like a boil on the tip of a nose in the lot filled with black, silver, and white cars. *If I stay in this boring awful town for long, this car goes.* To ensure that the coast was clear, she called Phoebe's landline. No answer.

She sat in the car observing the activities in the neighborhood. The mail truck was leaving and the FedEx deliveryman left a package at the house next door to Phoebe's, then drove away. Janelle couldn't see anyone tending to front yards. The street was like an Impressionist's garden painting, serene and peaceful. *Strike while the iron is hot, to quote Mother.*

Janelle shed her high heels and pulled on a pair of Ali's sweat pants, which was a challenging maneuver in her tiny car. She opened a black plastic garbage bag containing her camouflage equipment: Willoughby High baseball cap, a black hoodie, and a pair of Kayla's sandals. She exited the car, hiked up the loose fitting pants, and tightened the drawstring. She looked both ways then flip-flopped down the street, keeping her head lowered. When she was a few houses from Phoebe's, she saw a yappy dog across the street heading her way. She quickened her pace, walking as fast as the sandals allowed. When she arrived at Phoebe's house out of breath, she made a furtive look over her shoulder. The dog found another source of entertainment and scampered toward a squirrel.

None of Phoebe's old biddy friends were in sight. She'd have to work fast. In and out before Brad discovered her. With all the relatives and friends invading the house after the memorial service, it was a sure bet the door was unlocked.

Presto! She opened the door, walked into the house, closed the door behind her, and exhaled a huge breath. She threw off the damp hoodie and wiped her forehead with its sleeve. Janelle, now a cat burglar, crept from room to room trying to locate a logical hiding place she missed the last time she snooped. When that failed, she sought illogical places to search. She opened the hallway closet, then the pantry. She checked every shelf in the house, and the cookie jar. She lifted the lid on the tank of the guest bathroom toilet. She explored the linen closet, the washing machine, drawers, cabinets, and finally the garage. Nothing, nothing, nothing.

Janelle returned to the kitchen. She passed the shiny toaster and then backtracked. She checked her makeup. Janelle was horrified that her pancake makeup had dissolved like maple syrup and had cascaded down her cheeks.

"Who's here? Who's in here? Come out with your hands up or I'm going to shoot."

The shrill voice belonged to Evelyn Sheldon. Janelle was wrong about the absence of old biddies in the neighborhood. Evelyn had positioned herself at the bay window in her living room waiting for the commission of a crime to spark her dull life. Her lookout post gave her a direct view into Phoebe's house. She probably used binoculars to sharpen her spying skills.

"Hold on. Is that a real gun?"

"Yes, missy, and I can use it. What are you up to, Janelle? Why are you not in school?"

"School? I've been out of school for years. What's the matter with you?"

"I'm trying to protect Phoebe. Where is she anyway? Does she know you're here?"

"What the . . . ?"

"You better skedaddle. Stop lollygagging. Off you go."

"Don't you remember that Phoebe die—" Janelle paused. "Phoebe's at the drug store. She's tutoring me today."

"Wait on the porch. Phoebe doesn't like strangers in her house. What's your name?"

She seemed fine after the memorial service. Dementia? Alzheimer's? Maybe I can make this work to my advantage. "I'm going now. Do you want me to take you home?"

"Never mind about me. You get back to school." She shook the gun like a pointed finger and aimed it at Janelle.

"About that gun. I hope it's unloaded. May I take a look?"

The neighborhood's patrol officer hesitated.

"I'll give it back. Promise."

"Be careful with it. This gun belonged to my late husband and is probably as old as I am." She handed over the weapon to a nervous Janelle who examined the pistol. Janelle was no firearm expert, but she had researched weapons for a character in *Hot Night in NOLA* who killed her cheating husband. To ensure accuracy, Janelle went to a firing range to practice. She opened the gun and was relieved that it was unloaded. "You could do harm with this baby. I better get on my way." She handed the gun to Annie Oakley.

"One more thing. Don't call me by my given name until you grow up. Shows disrespect. My name is Mrs. Sheldon. Understand, girlie?"

"Yes, ma'am."

Janelle followed Mrs. Sheldon out the door but didn't lock it. She waited until Annie Oakley returned to her lookout post and slipped back inside the house for one more search. Finding nothing, she flip-flopped to her car.

I'll be more careful next time, Janelle decided, as she contemplated another tactic to invade Phoebe's home. *Like all my heroines, I do my best work at night.*

Chapter 27

Willoughby, GA – The coroner's office of Willoughby County confirmed today the cause of death of Janelle Jennings who died unexpectedly. The popular author and former resident of Willoughby died of blunt force trauma when she toppled off her six-inch high heel shoes. A toxicology report indicated Ms. Jennings's blood alcohol level was 0.431 making her legally impaired to drive. The report did not state whether she was legally impaired to walk.

Ali flipped on the switch to the porch fan and positioned herself in the white wicker rocker watching the driveway for Janelle's return from the Fickle Pickle. The fan hummed softly as the blades whirled, dispersing the humid Georgia air. The ever-faithful sentry Roxie sat upright, at her commander's side, ready for battle.

Ali reached for the Book Babes' newest selection from the adjacent wobbly wicker table. She read a few pages, closed the novel, and put it down. A tearjerker about malnourished orphans on a train didn't suit Ali's present mood. She needed to read a kick-butt Jack

Reacher book. Ali wanted to confront her sister about the meeting at the restaurant and all the chaos Janelle instigated since her arrival, but Ali had a history of not winning battles with her sister.

"Why do you always get to choose the food we eat?" she asked her sister when they were young. "We never have macarooni and cheese."

"Macaroni not macarooni. Ask Mother."

"Your sister won't eat it and I can't make two meals, now can I, dear? She doesn't eat white food."

"But the cheese covers the white part," Ali protested.

"Don't worry, you'll get plenty of macaroni and cheese at the school cafeteria," Janelle pointed out.

Ali chewed a handful of salmon-colored antacids she kept in her pocket, grinding the tablets into birdseed-sized pieces, as she rocked faster and faster in her chair. The aspirin Ali swallowed earlier calmed her throbbing headache. Despite her stomach's rumbling, food had no appeal. Roxie sensed her owner's agitation and jittered around Ali's feet. Ali shooed her into the shade garden. Roxie whimpered a bit but dismissed the rebuff when she spotted a gecko scuttling across the walkway. The gentle tinkling of the driftwood and sea-shell wind chimes that hung on a nearby maple tree usually calmed Ali. Today, the sound annoyed her.

Ali glanced at her watch. As each minute disappeared, her resolve to confront her sister decreased. *I'm a wimp.* Ali used the time to compose mentally the words she would use to lambast her sister. *Why didn't you include me in the meeting? Do you know I've been working on this project for a year? How dare you undermine my authority?*

Whom was Ali kidding? What "authority"? The book banquet committee was a volunteer group of Willoughby citizens who wanted to encourage reading in the community. Tired of waiting for Janelle, Ali left the porch and entered the kitchen to make a call.

"Hi, Ellen. Just me. So sorry." Sometimes a strong friendship doesn't require an explanation for bad behavior.

"No apology necessary. If Janelle were my sister, I'd do worse. Said she planned an award for you." Ellen hesitated. "Come to think of it, she never told us what kind of an award."

"What time did she leave?"

"Not long after the attack by the flying pickles."

"Do you think the others knew I was the culprit?" Ali felt her cheeks warming as she recalled propelling the fried pickle discs toward her sister.

"I blamed the assault on a boy sitting near you and Matt. The pickles were more powerful than if you slapped her surgically-altered face," Ellen said.

"I was rude."

"You're allowed."

"If Janelle drank too much wine at lunch, no telling what could happen," Ali said.

"She drank peach tea along with the rest of us. By the way, your sister charmed the committee. Wrapped them around her finger—the one with the emerald-cut diamond ring."

"More like a snake charmer," Ali said.

"I hope you noticed that only the Janelle lovers were there," Ellen said. "I'm going to my spin class. If I see her stumbling around town on those 'do me' shoes, I'll call you."

"One more thing, Ellen. Who paid for lunch?"

"Separate checks. Odd. When Janelle called me, she indicated we were her guests."

"Gotta go. Here she is."

Ellen warned, "Don't resort to violence. She's not worth a trip to the pen. Later."

"I'm home! I'm home!" Janelle shouted after entering the front door. Roxie moved swiftly to greet her new friend. "Did you miss me, little one?"

"Janelle, please," Ali said. "This is not your home and not your dog." Ali wondered when Janelle changed from the sophisticated brown and white outfit she was wearing at the restaurant to sloppy sweat pants and a hoodie.

"Don't be mad," Janelle said softly. "If you hear my side of the story, you'll understand. I don't want any more animosity between us. Kiss, kiss?" Janelle puckered her coral-stained lips and aimed for Ali's cheek, but missed when Ali turned away.

"I have some things I want you to hear," Ali said.

Kayla heard her aunt arrive and bounced down the stairs into the arms of Janelle.

"What a nice greeting," Janelle said, giving Ali a haughty look. "I could use a glass of water." Kayla hurried to the sink to fulfill her aunt's request. Janelle sat at the kitchen table, kicked off her sandals, and tossed the hoodie on the floor.

"Kayla. Stop. You don't have to wait on your aunt. She is capable of getting her own water, making her own bed, washing her own towels." Ali's forceful tone caused Janelle to flutter her mascara-laden eyelashes.

Kayla and Ali glared at each other intensely with their lips drawn into tight lines. Despite her mother's order, Kayla retrieved the requested water, placed the glass in front of Janelle, and with a smug look, took a seat at the table.

"Homework," Ali said. "You might want to look up the word *defiant*."

Kayla rolled her eyes and nudged the leg of the table with her foot. "You'll be here for dinner, won't you, Aunt Janie?" Her sweet demeanor returned when she addressed her aunt.

"Entirely up to your mother," Janelle said.

Kayla glared at Ali before she stomped up the stairs to her bedroom.

After Kayla left, Janelle went to the refrigerator and selected a bottle of Chardonnay. She held it up to Ali. "Join me?"

Ali shook her head.

"Let me explain about the luncheon today," Janelle said, as she uncorked the bottle and took a glass from the cupboard.

"What's to explain? You called a meeting and excluded me. Why? You don't have any connection to the book banquet. In fact, you've declined previous requests to make an appearance."

"I accepted an invitation for lunch. Simple as that."

"Janelle. THAT'S A BALD-FACED-DOWNRIGHT-DIRTY-DESPICABLE LIE. Ellen told me—"

"Ellen! I should have known your interfering bigmouth friend couldn't keep a secret."

"Janelle, when are you leaving?" Ali turned her head toward the window away from her sister.

"Oh, that's an excellent way to thank me."

"For what? Should I mention all the problems you've created since you've been here?"

"I wanted to plan a surprise for you at the book banquet. That's why I didn't include you. Now you've ruined it." She took a sip of wine. "I think the ladies enjoyed hearing about my exciting life compared with everyone else here in boring Willoughby."

"Does that include me? A boring life?"

Janelle shrugged her shoulders.

"What's this about a surprise?" Ali asked.

"You've worked so hard on the banquet. I realized you deserved recognition. I can't count the number of awards hanging in my office. You don't even have one. Unless you're hiding them somewhere." Janelle surveyed the kitchen with a sweep of her hand. "Wouldn't you like to have a plaque hanging on the wall? Or a little trophy to put on a shelf here in the kitchen where you spend so much time?"

"I don't need an award to boost my self-esteem, thank you very much."

"Well, Miss I-Have-It-All-Together, I guess it doesn't matter. You spoiled everything with your silliness at the Fickle Pickle. I'm going to rethink the award."

"Please leave. Go on upstairs and I'll call you when dinner is ready. Might be the last supper you get in this house. Go. Now." Ali waved her hands at Janelle as if she were shooing away a flock of clucking chickens.

"St. Alicia my foot. If they only knew."

"Janelle. Get out of here. Maybe you ought to go somewhere else tonight. We could use some peace in this house."

"Anything to make you happy." Janelle walked barefoot up the stairs carrying a glassful of wine. She paused midway. "Hate to disappoint Kayla."

Ali stood in the kitchen and watched her former buddy, Roxie, follow Janelle. "My child *AND* my dog."

Ali sat at the kitchen table and fiddled with a pencil. She picked up a piece of paper and shred it into tiny pieces. She picked up another piece. "Dear Janelle," she wrote. "The time has come. . ." The more Ali wrote, the less her hands shook.

Some people drink alcohol or take pills to relieve stress. Ali chose chocolate. After she finished her written rant to her sister, she thought, *to heck with my diet.* In the pantry, she pawed through cans of soup, cannellini beans, fire-roasted tomatoes, and jars of pasta sauce like a lunatic. AWOL were chocolate cookies, chocolate candy, chocolate anything.

Darn that Matt. He eliminated temptation as I requested. Why does he do everything I ask him? She licked her lips when she remembered a secreted box of Thin Mint Girl Scout cookies in the freezer, for emergency purposes only. As she opened the door, the chill from the freezer cooled Ali's face. She stood there while she chose a few cookies from the box and stuffed the frozen treats into her mouth. The squawking cuckoo clock reminded Ali to think about preparing dinner. She closed the freezer door and opened the refrigerator. She chose a variety of vegetables to chop and slice for stir-fry. With her chef's knife, she massacred the innocent bok choy, celery, carrots, onions, and red peppers.

The sound of the garage door opening signaled Matt's arrival home. Ali was too ashamed to call him at work to apologize for her behavior at the restaurant. She put down the knife, wiped her hands with a kitchen towel lying on the counter, untied her apron, and smoothed her hair.

Ali changed her mind. She didn't want to see the disappointment in his eyes. She put her apron back on and returned to the refrigerator to search for a package of skinless chicken breasts. She faced the sink with her back to the door, still slaughtering the vegetables, when Matt arrived at the kitchen door.

"Safe to enter? I don't want any more food thrown on my formerly clean shirt."

Ali slowly turned around to face Matt. He waved his white handkerchief in the air. "Don't shoot!"

"I'm so sorry." Her eyes reddened and tears flowed like an open waterspout down her flushed cheeks. "Must be the onions," she blubbered. Her sobs turned to heaves and her chin quivered. Matt put his arm around her waist and ushered her into the living room. They sat on the sofa. Neither one spoke. He rocked her back and forth as if he were soothing a teething Kayla years ago.

When the crying ceased, Matt left for the kitchen to brew a cup of tea. "Here's your favorite. Chamomile," he said when he returned. He took his thumb and wiped a bit of chocolate from her lip. "You two still at it?"

"She must leave. Tomorrow isn't soon enough."

"Let's get through dinner and then we'll discuss it. I'm going to change my clothes."

Those were *not* the words Ali wanted to hear. She wished Matt would rescue her and send Janelle packing. She wanted him to agree that Janelle acted like a squatter with no intentions of leaving.

Matt returned to the living room dressed in khaki shorts and a University of Georgia T-shirt. A few months ago, the shirt barely covered his beer belly, but now it hung loose.

"How does Thai sound?" Matt asked. "You don't need to cook tonight."

Ali turned her cheek to him when he tried to kiss her on the lips.

"No Thai? Mexican?"

"You choose."

"Be back soon." Matt paused. "Do you think you are overreacting? Other than the messes in the bathroom and the kitchen, it hasn't been so bad having Janelle around. Try to accept her for the self-absorbed person she is and ignore her or—" Matt hesitated. "Kick her out. I'll back you up with Kayla."

Tears welled up in Ali's eyes. She stood and kissed him on the lips. "Those were exactly the words I wanted to hear." Arguing with Janelle, always a losing battle, drained and tired Ali. She left the living room, and lumbered to the kitchen where she inspected the abandoned chicken originally destined for stir-fry. Ali dumped the unattractive mess into the garbage disposal feeling guilty about wasting food. She flipped the switch and watched the water swirl as the motor grinded. Bye-bye, chicken. How she wished she could toss her sister away so easily.

When Matt returned from the restaurant, he distributed plates, chopsticks, and napkins around the kitchen table. He put spoons in the containers. He poured Ali a glass of pinot grigio. "Sit down and relax. I'll get the girls."

"Kayla says she's not hungry," Matt reported, "but I told her to get her butt down here or else. No response from our honored guest."

"More like a *dis*honored guest to me. Besides, I told her to go somewhere else for dinner tonight."

Kayla trudged into the kitchen. "I'm not hungry," she said, crossing her arms.

"Please sit, Kayla," Matt said. He poured Kayla a glass of water and opened a bottle of Corona for himself. The threesome, with Roxie under the table, sat down for an unusually quiet meal.

Kayla broke the ice. "Why do you always fight with her, Mom? She only wanted to do something nice for you—giving you an award. Now she's going to leave our house. She may even leave Willoughby. Can't you make up with her?"

"Think whatever you want, Kayla. I've done nothing wrong."

"Show some respect for your mother, Kayla," Matt said. He continued to chow down, making comments, between bites, about how flavorful the Pad Thai tasted. The man could eat during a tornado.

Kayla used the chopsticks to inspect the food, took a few bites, and asked for permission to leave.

"Permission granted," Matt said. He followed Kayla toward the stairway. "You know how much your mother loves you. Try to cut her a little slack." He put his arms around her.

"Okay. I guess."

"We're overdue for our date night. Just the two of us. Check your busy social calendar."

"Sure, Dad. Soon." She shuffled up the stairs.

Ali's appetite made a comeback. She took seconds from the containers, finished the Pad Thai, and basil rolls Kayla left on her plate.

"I didn't want to mention this in front of Kayla, but I saw Brad at the gym today. He seemed fixated on how gorgeous Janelle is."

Ali couldn't and wouldn't picture Brad Patterson and Janelle as a couple and tried to dismiss that picture as she speared a shrimp.

Then she speared another and another. *Take that, Janelle, and that,* Ali thought, as she finished the tasty pink morsels. This was more fun than throwing pickles and not as dangerous as stabbing Janelle with a chopstick.

While Ali and Matt cleaned up the kitchen, Ellen called. "Janelle was seen at Classy Consignments."

"Consignments?" Ali asked. "Buying or selling?"

"Selling. She must need the money. Maybe she's broke. Yeah!" Ellen's words zapped Ali like a Taser.

"Broke! She'll never leave Willoughby," Ali groaned.

Chapter 28

Ali sat on the step of her porch enjoying the fragrant aroma of the gardenia plants blanketing their scent over the front yard garden. The sky was the color of a bowl of peaches and cream. Her walking shoes sat next to her as if they were puppies beckoning for adoption. Ali wished for an excuse to postpone her self-inflicted sentence of daily exercise that she put on a par with a bout of stomach flu, but the weather was uncooperative. Chance of rain zero percent.

The ringing telephone in the house was a grateful sound. "Hallelujah," Ali rejoiced to Roxie who was sniffing at her shoes. "A reprieve."

"Good morning, Ali. It is Ali, right?"

"Ali Lawrence at your service, Brad." His voice was easy to identify—deep, raspy, like Steven Tyler's.

"You and your sister still sound alike."

"Similarity stops there. Wish I had Janie's looks."

"She may be a former beauty queen but you're Miss Congeniality."

"What can I do for you, you sweet talker?"

"I need help sorting through my grandmother's belongings. The house looks like a museum overflowing with stuff from her travels," he said. "I don't know if these things are junk or have some value. Then, there's all of her underwear, et cetera. Embarrassing for me and I don't want her nosy friends in her bedroom. They already cleaned out the kitchen for me, which I have to admit was a big help."

"My mother's the expert. Not about the underwear—the other things. I'll give her a call."

"Could we keep this between you and me? Mimi's friends—you saw them at the memorial service. They've besieged me with offers to help but once I let them in, they'll never leave."

Even though Ali was grateful for a chance to forego exercise, sorting the possessions of a deceased 95-year-old sounded as inviting as a trip to the gynecologist. Ali put her right hand on her waist and grabbed a hunk of fat that had found a permanent home years ago and was as determined as super glue to stay.

"I sense hesitation," Brad said.

"Of course I'll help you, old friend. Can it wait until tomorrow?"

"Mimi signed a contract to remodel her house. Funny. For someone her age. The construction crew is coming early in the week. I'd like to at least organize this stuff ASAP."

"This afternoon should work, I suppose."

"You're a good sport, Ali. I owe you."

Good sport. How many times have I heard that expression? Matt makes the slightest request and I claim I'm too busy. For Brad, I drop everything.

She tied her shoes, hooked Roxie's leash to her rhinestone collar, and left for the park. She couldn't postpone exercise anymore. Many times Ellen tried to convince Ali to join the gym where she worked out. Being surrounded by flat bellies wearing cute and colorful workout clothes depressed Ali. Water aerobics was a negative—too many dimples and lumps on her cellulite-burdened thighs. Cycling was not an option. During her latest bike excursion, an inconveniently located tree totaled the bike, resulting in five stitches in her forehead. Walking was safe and easily accessible. So far, anyway.

***

Brad greeted Ali at the door of Phoebe's house. He wore dark indigo jeans and a starched white shirt with the sleeves rolled up revealing tanned arms. He was as desirable as a Calvin Klein model.

"I didn't recognize you. Your hair. Looks great."

Ali gave her hair a casual, sassy flip with her fingers. Since her Brazilian Blowout, she was not accustomed to compliments about her hair. Her sister was the reigning recipient of accolades. Ali walked in front of Brad so he couldn't see her blushing cheeks and entered the living room. She dug a rubber band out of her pocket and pulled her hair into a ponytail.

"Here it is. Welcome to Phoebe Patterson's Fine Art Collectibles and Other Stuff." Brad swept his long arm around the room almost touching the low ceiling. Empty boxes and packing paper filled the small living room.

"Don't make fun, Brad." A glass cat grooming itself caught Ali's attention. "Lalique," she appraised. "This one's a keeper."

"What about this ugly thing?" Brad held up a forest green bowl trimmed in gold with flying geese in the center.

Ali examined the bottom and edges of the item then shook her head. "Donation box."

"Seems your mother isn't the only expert."

Ali was impressed with her knowledge and recognition of the value of some of Phoebe's personal belongings. All the years Ali spent tagging along with her mother to estate sales and consignment stores paid off.

Ali recognized a teddy bear as Steiff, forlorn and lonely, waiting for a great-grandchild Brad had not produced. "Save this little guy. Might need it someday," Ali said to Brad who ignored her comment.

He pointed to a bowl covered with butterflies and bees. "Don't tell me this gaudy thing is worth anything?"

Ali pointed to the donation box. "I'll make an expert out of you before we're finished."

They continued sorting for several hours enjoying pleasant conversation about mutual friends and anecdotes about Phoebe. Every half hour a wooden cuckoo clock in the shape of a Black Forest chalet announced passing time—"coo-coo, coo-coo," was its plaintive sound.

They worked quickly filling boxes for donations, friends and relatives, and one for sale in Virginia's booth at Queen of Hearts. While Brad carried a box to the garage, Ali paused. She recalled Brad's comment about Ali's "expertise."

Ali remembered a conversation she overhead when she was young. "Mother, I don't enjoy scrounging around in dusty secondhand shops. Take Ali with you," was Janelle's response when Virginia had asked her to accompany her on a buying trip. Virginia's interest embarrassed Janelle even though the extra income paid for a wardrobe of pageant gowns. Those were the days before *Antiques Roadshow* and *Pawn Stars* inspired the country to hunt in attics and scour yard sales for treasures. Virginia was ahead of her time.

"I was surprised to learn from Mimi's lawyer that she had an impressive stock portfolio. She could have easily spruced up this house."

Brad's revelation that Phoebe had money surprised Ali. Phoebe lived a modest lifestyle except for exotic vacations she and Joe took every few years. Since Joe's death three years ago, the trips halted. Phoebe's house needed painting inside and out and the kitchen belonged in the American History Museum next to Archie Bunker's chair.

"If you come across anything you like, it's yours. Mimi cared for you. She told me you didn't like competing with your sister, but she always said you were the better writer."

"I suppose I recall her saying that," Ali said, as she set a brass candle snuffer down and gazed out the window. Her mind drifted to imagining her life if she had pursued her youthful dream of becoming a novelist.

Brad's voice interrupted Ali's thoughts. "Speaking of Janelle. What's her marital status? Divorced?"

"Sorry. What did you say? Janelle?"

"Her marital status?"

"Divorced again. I guess this one's final. Why the interest?"

"She does have a certain allure about her. Can't imagine she'll stay unattached long."

"Bradley Patterson. You can't be interested. She's not your type."

"Calm down, Ali. Merely an observation that she's still a hottie."

"With the help of a high-priced Beverly Hills doctor with a scalpel," Ali said. "Guess that sounded snarky."

Brad's cell phone rang. "Sorry. Should take this." When Brad finished his call, he joined Ali who had moved to Phoebe's bedroom.

"Guess I can learn more about Janelle's marital status tomorrow."

"Why tomorrow?"

"Janelle invited me to dinner and I accepted."

"Be careful. Her second husband fell off a boat and drowned. Besides, she probably wants to get into your—"

Brad interrupted Ali. "You were going to say 'safe deposit box,' I assume?"

Even when they were kids growing up together, Brad could make Ali laugh.

"A friendly dinner, that's all," he said. "Hate to bail on you, but I have an errand to run. Could you go through a couple of boxes in the bedroom closet? Do whatever you want with the contents. I trust you. I'm not the sentimental type and have already found a few photos and mementoes I'll keep."

"Aren't you the least bit nostalgic?"

"Not the least." He grabbed his car keys off a table in the hall and bolted out of the house slamming the door. After a few seconds, he returned. "Sorry, Ali. Thanks so much. I'll make it up to you. Pick out a restaurant. You, Matt, and me. My treat." He was about to shut the door for the second time when he called out again. "Let your hair down. Looks great."

Ali went to the mirror over Phoebe's dresser and removed the rubber band from her hair. She shook her straightened auburn tresses and let them cascade over her shoulders. She examined her reflection as though she were looking at a stranger. Ali found the rubber band in the bottom of her pocket and pulled her hair back into a ponytail.

Ali emptied Phoebe's closet of all the clothes destined for a trip to Goodwill and neatly stacked them on the bed. From the chest of drawers, she stuffed granny underwear, ruffled nightgowns, yellowed girdles, and lacy handkerchiefs into garbage bags. Ali whizzed from drawer to drawer until all that remained of Phoebe Patterson was the lingering scent of rose water.

Ali needed a break so she sat on Phoebe's bed and took a deep breath. She regretted committing to this project and was glad it was over. When the closet was empty, she found the two boxes Brad mentioned. They were light in weight so she decided to take them home.

She remembered Brad's comment that he wasn't sentimental. He may regret not keeping some of his family's history. Ali retrieved a photo album that Brad had placed in the trash pile. She sat on the lumpy brown and yellow plaid couch in the living room and turned each page. *No way were these going in the garbage.* Ali smiled as she looked at photos that traced Brad's life: as a toddler with strawberry ice cream covering his face, in Halloween costumes, Little League uniforms, and graduation caps and gowns. She'd keep them until

Brad had children and surprise him someday. Ali lifted an album marked "travels" and opened it. After flipping a few pages, she saw a photo of Phoebe, Joe, and Janelle in front of the Parthenon. "That can't be," she said aloud. She continued flipping. Another picture of the trio with the Leaning Tower of Pisa in the background. She continued to turn the pages until she came to the section marked "Spain." Phoebe, Joe, and Janelle were sitting at an outdoor café toasting each other with wine glasses. Ali was beginning to see her former English teacher in a much different light.

That's a coincidence. Both in Greece at the same time. In Italy and Spain at the same time.

Ali made a final check of all the closets and drawers. She went into Phoebe's office that contained hundreds of books that Brad planned to donate to the library. A row of books caught her eye. Curious, Ali pulled out the books one by one. They were all Janelle's books. Ali chuckled thinking that prim and proper Phoebe Patterson read racy romance novels.

Satisfied that she completed her commitment to Brad, Ali gathered the photo albums and the two boxes, locked the door, and put the boxes on the front seat of her pickup. She hesitated before she turned the ignition on. Ali was trying to remember the settings of Janelle's last three books—Greece, Italy, and Spain.

As she was leaving, Izzy, the neighborhood's mail carrier, honked the horn to get Ali's attention. "I've been holding a stack of magazines. Didn't want the mailbox to overflow. Think Matt will want them?"

"I'll take them. Thanks, Izzy." Ali went back into Phoebe's house and placed the stack of magazines on a living room table. She noticed a manila envelope sticking out from the middle of the stack. The addressee was Janelle at her New York City condo. Stamped on the front was the word "Undeliverable" and the return address was Phoebe's. Various scenarios spun through Ali's head. She didn't understand any of them. She took the envelope and climbed into her pickup, but before she started the engine, she called her mother on her cell.

"Mother, do you have a minute?"

"Yes, what it is, dear?"

"Did Janelle and Phoebe travel together?"

"Heavens no. Why would you think that?"

"They were in Europe at the same time."

"You must be mistaken. If Janelle took anyone on a trip, surely it would be me, not Phoebe Patterson. Why in the world would you ask such a question?"

"No reason. I'll see you later." Ali disconnected before her mother could pepper her with questions.

Driving home, Ali wondered about the photos of Janelle and the Pattersons in Europe. Then there was the "undeliverable" envelope. Janelle's life was as complicated as some of the characters in her books. The difference is that the books always had an ending. Ali had no idea how this tale would end.

Chapter 29

The banging of the screen door said that Kayla was home from a birthday party for a tennis friend. Ali was in the kitchen experimenting with a lemon pesto spread for Kitchen Bliss customers to sample the next day. She was also brewing a pot of a new line of tea. The pleasant aroma of orange peel and cinnamon filled the air. She tried, on many occasions, to encourage Ellen to create reasons to lure the many visitors to Willoughby Lane to enter the store. The food sampling was all that Ellen had agreed to. Despite flat sales compared with last year, Ellen was unconcerned. She blamed the big box stores and the mall. Her focus was on her handsome Pilates teacher, gym workouts, and training for a marathon. Kitchen Bliss was low on her priority list. Once the banquet was over, Ali planned to present new ideas for increasing traffic, especially since she and Matt might buy the store.

"Where is Aunt Janie?" Kayla asked. She joined Ali at the counter and snitched a taste of pesto with her finger.

"Aren't you forgetting something?"

"Every time I come home? I have to hug you?"

"Never too old," Ali said, opening her arms.

Kayla put one limp arm around her mother's waist and patted her twice on the back. "There," she said, stepping away before Ali could give her a real hug, "Happy now?"

Many of Ali's friends complained their daughters were less affectionate once they entered the fractious teen years, but that wasn't the case with Kayla, until Janelle's arrival.

Ali kissed Kayla on the cheek then pointed upstairs. In a few years, Ali would need a stepstool to kiss her growing daughter.

Kayla dashed up the stairway in search of her aunt with Roxie scampering close behind. Janelle's bedroom door was open, and she stood in front of her closet surveying the contents. Jasmine fragrance filled the room.

"I'm so glad you're here," Kayla said as she wrapped her arms around Janelle's waist. "You smell so nice. Mom never wears perfume."

Janelle hugged her niece and said, "You can use mine anytime."

"Awesome. I'll wait for a special occasion." Kayla pulled off her messenger bag, collapsed on one of the beds, and crossed her legs yogi style.

"Help me choose an outfit to wear tonight for my date with Mr. Brad."

"Aren't Nana and Gramps coming over tonight?"

"They'll have plenty of chances for my company. So what do you think?" Janelle held up several dresses for Kayla's approval.

"First of all, where are you going?"

"I don't know. I invited him. Any suggestions?"

"Indigo on The Lane is popular. You could sit on the patio. Might be romantic."

"I'm not an alfresco person, honey."

"Alfredo? As in fettuccine?"

"No, alfresco, outside, outdoors. Italian."

Kayla pulled her eco-friendly cork journal out of her bag and made a note. "I want to go to Italy with you. Mom says to save my money. Dad says not till I'm in college."

"I wanted to take you to Italy last year, but your mother said no."

"Really?" Kayla stammered. "Mom said no? Dad too?"

"Let's not talk about it now. I don't want to be upset when I go out with Brad."

"I can't believe they would do that to me."

"You know, my book, *Amore Amore,* was set in Italy. I'll take you. We'll go to Italy and rent a villa in Tuscany."

"That would be sweet," Kayla said softly. She was still stuck on her parents denying a trip to Italy. "This summer? Before school begins in the fall?"

Janelle hesitated. She turned her back to Kayla and picked up a jade green blouse from several she had placed on the bed. "Have to wait until my next book is published and it has to sell lots of copies. Perhaps next year. Meanwhile, study the Italian language."

"But all your books are best sellers."

How Janelle wished that were true. Sales had plummeted after her last divorce. The reviewers said she had lost her spark. Her books were "depressing and maudlin," another reviewer wrote. Fortunately, her publisher believed she had another best seller in her.

Janelle tried on several dresses, skirts, and tops, before they decided—a Celtic green silk dress with a draped-V neck. Janelle paraded back and forth in the small room. "Does the skirt swish when I walk?"

"Oh, yes. Looks good with your pointy shoes."

Kayla followed her aunt into the bathroom and sat on the toilet with the lid down. She watched Janelle apply moisturizer, primer, foundation, cheek color, two kinds of eyebrow makeup, eye shadows, eyelash base, lip base, lip liner, and several coats of mascara. She used a variety of brushes, sponges, and an eyelash curler. "Now for the pièce de rèsistance." She put on volcano red lipstick topped with a coat of super-shiny gloss.

"Wow! I didn't know there were so many different kinds of makeup," Kayla marveled. "Mom never wears any and I don't think she or Dad like me to wear too much."

"Guess we'll have to have a makeup lesson one day soon. I'll show you all my tricks."

"You are so beautiful. You don't need any makeup," Kayla said.

Janelle hesitated.

"Is something wrong?"

"No, no. Thinking about another time, when your mother and I were young."

In their teenage years, Janelle would ask Ali for advice on what to wear before a big date. "I'm not good at fashion," Ali would say. "But I think your red sweater with the stripes on the cuffs and the collar is pretty."

"If you would ever quit growing, I'd give it to you."

"I can't help it if I grow."

"But you can help stuffing food in your mouth."

Janelle continued to evaluate herself in the mirror.

"Why aren't you and Mom friends? I would love to have a sister."

"We are close. A different kind of close. We are sisters forever because we have the same parents and we have you. We'll talk more about sisters later." Janelle gave her niece an air kiss to prevent smeared lipstick. She walked down the stairs on her stepladder shoes with the balance of a tightrope acrobat.

"Give my regrets to the folks," Janelle said to Ali who was in the kitchen preparing dinner. "You sure spend a lot of time in the kitchen, Li'l Sis."

"They'll be disappointed."

"You'll think of an excuse," Janelle said as she walked out the front door.

When the sisters were young, Ali felt guilty about lying to their parents about Janelle's whereabouts or what time she returned home from a date. But, Ali couldn't resist the incentives her sister offered: money, borrowing an oversized sweater, or the best bribe of all—spending time with Janelle and her friends.

Janelle stood on the porch waiting for Brad. He arrived in a Mercedes convertible with the top down. He exited the car and helped Janelle into the passenger side.

"Where to?" he asked.

"I'll let you choose the restaurant, Brad, since *you* are the authority. How many restaurants do you own?"

"None at the moment. I sold my restaurants in New York, Baltimore, and D.C."

"Aren't you too young to retire?"

Brad's wide grin revealed white teeth and Mario Lopez-like dimples.

"Would you mind putting the top up? My hair, you know."

He acquiesced, as most men did for Janelle, and activated a button to close the top.

Janelle stroked the leather seat as she would a lover's arm. "I requested a car like this at the airport but no luck." She put her head back and breathed a sigh of familiarity.

"No retirement for me. I made some money, but I'm going to reinvest in the restaurant business. Looking for somewhere to settle. New York is exciting, but it never felt like home. Plus, the taxes were killing me. I miss the South and especially Willoughby."

"Certainly not Willoughby. So boring for sophisticates like you and me."

"I think Willoughby would suit me fine. In fact, I noticed some potential properties along Willoughby Lane. Besides, my grandmother left her house to me."

"You'll sell it, of course."

"Don't know. Will wait for the remodeling. Where to?"

He parked his car in the back lot of the yellow stucco restaurant he was considering buying. They proceeded along the walkway passing an attractive patio. "If you could design a restaurant in Willoughby, what would you choose, Janelle?"

"Upscale, refined, expensive, beautifully decorated. I don't care a thing about food. Ambience is important to me."

"Hmm. Upscale, refined, expensive, beautifully decorated. Sounds like my charming dinner companion."

Janelle gave an impish, coquettish smile.

The hostess seated the couple in the front of the restaurant, but Janelle requested another table.

"What's wrong with this table?" Brad asked.

"I don't want anyone to recognize me. So embarrassing when fans ask for autographs while I have a mouthful of lettuce."

"I hope this is better for you, ma'am," the hostess said as she led the couple to another table.

Janelle's eyebrows rose at the "ma'am."

"This is fine. Thank you," Brad said to the young woman. Fine for Brad but not for Janelle.

"Do you think we're too close to the kitchen? So noisy. I'm feeling a draft from the air conditioning. Must be sitting underneath it." Janelle looked up at the ceiling.

"Perhaps a table on our patio will suit you better, ma'am," the patient hostess suggested.

"No, no, no. Too humid. How about that table by the window in the back?"

The hostess smiled, collected the menus, and led Janelle and Brad to a third table. A female server approached the couple and asked if they would like a cocktail or perhaps a bottle of wine.

"Oh, please, Brad. Could we order a bottle of champagne?" Janelle whined.

"Bring a glass of anything bubbly for the lady. Please bring me a glass of the house cabernet sauvignon."

"The house wine? Really?" Janelle asked.

"Might find a surprise."

"I wish we had a male server. Don't you think they do a much better job?"

"Good service depends entirely on the competency of the individual not the gender."

Janelle had no comeback. She wasn't accustomed to men disagreeing with her, at least not to her face.

Brad sipped his wine and Janelle gulped her sparkling wine.

"Oh, look. My glass is empty," Janelle said.

Brad ordered a second and then a third glass for her.

The server asked twice to take their orders, and both times Janelle shooed her away. On the server's third attempt, Brad indicated they were ready.

"Oh, please order for me, Brad; I'm not hard to please."

"You couldn't pay me to order for you." He thrust the menu toward her. "Choose something. Please. I'm hungry."

Janelle questioned the server about many items on the menu and finally decided on a piece of grilled fish, no butter, no sauce, and an arugula and spinach salad with no dressing.

"Let's talk about your dear grandmother."

"What do you want to know? I think you and she had kept in touch. You probably know as much as I do."

While Janelle rambled on about how much she respected Phoebe and what a great influence she was on her students, Brad assessed her. If it weren't for some heavy-duty bags under her eyes, she was still a beauty. She ignored him in high school but maybe now that he was financially successful, she might be interested. But was he?

"Oh, no. I can't eat that," Janelle protested when the server placed the plate in front of her. "What is this? I said grilled, no butter, no sauce. I can't eat this."

"I'm so sorry, ma'am," the server said as she picked up Janelle's plate. "Would you like to make another selection? I'll put a rush on your order."

"No. The salad is all I need."

"My food looks great and superbly plated," Brad said to the poised server.

"Another," Janelle said while pointing to her empty glass.

Brad frowned at Janelle. "Okay, Janelle. Come clean. As much as I enjoy sitting across the table from a gorgeous woman, you're up to something. You've never paid attention to me until now."

Tears pooled in her eyes and dripped down her cheeks. "At the memorial service you said Phoebe left something for me." Janelle took her napkin and dabbed at her right twitchy eye. "I might be able to use a little—"

Brad fiddled with the stem of his wine glass. "I believe I said 'might' have. Sorry if I misled you."

"So did she or not leave anything for me," she demanded.

"Haven't found anything yet."

Wrinkles creased Janelle's moist forehead. "I'm going to the powder room." She stood, wobbling on her six-inch skyscraper shoes. When Brad tried to steady her she fell, and grabbed the tablecloth as she went down. Red wine splattered like paint on a Jackson Pollock canvas to the nearby table. Food scattered on the floor, plates broke, and the entire restaurant slid into a shocked silence.

"No problem," the composed server said as she motioned to the staff to help her clean up the mess Janelle created. The staff left Janelle flat on her back flaying hands and legs like a fish flopping on the deck of a boat.

Ignoring Janelle for a moment, Brad took a wad of bills from his gold money clip and handed it to the hostess. "After my bill is paid, please share this with the staff. I apologize for my dinner companion's behavior."

"Is she someone famous?" the hostess asked. "She looks so familiar."

"More like infamous," he said. He extended his hand to Janelle who was wearing a look of horror as he pulled her up from the floor. Brad lifted her and carried her out the door as the patrons of the restaurant applauded. This was no Richard Gere/Deborah Winger moment, however. They were probably thinking good riddance. Brad took Janelle to his car, dropped her into the seat, and put the top down. "Maybe some fresh air will help you," he said.

***

Ali looked up from her laptop in the kitchen when she saw the lights of Brad's car in the driveway. She watched as he exited the car and brought his date to the front door. He opened the unlocked door and called out, "She's all yours."

Janelle dragged inside. Her skin was greenish-gray and her shoulders drooped. She tossed her shoes into a corner.

"What happened to your hair?" Ali asked.

"Convertible."

"The date not so hot?" She motioned for Janelle to sit.

"I think I blew it. I know he still likes me though."

"Coffee? Water?"

"I didn't eat much. Probably drank one glass of champagne too many on an empty stomach. How about one of your grilled cheese sandwiches you used to make when we were kids?"

Ali was flattered that Janelle remembered. She took out a pan, bread, cheese, butter, and mayonnaise.

"Your secret ingredient. I forgot about the mayo." Janelle placed one elbow on the table, her palm to her forehead, as she inhaled the aroma of melted cheese. "Sorry for your trouble. Don't think I can eat it though."

Ali pushed the plate closer to Janelle. "You'll feel better in the morning if you eat a little."

Janelle took a couple of bites and then pushed the plate away. "Thank you," she said.

Ali watched her sister shuffle away with her head hanging. She wanted to run to her and give her a big hug but decided otherwise. *Maybe my life isn't so boring,* Ali decided. She stared at the abandoned sandwich with cheddar oozing out of the sides. Her mouth watered as she reached across the table and pulled the plate toward her. She took a bite and licked her lips before taking another bite. She calculated the calories: two slices of cheese, butter, mayo, bread. Ali took the plate to the sink and tossed the scrumptious sandwich grilled to a light brown into the garbage disposal.

Chapter 30

Kayla bounded through the front door and called out, "Anybody home?"

"Only little ole me, in the sunroom," Janelle said.

"Did you have fun last night with Mr. Brad?"

"Fabulous. I think he's interested. Why shouldn't he be? We have so much in common." Janelle crossed her fingers behind her back.

"Wow! That would be a great way to keep you here forever."

"We'll have to give the relationship time to develop. Want to come with me on an errand, sweetie?"

"Shopping? And then dinner?"

"No shopping. Not today. Can you keep a secret?" Janelle asked

"Sure."

"You and I are going to the bank."

"Can't you go to an ATM?" Kayla asked.

"I don't want cash. I want to show you some things."

"Can I drive?" Kayla asked as they left the house.

"What kind of driver's thing do you have? Permit? License?"

"Permit. With an adult over twenty-one."

"Guess I qualify. Barely though."

Kayla giggled.

"Here are the keys."

Kayla opened the driver side and slid in behind the wheel. She buckled her seat belt and adjusted the rear view mirror.

Janelle walked around to the passenger side. "Oh no. Here comes troublemaker Ellen. Better switch places. I never did like that big mouth and she'll tell your mother I let you drive."

"But we're legal."

"Believe me, your mother would not approve."

Ellen observed Janelle exiting the passenger side and moving to the driver's side. She waved and approached the car.

"Hey. Where are you off to?" Ellen asked. She stopped and approached Janelle's side of the car.

"Nowhere special, Aunt Ellen. Some errands."

Janelle ignored Ellen while she pretended to look for something in her purse.

"You in town for long?" Ellen promised she would try to pry the information out of Janelle.

"Don't know. Gotta run," Janelle said as she turned the key in the ignition. She put the car in reverse and waited until Ellen backed far away from the car. "Can't afford to break someone else's leg."

Ellen put her hands on her hips and shook her head. She resumed jogging while calling Ali on her cell.

"You don't like Aunt Ellen much, do you?"

"*Aunt* Ellen. I thought I was your only aunt."

"My favorite."

Kayla and she high-fived.

"Guess you don't drive much."

"Is it that obvious?" An impatient driver was on her bumper leaning on his horn. Janelle continued at a sluggish speed hugging the steering wheel as if it were about to fall off. When they reached the bank, she parked under a crepe myrtle bursting with pink blossoms and then she fished around in her purse until she found a tiny red key holder.

The two went into the bank where Janelle asked for access to her safe deposit box. A friendly male employee asked for identification and showed her to the sign-in area. He led Janelle and Kayla to a room secured behind heavy glass doors.

"On the top," Janelle directed the young man. The employee retrieved a stepladder, climbed to the top, and inserted his key into one of the two locks. She handed her key to him. He inserted it, removed the metal box, and handed it to Janelle.

"If I can be of any assistance, please let me know. My name is Justin." He directed his comment to Kayla and handed her his business card.

Janelle snatched the card out of his hand. "Okay. Fine. Leave us alone."

"Why were you so cranky to him? He's awfully cute," Kayla said after the young man left.

"But *awfully* old for you."

When they were alone Janelle took the medium-sized box to a nearby table with chairs.

"Is this like a vault?"

"Holds all the safe deposit boxes. Your parents probably have one. I have to add you to the rental agreement so you can access it when I'm dead."

Janelle opened the gray metal lid to reveal multiple jewelry boxes in various sizes and colors.

"See anything you like?" Janelle asked as she opened each box and grinned as though she were looking at a picture of a loved one. She caressed a tennis bracelet with diamonds almost as big as marbles; she stroked a smoky topaz suspended on a thick gold chain, and slipped a jade ring on her finger. She continued to pick up the boxes and stacked them on the small table until they stood almost a foot high.

"Do you like this ring?" Janelle asked as she held her hand up to the light and watched a bluish-green stone shimmer. "Reminds me of the Caribbean Sea." She put it on Kayla's finger.

"I'm not into bling so much, but these are beautiful. How did you get so many?" Kayla asked as she examined the ring.

"Gifts from some of my ex-husbands. Bought with my money, probably. Pick out something to take home. When you reach a milestone, a graduation, something major, I'll give you another piece."

"They're all so pretty."

"What did you decide?" Janelle asked after a few minutes.

"May I please have the green pendant?"

"Emeralds are always an excellent choice," Janelle said as she put the jewel into a velvet-lined box and handed it to Kayla. "The stones of prosperity and riches. Worked for a while. They also promote domestic bliss. Didn't work for me."

"What's the occasion? It's not my birthday or anything."

"What good are they locked away? Think of these things as your inheritance. I'm contemplating selling some of them. Most don't have pleasant memories attached anyway."

Janelle took three of the jewelry boxes and put them in her purse. She stood to leave but decided to take two more of the small boxes, one pale blue and one white. She buried them in the bottom of her purse. She patted the lid of the box and then called for Justin.

"Thank you, Aunt Janie." Kayla took out her journal and wrote a note reminding her to search "emeralds" on the Internet.

As they were walking to the car, Janelle said, "By the way. Better not mention to any one that I'm selling some of my things. Makes me look poor."

"How could anyone think you're poor, Aunt Janie."

"That may change if I don't finish . . ."

"Finish what?" Kayla asked.

To: Book Babes
Fm: kbellen
Re: Ali caught Janelle-itis

We need to get the old Ali back. I'm calling an emergency meeting at my house tonight at 7 p.m. I'll tell Ali to arrive at 7:30. Wine provided and plenty of it. This is serious. Janelle invited her sycophants from the banquet committee to lunch at the Fickle Pickle: Lisa, Vanessa, Delaney, and Ethyl. Why did she invite me? Ali lost it when she saw us and threw pickles at Janelle. J claims she wants to give Ali a special award. Ali needs our help.

When Ali arrived promptly at 7:30 p.m. at Ellen's house she was surprised to see so many cars parked in the circular driveway. Usually, one or two members were late or absent for the monthly meeting of the Book Babes. Based on the number of cars, all six members were present.

The group formed twenty years ago because of their love of reading, but the bond that united them was camaraderie. Ali cherished the friendships that took root in Willoughby and continued to flourish during joyous or sad times.

After parking on the street, Ali approached Ellen's two-story Georgian brick home she had inherited from her parents. The front door was ajar, so Ali pushed it open and followed the cacophony of women's voices that led to the den. The enticing aroma of freshly brewed coffee filled the room.

Jackie Glassen motioned to Ali to sit next to her on Ellen's red leather sofa. "Try one of the lemon tarts," she whispered to Ali.

"Can't. Diet." She coveted the tempting treats on the table in front of the sofa within an arm's reach, but selected a carrot stick.

Ellen came behind the sofa, leaned over Ali's shoulder, and handed her a glass of white wine. "Doctor's orders."

The conversations tapered off. The group directed their attention to Ali. "Did I miss something?" she asked the now quiet group.

Ellen ignored Ali's question. "The monthly meeting of Book Babes is open and ready for discussion," she said. Ellen asked members to score the book. The ratings ranged from a high of ten to a low of five with two abstaining because they hadn't read it.

"Okay. Forget about the book. We have an elephant in the room," Diane said.

Most members verbalized agreement. Jackie put a lemon tart on a plate and handed it to Ali. "Here. You're going to need this."

"What can we do about her?" Sally asked. "She's a star; everyone in town loves her."

"But she's causing our friend to suffer. We can't let her continue the same old crap she did to Ali in high school," Ellen said.

"She ordered an outrageously expensive floral arrangement for Phoebe's funeral and Matt paid for it," Jill said.

"When we met at the restaurant she tried to undermine all the decisions Ali had made," Ellen reported. "She even suggested that Ali needed mental health counseling."

Ali put her hand on her neck anticipating the tiny bumps that emerged when she experienced stress. She craved a glass of water, not to drink but to pour on her head. Ali didn't have to ask if the *her* and the *she* her friends referred to was Janelle.

"We know about the pickle throwing," Jill said with her head lowered. "We decided Janelle deserved more than a pickle."

Ali scowled at Ellen who said, "Sorry."

"I saw Janelle at the cleaners. She was having an argument with the owner because he couldn't get a red stain out of a tablecloth. Why would she have a tablecloth?" Diane asked.

"A *white* tablecloth? Oh, no. My Thanksgiving-Christmas tablecloth?"

Gasps from the group.

"That accounts for at least one of Janelle's mysterious errands," Ali said.

"Something else but I don't know if I should mention. . ." Sally said.

"SAY IT," the group responded.

"I saw Janelle at Macy's in the china and crystal department. She bought one Waterford wine glass."

"Was the pattern Lismore?" Ali asked.

"Couldn't tell."

"I told Kayla not to use those glasses. A wedding gift from you, Ellen."

"A broken glass, a stained tablecloth. So what. The real damage Janelle does is to your spirit, your confidence," Ellen said.

"She has a huge fan base. Somebody likes her," Ali said.

"Sure, we admire her book selling accomplishments," Diane said. "But look at the damage she's causing on the way to success: hurt feelings, unpaid bills, and backstabbing you."

"What's my alternative? She had indicated she wanted to stay here. Mother and Kayla encouraged her."

"You have to get rid of your sister," Diane said.

"Ask her to leave town as soon as the book banquet is over," Ellen advised. "Be honest with yourself, Ali. Your personality changes when Janelle's around. We want the old Ali back."

"At least, ask her to move into your parents' home. Or into the Willoughby Inn. You have to distance yourself from her. Let your parents deal with her," Diane said.

"If Janelle leaves, I'll be persona non grata with Kayla. Besides, I think Janelle's in financial trouble. I should help her," Ali said.

More gasps from the group. This was one gasping group.

"Why are you defending Janelle? She's so mean to you," said Jackie who spoke between bites of a lemon tart.

"I have to help her. After all, she's my sister." Ali couldn't believe the words she spoke. Was she trying to protect her sister? "I'm grateful for your concern. I have to come to terms with her."

"We've offered advice and now it's up to you to take action or remain a bitter doormat."

Ali knitted her eyebrows together and she bit her upper lip before she spoke. "Nothing like a close friend to tell the truth," she said, looking at Ellen. "Even though it hurts."

Chapter 31

"Hello. Anyone home?" a male voice said through the screen door at the Lawrence home. "Hello! Hello!" the visitor shouted as he repeatedly punched the doorbell. Janelle was stretched out on the sofa in the sunroom taking a nap. Roxie was on the floor nearby. At the sound of the bell, Roxie, in guard dog mode, raced to the door barking along the way.

"Can't someone answer the doorbell?" Janelle shouted to an empty house. Reluctantly, she arose from her snoozing alcove. "Why is it so damn dark in here?" she said, forgetting about the sleep mask strapped around her head. She stood on wobbly legs, lost her balance, and bumped into the end table knocking over a brass lamp. "Damn. More ammunition for Ali to use to evict me."

Janelle pulled off the sleep mask and threw it on the floor. "Am I a maid around here?" She heaved a big sigh and sauntered toward the front door. "Wait a minute. Hold on. I'm coming."

"About time. I've been ringing the damn doorbell for ten minutes," the visitor said when Janelle reached the door. "I was about to climb through a window."

"What the hell are you doing here, Ken? How did you find me?"

"You told me to come. Remember? Yesterday? Our phone conversation?"

"I haven't talked to you since I've been in Willoughby. I've been—"

"Avoiding me. Open the door for Pete's sake. Hotter than hell out here."

Janelle opened the door. "Follow me." She led Ken to the sunroom. He removed a tight fitting blazer revealing a wrinkled pale yellow shirt with dark rings underneath his armpits. He loosened his collar and tie, and tossed his crumpled jacket on a nearby chair.

"Pick up that lamp, for me. Not broken, I hope." Janelle returned to her recumbent position. She watched Ken place the lamp on the table. He picked up her sleep mask and tossed it to her.

"What happened in here? How'd the lamp get on the floor?"

"The dog. Roxie."

Little Roxie's ears perked up when she heard her name called, unaware of the false accusation.

"I could use a glass of water," Ken said. "Hotter than hell in this town."

"You already gave one weather report. Help yourself." Janelle pointed to the kitchen. "Bring me a glass, too. I must be dehydrated. My skin feels wrinkly." She pinched the skin on her wrist to check elasticity. "Too much coffee."

"Do you want a bowl of peeled grapes and a gaggle of young men, too, Cleopatra?"

Roxie sniffed at Ken's shoes and then trailed him into the kitchen.

Janelle heard Ken opening and banging cupboard doors. He returned to the sunroom with two coffee mugs and set them on the table in front of Janelle. "Couldn't find any damn water glasses." He flopped into a club chair and gulped the water emptying the mug. He took off his shoes and propped his feet on the coffee table.

"Janelle, I'm worried about you. You don't answer my phone calls, texts, e-mails. Now you say you don't remember our phone conversation yesterday. How do you think I knew you were hiding out in Willoughby?"

"Not hiding. Get my phone in the kitchen."

"Yes, your highness, and if you don't produce the damn manuscript, you won't have me as your manservant." He shook his head as he shuffled toward the kitchen. "Don't get paid enough for this."

When Ken returned with her phone, Janelle checked for recent incoming calls. "I see a call from you yesterday. Interesting."

"Have you been drinking again, Janelle?"

"I swear I did *not* black out. I repeat. I have not spoken to you since I've been in Willoughby."

"Someone who sounded like you sure did talk to me. At least the voice did. Not the words. The person I spoke with was Georgia peach sweet."

"Tell me again. How did you know I was here?" Janelle asked.

"I asked if you were with your sister. You didn't answer so I guessed."

Janelle placed the phone in her lap. She patted her hand on the sofa encouraging her furry friend to join her. She pulled on her ear lobe and twisted the large sparkling diamond stud earring back and forth.

"Okay, Janelle. Enough of the suspense. Out with it."

"I'm thinking. I'm thinking."

Janelle wasn't paying attention to Ken's ramblings. "Reminds me of my book—*The Twins of Terror Falls.*"

"I remember that one. Stayed on the bestseller's list for months. Paid for my vacation to the French Riviera."

"Must have been Ali who answered my phone. We pretended to be each other in high school. Our voices still sound alike. Mine is more melodious, though. Don't you think?"

"Should have known it wasn't you. Ali, or someone, said, 'I'm sorry.' Never heard those words from your mouth in the twenty years I've known you."

"I'll handle my sister later. I have to deal with you now."

"Forget about me. You've missed one deadline. Why are you purposely sabotaging your career?"

"You're concerned about your commission and my publisher's anxious about the advance he sent me. Everyone wants something from me."

Janelle stood. Ken stood. They faced each other. Without her shoes, Janelle and Ken were toe to toe.

His fleshy face was as red and round as a cherry tomato. "By the way, you look like hell," he said.

"These are my lounging clothes. Everything's casual around here."

"Since when are brown stains on your white shirt 'casual'? Did you sleep in those pants? What's going on with your hair?" Ken asked.

"You don't look so great yourself, Kenny baby. Taken a shower in the last forty-eight hours?" She attempted to fluff her hair with her fingers.

"You wouldn't look so good either if you had to fly stand-by, stuffed into the middle seat in coach, with a screaming baby in the next seat, who by the way, puked all over me. All avoidable if you would give me the—"

"OKAY. OKAY. Calm down. You look apoplectic. Taking your blood pressure meds?"

Before Ken could answer, they heard Ali at the front door.

"I'm home," Ali called out, as she headed toward the kitchen carrying two recyclable shopping bags of groceries from Publix. "Whose car is that? Where are you, Janelle? How many times do I have to tell you to close the front door?"

"In here," Janelle said. "Time to meet my sister, the con artist."

Ken stood when Ali entered the sunroom and offered his moist hand. "How do you do? I'm Ken Luzi, Janelle's agent. All the way from New York City. Or, should I say the Big Apple? Nice to put the voice with the face."

Ali shook Ken's sweaty hand. "Guess I'm busted. Would you like a glass of iced tea?" she asked as she ruefully glanced at Janelle.

"Thank you for the offer, Ali," he said, as he glared at Janelle. "May I help you?"

"No need, Ken. Make yourself comfortable." When she returned to the kitchen, she washed her hands.

"*Someone* in the family has manners," Ken said to Janelle when they were alone. He pulled a white handkerchief from his pants pocket and wiped his shiny pate. He noticed a white spot on his pants and rubbed it off with the handkerchief. "Guess you never learned Southern hospitality."

"I know all about hospitality. Ask anyone. They will tell you I am the essence of hospitality, Southern or otherwise."

"You're the essence of changing the subject. Manuscript. MAN-U-SCRIPT."

"Don't talk so loud. I don't want my sister to hear our conversation."

"Give me *something*, Janelle. Tell me about the plot. The characters. The setting. Do I need to hire a ghostwriter, a shrink?"

"No. No ghostwriter. How could you even think such a thing?"

"Knock, knock. Anyone home?" Virginia said as she opened the unlocked door and joined Ali in the kitchen. "Who's here? Whose car is that?"

"Hello to you, too, Mother. It's Janelle's agent. Ken Luzi. 'All the way from New York City, the Big Apple.'"

"Why is he here?" Virginia asked.

"I have no idea. Use your well-honed interrogation skills and you should know in ten minutes or less." Ali picked up the strawberry kitchen timer and showed it to her mother.

"Is the tea for our visitor?" Virginia asked, shooing the strawberry away.

Ali nodded.

"Let's put it on a pretty tray with a doily. Any cookies?" Virginia nudged Ali out of her way and then glimpsed around the corner to observe the visitor.

"Look at him," Ali said. "Does he look like he needs a cookie, Mother? Any minute all the buttons on his shirt are going to pop. He needs a shower, too. Smells like vomit."

"Doesn't matter. Where are your manners? He must be important to Janelle's career. We have to make a good impression."

"Why? Are you writing a book, too?"

"I don't know where your sarcasm comes from, Alicia. Not from my side of the family. By the way, you might want to put on a touch of lipstick."

"Whose car is that?" Kayla shouted. She let the screen door bang shut, dropped her backpack on the floor, and joined Ali and Virginia in the kitchen. "Hi, Nana," she said to Virginia. "You, too, Mom."

"Ken Luzi. Janelle's agent. 'All the way from New York City, the Big Apple,'" Ali said.

"Her agent? From New York City? Sweet."

Virginia placed a glass of tea on a small black lacquered tray decorated with strawberries. "Where are the lemons?" she asked Ali.

"If that's for the agent, let me take it in." Kayla picked up the tray.

Virginia took the tray from her granddaughter. "No cookie. No doily. Shameful," Virginia said.

"Your grandmother's pulling the welcome wagon today, Kayla."

"What?"

"Before your time."

"By the way, Alicia, please pull the weeds from your garden I've worked so hard at perfecting."

Ali raised her eyebrows. "I'll add that to the list, Mother."

Kayla followed Virginia into the sunroom where Janelle and Ken were sitting side by side on the sofa with their heads together in hushed conversation.

"Where are your manners, Janelle? Do I have to introduce myself?" Virginia set the tray on the glass-topped table in front of the sofa.

Janelle stayed seated, pointed her left hand toward the agent, and her right hand toward her family. "Ken. Mother. Kayla."

Ken stood, wiped the perspiration from his palm on his pants, and extended his hand to Virginia and Kayla.

"You ladies certainly have the pretty gene," Ken gushed. "The family resemblance is strong."

Virginia feigned embarrassment. Kayla replied "thank you" and then wiped her hand on her shorts.

Ali overheard Ken's "pretty" comment and knew he wasn't talking about her. *Would he have made the same comment with me in the room?* She carried a pitcher of iced tea and glasses on a larger and heavier tray than the strawberry one Virginia chose, and joined the group.

"It's too crowded and hot in here. Let's move to the living room where our guest will be more comfortable," Virginia said. She was skilled at directing any scene, not unlike another family member.

Ken took Virginia by the elbow and escorted her into the living room with Kayla trailing. Ali lifted the heavy tray from the table and brought up the rear.

Returning from work earlier than usual, Matt followed the noise of conversation into the living room. "Whose car is that?"

Ali wanted to scream, *AGENT. KEN. NEW YORK CITY. BIG APPLE.*

Matt introduced himself to Ken, since Janelle didn't offer, and the two men shook hands. "Welcome to Willoughby. What's the occasion?"

"Janelle and I have some pending business to finalize. Shouldn't take too long." He scowled at Janelle who returned the look.

Ali poured and distributed tea and took the empty tray to the kitchen. She groaned when she looked out the bay window and saw her father coming up the walkway. She beat him to the doorway. "The car. It's Janelle's agent. Ken. From New York City."

"What car?" He turned to look over his shoulder at the driveway. "That black SUV? Didn't notice."

"The entertainment's in the living room," Ali said as she kissed her dad on the cheek.

"So what are your plans, Mr. Luzi?" Virginia asked with a coquettish tilt of her head. "I would love to give you a tour of Willoughby."

"My plans depend on Janelle," Ken said.

"I spilled something all over my blouse. I'll be right back. Don't tell any of my secrets, Kenny," Janelle said.

"My husband and I would love to have you join our family tonight for an impromptu dinner. Isn't that right, Ed?" Virginia said as she scanned the room. "Where are you? I heard you come in."

"I'm right here. Making myself a cocktail. Not in the mood for tea," Ed said standing at the bar. "You look like you could use a stiff drink yourself, Kent."

"It's Ken," Virginia corrected. "His hearing, you know, at his age." She pointed to her ear.

"What's your pleasure, Kenny?" Ed asked. "How about a manhattan for the man from Manhattan?" No one laughed at Ed's joke except Kenny, the man.

"A manhattan. You were reading my mind."

Ed knew his way around the Lawrence bar. He put the cocktail ingredients into a shaker filled with ice and then strained the contents into a glass, plopping a maraschino cherry on top. "Sorry. No chilled glasses."

Ken took the glass and saluted Ed the bartender. "Works for me."

"Has anyone given Roxie a bath lately?" Ed asked. "What's that strange smell in here?"

No one answered his question but several pairs of eyes focused toward Ken.

The cocktail hour continued with Ken entertaining the family with stories of Janelle's book signings and zealous fans.

Virginia announced the dinnertime of eight o'clock. "Unless that's too early for a sophisticated New Yorker?"

"Eight o'clock it is, Mrs. Lawrence." He took her hand with both of his. "I can see where Janelle inherited her sparkling blue eyes." He retrieved his jacket and searched for business cards to distribute. "Never know when there might be another author in the family."

Ed and Matt exchanged a "who is this character?" glance. Ed was more direct. "He's full of B.S. and smells like it, too."

"Agreed."

"Besides, since when did we start eating dinner at eight o'clock? This family—," Ed grunted.

Janelle returned to the living room looking refreshed with spotless clothes in bright greens and yellows and wearing strappy black sandals. As usual, her perfume entered the room before she did. She performed a miracle with her hair and applied fresh makeup. Nothing could camouflage the dark circle under her eyes. "What's at eight o'clock? What did I miss?"

"Your mother's invited the whole gang to our house tonight. Should be a gas," Ed said.

"I don't think so. Ken and I have business to take care—," Janelle said.

"We can talk business tomorrow, Janelle. I will be pleased to spend time with your family." He gave her a snide smile and crossed his arms.

"One taste of Virginia's food and he'll be on the next plane to New York," Ed whispered to Matt.

The house cleared out—Ken to the Willoughby Inn, hopefully to shower and change clothing; Kayla to tennis practice, followed by a team pizza party; and Virginia and Ed to their home for dinner preparation. Matt went to his computer in the den and Ali sat at the kitchen table with her laptop checking emails about the book banquet. After about an hour, Matt joined Ali in the kitchen; he took her hand and led her to the front porch. "Let's take a break." From where they were sitting, they could see their neighbor, Mr. Fenny, sneaking a cigarette on his side of the house. The smoke drifted into the yard.

"Mrs. Fenny must know he smokes," Ali said. "The smell alone."

"Maybe that's what old married people do. Pretend they don't know something about the spouse. Sometimes I think that we do some pretending," Matt said.

"About what?"

"You pretend you're happy with the life we have."

"I'm happy." She paused. "Guess that didn't sound convincing, did it? I'm unhappy when Janelle's around. Does that sound better?"

"Don't let Janelle upend you. If I had a brother who acted like Janelle, I'd belt him one and tell him to shut up."

"I can't. Girls don't resort to boxing matches."

"Perhaps the situation with Janelle warrants at least a hair-pulling cat fight."

"Please, Matt. I couldn't hit Janelle."

"That's a relief. I wouldn't hit you either, Li'l Sis. No matter what."

Ali jumped from her chair. "Why are you always sneaking up on me, Janelle?"

"Sorry. Guess my mea culpas are countless since I've been here. I AM SO VERY SORRY for whatever I've done to upset you, Ali."

"If you don't know why you're apologizing, then your apology is worthless," Ali shot back.

"See. I can't win, Matt." With upturned palms, Janelle turned to face Matt and moved closer to him. She had changed her outfit. Now she wore a saffron yellow curve-hugging sheath, white strappy low-heeled sandals, and multiple strands of gold chains around her neck.

"You look nice, Janelle. A little dressed up for dinner at the folks' house." As Matt spoke, he noticed a black Escalade in the driveway. Ken Luzi exited the driver side of the SUV and opened the passenger door, and helped Virginia step down. He took her by the arm and escorted her to the front porch. Ed stayed glued in the back seat with his arms crossed over his chest. Janelle, Ali, and Matt met them on the porch.

"Why aren't you dressed, Alicia?" Virginia asked. "Matt, you can't wear those shorts to Bones. Didn't you get the message?"

Janelle chirped, "Oh, my fault. I forgot to tell them that Ken is treating us to dinner tonight. He didn't want Mother to trouble herself."

"We'll wait for you," Ken said. "Ed can make another one of those terrific manhattans."

Matt explained that they were both tired and didn't want to leave until Kayla returned home. "Have fun. We'll leave the door unlocked for you, Janelle."

Ali sat in one of the rocking chairs on the porch. Before the Escalade left the driveway, she began, "Another example of—"

"Ali, drop it. You wouldn't want to go anyway. Your mother will fawn over Ken as if he were Richard Castle's agent and Janelle will tell one outrageous story after another. Your father will grumble and complain about how he should be home watching the Braves. Wouldn't you rather sit here with your ever lovin' husband?" He took her hand and kissed it. "All I want in the world is your happiness. Won't you do that for me? Give me a little smile, babe. A little smile on your pretty face." He put his fingers on the corners of her bottom lip and turned her depressed mouth upward.

"Stop it. Stop it." She laughed before she brushed his hands away.

"Let's get out of here. I'll get your walking shoes and leave a note for Kayla. We can eat somewhere on The Lane."

Fisticuffs? Hair pulling? Catfight? One more chance, Ali decided. *I'll give Janelle one more chance and then POW! POW! Take this. Take this again. Take that. A slap across her face and a punch to her stomach. Oh, I couldn't. I just couldn't, but what fun to think about it.*

"Ready?" Matt asked as he returned to the porch with Ali's dilapidated shoes.

"I've never felt better."

Chapter 32

A li was puzzled to find Matt at home during the day. She tried to recall how many times he had done that in the last month. Two times? Three? "Is something wrong, hon?"

He ran his hand through his hair. "Needed a break from the dealership. Not much going on." He took off his sunglasses and pinched his eyebrows together forming a small v on his forehead.

Ali recalled that Matt was wearing a black Graham Auto polo shirt when he left this morning. Now he was wearing a white one. Maybe she was wrong. She wasn't wrong about wet hair along the nape of his neck.

"Have you eaten? I'll make sandwiches," Matt volunteered.

"Not hungry. Thanks."

"I'll make your favorite. Roast beef, arugula, horseradish."

"We're out of roast beef."

"I'll go to the store tomorrow," he said.

She sat across from him at the table and watched him eat a turkey and Havarti sandwich on rye while he read *Automotive News*.

"Don't you think she's a bad influence on Kayla?" Ali asked.

"Who?"

"Who do you think? Lady Gaga?"

"I didn't realize you were bringing up this family's favorite topic." Matt put the magazine aside and took a gulp of iced tea.

Ali thought Janelle was interrupting their everyday routine. Matt disagreed and said that Janelle added some excitement to their lives. "She won't stay forever. I think she's entertaining. Never a dull moment with Janelle around."

"Do you think we lead a dull life?" Ali asked.

Like a skilled politician, Matt sidestepped the question. "We lead a great life." He reached for the magazine and flipped a page.

"Sometimes I wonder where we would be and what we would be doing if we had vamoosed out of Willoughby," Ali said. The woulda-coulda-shoulda refrain frequented Ali and Matt's discussions about the life they led.

"Janelle has dangled a lifestyle that is unobtainable for most folks. I suppose Lady Gaga has done that, too. I don't find anything problematic except some questionable clothing choices Kayla's made under the guidance of her aunt." Matt stood from the table, gave Ali a peck on the top of her head. "Relax. You worry too much." He took his plate to the sink. "See you tonight."

Ali waved her hand as if to say *whatever*.

"What's the matter, Li'l Sis?"

"Yikes! Why do you always sneak up on me, Janelle?"

"Should I ring a bell before I enter your sacred sanctum?" Janelle sashayed into the kitchen wearing a black and white animal print robe trimmed in white lace. "You look despondent. You're wearing the same frown I portrayed on Amanda Lilenthal in my book *Harbormaster's Secret.*"

When the sisters were in high school, Ali learned the consequences of sharing a secret with Janelle. "What do you think about Benny Greenway?" Ali asked Janelle one fateful day.

"Greenway? For what? A lab partner yes, but a boyfriend? No way."

"Just asking."

Several days later Ali was shocked to find "Ali + Benny" signs on Ali's locker and in the girls' restroom. Ali confronted her sister in the hallway at school. "Did you break into my diary?"

"Of course not. Why would I want to read your boring diary?"

If Benny had been a high school super star, Janelle might have laughed at Ali's crush. Because he was the quintessential nerd of Willoughby High, Janelle took great pleasure with broadcasting the news to the entire school.

"Please make her stop, Dad. I'm humiliated. The worst part is that now Benny won't even talk to me."

Virginia dismissed Janelle's prank, but Ed grounded her for two weeks. Of course, she found ways to sneak out of the house.

That was a long time ago, Ali thought. "I think Matt is involved in an affair."

"What kind of an 'affair'? Business?"

"Another woman kind of affair. Adultery. Cheating. Playing around."

"Matt? I don't think so. He's crazy in love with you. Always has been. Always will. Believe me, I know the signs. I based my male antagonist in *Billionaire's Dilemma* on my second husband. Both were the consummate cheaters. Why are you suspicious?"

"I've noticed a few signs," Ali said.

"Such as?"

"He's been coming home for lunch with wet hair."

"Lunch? Wet hair? Not exactly grounds for divorce. Give me more information, Ali."

"He's distracted. Doesn't seem to notice me."

"Hard to notice someone who's never around. Between your little book banquet—Sorry, I mean, your important book banquet, and taking care of Mother and Dad, and who knows what else, you never have time for him."

This was the first time Janelle acknowledged the time that Ali spent with their parents.

"Only one way to find out. We'll spy on him like I did in —"

"Let me guess," Ali said. "One of your books. *Passion in Paris.*"

The sisters shared a rare laugh.

"That felt good, Janelle. Laughing together, I mean." Ali paused. "Remember all the April Fool's tricks we used to play on Dad? Or the times you practiced putting makeup on me and I always ended up looking either like a clown or a ghoul?"

Janelle quickly changed the subject. "You know I don't remember our youth the same way you do. Now, back to adultery. I've had plenty of real life experience spying on all my exes except the first, Howard." Intrigue and tension fueled Janelle's existence not only in her books but also in her life. This was one of the reasons, according to the critics, why her novels were so popular, real page-turners.

"Where should we start?" Janelle asked.

"Too sneaky. I would never spy on my husband."

Janelle poured herself a cup of coffee. "Suit yourself. I'll be upstairs. Working. Then I have some errands to run."

"By the way, Janelle. Please don't tell Matt we had this conversation."

"Don't worry. My lips are sealed." She took a finger to her mouth and imitated zipping her lips. "Have I ever let you down?"

"That's what I'm worried about," Ali said. When Ali was positive that Janelle had retreated to her bedroom, she made a phone call. "What are you doing?" she asked Ellen.

"Bookkeeping."

"Can you leave? Right now?"

"Well, I guess. Bailey's here."

"Pick me up," Ali said.

"What—?"

"I'll explain when you get here." Ali walked to the end of her driveway waiting for Ellen.

"Where are we going?" Ellen asked as Ali climbed into the back seat of Ellen's silver metallic Mini Cooper.

"To see Matt."

"Why?"

"To check if he's working."

"Why don't you call him?" Ellen asked.

"He gave me some convoluted story about how the phone lines are always down because of the installation of a new system. I can only reach him on his cell. I tried anyway but the call went to voice mail at the dealership."

"Yes, that does sound suspicious—but not incriminating."

"In case he sees us, make up a story. Say you're in the market for a new car. I'll crouch down in the backseat."

"Matt will never believe that one. My car's new."

"Say an overwhelming sense of patriotism came over you. Tell him anything. It won't matter because he won't be there."

Ellen steered her spy mobile into the entrance of the dealership. Five or six salespeople, men and women, were standing in the front of the building. They were all dressed in dark jackets and white polo shirts. They looked like melting hot fudge sundaes in the heat.

"Drive slowly. Over by the side. If he's here, he'll be in the tower."

The front of the dealership was glass. Ali scanned the floor of the dealership and the tower where Matt positioned himself answering questions and giving instructions to the sales staff.

"He could be in the men's room. Or getting a cup of coffee," Ellen suggested.

"Drive to the back. Let's look for his car."

Ellen followed Ali's instructions and drove behind the dealership but still no sight of Matt or his car.

"What symptoms have you noticed?"

"He's not sick. Not physically anyway. Odd behavior. Coming home for lunch. Showers in the middle of the day."

"Hmm. Showers?"

"Where else would a man go if he lost his job and is afraid to tell his wife?" Ali asked the worldly Ellen. "A bar? A gentleman's club?"

"Not Matt," Ellen said.

Ali sat up from a crammed position in the back seat. "The gym. He loves that gym. He goes every chance he has since we began this insane diet. Turn right on Alpharetta Highway and go to 24-Hour Workout. That's where he is." *That's where he has to be.*

They drove around the parking lot of the fitness center. Ali slumped low in the back seat forgetting that her red hair might be noticeable to anyone walking by. When they reached the parking lot that was not visible from the street, Ellen yelled, "Bingo! His car."

"You go in and find out what he's doing. I don't want to look like a suspicious wife even though I am a suspicious wife."

"As if I'm dressed to work out?" Ellen was wearing a green and white tunic over leggings and ballet flats. "What should I say?"

"Think of something. Say you want membership information. Do they have a pool? What's the fee? I don't know. Get in there, please."

Ellen easily found Matt. He stood by the reception counter, wiping his forehead and neck with a sweat-drenched towel, while talking to an attractive young female employee. Ellen pretended she was looking for something in her purse to give Matt time to exit. He didn't seem to mind that she saw him.

"Ellen. I didn't know you were a member here."

"I'm thinking about switching gyms."

"Would you like a tour?" the young woman asked Ellen.

"I'll show her around."

"Oh darn. There's my phone." Ellen took her phone out of her purse and faked a conversation. "Sorry. Gotta run."

Matt shook his head while he watched her leave.

Meanwhile, Ali sat up in the car twirling a piece of hair around a finger with one hand and chewing on the fingernails of her other hand. She kept a close eye on the door, hoping Ellen would return with good news.

Ellen exited the gym and gave Ali the A-OK sign. "He's working out, that's it," she reported when she joined Ali in the car. "Some flirting with the tight body at the counter, but he had plenty of time to avoid me and he chose not to. He spoke to me first."

"Something's off. If he's not having an affair, something major is wrong at work and he doesn't want to tell me."

Chapter 33

The dream went like this: Phoebe Patterson, in the persona of a wicked witch, apple in hand, placed a curse on Janelle. "Janelle Jennings, forever you are doomed to live out your days in Willoughby. Willoughby, Georgia," the grotesque witch snarled. Gasping for air, Janelle sat up in bed and tore off her sleep mask. She decided a shot of tequila would quiet her nighttime demons. She was at the foot of the stairs, close to Ali and Matt's bedroom, when she bumped into a dark figure. Too frightened to scream, she dashed to the front door to escape, but before she reached her destination, Matt grabbed her by the arm. "Geez," she shrieked.

"What's the matter with you, Janelle?" Matt said, barely above a whisper, chasing after her before she left the house.

"Couldn't sleep. Need a drink."

"Now I need one, too. Hope you didn't wake Ali."

"What the heck are you doing here?"

"I live here. Remember?" Matt took her by the arm, ushered her into the living room, and closed the French doors. Janelle immediately headed for the bar.

"Looking for the tequila?"

"Need something to calm me down. Cognac, wine—I'll take anything. No beer. Definitely no beer. Too many carbs."

"I'll meet you in the kitchen. Less likely to wake Ali. And, be quiet—if you're capable."

Janelle tiptoed into the Command Center, aka the Lawrence household's kitchen. She settled into a captain's chair with a comfortable squishy cushion underneath her bottom.

Matt brought a bottle of Josè Cuervo and two glasses to the table. "Salt? Lime?" he asked.

"Skip the accoutrements. Pour."

"I don't picture the glamorous Janelle Jennings as a shot glass gal."

"What I do in the privacy of my own home or hotel suite is my business."

"Speaking of homes. Your sister is concerned that you don't have a home." He poured the clear liquid into the glasses.

"She's worried I'll never leave Willoughby. Is that what you wanted to say and needed another shot to bolster your courage? I didn't think you were afraid of anything, Matty, especially little ole me." She tapped the bottom of her glass on the table.

Janelle noticed Matt looking at her chest. In mock modesty, she crisscrossed her arms and placed them on her bosom. "Sorry. Hope my girls aren't a distraction. Forgot my robe."

Matty filled both glasses.

"Ali thinks you're having an affair. She probably suspects me as the home wrecker. Isn't that priceless? Of course, it isn't completely impossible. Two of my characters in *The Secret Summer in Sahara*, a sister-in-law and brother-in-law, had a torrid love affair that ended badly. Death by camel. I don't know how I wrote such a tragic and immoral story."

"Immoral? Janelle, you are a gem."

"I have my principles."

"Why would Ali think I'm having an affair?"

"Odd hours, distraction, showers in the middle of the day. She came to her big sister for advice so I briefed her in the skill of identifying a cheating spouse. But now she knows it isn't true because she and Ellen followed—"

"She followed me?"

"She was thinking about it, but I told her not to. I told her to let me handle it."

"Sounds like one of your alcohol-induced delusions—not Ali."

"I don't drink much anymore. Only under stress." She circled her finger around the rim of the glass. "Being in Willoughby with the parents and Ali is filled with stress."

"I find it hard to believe that Ali doesn't trust me. If anyone were going to have an affair, she's the one with opportunity. I can account for every minute of my day. Most of the time I have no idea where she is or what she's doing: book banquet committee, Kitchen Bliss, delivering food for showers."

"Your situation reminds me of . . ."

"Let me guess. One of your romance novels. Do you always have to relate real life situations to your books?"

"Now, Matty Boy."

"Furthermore, my name is Matt, not Matty Boy. I'm Matt. Got it? Like the character in your book The Flame that Fizzled or whatever you called it."

"*The Secret of the Flaming Fury.* I modeled the protagonist's lover after you. Oh, Matty—I mean, Matt. I thought we had such a good relationship and now you're turning on me. Why so mad at your dear sister-in-law?" the mistress of fake coyness purred.

"You can cut the crap, Janelle. I'm in no mood for your shenanigans. I have my own problems and one of them is sitting at this table. Another thing, Ali was hurt when you named a particularly dowdy character in one of your books *Alicia*. That was unkind." He poured another shot of tequila and knocked it back.

"I write fiction. That particular Alicia was not our Ali. Mother's right. Ali is excessively sensitive."

"You could use a big dose of sensitivity, Janelle."

"I apologize. There, I said it. I know I get on Ali's nerves, but I have problems you can't imagine." She stopped short of revealing her situation.

They went back and forth, Matt defending Ali, and Janelle defending Janelle. Janelle was on the verge of divulging her sad story. One more swallow of tequila and she would have. Janelle and Matt stopped talking when they heard someone in the hallway.

"What's going on in here?" Ali asked. "Am I missing the pajama party, or by the looks of Janelle, a Victoria Secret party?"

"We're having a chat," Janelle said. "Oh, look at the doggies on your PJ's. So cute."

"At least I'm more modest than that flimsy thing you're wearing. Can I join the 'chat'? Or, do I need tequila to participate?"

"Neither one of us could sleep. Didn't want to wake you. Sorry," Matt said. He didn't seem embarrassed or guilty. "Janelle told me you thought I was cheating on you. Is that true?"

Janelle blurted out—"I told him I convinced you it wasn't true."

"I'd like to hear Ali's version."

Ali glanced from her sister and then to Matt. "I don't know what you're talking about."

Matt put the top on the tequila bottle and took the shot glasses to the sink. "You've had enough, Janelle. Ali and I are going to bed." When they were in their bedroom, Matt said, "Your sister is a crazy troublemaker. You would never spy on me."

"As I said, I don't know what she's talking about." Ali took his hand, led him to their bed, and turned out the light.

Chapter 34

"Sorry for my rudeness, Aunt Janie, but we haven't done our favorite fun thing since you've been here."

Janelle was sitting on the sofa in the sunroom playing solitaire on her laptop. "What's that, borrowing all my clothes, sweetie?" she answered without looking at Kayla.

"No, shopping. Some cool stores have opened up since you were here. Within walking distance. Better than the mall."

"Oh, that. Not quite yet. My novel is still in need of some rewriting. As soon as it's finished, we'll have a big day, and go shopping, and then somewhere fancy for lunch." Janelle returned to her game.

Kayla leaned over to check her aunt's computer screen. "If you don't mind me saying so, shouldn't you be writing instead of playing cards?"

"Aren't you brash? Are you turning on me like your mother?" She shut the lid on the laptop.

Kayla and Janelle sat side by side then turned their heads to look at each other.

Janelle broke the fence of silence. "Promise not to tell your mom?"

"Cross my heart."

"My financial situation is, well, shall we say, precarious at the moment. This is all due to a scheme by the name of Ponzi and my greedy ex-husbands."

Kayla sensed her aunt's discomfort and remained quiet.

Janelle continued. "If it's too good to be true, it probably is."

"Sounds like a Nana saying."

"Your grandmother's saying is true. I imagined I could make a lot of easy money but then it exploded. I'm in a bad way financially. You mustn't tell your parents. I have to finish my book, get it to my publisher, pack my bags, and promote the hell—excuse me, your mother doesn't like me to swear in front of you—promote it. Facebook, Twitter, LinkedIn, the world."

"What's stopping you, Aunt Janie? If it's too noisy here, go to the library. I know a perfect spot where you could have privacy and write all day long."

"Not as easy as that, Kayla." Janelle put her head in her lap and began to cry. "I've been a fool. I think I should forget about the book and start a new life. Declare bankruptcy."

"Thank you for telling me this. You make me feel like an adult."

"Another thing. Your mother hates me and wants me to leave."

"Oh, Aunt Janie, why do you care about what Mom says? She's been so grouchy lately and she's, like, totally jealous of you."

"Don't disrespect your mother. You're lucky to have her. Besides, this is her house and your dad's, not yours. You should be more grateful, Kayla, and not so self-centered."

Kayla stood up. The harsh words from Janelle stung like a slap on the cheek. What happened to the aunt who treated Kayla like a princess, but all of a sudden sounded like her grouchy mother? "I'm going to take Roxie for a walk." She turned around and said, "Nana also says, 'It could be worse.'" She slammed the door and left.

Janelle regretted speaking to Kayla that way. Now she would go straight to her mother and tell all. Then she'd tell Matt, and the parents, and all of Willoughby. . . fodder for the tabloids. Janelle had given all her female protagonists intuition and skepticism when choosing husbands, but she couldn't do the same for herself. *If my readers know the truth, I'll lose credibility. I truly loved my first husband, Howard, but I was too selfish to give him the life and kids he wanted. It was downhill after him. I caught Miles, number two, on our sailboat with my former personal assistant. Wasn't my fault he jumped overboard and drowned. Number three, Philip, loved luxurious cars and exotic dancers. I have to adjust my gold-digger radar or swear off men and become celibate. About Gerald. Can't stand to think about that one.*

Janelle knew that if she could find the outline of the partial manuscript that Phoebe was supposed to write, she could whip out the final copy, get it to her publisher, and breathe a sigh of relief. Without Phoebe's help and guidance, Janelle doubted herself. Why did she ever let Phoebe talk her into this charade? If Phoebe's righteous friends were aware of the facts, Phoebe would fall off her pedestal so fast the entire town of Willoughby would rock from the crash.

Janelle imagined what the old biddies would say. "How could Phoebe stoop to write such trash?" "I'm so disappointed." "How much of the writing do you think Janelle did versus Phoebe?" "Janelle was acting strange at Phoebe's memorial service." "This will kill Virginia." "It serves Virginia right for all her braggadocio about that trampy daughter of hers." *This is mild compared to what some of them will say,* Janelle mused.

"Willoughby, GA–Phoebe Patterson, former mayor of Willoughby and respected educator, was revealed as the co-author of eighteen best-selling romance novels. The news that Mrs. Patterson wrote steamy, racy books was received with mixed responses in the community. 'I'm absolutely shocked and disappointed with Phoebe,' said Mrs. Harriet Bell, president of the Willoughby Library Association. 'This is surely a black mark on the reputation of our fine community,' she added. Other viewpoints expressed an opposite opinion. 'I'm pleased to know that Phoebe had another side to her stuffy self,' said a person who chose to remain anonymous. The truth was exposed when the *Willoughby News & Record* obtained an e-mail allegedly sent to Janelle Jennings, Mrs. Patterson's co-author. Ms. Jennings was unavailable for comment. Mrs. Patterson died recently so she, too, could not be reached for comment."

Chapter 35

"**G**ramps, I have to talk to you. It's really, really important," Kayla said from her cell phone.

"What's so important?"

"Can you meet me at the park? Privately?"

"I always have time for my favorite girl."

Ed and Kayla often met at the pond in Willoughby Park. They enjoyed sitting on a bench while discussing their lives, and watching mother ducks and their ducklings swim around the perimeter of the pond. Not as pleasant was stepping over the slippery goop deposited by the annoying Canada geese that populated the park. A flock of ten paraded around the walking trail. Their elegant long black arched necks demanded authority. Their irritating honking dissuaded dogs or small children from approaching them and interrupted the otherwise serene atmosphere.

The visitors to the park included parents jogging in packs while pushing strollers and many dog lovers exercising their precious pets. Majestic trees formed a canopy over the graveled walking trails making the park an ideal spot to exercise during hot Georgia summers.

Ed arrived before Kayla. He found an empty bench facing the American flag hanging on a tall pole positioned on the peninsula of the pond. Clouds puffy as meringue glided across the Carolina blue sky. He tipped his Braves baseball cap to his neighbor, Mrs. Tyler, whose Golden Lab pulled her along the path. Ed was more curious than concerned about Kayla's urgent phone call. Teenagers often found drama in minor events of life.

Kayla arrived out of breath. "Thanks for meeting me." She reached for Roxie and placed her on the bench next to Gramps. She gave Roxie some pats on the head and scratched her belly.

Ed brought a small bag with an apple, an orange, and a treat for Roxie. "I guessed you and Roxie might need a snack after school." He waited for Kayla to bring up the "really, really important" matter.

She took the apple and put it in her lap. Kayla launched into a recap of Janelle's revelation that she was broke and would have to declare bankruptcy.

Ed moved his head up and down a few times and made comments like *hmm, you don't say*. He turned his body slightly so he could make direct eye contact with Kayla and give her his full attention.

"She said it's all some guy's fault," Kayla asserted.

"What guy? An ex? Her last husband? Gerald?"

"A Mr. Bonsee. Maybe it was Pondzee."

Ed repeated Kayla's words. "Could it be Ponzi?"

"Yes, I think so. That's it."

"Ponzi is the name of a scheme to cheat people out of their money. When you go home, Google it. P-O-N-Z-I. I think Janelle's desire to get rich quick replaced common sense."

"She told me her last husband talked her into it."

"I never did like that fellow. Gerald. I think. Sleazy."

"What can we do?"

"Who knows about this?"

"Aunt Janie told me not to tell Mom and Dad, but she didn't say not to tell you."

"That was wise of you. Whatever happens, we can't tell your grandmother. This would kill her. She wouldn't be able to face her friends."

"Nana likes Aunt Janie better than Mom, doesn't she?"

"Parents love all their children equally. If Janie lived in Willoughby, your grandmother and your aunt might get on each other's nerves."

"But what can we do? We have to help her."

"Let's sit on it for a while. Sometimes things work themselves out. What about her new book? Shouldn't that be coming out soon? Wouldn't that take care of her money woes?"

"She must have writer's block or something because I haven't seen her working since she's been here. I'm so worried about her, even though she was horrible to me today."

"You're too young to worry about your aunt. You have two jobs—excel in school and follow through on your forehand. I bet you've been ignoring your studies since your aunt's been here."

Kayla lowered her head and rubbed Roxie's leash between her fingers. She scraped her Reeboks along the ground. Roxie turned her head back and forth between grandfather and granddaughter hoping for a treat. Kayla removed the brown bone-shaped biscuit from the bag and put it in front of Roxie who grabbed it, broke it into several pieces, and then chewed each piece one by one.

"I should have aced my algebra test. Mom will blame it all on Aunt Janie. I heard her tell Dad that she's a distraction and a bad influence on me. I think she wants her to move in with you and Nana."

"I'm glad we had this talk. Let me worry about it." The two sat silently looking at the ducks in the pond. He took her hands. "Squeeze my hands tight. Close your eyes. Now, all your worries are mine. You and Roxie run home, get some exercise that way, and then hit the books."

She opened her eyes but still gripped her grandfather's hands. "I love you, Gramps." Kayla dropped his hands and gave Ed a serious hug.

"Back at you, sweet pea, and don't forget about your forehand."

Ed continued to sit on the bench as he watched Kayla and Roxie jog around the pond and head home. He observed a proud mother duck leading her ducklings across the water. They would follow her anywhere, not unlike Kayla's devotion to the aunt she worshipped. Ali claimed she was not jealous of Janelle. Perhaps she was right. Jealousy was not the issue between the two women. Ali wanted to protect Kayla from Janelle.

Ed took a bite of the crisp apple Kayla left on the bench. He decided he wouldn't do a darn thing about Janelle's mess. She would have to clean it up by herself. *If only my shoe sanitizer took off, or the Shark Tank bankrolled me, or QVC came calling. Or, maybe I'll win the Powerball.* He pulled out his wallet and searched for a business card.

Chapter 36

The following day Ali heard the honking of Janelle's rental car in the driveway and went to the window. *Is that sound the equivalent of ringing a bell for a maid?* She opened the front door and met her sister in the driveway. Janelle's car exiting skills had improved since her arrival. Ali shaded her eyes from the sun with her hand and squinted to see what Janelle was doing. Janelle collected multiple Nordstrom's shopping bags from the trunk.

"Where's Ken?" Ali asked.

"On his way back to New York. Help me with these."

Ali and Janelle walked into the house carrying the shopping bags and put them on the kitchen table. Janelle removed her Jackie O sunglasses. She took off her five-inch platform sandals and placed them under the table. Roxie sniffed at Janelle's toes.

"What about taking Kayla shopping? She's counting on it."

"Don't tell her. I needed some new clothes and I still had one credit card. Help me upstairs with these bags."

"This reminds me of those secret shopping excursions you and Mother took when we were young."

"What?"

The sisters and Roxie walked upstairs.

"You and Mother left on Saturday mornings and returned home with shopping bags from Rich's. You took the bags into our room and dumped the contents on your bed. I remember sitting on the window seat admiring the beautiful clothes."

Janelle set the bags on her bed.

"You didn't enjoy shopping. You always had your nose in a book." Janelle turned to face her sister and straightened the collar on Ali's white polo shirt.

Janelle held up a shimmery silver blouse with a low-cut neckline. "What do you think of this color for me? Too bland?" She put it back in the bag and brought out another blouse.

"You two snuck away like thieves," Ali recalled.

"Mother insisted I have stylish clothes for the parties I attended. Of course, I had to wear special outfits for the beauty pageants. Didn't we bring you something?"

"Underwear. Always underwear."

"Who can't use underwear? My guess is that your underwear today could use an update."

Janelle wasn't paying attention to Ali. She removed a red leather hobo purse with a large gold clasp from one of the bags and set it on the bedside table. She admired the purse as though it were a piece of priceless sculpture.

"Did it ever occur to you to bring me a blouse, a sweater?"

"Believe me, those shopping trips with Mother were not pleasant. She was so opinionated about what I wore. She vetoed most of my choices. Anyway, I gave you lots of my clothes until you grew out of my size two."

"Hand-me-downs with cigarette burns weren't much of a gift."

"You're blaming the wrong person. I was a kid. Mother was to blame. Be upset with her, not me. Besides, she took you on her antique shopping."

"Only because you didn't want to go."

Janelle thought for a moment. "You and Dad did your own thing. Didn't he take you to the movies or something?"

"Our dear dad always found something to keep me busy while you shopped. I lied to him and told him I hated shopping."

"So what do you want from me, Cinderella? I can't rectify what happened a hundred years ago. Do you want to go shopping? Is that what it is? Let's go. I'll buy you all the damn clothes in the store if it will make you stop wallowing in a pool of imagined favoritism by our mother."

"What will you use for money? My credit card? Like you did at the hair salon?"

"I found a credit card stuck in the bottom of my purse that my ex Gerald hadn't maxed out. I'm having a short-term financial setback. By the way, you're still wearing your apron from the store."

Ali glanced down and realized she left work in such a hurry she forgot to take off the green apron with the Kitchen Bliss logo. Ali had gone to the grocery store, post office, and library wearing the apron. Ellen should give her an advertising bonus.

"So what? I'll wear it all day and night if I want. Maybe I'll take off my clothes and wear nothing but the apron. What difference does it make to you? Do I still embarrass you? Even as an adult?"

"Matt said you have a mental health issue."

Ali was silent for a moment. "Matt? You're making that up."

"He didn't use those exact words but it was close. He thinks you're insanely jealous of my success. That was the word he used—'insane.'" She used air quotes around insane.

"You want to see insane? Watch me."

Ali felt her face warm. She touched her neck to feel the tiny familiar bumps that emerged under stressful conditions. Ali went to the hall closet and yanked out one of Janelle's suitcases. She jerked the bag so fast the others tumbled to the floor.

"What are you doing?"

"I'm packing your clothes. You can go to Mother's. This living arrangement isn't working."

"Careful. Those clothes are expensive. Guess you wouldn't know about expensive clothes. You chose bland and cheap a long time ago."

"Get out of here, Janelle. I mean it."

"You need something to calm you down. How about a Xanax?" Janelle reached for her purse. "You're overreacting."

"I'm supposed to what? Go along with all your crap? Besides, I can't trust you. Why did you tell Matt I thought he was having an affair? I told you in confidence."

Janelle approached Ali with open arms. "I'll give you that. I am sorry. Truce? For Kayla's sake."

Ali grabbed clothes on hangers from the closet and threw them onto the bed. She took a few steps toward her sister and pushed her right hand against her sister's chest. "GET OUT OF HERE."

Janelle's mouth dropped open. She reared back on her heels, lost her balance, and caught herself on the dresser. She composed herself and appeared to contemplate her next move. She raised her hands, and shoved Ali who fell on her back onto the bed barely missing the headboard.

"Get out," Ali shouted again.

Ali pushed up off the bed. She stood, untied and removed the apron, and threw it toward Janelle. The apron ties flew like a lariat slapping Janelle's cheek.

Janelle wadded the apron and threw it back at Ali. The two sisters squared off. Sensing danger, Roxie ran around the room in circles, yelping and barking. Ali turned away from her sister, grabbed some of the clothes from the bed, pushed the screen from the open window, and flung them onto the front lawn. The screen along with Janelle's clothes sailed to the ground.

"How could you?" Janelle shrieked. "Go get my clothes. Now."

"Mom. Aunt Janie. I'm home. What's the screaming about? Are you two fighting?"

At the sound of Kayla's voice, Roxie scurried down the stairs and jumped into her open arms. "Poor Roxie? Too much noise?" Kayla cradled the shivering dog like a baby and held her close.

"Enjoy the company of your 'expensive' clothes, Janelle. I'm going to enjoy the company of my daughter. A daughter you don't have." Ali went down the stairs two at a time holding onto the railing.

"What the heck?" wide-eyed Kayla asked.

"Your aunt and I were having a slight disagreement. Sorry if we were a bit loud. Why don't you take Roxie in the backyard? Your aunt will be down in a minute."

"Mom, you know Roxie doesn't like loud noises. You were into more than a 'slight disagreement.'" Kayla gave her mother the look that said *can't you two get along?*

After Kayla and Roxie left, Ali and Janelle hurried outside to retrieve the ejected clothes. They sprinted upstairs and threw them on the bed. Janelle began hanging some of the clothes in the small closet, ignoring Ali's ultimatum to leave.

"I don't want Kayla to know how childish we behave. She adores you and there's nothing I can do about that," Ali admitted to Janelle's back.

"You started it," Janelle said without turning around.

Ali slammed the bedroom door and stomped downstairs. She sat on the steps in the backyard, and watched Roxie and Kayla play fetch with a tennis ball. Roxie brought Ali the ball inviting her to join the game. Her trembling hand reached for the ball but dropped it. Ali had been so close to slugging her sister's wrinkle-free face that the idea sickened her. After her breathing returned to normal, she left the backyard. On her way to the bathroom to drink a bottle of Pepto-Bismol, she and her sister were face to face.

Ali spoke first. "We're childish."

"We're silly," Janelle agreed. "Truce?"

"For Kayla's sake, yes. A truce. I still want you out of here, Janelle."

"Don't worry. I won't be around much longer."

Did I hear correctly? Yeah! Peace at last.

Later on, Janelle entered Kayla's bedroom and placed a shopping bag from Nordstrom's with a note on her bed.

Chapter 37

"So here you are. In the sunroom. Not in the kitchen. Looking for a change of scenery?" Janelle placed a black and white Chandlery gift bag tied with pink and red chiffon ribbon on the table in front of Ali.

Ali didn't look up from the book she was reading.

Roxie jumped from Ali's lap and ran to Janelle.

"I haven't seen you read a book since I've been here. When we were kids, you were a reading machine. Are you sick?"

"I'm fine. Thanks for asking." Ali looked up from the book. "By the way, I haven't seen you working on your manuscript."

Without addressing the question, Janelle said, "A little bright in here, don't you think?" Janelle closed the white plantation shutters, blocking the bright afternoon sun; she rearranged the pillows on the sofa where her sister sat.

"What about our truce? This is my home and not yours. I'll do the decorating. Put your sunglasses on if it's too bright in here." Ali stood to reopen the shutters and her book fell to the floor. "Sorry. That sounded rude." She repositioned the pillows, returned to the sofa, and continued reading.

Earlier, Kayla had implored the two sisters to show politeness to each other. St. Ali was making an effort but her halo was slipping.

"No worries." Janelle kicked off her black patent-leather stepladder shoes and sat in the swivel club chair across from Ali. "What are you reading?"

"A biography of Marie Antoinette," Ali lied.

"I vaguely recall something about writing our biographies for each other," Janelle said. "For a class assignment, from Phoebe maybe?" She turned the chair away from Ali and motioned for Roxie to jump into her lap.

"It's as fresh in my memory as what I ate for breakfast. Phoebe gave the same assignment to all her English class students at the beginning of the school year. Every year. So we should both have four."

"You have a memory like a vise," Janelle said. "You won't let go of the past."

"You said it would be *fun* to write each other's biography. You tricked me. After I wrote yours when I was a freshman, you claimed you didn't have time for mine—the night before the assignment was due," Ali said.

"You were a better write—I mean, you had more time for homework. All my beauty pageants, cheerleading practice, and dating kept me busy. We both received A's, as I recall."

"I should have received two A's, one for you and one for me."

"Might be fun to resurrect those bios," Janelle said. "Never know what we might find."

"There are a zillion boxes in the garage. Probably some high school stuff in there. I promised Matt I'd get rid of most of it. After the banquet."

"Where are the boxes?"

"In the far corner. Marked *Alicia*. Might be two."

"I'll get them. While I'm gone, open your gift. Aren't you curious?" Janelle asked. She waved the bag in front of Ali.

"Still bribing me."

Barefooted, Janelle left the sunroom to retrieve the boxes with Roxie following. When Janelle was sure Ali couldn't see her, she gave Roxie a doggy cookie.

Ali regarded the attractive black and white bag that Janelle left on the table. She picked it up and then put it down. Overwhelmed with curiosity, she untied the ribbons and pulled out the colorful tissue. A lovely fragrance wafted from the bag when she peeked into it. She removed two small boxes affixed with intricate gold labels.

"So, what do you think?" Janelle asked when she returned to the sunroom. "I poked into your bathroom and couldn't find any girly creams or lotions."

"Thank you. This is a lovely gift. Things I would never buy for myself." She opened one of the containers and applied the fragrant lotion to her hands.

"Let's see if we can find anything interesting," Janelle said as she opened the box marked "Alicia."

The sisters searched through the items while laughing or groaning at the pictures of themselves in preposterous hairstyles and clothing of their youth. Many of the photos were of a tiara-wearing Janelle in ball gowns appropriate for a red carpet walk at a movie premiere.

"Look at this," Ali said. The photo was of a young Ali wearing her sister's crown placed in a crooked position on Ali's wild hair. "I remember when you put this on my head cockeyed. Why didn't you straighten it?"

"You had too much hair for a proper crown."

"Always about the hair."

"Why aren't there more photos of you? This is your memory box."

"Mother and Dad weren't interested in taking photos. You insisted that I was the better photographer, but I think you liked to practice posing."

"I was a little self-centered, wasn't I?"

Ali wanted to shout, *You bet your skinny butt you were,* but merely nodded in agreement. After Janelle left for college, Ali gave her 35mm camera and rolls of film to a friend. She hated taking all those pictures especially since Virginia relegated photos of Ali in less observable places around the house.

Janelle took a faded green folder from the box. "Look at these. Newspaper clippings and beauty pageant programs. You saved so many of my things, Ali."

"I was proud of you."

Janelle pulled out a blue ribbon with faded gold letters. "This was for the Miss Snowflake Pageant. Here's another one for the Little Miss Georgia Peach contest. I won those. First place."

"Seems to me you stopped entering the contests in high school," Ali said. "Why?"

"I wasn't as cute as I aged. Always a runner-up. Don't you remember? Every loss crushed Mother. At least according to her, second place was a loser. She pushed me to enter the Miss Georgia pageant and thought I had Miss America potential. We had a huge battle, and I told her no more of those silly pageants."

"But you were Miss Willoughby County and prom queen twice."

"I suppose." Janelle held up the ribbons and draped them across her chest and then continued searching the box. "Enough with nostalgia. I'll take care of dinner tonight and you get back to reading. We'll finish later."

Ali reflected on Janelle's stunning statement. If Virginia had been the driving force behind Janelle's foray into the world of beauty pageants, perhaps Ali had misjudged her sister for all these years. If Janelle and Ali's relationship had been better, maybe Janelle could have gone to Ali for support and commiseration.

From the doorway, Roxie whimpered as she watched her friend leave with treats in her pocket.

Ali doubted whether her sister knew how to operate a microwave, not to mention dinner for four people. "Janelle," Ali called out. "The takeout menus are on the bulletin board."

Ali took another folder from the box. A pink envelope decorated with Janelle's precise handwriting caught her attention. Inside was a piece of rose-colored stationery:

> *My dearest sister: If you die before me, which you probably won't because I'm older, this is what I will write for your obituary:*
>
> *Alicia Maureen Withrow_____(I'll leave this blank for your husband's name) who was known as Ali, led a happy life as a wife and homemaker in Willoughby, GA. She was the mother to four children who are all successful in their chosen professions. Alicia has a famous sister who is now touring the world promoting her latest blockbuster movie.*

Ali shook her head and continued to browse through the mementoes.

"Pizza? You must have the wrong address," Matt said to the Piece of Pisa deliveryman at the front door.

"Pizza. Yeah!" Kayla shouted. The enticing aroma of pepperoni brought the family, including Roxie, to the kitchen.

"Why did you pay, Matt?" Janelle asked innocently. "This was my treat."

"Another time."

Kayla, Matt, and Ali watched with amusement when Janelle selected a slice, folded it, and stuffed it in her mouth. She chose a second slice of the pizza covered with sausage and three kinds of cheese.

"Yummy. I had forgotten how much I like pizza," she mumbled between bites of the crust. "You people are a bad influence on me." Janelle tried to sneak a piece of pepperoni to her new friend.

"I saw that Janelle. We don't feed Roxie from the table," Matt admonished. "The vet says she's gaining weight."

"Do you have any beer?" Janelle asked, sneaking Roxie a sliver of sausage despite Matt's warning.

"Beer and pizza," Ali said. "Guess we are a bad influence."

Kayla, ever Janelle's handmaiden, went to the refrigerator and returned with a glass and a bottle of beer.

"I'll have one, too," Matt said.

"Do they have pizza in Italy, Aunt Janie?"

"Oh, the food is *buono molto*. The olive oil. The cheese. The gelato. The wine. The men."

"Wine?" Ali asked. "If and when you take Kayla to Italy, no wine."

"And, forget about the men," her dad added.

Janelle and Kayla shared a conspiratorial look.

After the family finished their meal, Janelle made an offer to clean up.

"You must be kidding," Matt said.

Remembering the truce, Ali said, "Thank you for the offer, Janelle."

"In that case, guess I'll go up to my office. That's what I'm calling my bedroom."

Kayla jumped up to follow her aunt.

Matt said, "Upstairs, young lady. You need to study—by yourself. Your aunt's room is off limits. Did you hear that, Janelle?"

Kayla rolled her eyes and headed upstairs.

Matt gathered the empty pizza boxes and put them in the garbage.

"What's in those boxes in the sunroom?" Matt asked.

"More of Phoebe's things. Guess I'll look through them now and get it over with."

"Need some help?"

"Old lady stuff. The box is light. Probably linens and handiwork from her travels."

Roxie entered the room and whimpered at Matt's feet. "Guess Roxie wants to take a walk."

Ali went to the sunroom to open the remaining box. She found a yellow and vermillion scarf made of a lustrous fabric and draped it around her shoulders. Ali closed her eyes and imagined standing in front of the Taj Mahal holding Matt's hand, or riding an elephant in Jaipur. She hoped she wouldn't have to wait until she was Phoebe's age to explore the world. Once Kayla was educated, if they had any money, they would take a long adventurous trip.

When she lifted another piece of fabric, something slid to the bottom of the box. Ali picked up a CD and read the title of one of Janelle's books—*Lust and Luck in Las Vegas* by Janelle Jennings. She held it in her hands, turning it over, scrutinizing it. Ali looked around the empty sunroom. She had the unsettling feeling she was holding contraband. This was the same guilty feeling that gripped her when Matt caught her in the kitchen at two a.m. eating a bowl of double chocolate fudge ice cream, sabotaging her so-called diet. She shoved the box into a corner out of sight.

Ali took the CD into the den. She had to work fast before Matt returned. He would accuse her of being overly suspicious of Janelle. Ali slid the CD into the computer and waited for the contents to appear on the screen. A manuscript, *Lust and Luck in Las Vegas,* popped up. Even though Ali had read all of Janelle's books, she barely recalled this one. The first sentence sounded like Janelle.

In desperation to escape the clutches of her abusive husband, Loralee Livingstone threw a few items into a brown paper bag: blow dryer, curling iron, makeup, and deodorant. She may be destitute but proper personal hygiene and an attractive appearance would help her survive any emergency. A few miles south of Las Vegas, the dented pickup with a missing bumper that she was driving sputtered to a halt. Loralee stepped out of the rusted truck and kicked one of its tires. "He didn't even have the decency to fill up the gas tank," she wailed to the dark and deserted desert.

Definitely Janelle.

Ali peered around the corner of the den to make sure the coast was clear. No Janelle. No Kayla. No Matt. No Roxie.

She went to the bookcase behind the desk where Janelle's books were enshrined, taking up an entire shelf. Ali pulled out the Las Vegas book. On the cover were a glamorous woman and a gorgeous man, both with spray tans and glistening skin wearing shirts unbuttoned to their navels. The contents of the CD and the book appeared identical.

While Ali was deciding whether to share this curious information with Matt, he appeared in the doorway. She turned to him and said, "Come here!"

"Okay. I'm coming."

"Look what I found." She still had the multicolored scarf draped around her shoulders.

"Exotic."

"Not this." Ali threw the scarf on the desk. "*This*. It's a CD of one of Janelle's books."

"So. What's the problem? Where did you find it?"

"At Phoebe's. Bring me the box in the sunroom. Maybe there are more. Please."

They sat next to each other at the computer while Matt inserted and ejected each CD after checking the contents.

"I don't get it," Ali wondered. "What're these doing in Phoebe's possession? Manuscripts with edits. See all the comments in red? A teacher thing."

"Was Phoebe Janelle's editor?" Matt asked. "You said they kept in touch."

"Phoebe wouldn't read these kinds of books, let alone edit them," Ali said. "No way would she want her name associated with lust or anything else in Las Vegas."

"That's the point. She didn't want anyone to know she worked with Janelle. The proof is here. There's no other explanation and Pee Pee's not around to corroborate or confess."

"Don't call her that. It's disrespectful."

"Sorry. But, why do we care if Phoebe was the editor? What difference does it make to us?"

"Maybe *you* don't care, but I sure do."

"All writers have editors. Janelle chose not to identify hers," Matt said. "Lower your voice. We don't need Janelle down here."

"We should give a damn because first of all she's shoved her success into my face for years and secondly we need to 'care' otherwise we'll be stuck with Janelle forever. I think she's in financial trouble and needs the income from another book." Ali returned to scanning the CDs on the computer screen.

"Jeez Louise! I forgot about the envelope," she shouted.

"Be quiet." He put his finger to his pursed lips.

"A manila envelope on the front seat of the pickup. Bring it in," Ali said, lowering her voice an octave. "Please," she added.

Matt retrieved the envelope Ali had found stuck between the stack of magazines Izzy had given her. He placed it next to the computer where Ali was sitting.

"I have a bad feeling about this. Here, you open it." She changed her mind. "No, I'll do it." She snatched the envelope from Matt and removed a piece of Phoebe's personalized ecru stationery. "No, you better read it." Her hands were trembling and she felt her face warming—a prelude to a red and itchy rash.

Matt read:

February 14

Janelle – I'm too old for this. I've enjoyed our partnership and the extra income. Our books have afforded Joe and me the opportunity to take many memorable trips throughout the world and comfort in our old age. You're on your own now, dear, but don't worry, I know you can do it. Sorry the enclosed outline is skimpy. I'm too tired to continue. Hope you can read my handwriting.

Fondly, Phoebe

"Phoebe wrote the books," Ali screamed. "I'm so mad I could swear."

"I get your anger, but do it quietly."

Ali grabbed the batch of CDs and one by one threw them on the floor. Some of the plastic holders crashed into furniture and cracked.

"Whoa," Matt warned. "This is your evidence. Without proof, Janelle will deny her partnership with Phoebe. I can hear Virginia now—'You've always been jealous of your sister. How dare you accuse her of deception?' Kayla will turn against the messenger. You can't win."

They gathered the CDs from the floor.

Ali grabbed Janelle's books from the shelves and flung them onto the floor. "These books are leaving this house. Burn them. Shred them. I don't give a damn what you do with them but get them the hell out of here."

"Stop for a second. What about Phoebe's role? She's complicit, too."

"She did it for the money."

"What do you think your sister did it for?"

"To make me miserable." As if in slow motion, Ali drifted to the floor into a seated position and landed on her tailbone. "Ow. That hurt." She realigned herself and sat with her legs crossed.

"Seriously? 'To make you miserable.' So now what's your plan? Ruin her? Retaliate? Get her back for all the grief she has tossed your way? This will hurt Virginia and Kayla as much as it will hurt Janelle."

"I don't know what I'm going to do and I don't know what I feel besides anger."

"Let's sleep on it." He repositioned the books on the shelf.

Ali continued, "For years she's made me feel inferior and inconsequential. If Janelle didn't have Phoebe, *she* might be the inferior and inconsequential one."

Matt extended his arms to Ali and pulled her up off the floor. "I'm going to bed. Nothing we can do tonight unless you want to pull her out of bed and confront her, which might wake Kayla." He faced Ali, put his arms around her waist, kissed her cheek and her neck. He moved his hands under her sweater and unfastened her bra.

"I'm not in the mood, Matt. I need time to process this giant fraud that Janelle has created."

"Have you noticed you're never 'in the mood' when your sister's around?" He gave her a cursory kiss on the lips before he left the room.

Ali took the envelope with Phoebe's note and outline to the kitchen. She took two aspirins and drank a glass of water. Her head felt like it was in a vise, the muscles in her back tightened, and her stomach churned. She sat at the kitchen table staring out the window at darkness. She recalled the years of politely acknowledging her sister's success to friends and neighbors—unearned, fraudulent, and deceitful achievement. Ali's mood turned from shock and anger to glee when she considered the possibilities for pain she could afflict on Janelle Jennings.

Ali laid Phoebe's letter and notes on the table. The handwriting on the outline was shaky and difficult to decipher. Ali went to her junk drawer, found a small magnifying glass, and put on her reading glasses. Ali could make out a few words. Phoebe reminded Janelle to introduce the reader to the setting, state the characters' goals, and create conflict. She should develop obstacles and find a resolution. There was something about a cover conference.

Not much to work with, nothing specific. What setting? What characters? What conflict? Evidently, it had been a formula that worked for eighteen books. Ali continued sitting at the table scribbling on a pad of paper she kept on the table. She knew that opening the envelope addressed to Janelle was sneaky. She doodled on the paper writing. *Alicia Lawrence novelist. Alicia Lawrence author of best sellers.*

"What am I thinking?" she said aloud. The discovery of the outline, if that's what this piece of yellow-lined paper with Phoebe's scratchy handwriting was, would solve both sisters' dilemmas. Janelle would take the outline, finish her novel, and leave Willoughby. Then, Ali would resume her peaceful life. Or, for retribution and revenge, Ali could hold onto Phoebe's notes.

Perhaps St. Alicia's not so saintly after all.

Chapter 38

To: Willoughby Book Banquet Committee
Fm: alilawrence
Subject: Laurel Atwood canceled

I rec'd a disappointing phone call from Laurel's agent. Laurel broke both her arms. Is unable to speak at the banquet. Guess I should say she could speak but hard to travel without the use of her arms. As you know, Laurel agreed to waive her fee and she is our major draw. We're sold out. Need to decide how to handle.

At the urging of some committee members, I'll invite my sister to attend our next meeting. And Brad too. Let's meet at Maggie's at 10 a.m. tomorrow. Please do your best to attend.

Ali

"Did you ask her to speak? For free?" Ali asked Ellen as they walked along Willoughby River crowded with joggers despite the humidity.

"I asked but no commitment. She wasn't eager to waive the fee. Claimed her people wouldn't approve."

"What people? She fired Bobby and I think she's worn down Ken."

"Did you try the blackmail part?"

"Not yet. Let's watch her reaction when she sits face to face with the committee members. I wonder what excuse she'll fabricate, if she turns them down."

"See you in a bit," Ali said. She returned home and dressed for the meeting.

Ali went to the rear of the Tea Shoppe. Maggie had placed a water pitcher and glasses in the middle of the reserved table. No tempting treats today. All members were present including Janelle. Ali distributed agendas and then welcomed Janelle. "The committee requested your attendance, so please feel free to speak." She took a sip of water. "I've invited Brad Patterson but he must be running—"

"Sorry, ladies," Brad said as he joined the group. "Excuse the way I'm dressed. Came straight from the gym."

"No apologies necessary," Vanessa said as she assessed his athletic body and "just had a swim" hair.

Janelle motioned to him to sit next to her even though the empty chair was across the table next to Ali. "Let's make room for Brad. Please sit over here." After some musical chairs, Brad took his place next to Janelle.

Ali noticed that Janelle sat practically in Brad's lap. He smiled and whispered something into her ear.

"I'm not sure why I was invited but I'm glad to be here," Brad said.

"We have two problems," Ali said. "We can't afford to pay a speaker's fee to Laurel's replacement, and we're over budget on food."

"One solution is sitting right here at the table," Ethyl suggested, as the committee directed its focus at Janelle.

"I haven't been asked, if that's what you mean," Janelle replied.

Ali's face reddened because she'd been asking Janelle for years.

"We're asking right now," Ethyl said. "Please, Janelle, we need your help."

"It's up to my sister," Janelle said as she tilted her head and pursed her lips.

"Of course, we want you to speak," Ali said. "In fact, we'll be delighted." She clenched her hand.

"Do you want us to beg?" Ellen asked.

Janelle gave Ellen the stink eye. "I suppose I could waive my fee, but you must not tell my agent. He'd be so upset with me."

"Why?" Ellen asked.

"He's funny that way. But sure, I'll be glad to help your banquet." The pro-Janellers clapped while the con-Janellers observed.

"Now, about a few details, if I'm the keynote speaker." She asked questions and made demands about the color scheme, menu, schedule, the flowers, publicity.

Ali tapped a pencil against a water glass. "I doubt that Brad wants to hear about the minutiae. We want you to accept the posthumous award for your grandmother."

"It's my honor. Something else. I might be able to solicit donations for the menu. Leave it to me. Anything else?"

"Thank you so much, Brad. You are our savior, our benefactor, our knight—" Janelle said.

"Thanks for the gratitude, Janelle. Have to attend another meeting." He stood to leave. "Great to be with you, ladies. Thanks for honoring my grandmother. I'm grateful."

"But..." Janelle's attempt to pull him back didn't work. "He's a busy man; we were lucky he joined us."

"Back to business," Ali said. "Any other items for discussion?"

Janelle watched Brad leave the store. When she thought no one was looking, she sent a text: *I don't believe you. Phoebe left something for me and I want it now!*

Chapter 39

"Did Kayla eat breakfast before she left?" Ali asked Matt when he joined her in the bedroom and delivered her daily dose of caffeine in an oversized mug with the inscription: "Put Your Big Girl Panties On."

"Mmm. Cinnamon hazelnut. Smells divine." She grasped the mug, contemplating the message she held between her hands.

He opened the shutters to let the bright morning sun in. "Kayla drank a new recipe of mine. A kale, carrot, yogurt, banana smoothie. Think she liked it."

"I doubt it, but I give you full credit for trying to convert her."

"How are you feeling? Tonight's the big night. I hope you got your beauty sleep. You tossed and turned way past midnight. Thinking about your discovery, I suppose."

"My problem is wondering why you aren't taking this more seriously," Ali asked. "You know how Janelle treats me. How she's treated me my entire life."

"Okay. I'm leaving the room and will reenter." Matt walked to the threshold of the bedroom, turned around, and faced Ali. "How could the witch do this to you?" He paused. "Does that sound better?"

"You make it difficult for me to stay mad at you. Thanks for the java, sweetheart. See you at the banquet." Ali blew him a kiss.

Ali mentally composed the words she would say to confront her sister before the banquet that night. She opened her laptop on the kitchen table and began to write the revelation that Phoebe was Janelle's ghostwriter. Ali's emotions alternated between anger toward her sister and fear for her own mental health. Hot vs. cold. Love vs. hate. Admiration vs. jealousy. Ali was tired of this tug of war and wanted to end it. She would have to take the first step and maybe now was the opportunity she needed.

Ali looked up from the laptop when Janelle entered the kitchen. "Breakfast?"

"I'll make something. Thanks though," Janelle said. Ali observed her putting a carb into the toaster. Then she poured tomato juice into a tall glass.

"Brad told me you helped him clear out some of Phoebe's things. You didn't happen to find anything for me, did you?"

"Why would Phoebe leave you anything?" Ali planned to prolong tormenting Janelle.

"Didn't I tell you? Phoebe and I stayed in touch. She followed my career and often wrote me fan letters."

"Phoebe? A fan? The doyenne of the Willoughby literary community a fan of your racy novels?"

"I suppose it does seem out of character. Are you sure you didn't find anything?"

"Give me an example," Ali said.

"A letter? A CD? She always sent..." Janelle hesitated. "You know something, Ali. I can tell by the devious look in your eyes and that half smile of yours. You're persecuting me because of some ill-contrived notion in your head, aren't you?"

Ali picked up the Chandlery bag she had filled with the CDs of Janelle's books. She shook the bag so the contents sounded like clapping hands.

"Yes, I found some items. CDs with all your stories on them."

"Your point is?"

"Why would Phoebe have these?" Ali asked.

Janelle left the bagel in the toaster and sat at the table. She put her head in her hands.

"She was more than an editor?"

"You may as well know. I'm ruined anyway," Janelle blubbered. She stood and walked to the liquor cabinet and returned with a bottle of vodka. She poured a generous amount into her tomato juice glass. "Before you say it, yes, it's early for a cocktail. This won't hurt me."

"Phoebe wrote your books. She was your ghostwriter."

"Do you think Phoebe would want her old lady friends to know she wrote *Hot Night in NOLA* or *Passionate Paris*? Absolutely not."

"How did it start?"

"Innocently. After my first book, Phoebe sent me a fan letter. She said she had some ideas for other novels in the same genre and sent me a first draft. I made a couple of changes, not many. Phoebe didn't want authorship credit. We worked out a financial agreement, and she said the money would give her security in her old age. Phoebe loved living a wild and reckless life through the pages of my— rather, *our* novels."

"You did some of the writing?"

"It was a partnership. For example, when Samantha Queensbury in *In Search of Eros* went to Greece to hunt down her archaeologist lover, I traveled to Greece and wrote about the countryside, the food, the clear blue water, the ouzo, and, of course, the sexy men. Phoebe traveled, too. She excelled at adding the international flavor. She could have been a travel writer."

"I remember when you took that trip. Right after one of your divorces. Mother was disappointed you didn't invite her to join you."

"Probably should have. She would love Greece. So would you."

"So, how much did you pay Phoebe?" Ali asked.

"I paid her generously—quarterly. If I was one day late, she'd let me know. The reason, I think, she hasn't left me an outline is because I haven't paid her from my latest advance. She wanted money upfront. Guess she didn't trust me."

Ali regarded her sister in disbelief. Janelle had aged in the short time since she had arrived in Willoughby. Her hair was disheveled and her gel manicure needed a visit to the nail doc.

"My point is, Janelle, you contributed more to these books than you think. You don't need Phoebe."

"I can't write by myself. I'm finished. I'll have to sell more jewelry, return my advance, and take Philip—number three, remember him, don't you?—back to court to try to reduce the alimony the bum is extracting from me. Now, Miles—number two, I think you liked him—he's no problem since he fell off the sailboat I bought him and drowned. Hmm. That reminds me. I should sell that boat. I'll put Ken on that right away. Can't bear to think about Gerald, the last one, that lousy, two-bit con artist." Janelle took a swig of the tomato juice after she ended her diatribe.

"Why didn't you and Phoebe share authorship, like many famous authors do?"

"I suggested that in the beginning. You probably find that hard to believe, but I did. Phoebe refused. I didn't push her. I should have persuaded Phoebe to choose a pseudonym, but I didn't press the issue. After the first couple of books, it was a moot point. The pretense is over. I'm finished. I'm a fraud." She put her head on the table and sobbed. Between sobs, she told Ali that she didn't know how to change her lifestyle. "I can't be poor. I can't live like you do."

Ali didn't realize she was poor, but if Matt lost his job or took a pay cut, poverty might become reality. "You have written—or, should I say, co-written eighteen novels. Don't you have the hang of it yet?"

"I proposed the plot. Phoebe sent me a detailed outline and photos clipped from magazines the way she pictured the characters. I took it from there." After a beat Janelle said, "I returned my manuscript to Phoebe for proofing. She'd grade me—like in high school. If she gave me a failing grade, I worked hard to improve, and sent it back to her. My editor said he never found grammatical or punctuation errors."

Janelle took a sip of the cocktail. "I could relate to most of the plots. It was like writing excerpts from my life—talented heroines tricked or seduced by handsome, nefarious men. Nevertheless, the heroine always was victorious. I worked hard." Janelle put her elbows on the table and cradled her head in her hands. She bellowed so loud Roxie came running to investigate the source of the frightening sound.

As Janelle gasped for breath between bellows, Ali pulled Janelle's head up by her hair and slapped her lightly on either side of her face.

"Damn you, Ali. That hurt."

"Snap out of it. You are downright maudlin. When did you ever give up anything? How many times were you a runner up in a beauty pageant, but you kept trying until you won? You can't give up now."

Janelle blew her nose and stammered, "Two beauty pageant titles plus Miss Willoughby County and twice for prom queen." She stopped sniffing and blowing. "Wasn't much to show for all the energy Mother and I spent."

"Do I have to slap you again?"

"I'm tired of living a lie. I think I should go away. Permanently. Will you write a glowing obituary about me and distribute it. Don't forget Facebook. Make sure you use a photo from a few years ago.

I'll fade away. Change my name. Find a job somewhere. I could wait tables or join a commune. Are there still communes? Where are they? I don't like hot weather. I know fashion. I could get a job at Macy's."

"It's against the law to fake a death. Don't get me involved. You can write your own obit and mail it from the commune or the coffee shop where you'll wait tables."

Janelle returned her head to the table and moaned and groaned some more.

"You have income? Royalties? Investments? Your condo in New York? "

Janelle made no mention of money she lost in the Ponzi scheme. "No condo. Philip stole it from me in the divorce. Or maybe it was Gerald. I'm homeless."

"You must be kidding," Ali said. *Now she'll never leave Willoughby.* "You must have something."

Janelle lifted her head and accepted the tissue Ali offered her. "Not much. A few pieces of jewelry. I sold the rest. While I've been here." She blew her nose a couple of times. "You were a good writer. Didn't you help me with some book reports or something? "

"Something like that."

"Let's team up again. We'll form a creative partnership. I'll give you credit. Janelle Jennings with Alicia Lawrence."

"How about Janelle Jennings *and* Alicia Lawrence? Or, Alicia Lawrence *with* Janelle Jennings."

"Whatever you want, Li'l Sis."

"We can't live in the same house without discord and you want to write a book with me. Do you realize how close proximity will drive us both nuts?"

"I'll change. I promise."

"I don't even know if I can write anymore. The library's newsletter is about the only writing I've done lately and a few obituaries I embellish. Besides, why should I help you?"

Ali considered the consequences if she didn't help her sister. "I'll think about it," Ali said as she left with Roxie. She paused at the doorway, turned around to face Janelle. "I've thought about it. You'd better come up with an alternative. We can't work together."

Janelle moved from the table and snatched her purse that was sitting on a nearby chair. She pulled out a bottle of pills and popped one in her mouth.

Ali pulled her cell from her pocket and called Ellen.

"You've reached Ellen Mannerly. Please leave a message."

"She's a fraud. She didn't write all those books by herself. Phoebe was her ghostwriter. I can't believe this is happening. And then you'll never guess what she asked me to do—write with her. Can you believe that?" Ali hung up.

Ellen returned the call. "You've always wanted to write a novel."

"But that was a long time ago."

"You've got a big decision in your hands. I can't help you."

This is one time in my life when chocolate won't help.

Chapter 40

The landline phone rang while Ali was getting dressed for the banquet. "Kayla. Please get that." The ringing continued. Ali walked to the phone in her underwear. "Ken. How nice to hear from you. I suppose you want Janelle."

"I was hoping to talk to you. Privately. Without Janelle knowing. Is this a good time?"

Ali took the phone into her bedroom and closed the door. "Have to dress for the banquet but I have time."

"I'm at the Willoughby Inn. So worried about Janelle I thought I should make another visit. On my way to Savannah. I'm hoping you can shed some light on Janelle's odd behavior. We have a relationship more than author and agent. Perhaps you didn't know."

Ali couldn't hide her shock. She stammered something and then said, "I didn't know."

"Not a romantic relationship. Janelle's hardly my type. Kidding, of course. She'd never give a short fat man a minute's notice. We have a sibling relationship. In fact, I have her power of attorney and have witnessed her last two weddings. You've probably noticed that we bicker back and forth like brother and sister."

Ali wondered what was coming next.

"Something's wrong and I'm worried. Her finances are in a huge mess."

"We're in no position to help her."

"Here's how you *can* help. She must finish her book. It's imperative. Maybe this big speaking fee from the banquet will keep the creditors off, for now. If she's not worried about bills, maybe she can relax and concentrate on writing."

"Speaking fee?"

"For replacing Laurel Atwood."

"Ah yes. Maybe that will help." Ali had to bite her tongue to prevent her from revealing Janelle's lie.

"I don't know what I can do, Ken. I want to help her."

"She admires you."

"Ha. You're kidding."

"She's confided in me that she'd like to slow down and move to Willoughby. Lead a life that's not so egocentric."

Ken's announcement baffled Ali. "I find it hard to believe that Janelle would be happy in Willoughby. Anyway, what can I do?" she repeated as she looked at the clock on the bedside table.

"Find out what's going on and report back to me. You have my card?"

"Somewhere."

He gave her his cell number. "Will you call me if you learn anything?"

"Are you coming to the banquet tonight?"

"Yes."

"We're sold out but we'll find a seat."

"That brings up another subject. I took the liberty of sending out a news release announcing Janelle's appearance tonight and updating her website. Your dad's idea."

"Oh boy."

"One more thing. Please don't tell her I'm coming. I'll stand in the back and observe. A million thanks, Ali. You're a real Georgia peach." He hung up.

"I want to go back to sleep," she said to Roxie who was taking a nap on the bed.

Before leaving for the banquet, Ali tilted the freestanding oak mirror in her bedroom for a final head-to-toe evaluation. As she scrunched up her face and shook her head in disappointment, the chandelier earrings Janelle insisted she wear made swishing noises. Ali preferred mute earrings. She unhooked the golden strands and chose a simple pair of quiet pearl studs from her limited jewelry collection. The lime green and lemon yellow floral cotton chiffon dress she purchased from the clearance rack at Macy's was a departure from her more conservative wardrobe choices. Although the dress was sleeveless, the jacket covered her untoned arms. A discarded flower arrangement or the produce department at Kroger's came to Ali's mind when she saw her reflection in the mirror. Ali rarely looked into the mirror, taking the attitude that what she didn't know wouldn't hurt her. If Matt had been home, he would say she was beautiful because that's what he always said.

"Kayla, would you come in here for a minute?"

"In a sec, Mom." Kayla was sending selfies to her friend Emily. Kayla was proud of her hot pink halter dress with sugar-white polka dots and pleated skirt that Janelle had surprised her with along with a pair of black patent leather ballet flats.

"Mom's calling. Probably needs a wardrobe consultation."

While Kayla was skipping into her parents' bedroom lifting the sides of her polka-dotted skirt like a carefree kindergartner, the doorbell rang. "Wait a sec, Mom. Someone's at the door." Kayla opened the door to face Logan who was clutching something behind his back.

"Here," he said, as he shoved flowers toward Kayla.

"Wow. A corsage? But why?"

Logan hung his head and turned to leave. "I told my dad it was a bad idea."

"No, I didn't mean that. The flowers are beautiful. Pink and purple."

"The woman in the flower shop helped me. She said you could wear it on your wrist, or pin it to your purse, or pin it to your dress. I wanted you to have something special from me because you're so excited about your aunt's speech tonight."

"Thank you, Logan." Kayla hesitated. "You're a good friend."

"You look pretty," he said in a hushed voice.

"Kayla. Where are you?" Ali shouted.

"Sorry, I gotta go." She leaned over and kissed him on the lips before she went inside.

Logan walked to his bike, which was leaning up against the porch column, and touched his lips.

"What's up, Mom?"

"How do I look? Are these shoes okay with this dress?"

Kayla circled her mother like a judge at the Westminster Kennel Club Dog Show. She placed a finger on the side of her cheek and tilted her head. "A higher heel would be more flattering to your ankles but the neutral color of the kitten heel defuses the bright colors of the dress," newly self-appointed fashionista Kayla critiqued. "I think the dress works for you. You look pretty, Mom. It's about time you gave up wearing beige."

"Oh, I'm so glad you approve. Thank you." She gave her daughter a hug, being careful not to smear her lipstick.

"Look at you. You're adorable. Where did this come from?"

"Aunt Janelle didn't have time to take me shopping. She picked this out. With you in mind. Not too short, not too revealing," Kayla said with a smile referring to previous discussions with her mom about appropriate attire for a teenager.

"Are you wearing perfume? Smells like Janelle."

"She let me spray a little on my wrists." Before Ali could respond Kayla said, "You should wear lipstick more often."

"What's this?" Ali held the emerald pendant hanging around Kayla's neck and examined it. "Where did it come from?"

"Aunt Janie gave it to me."

"A nice gesture. Don't lose it. Looks expensive." Ali examined the sparkling jewel. "And the corsage?"

Kayla raised her wrist. "Logan."

"He's a thoughtful young man." Ali glanced at her watch. "Where is Janelle? I haven't heard any movement upstairs. She needs hours to get ready even for a trip to the mailbox."

Kayla's face reddened as she faced her mother.

"Something wrong, honey?"

"I don't think Aunt Janie is feeling too great. I helped her upstairs and put her to bed. Maybe I should have told you sooner."

"What's wrong with her?" Ali asked.

"She was shaky on her feet and was slurring her words. I thought a long nap would help."

"I'm not surprised. She drank almost a whole bottle of vodka laced with tomato juice."

"She can handle it. I don't think she's drunk, if that's what you mean." She gave her mother that all too familiar *why do you always pick on her* expression.

"Better check," Ali said.

Mother and daughter raced up the stairs and entered Janelle's bedroom without knocking. Janelle was lying on the side of the bed with the fingertips of one dangling arm touching the carpet. Her mouth was open and saliva dripped down her chin like a leaky faucet. Her cockeyed red silk eye mask gave her a demented look. Since stroke victims probably can't snore, Dr. Ali made a diagnosis:

drunk and out of commission. Prognosis: a severe headache in the morning.

"Janelle, wake up. Now!" Ali bent over the bed and shook her sister's shoulder.

"Why are you so mean to her? She needs to sleep a little," Kayla said.

"How could you, Janelle? I know our 'little' book banquet is insignificant to you, but many people have spent countless volunteer hours in preparation. We have a sold-out crowd. You have no license to swoop into town on your glitzy broom and disrespect the committee members and me. Get into the bathroom and try to get ahold of yourself." Ali immediately regretted her outburst, especially in front of Kayla, but a demonic force grasped her. Days of bottled up anger spewed from her mouth like a projectile. "I'm warning you, Janelle. I will not cover for you or make lame excuses this time. I will speak from the podium into the microphone, as loud as I can, and tell the audience that you are a no-show tonight because you decided to check into the Betty Ford clinic."

Ali moved toward the door. She turned around facing Kayla who knelt at the side of Janelle's bed. "Kayla, help your aunt. Don't leave her alone for a minute. We need her tonight, even though I hate to admit that."

"You called me a switch. Xan...Xanash...fell asleep," Janelle muttered as she pushed her bangs off her forehead. She wiped her wet face with the back of her hand. With Kayla's help, she sat up.

"Waz the time?"

"Time for you to think about someone other than yourself. Call your dad, Kayla, and tell him to pick up you and our keynote speaker, if she sobers up. Make sure she wears something modest and no boobs hanging out of her dress. No stilettos. Be there by seven o'clock."

"What if she's actually sick?" Kayla asked.

"Don't worry about your aunt. Call your dad. I'm leaving."

Chapter 41

When Ali entered the community center's banquet room, she admitted its appearance benefited from Janelle's suggestions to the decorations committee. The women had transformed the beige non-descript room into a colorful and festive banquet hall.

Janelle requested red and black for the color theme to coincide with the cover of her supposedly soon-to-be published book. This forced the committee to return the previously purchased pastel colored decorations to Party City.

"Whatever Janelle wants Janelle gets, I suppose. Some things never change," Maggie opined when she met Ali at the front door.

"Oh, it's so beautiful. It looks like a Valentine's Day dance," gushed Lisa, observing the scene. "Wish we could get our husbands to attend."

Low towers of Janelle's books were stacked in the middle of the tables covered in red plastic. The book banquet committee had stockpiled these books for years in the hope that the local girl who became a famous author would one day speak at the banquet. Plastic tiaras purchased at a dollar store sat on top of each stack of books.

Ali made a furtive trip to a table in the rear of the room and turned its tiara upside down.

Red and black balloons were in abundance. If Ali chose, she could burst Janelle's balloon tonight and reveal her as a fraud. One negative to this potential exposé was that Kayla and Virginia would never forgive Ali. In addition, the truth would tarnish Phoebe's reputation as an esteemed and admired Willoughby resident. Ali proceeded to her assigned table and found her place card positioned next to her sister. She switched the place cards so that Matt served as a barricade between the two. Ali put her index cards with notes in her pocket and put her purse on the chair. She had memorized acknowledgment of special guests. The cards listed everyone else who deserved gratitude and recognition along with the winners of the student-writing contest.

Ali checked her watch. Only an hour before her introduction of Janelle and she hadn't decided which road to take—an adoring sister or a truthful, albeit spiteful, one. She could give the usual and expected accolades, expressing pride in her sister's accomplishments. She could tell the crowd how grateful the committee was to Janelle for agreeing to replace Laurel Atwood. Or, she could expose Janelle.

Ali stayed up the previous night and into the morning thinking about how to accomplish the betrayal without portraying herself as a jealous, untalented sibling who would never equal her sister's acclaimed reputation. About two a.m., Ali decided to take a sarcastic approach. "Ladies and gentlemen," she would begin. "We are here tonight to honor all writers, famous and not so famous and to recognize our own deceased Phoebe Patterson. Mrs. Patterson was a best-selling novelist who sold millions of books. You weren't aware of that were you? This humble woman never spoke of her success. Now, will Janelle Jennings, my duplicitous sister, please join me and reveal the secret she and Mrs. Patterson have shared for years."

Oh, you wouldn't do that, Ali. Or would you?

Ali walked to the buffet table that continued the red and black color theme. She admired the variety of entrées and the medley of enticing salads. Thanks to Brad and his contacts, the food was impressive. Shrimp and grits, pecan-crusted chicken, medallions of beef, and spinach and Portobello mushroom lasagna filled silver chafing dishes. Jill's eye-catching floral centerpiece of blood red roses, hot pink Stargazer lilies, and vermillion tulips was nestled into a black Grecian urn.

A separate table displayed Maggie's luscious lemon bars and Virginia's triple chocolate brownies. She hoped her mother saved a batch of her ultra-rich decadent dessert for family consumption.

"The centerpiece is dazzling, but looks expensive. You should submit a bill to the committee," Ali said when Jill asked for an opinion.

"No worries. Brad paid for it. Told me to keep it a secret. He said it was in honor of Phoebe even though she wasn't partial to cut flowers. I think it's a little over the top, but he likes it."

Ali approached the podium to check the mike. She surveyed the room to imagine her reaction when two-hundred pairs of eyes focused on her. Although public speaking made her anxious, she was more apprehensive about introducing her sister because the consequences were significant.

"There you are," Ellen said. "Have you decided? What're you going to say? Are you okay?"

Ali stepped down to answer Ellen. "I'm shaking all over. Even my hair is nervous." She twirled a piece of hair around a finger. "I wish I had never found those darn CDs. Do you think you could sneak a tiny piece of one of Mother's brownies to me? Chocolate is so calming."

"No. You'll have to wait. You don't want to address the audience with chocolate between your teeth. And keep your hands off your hair."

"Thanks, my good friend. Have to make the rounds."

Early arrivals packed the non-alcoholic bar, sipping punch and soft drinks. Most would have preferred a cocktail or a glass of wine, but local government prohibited alcohol on city-owned properties.

When Ali found the Book Babes' table, her friends encircled her and complimented her appearance. *How do we manage without girlfriends?* Ali couldn't remember Janelle mentioning female friends. She surrounded herself with members of the male species: agent, editor, personal assistant, publicist, hair stylist. Wasn't much different in high school, as Ali recalled.

Ali circulated the room congratulating volunteers for the decorations and the beautiful buffet table. Every few minutes she removed index cards from her pocket with names of people she would acknowledge. The cards were beginning to warp as Ali's hands moistened. While rereading the names, she searched the room for Mrs. Knox. Ali asked Vanessa, "Where is Mrs. Knox? She made a substantial donation."

"She snuck outside to take a quick smoke. She doesn't care if this is a non-smoking facility inside and out. Who's going to forbid her from doing what she wants?" Vanessa said.

Sounds like someone I know, Ali thought.

"Shouldn't Janelle be here by now?" Vanessa wondered.

"She had to take a call from her publicist. The life of a busy author," Ali lied. The longer Janelle was in town, the more Ali's nose grew. "Will you please put a glass of water on the lectern for her?"

An out of breath Lisa reported to Ali. "People are arriving without tickets; they are adamant about staying. One lady said she had bought every book Janelle had written and she was going to hear Janelle speak if she had to climb through a window."

"As long as they don't expect dinner, we can set up chairs around the perimeter of the room. Hope the fire marshal doesn't catch us. Make them pay the full amount. After the ticket holders have eaten, they can help themselves to whatever's left. That might satisfy Janelle's fans. How many are out there?"

"I didn't count. At least fifty."

"Fifty? You're kidding. We can't accommodate that many," Ali said.

"Got a riot on our hands," Lisa said.

"Let the first twenty-five in. After they take their seats, we'll talk to the others. Need time to think of a solution."

"You'll think of something."

Ali scanned the room until she found Diane. "Will you host a private book signing at your store tomorrow? For Janelle's fans we turned away. They have their own books, if that's a problem."

"What?"

"Could you open early? I'll explain later. Ask Maggie if she can supply scones and coffee cake. Find a clipboard. Get the names of the people in line. Tell the crowd we'll have a VIP event in the morning. Everyone wants VIP status."

Ali didn't wait for Diane to respond. She glanced at her watch— five minutes to seven and no Janelle. Ali pulled out her cell and called her husband.

"Relax. See you in five," Matt said when he answered the phone. "That woman takes forever to get dressed." He paused. "She looks great."

"I don't care if she's wearing a paper bag. Get her here. Now."

Seven o'clock. Time to start. Why penalize punctuality?

Ali couldn't find Ellen in the crowd so she called her cell and asked her to go to the podium and ask everyone to line up at the buffet by table numbers. "I need time to think," Ali said.

Lisa scurried back inside. "We found a few more chairs and squeezed in thirty. Good idea to send Diane out there. I think they are appeased. You sure can think on your feet, Ali. Hope you'll take the job of chair again next year."

"Let's get through tonight," Ali replied. She observed the outside scene from a window at the back. A long line of women and a few men stretched around the building. She was shocked when she saw that they were holding books—not one or two but three or four. The loyalty of Janelle's fans amazed her. After Laurel Atwood canceled, Ali decided only ticket holders would learn of the change in speakers. No one complained or asked for a refund. Ali could *thank* Ken for the long line of Janelle's fans.

Janelle often bragged that she had more devoted fans than Laurel Atwood. Ali considered that statement another one of Janelle's exaggerations. Evidently not, if the number of people was any measurement. If Janelle had agreed to speak in previous years, the book committee would have made a huge profit. They would have doubled the price of the tickets and moved to an upscale venue rather than the modest community center.

Matt drove to the passenger drop off at the center. Janelle, Kayla, Virginia, and Ed exited the car. Janelle's fans immediately recognized her and began to clap. She was steady on her feet and wisely chose ballet flats thanks to Kayla's influence. Janelle walked up the line of fans toward the entrance, greeting each person, signing books, and thanking them for their loyalty. At seven p.m., the need for Janelle to wear huge sunglasses was pointless. Maybe she was adding to her glamorous reputation or hiding bloodshot eyes. Kayla walked beside her aunt opening books for Janelle to sign. Janelle handed her Kate Spade clutch to Virginia to hold. Her brilliant red lipstick made her white teeth luminescent. Regardless of the flat shoes, dressed in a gold metallic lace sheath with an asymmetric neckline spliced on one shoulder, the diva had arrived.

Harriett Bell, president of the library association, greeted the Withrows and the Lawrences and ushered them to their seats. Several library board members stopped by to pay homage to Janelle.

Ali found Kayla and said, "Please get your aunt a plate of food, pasta salad, biscuits and butter—anything that has lots of fat."

"She won't eat that kind of food."

"She will tonight. Tell her I said so."

Kayla said something to Janelle, and headed to the buffet table. Ali noticed that she politely, but confidently, went to the front of the line. Kayla had not inherited her mother's meekness gene. Ali preferred to ignore Janelle, but that would be difficult tonight since her sister was the featured speaker. She sucked up her annoyance, approached Janelle, and admitted, "You look beautiful. No black and red—to match your book cover?"

"Now, I wouldn't want to blend in with the table decorations, would I?"

"That's a smart-alecky comment for someone whose reputation is about to disintegrate."

Janelle shrugged her shoulders.

Matt joined his family at their table in front of the podium along with two library board members. Ali searched the room and found Brad mingling with his grandmother's cronies. He wore a navy blue blazer, crisp white shirt, lavender tie, and contrasting pocket scarf. His scruffy beard could put him on the cover of *GQ*. A young woman with long blond hair and a curvaceous body was clinging to his arm. When she stepped away from Brad, Ali said, "You're at the table next to us. Is that your date?"

"Let's say she's an old friend." He winked at Ali.

"Not so old," Ali countered. "Gorgeous, too. Be careful of beautiful women."

"Maybe I should introduce her to Janelle," Brad smirked.

"You're mean." Ali shook her finger at him. "She has enough on her mind tonight. See you later."

Ali returned to her table where questions addressed to a subdued and polite Janelle dominated the conversation.

"What did Brad have to say?" Janelle asked. "I see he brought one of Kayla's classmates."

"Looks her age, up close. Late twenties," Ali said with a smile.

A photographer from the *Willoughby News & Record* approached Ali and asked her to pose with her sister. "No way—I mean, let's get a photo of Janelle with some of the donors and volunteers." Ali could see her mother eyeing the photographer with the goal of finagling herself into the photos. Ali had no desire to see her photo in the paper next to her beautiful sister.

When most people had finished their dinner and were enjoying dessert, Ali decided it was showdown time. She took her place at the podium, turned on the mike, and scanned the audience. "Welcome," she said while making eye contact with Matt who pointed to his ear and mouthed *louder*. She fumbled her index cards and watched them sail to the floor. A few hushed "oohs" were heard from friends who shared Ali's pain. She left the notes on the floor because she didn't need them. She had made her decision.

Chapter 42

"**W**elcome," she repeated in a slightly stronger and more confident voice. She removed her reading glasses. "Sorry. I already said that. Well, I guess I must want to doubly welcome you since I said it twice." The audience politely laughed. Ali thanked the benefactors and volunteers of the book banquet. She acknowledged Willoughby's popular mayor, who made an appearance before he moved on to the next community event. She didn't know if her nervousness was caused by fear of public speaking or because of what she was about to reveal. She took a sip of water from the glass she had requested earlier for Janelle.

After a deep breath, she took off. "I'm overflowing with happiness tonight. I'm so proud of our community for supporting reading, authors, independent booksellers, our beloved libraries, and even eBooks. We must embrace all forms of literature, but for most of us here tonight, we want to hold a traditional book in our hands." The crowd applauded. Ali sipped more water, and then announced the awards for the best short story by middle and high school students. "We'll present these awards at end-of-the-year ceremonies at the schools. Our goal next year is to expand the contest and solicit entries from adult writers." After her pulse returned to normal, she said, "We have another announcement."

Janelle curled her fingers until the knuckles whitened.

"Will Bradley Patterson, Phoebe Patterson's devoted grandson, please join me?"

Brad went to the podium and kissed Ali on the cheek.

"We are presenting a posthumous award to Phoebe Patterson for making the most impact on Willoughby's reading community. In the future, this award will be named in honor of Mrs. Patterson." Ali handed Brad a framed certificate and then stepped back.

Brad's comments about his grandmother were as poignant as they were at her memorial service. "As you know, my grandmother was the founder and a supporter of the Willoughby Book Awards Banquet. She left in her will a gift of $25,000 to this group." He glanced at Janelle who took a sip of water.

Ali stared at Brad in disbelief. She recalled Brad saying Phoebe had money invested in stock. *Was this donation Phoebe's money or Brad's?*

The audience was shocked into silence by this generous gift from a woman they assumed lived on a modest income. When Ali encouraged the audience to applaud, they gave a standing ovation. After the audience quieted, Brad continued. "I'm placing my trust in Ali Lawrence's hands. She and her committee will decide how to allocate the money. For many years, my grandmother had supported aspiring writers with potential." Brad looked at Janelle. "Perhaps the committee will find a way to continue Mimi's desire to encourage writers."

The audience went wild with applause. Brad left the podium and Ali took his place at the microphone.

Ali was surprised as anyone in the audience. She tried to think of a comment and took a sip of water to kill time. "With this magnanimous gift from Mrs. Patterson, we will expand our program and have a true festival which will rival all cities our size in the country."

More applause. "I have another reason for joy tonight." Ali paused and stared at her sister, whose complexion, though not as radiant as usual, was several shades of green lighter than it had been earlier. Then she looked at Kayla and Virginia who beamed with pride.

"Willoughby's darling daughter and popular novelist stepped in at the last minute to replace Laurel Atwood." The audience applauded and Janelle gave a royal wave to acknowledge the adulation. "In addition, she agreed to forego her usual speaking engagement fee." Ali scanned the back of the room, looking for Ken. "I was proud of my sister when we were young and my pride is a hundred-fold tonight. Please help welcome, our own, Janelle Jennings." *Was that a tear in Janelle's eye?*

Janelle heaved a big sigh of relief. Matt escorted Janelle to the dais and handed her over to Ali. Janelle was steady on her feet so maybe there was hope that she wouldn't pass out before she finished speaking. The sisters hugged. Ali returned to her seat next to her husband.

Matt kissed her hand. "You took the high road. Congratulations."

"Fasten your seat belt." She paused. "I still have another opportunity to speak."

Matt gave Ali a puzzled look.

"Thank you, my darling sister." Janelle hesitated. "And Willoughby Book Awards Banquet—you assumed that I ignored your wonderful event. Admit it. You did, didn't you?"

A few people said "yes" and nervous giggles rippled through the room.

"Oh, I know there are more of you out there. You thought Janelle Jennings said this lovely banquet wasn't a big enough audience, didn't you?"

The entire audience applauded.

"Here I am, hanging my head in shame for ignoring this town and the people who discovered my talent. My excuses were always valid. Nevertheless, I should have allowed time for you and for my family."

Ali looked toward Ellen who wrinkled her face and stuck her tongue out as if to say *icky*.

Janelle extended her arms to her family. The multiple rows of thin, gold bracelets she wore jangled like wind chimes on a blustery day. She stretched her arms again to include the audience. More applause. They loved the woman. *She should run for public office.*

"I'm not unlike some of my more outrageous characters, each of whom had a serious character flaw. Since you read my books, you know that my heroines redeem themselves. That's what I am doing tonight. I'm going to redeem myself and give ten percent—" She paused. "Correction. Make that fifteen percent of the profits from my next book to the Willoughby Book Awards Banquet." This announcement generated another standing ovation.

Janelle's announcement shocked Ali, but she was pleased with her sister for pledging a financial donation. In Janelle's twisted way, she was trying to make amends with Ali by contributing to her favorite project. Only one problem, Janelle hadn't written the book. She might never write another book since Phoebe was dead.

Janelle continued speaking. She gave an animated and engaging recap of her life as a writer—or half a writer, if the audience knew Janelle's secret. At the end of her presentation she said, "Now I'd like to call my sister and the banquet committee to come forward."

"This was not part of the plan," Jill grumbled to Maggie.

With Janelle's encouragement, they approached the stage and climbed the steps. Ellen remained seated with her arms folded, staring at Janelle.

"A round of applause for this hard working committee," Janelle said once the uncomfortable committee members had gathered on the stage. "Now for the pièce de résistance. On behalf of a grateful town, please accept this token of our appreciation to our very own, my sister, my friend—Ali Lawrence—for her hard work and dedication." Janelle turned her back and took something from one of the community center's employees. It was a twenty-four inch plastic trophy with an imitation gold Lady Victory on top. Although the audience clapped, a few chortles were audible.

"If that's not the ugliest thing I've ever seen," Ed said to Matt. "Where in the hell are you going to put it?"

"How about your workshop?"

The committee members seemed puzzled as they exchanged glances. "I thought we agreed to a little plaque," Maggie said to Diane.

"Let's get the heck off this stage," Jackie said. "This is humiliating."

Ali stood back so her sister could wrap up her speech, but Janelle grabbed her arm so hard the trophy fell to the ground and poor Lady Victory lost her head.

"Never mind, about that," Janelle mumbled to a stunned Ali. "One more announcement," Janelle directed to the audience.

"As if that wasn't enough," Matt said to Ed. "What now?"

"I am pleased to announce that I will co-author my next book with someone I love and admire. My fabulous sister, Ali Withrow Lawrence, will collaborate with me for my next book. "Won't you?" Janelle said into Ali's ear as they hugged. "I need your help." Janelle waited for the audience's reaction. A few people applauded and others murmured to each other.

Ed, Matt, Virginia, and Kayla looked at each other. Virginia and Kayla applauded. Ed and Matt shook their heads.

"Anything for the family. That's our Ali," Ed said.

"Won't hold my breath," Matt said.

Ali felt as though an arctic blast had invaded the room. She rubbed her hands together and held her jacket close to her body.

Her euphoria from Brad's announcement of the $25,000 donation vanished. A million scenarios pulsated in Ali's head. She wanted to write a novel, didn't she? Hadn't that always been her secret, unspoken except to a few trusted people? Still stunned, Ali thanked Janelle and the audience and the evening was over. Ali stood at the podium and watched Janelle's fans approach her.

When Ali joined her family, Matt put his arms around her and kissed her on the lips. Ali remembered others offering congratulations, but the rest of the evening was a blur. Ali considered options. If Matt was serious about buying the store, she wouldn't have time for Janelle. But, if he was unemployed, she would jump in, grit her teeth, and co-write a novel as a source of income even though there was no guarantee that the book would sell. Maybe they could divide the writing and meet on the computer. Ali could set the ground rules. *What am I thinking? This will never work. Janelle will have to find a ghostwriter to replace Phoebe, finish the book, and get out of my Willoughby.*

Ali never saw Ken, so she assumed he changed his mind and didn't attend. As she was leaving, she received a text message. She read it unassisted. "Thanks. I knew you'd come through. She doesn't need to know I was here. KL"

Chapter 43

The piercing drumming sound of a red-bellied woodpecker that frequented the Lawrence's metal gutters during mating season awakened Ali from another night of restless sleep. Sunlight streamed through the half-opened shutters. She kept her eyes closed and stretched her arm across the bed searching for Matt. When she turned over and opened her eyes, she felt the empty space.

"I wish Woody would hurry up and find a wife," Ali said to Matt when he entered their bedroom.

"You were having some wild dreams last night," Matt said. "Still upset with your sister?" He kissed Ali on top of her mussed hair. "She placed you in an awkward situation announcing you were going to co-write with her."

"How did I react? Shocked? Angry?"

"All of the above and then some," Matt said.

Ali mumbled, "Coffee, please. I need an extra strong brew this morning." She sat up and leaned against the headboard. Janelle's announcement reverberated in Ali's head like a clanging bell at a boxing match.

Matt handed the mug to her, which read, "Stressed is desserts spelled backwards." She hugged it with both hands and inhaled the French roast. "Is the Queen of Deception up?" Ali asked.

Matt sat on the side of the bed. "She wasn't a few minutes ago. Aren't you at least flattered that she wants you to write with her?"

"She's desperate. Janelle has no money to hire a ghostwriter and she thinks she can subject me to servitude. I'm not bailing her out of this mess."

"Do what makes you happy. Words of advice—make sure you have no regrets."

"Hope we have a decent turnout at the bookstore, not for Janelle's benefit, but for all my friends who jumped in at a moment's notice to organize the event. Thanks for the coffee, hon, and for all the support. Sorry I get so crazy. I'll make it up to you, if you know what I mean."

Matt gave her the thumbs-up sign.

She glanced at the bedside clock—time to get dressed. This morning Ali didn't fret about what to wear. No longer would she allow Janelle's opinion to influence her hairstyle, clothing choices, or home decorating. For the first time, Ali felt in control of the relationship. She had the upper hand and planned to use it.

Ali searched the closet for her favorite denim skirt and white Mexican embroidered peasant blouse, but couldn't find them. She loved that blouse even though Virginia called it a hippie shirt. She noticed that her closet seemed sparse. Ali didn't remember having so many empty hangers. She searched for another favorite outfit and then another. Her worn brown loafers were missing, too. There was only one explanation—*Janelle*. Ali tried on a pair of turquoise paisley pants she bought on sale hoping that one day she could squeeze into them without the aid of shapewear. She took a deep breath, pulled them on, and easily fastened the buttons. *Yeah!* She hadn't weighed herself in several weeks. This was a much better measurement—pants that fit and that didn't impede breathing. One of her many white blouses was relatively wrinkle-free so she chose that and tied the red and gold scarf from Phoebe's box under the collar. *Janelle wouldn't approve of my color choices, but I don't care.* She reached for her go-to pearl stud earrings and held them in her hands. *Conventional. Classic. Boring.* She noticed a pair of silvery dangling earrings she bought at a crafts fair but never felt comfortable wearing. *Why not?* A quick application of makeup followed by an approving glance in the mirror and she was ready to face her sister.

Ali found Janelle slouched at the kitchen table with Roxie sitting at her feet. Janelle was dressed and appeared ready for the book signing. Her eyelids were puffy, her skin was sallow, and she had applied too much cheek color—telltale signs of sleep deprivation. Her black and brown outfit matched her funereal expression.

"I'm missing some clothes, Janelle. You wouldn't happen to know what happened to them?"

"Good morning to you, too. Why would I know?"

"I don't think Stacy and Clinton from *What Not to Wear* invaded my closet."

"I don't know what you're talking about." Janelle bent down to pet Roxie. "About last night. You could have ruined me."

"Saving your reputation wasn't my motive. I wanted to shield Kayla and Mother from embarrassment."

"I was terrified you were going to expose me. If you had, I wouldn't have blamed you. My sisterly attributes are lacking."

Ali's eyes widened. Janelle had never taken responsibility for her transgressions and certainly not for being a lousy sister.

"Why didn't you discuss your announcement last night with me? I told you no. Remember? I said we couldn't work together."

"A girl can hope." Janelle folded her hands as though in prayer and pointed her eyes toward the ceiling.

"Swear you don't know what happened to my clothes?"

"Why would I lie about something silly like your clothes?" Janelle paused. "Although it has occurred to me that your wardrobe—"

"Stop there, Janelle. Leave my wardrobe alone."

"You look nice *today*. White suits you. The red and gold scarf with the turquoise pants is. . . is unique."

Ali continued sipping her coffee. She picked up the *Willoughby News & Record* and turned to the obituary page. After a few minutes of silence, she removed her glasses and looked at Janelle. "We could have been best friends. I worshipped you when we were young. Like Kayla adores you, or used to until she began to see some cracks in your façade."

"You're jealous of Kayla's relationship with me," Janelle said softly. "I've tried bribery to win her love. Ironic, isn't it? You're jealous of me and vice versa."

"Why in the world are you jealous of me, Janelle?"

"Having a daughter is a precious gift that I will never have."

Ali choked on her coffee. "Went down the wrong way." Too many years of manipulation and lies had kept a cover on the warm feelings beginning to percolate inside Ali. Janelle had many opportunities over the years to express pride in her sister but chose to demean and ridicule her instead. Ali quickly changed the subject, a trick she learned from her sister. "About this trip to Italy you keep dangling in front of Kayla—"

"I promise you, Ali. I will follow through. My finances are—well . . . my finances are compromised at the moment."

"Coulda fooled me. Seems like you've been doing some shopping while you've been here—Nordstrom's. You even bought a present for me at the Chandlery."

"Ken gave me a personal loan. I have to keep up appearances."

"I thought you said you found a credit card in the bottom of a purse."

"That, too."

"So how are you going to fix your finances?"

"I must find someone I respect to write with me, Li'l Sis." She paused, took Ali's hands, and pleaded. "Phoebe predicted you had writing potential."

Ali's feelings continued to percolate. "Janelle, that was years ago."

"You've read lots of books."

"I see a lot of movies but that doesn't make me an actress."

"What about all those obituaries you write? Talk about fiction."

"That's none of your business," Ali snapped.

"You could try."

"Try what? You're not listening to me. I'm not the star-struck teenager who hung on your every word and did whatever you asked."

"Try writing. With me. Get me through this book."

"I don't know, Janelle." Ali was weakening as visions of many unfinished manuscripts stacked on the floor of her closet flashed before her.

"Do you have ideas about a plot, setting, characters, anything?" Ali asked. "How can I help you if you don't give me something to work with?"

"I think Phoebe left me an outline for another book but damn that Brad; he's keeping it from me."

"Why do you think she left something?"

"He keeps toying with me, saying Phoebe might have or may have left me something."

"Why is this outline so important?"

"I can't write without it. Psychological, I guess. I need Phoebe."

Ali wondered why Janelle hadn't considered Phoebe's age and that perhaps she should have prepared for the time when she wouldn't be around to help her.

"What's it worth to you?"

"What do you mean? You'll talk to Brad? I know he likes you. Will you do this for me, Li'l Sis?"

"Cut the malarkey, Janelle." Ali walked to a kitchen drawer and withdrew Phoebe's letter and the yellow-lined paper. She tossed it toward her sister.

Janelle examined both pieces of paper. "Thank you, Lord, now I *will* go to church." After a few minutes, she tossed the note back to Ali. "What the hell is this? Was she that feeble? I can't read a word. This is useless."

"What's your deadline?" Ali asked.

"Yesterday."

"Janelle! You've lost it now. You think we can sit down and write a book, in what, a month, two months, three months?"

"Phoebe could do it."

"I'm not freaking Phoebe. Excuse me. I didn't mean to disrespect her."

Janelle fiddled with a pencil on the table. "You might not understand this, but if I don't have a new book out soon, my fans will desert me. Human nature, I suppose."

"Call your agent. Maybe Ken can find a ghostwriter who will postpone an upfront fee."

"Ken? You're crazy! He can never know. Never. Never!"

"Calm down," Ali ordered.

Janelle's face turned to fury when Ali mentioned Ken.

"We're expected at the bookstore in fifteen minutes. You have fans to meet and greet. We'll talk about my writing or not writing with you later. Regardless, there's going to be some big changes around here—beginning today."

"What changes?"

"You'll see."

Chapter 44

Before the sisters headed out the door for the short walk to the bookstore, Ali said, "You could use a brighter lipstick. That color ages you."

Janelle's hand flew to her lips. "You could have told me sooner," she snipped, as she dug around in her purse for lipstick.

"Imagine. I'm giving my sister makeup advice," Ali said to Roxie.

The special event at the bookstore was a far better experience than Ali had imagined. Maggie and Diane set up small tables around the store laden with scrumptious breakfast treats and aromatic coffee and specialty teas. Jill had brought the previous night's flower arrangement plus leftover paper goods. Diane posted a sign on the door: "Closed until 11:30 a.m. due to a VIP Book Signing with Janelle Jennings." Jill positioned herself at the door, with a clipboard, checking off the names of those who signed up the night before, but after a while, she let everyone in.

Diane was busy at the checkout counter. Customers were in such cheerful moods they not only bought Janelle's book but also books by other authors. Maggie prepared cards that told the customers where they could buy her popular lemon scones. Jill had placed a sign saying, "Flowers by Jill" next to the arrangement she brought. Virginia flitted around the room making sure the attendees knew she was the Mother of the Author. Everyone was mellow. Well, maybe not everyone. Janelle's freeze-frame smile contrasted with a deep furrow between her eyes. Promptly at 11:30 a.m., Diane opened the doors to the public. Janelle continued talking to her fans and autographing books. After most of the customers had left, Janelle found Ali and grabbed her by the arm. "Brad sent me a text. He left something for me at your house. On the doorstep. Let's go."

"Where's Mother?" Ali wondered as she looked around the bookstore.

"She left. Said she had something to do at home."

Janelle made a gracious exit and the two sisters hurriedly walked the three blocks to Ali's house. As Brad said, a package waited at the door. A frantic Janelle told Ali to hurry up and unlock the front door.

"Let me do that." Janelle seized the key from Ali but fumbled it. Ali grabbed the key from Janelle and opened the door.

Janelle snatched the package and raced to the kitchen table. "Scissors. Knife," Janelle demanded like a surgeon asking for instruments.

"Slow down, Janelle." Ali used a paring knife to open the package. Inside the large box was another box.

"He's toying with me." The last box was a small jewelry box tied with black and red ribbon.

"Oh, damn! Why would Phoebe leave me jewelry?" Janelle yelled. She opened the box. "What the…" She tried to hand a black flash drive to Ali but it slipped from her clammy hand.

Roxie ran to investigate.

"Go away, you pest."

Roxie snatched the flash drive in her mouth and darted to the sunroom away from her former friend.

An expensive veterinarian bill flashed into Ali's mind, not to mention a potential plot in the pet cemetery. She chased Roxie into the sunroom. "Here, girl. Come here, Roxie. No. No. Please."

Roxie turned around to face the two sisters. A corner of the flash drive peeked out from the side of her mouth. It was a standoff—Roxie vs. The Sisters.

"Go get a cookie!" Ali yelled to Janelle. At the sound of "cookie," Roxie dropped the purloined item and hurried toward Janelle.

"I've got it," Ali said, wiping Roxie's saliva off the flash drive with the hem of her blouse.

Janelle made a U-turn, and raced to the den leaving a disappointed Roxie behind.

Ali inserted the flash drive into the computer. One file appeared. The label read: "For Janelle's Eyes Only on the Event of Phoebe Patterson's Passing."

"Open it! Open it!"

Ali clicked the open file button.

"What the hell is this?" Janelle screeched.

The two sisters stared at a picture of an x-ray. It appeared to be a broken leg.

Chapter 45

"So what's this x-ray thing all about?" Janelle paced around the den with her hands curled into balls. Her face was pale as the blood receded from her skin.

"Someone's playing a joke on you, Janelle. Don't you get it?"

"If I got it, I wouldn't be asking you."

"Leg bone. X-ray."

"Oh, damn that Brad. I guess he never forgave me for breaking his leg. I did apologize, didn't I?" Janelle pleaded with Ali for a response.

"You're the only one who can answer that."

"Do you think Phoebe left this for me? Is this a clue? Maybe it's supposed to mean something."

The sisters sat near the computer starting at the x-ray on the computer screen.

"I think it's a clue," Janelle said.

"I think it's a joke."

***

Earlier that day at the Withrow home, Virginia called out to Ed, "I'm leaving. Hope you have everything under control."

"On schedule, Chief."

"I still don't understand why the cloak and dagger? If this was Janelle's idea, why are we doing this while she's at the book signing?"

"More fun this way. Imagine the look on her face. She'll be so pleased."

"Seems strange," Virginia said. "But I'm thrilled. Better late than never."

"See you around eleven?"

"If I can sneak away by then," Virginia said.

Ed checked his watch then called Matt at the dealership. "What are you doing?"

"Working. Why?"

"I need help with a project. Won't take long."

"Can it wait until I get home tonight? Pretty busy."

"No, we have to move while the coast is clear," Ed explained.

"Why?"

"No time for a Q&A. Meet me at your house."

Matt smiled at Ed's request for help with a mysterious assignment—probably related to one of his inventions. The timing was not good. The rumor circulating the dealership was that major personnel changes were looming. Regardless, he acquiesced to his father-in-law's appeal.

Ed stood at the front door with Roxie at his side when Matt arrived home.

"Why the urgency?" Matt asked.

"We're moving Janelle out of your house and into ours, while the girls are at the book signing. Have to move fast."

"Whoa! I don't get it. Why can't you wait for Janelle and Ali? Why now?"

"Because they don't know the plan. Don't you see? Janelle will come here to your house and find her belongings missing. I've written a note saying that if she knows what's good for her she'll leave with a happy face. Virginia's waiting for us."

"You are one brave man," Matt said, "but slightly loony. You know Janelle will go postal."

"Not my concern. Ali asked if I would get Janelle out of your house. She didn't ask when. One thing though, and this is important, son. Virginia must think Janelle made the decision to move. Virginia would be devastated if she knew the truth."

"What *does* Virginia think?"

"I told her this was a surprise. Saving Janelle the trouble of packing and unpacking. Something like that. She's suspicious though."

The two conspirators walked upstairs to Janelle's bedroom with Roxie close behind.

"What's the plan? Pack all her clothes?"

"It's the only way. Have to empty the closet, drawers, bathroom, all that makeup stuff women use."

"Seems sneaky and extreme. Love it," Matt said. He moseyed over to the dresser, opened a drawer, and cautiously peeked. "This is too creepy. I'm not touching her underwear." He slammed the drawer. "How about if you do the packing and I'll do the carrying?"

"I changed her diapers so I guess underwear won't embarrass me." Ed opened the drawer where Janelle kept her lacy bras, thong panties, and black thigh-high stockings. "Geez. Forget about this stuff." He firmly closed the drawer and joined Matt in front of the crammed closet.

Although Virginia instructed Ed to handle the clothes gently, the two men awkwardly folded Janelle's garments and stuffed them in the suitcases Ed had retrieved from the hallway closet. "No instructions about the shoes," he added. The two evictors haphazardly tossed shoes into a large black garbage bag along with several purses.

From the bedroom, they moved to the bathroom where Janelle's perfume assaulted them.

"I'll be glad to get that smell out of my house," Matt said. They tossed jars of Janelle's beauty treatments into a second black garbage bag. "Whoops," Ed said, as some of the glass bottles clanked against each other.

After several trips up and down the staircase, Matt said, "You shouldn't be doing this, Ed."

"Yes, I should. My daughters can't live together. I'm sick and tired of all this commotion. Ali says Janelle's too critical of her, Janelle says Ali hates her, and Virginia's endless praise of Janelle irritates Ali. On and on. Women—can't live with them and can't live without them."

"No. I meant going up and down the stairs."

"Oh, that. Maybe I will take a short rest. I could use a beer. You interested?"

Matt shook his head. "Too early for me. Besides, I have to get back to work." He continued carrying Janelle's suitcases to his and Ed's cars.

They drove separately to the Withrow home, with Roxie accompanying Ed, where a cheery Virginia greeted them at the door. Wearing an apron, high heels, and a pearl necklace, she could have been mistaken for June Cleaver.

"This is wonderful. Janelle has finally decided to move in with her parents. Would have happened sooner," Virginia said, "if you"—pointing a finger at Ed—"had moved all your stuff out of your junk-filled office." She glared at her husband.

"How many times do I have to tell you, Virginia? Not junk. Inventions." He shook his head back and forth. "Wasn't my idea to move all my things. But I made the sacrifice in order to improve family harmony—mainly *my* harmony." He took a seat in the living room in his Mission style well-used leather recliner with a burn hole on the cushion. With the chair reclined and a remote in his hand, it was evident that his role in the caper was finished.

"How'd you convince Virginia to let you bring this chair in here? Didn't she ban it from the living room?"

"Compromise, young man, compromise."

"Pretty soon you'll be smoking your pipe in here, too."

"You never know what's coming around the bend," Ed said. He continued relaxing while Matt carried multiple designer suitcases and the black garbage bags into the house. A few high heels were poking out of one of the bags and some jars had broken, leaving a trail of expensive white goop in their wake.

Virginia gave Matt specific instructions. "We're going to hang her beautiful clothes by color. This is the way I taught Janelle to organize her closet. Ali never cared about clothes."

"We?"

"Won't take long. I want everything perfect for Janelle's return."

Reluctantly, Matt called out the colors of the clothes before handing them to his mother-in-law. "Red. Blue. Brown. Black. More black."

"I bought these padded scented hangers for Janelle. I doubt that Ali has any quite like this."

He sniffed one of the lavender scented hangers and coughed. "Whew!"

Virginia held up a short black sheath with a rhinestone collar. "I'd look good in this." She held it close to her body and stood in front of the mirror. "If Ali would lose some weight maybe she could wear—"

"That's it, Virginia. She can hang up her own damn clothes! I'm outta of here."

Before Matt left he turned to face his mother-in-law. "I never say too much to you, and I regret that. You don't appreciate Ali. Stop comparing her with Janelle. Bad enough she endures abuse from her sister, but from her mother? What's the matter with you?"

Virginia clutched the black dress tighter and faced Matt with her mouth agape.

"Who gives a damn about padded smelly hangers anyway?" He picked up one and flung it toward a wastebasket in the corner of the room. Matt went into the living room to find Ed, with Roxie in his lap, connected to TV Ears watching a John Wayne movie.

"I was hard on your wife," Matt said.

"She probably deserved it," Ed said while watching The Duke saddle up.

"Janelle will explode when she finds out what we did. I don't plan to stay for the fireworks."

The two men knuckle bumped then Ed returned to spending his morning with John Wayne.

When Matt returned to the dealership, he found a note on his desk: "Please see me." A summons from Ellis was like anticipating a deluge without an umbrella.

Later in the day, Kayla returned home. "Where is she? Her car's not here," Kayla said, as she dumped her backpack on the floor.

"Hi, Mom. I'm home," would be a preferable greeting, but Ali surrendered to that battle since Janelle's arrival.

"At your grandparents' house, I suspect," Ali responded from the kitchen table. She pretended to focus on the newspaper with her reading glasses on her head.

"I'll take Roxie for a walk and visit them," Kayla said. She took Roxie's pink leash from a hook on the wall behind the kitchen door and attached it to her dog's collar.

"Before you go, I have something to tell you." Ali took her glasses off her head and motioned to Kayla to sit down.

Kayla wrinkled her forehead. "What?" She remained standing, glaring at her mother.

"Your aunt will live with Nana and Gramps for the time being."

"Why? What did *you* do?" Kayla snarled. "Did you make her leave?"

"She's two blocks from here. You can see her anytime. Besides, she's leaving Willoughby."

"But I liked having her around. She didn't treat me like a child, like you do."

"Kayla. Please sit down and talk to me. I'm not the enemy."

"Yes, you are the enemy. What about last summer? How could you do that to me? Why do you treat me like a baby? I'm so mad I don't know what to do. Why do you keep me from having any fun? I bet it was your idea. Dad wouldn't do this to me."

"Kayla. Calm down. I have no idea what you're talking about."

"She told me. She wanted to take me to Italy last summer and you said no. You even said no to a trip to California. Why? Because you've never been anywhere doesn't mean I can't." Kayla was gasping for air and her face was as red as Ali's strawberry timer.

"Janelle never asked. . ." Ali approached Kayla and tried to put her arms around her. *Darn that Janelle. She never asked to take Kayla anywhere.*

"Leave me alone. I'm going to Gramps and Nana's and I don't feel like ever coming back." Kayla jumped over her backpack and slammed the door behind her. Abandoned Roxie whimpered at the screen door as she watched Kayla leave.

Ali unhooked Roxie's leash and hung it behind the door. She made a phone call. "Glad you answered, Dad. Kayla's on her way. Try to calm her down."

"Okay, Gingersnap. I'll do my best."

"Is Janelle mad at you?"

"You could say that. But, we haven't had any time to talk so this might work out."

"I'm so sorry, Dad."

"No problem. Virginia's elated."

"You can't know how wonderful it is to have her gone."

"Don't count your chickens, to quote your mother," Ed said. "Only been a couple of hours and already our house is in turmoil."

Ali felt her stomach tighten when she pictured Janelle returning. "Don't send her back. Please."

"We'll talk later." He hung up the phone.

Janelle turned to wine or Xanax when she was nervous. Ali chose chocolate. She went to the pantry in search of her drug of choice but shook off her diet sabotaging cravings when she snapped her waistband. She moved to the bay window and observed the activity on Plum Court. Lingering yellow pollen tinged the cars passing by. Willoughby could use a cleansing rain not unlike the fresh feeling Ali felt with Janelle gone. She took a stack of folders and went to the den to work at the computer. When she was settling in and answering her e-mail, she heard Kayla bound through the door and up the stairs.

"What's wrong?" Ali called out.

Kayla replied by banging her bedroom door so hard that pictures hanging on the wall outside her room shook.

Ali followed Kayla upstairs and gingerly knocked on her bedroom door. "I know something's wrong. Won't you tell me?"

"Leave me alone."

Ali was accustomed to this reaction of Kayla's and wrote it off to teenage angst. Instead of worrying over Kayla's petulant attitude, which, according to Ed, would disappear in a few years, Ali returned to the computer. Follow-up work for the book banquet was mounting. She had e-mails to answer and notes of gratitude to write to the sponsors. She had received sensible suggestions for improving next year's banquet. She had decided to set up a planning committee to share ideas and to decide how to use Phoebe's $25,000 gift. Historically, the planning committee elected next year's chairperson immediately following the banquet. Ali would be flattered to continue her role, but with Matt's job in jeopardy, Janelle begging for help, and the possibility of buying the kitchen store, she decided to decline the position, if asked. After several hours at the computer, the cuckoo clock in the kitchen reminded Ali it was time to prepare dinner.

Kayla entered the den. "I'm sorry."

Ali jumped. "You surprised me."

Kayla turned to leave.

"Come back, honey. I'm confused. So unconfuse me."

Kayla's eyes were red. She wiped her nose with the back of her hand.

"I'm so stupid."

"Not so."

"I asked Aunt Janelle why she left and she told me to leave her alone and a lot of other mean things."

"Sort of like what you say to me? That's Janelle's mantra."

Kayla shrugged her shoulders.

"The people we love the most have the power to hurt us the most," Ali said. "Your aunt is crazy about you."

Kayla laughed. "You're defending her? She did the same for you. She told me this was your house and I should follow your rules."

"Really?"

"I've acted like a kid."

Ali wanted to remind her that she *was* a kid but dropped that idea—why ruin the moment? Instead, Ali gave Kayla a hug, which Kayla returned. They embraced for several minutes.

"When you're ready, you can talk to me about how Janelle hurt you."

"First of all I have to tell you something." Kayla picked up Roxie and held her close. "I'm the one who threw out your clothes. I'm sorry, Mom. I know that was wrong."

Ali let Kayla stew before she replied. "Yes, it was wrong not asking me." She took a step closer to her daughter and waited a beat. "But, most of the clothes were outdated. Maybe you did me a favor. Let's agree to an annual appraisal of my clothes. I know I need help."

"Thanks, Mom," a relieved Kayla said as she placed Roxie on the floor.

"Want to give me a hint about what Janelle did? You were mad at me when you left and now it's Janelle who's on your list of enemies."

"She gave me the emerald pendant I wore to the banquet. Then she asked for it back. She makes one promise after another that she doesn't keep. Shopping, a trip to Italy. Then when she doesn't feel like having me around, she kicks me out," Kayla revealed.

"I think a Nana quote is in order," Ali said to Kayla. "We can choose our friends but not our relatives."

Chapter 46

Ellen stopped running along Riverside Drive and bent at her waist to catch her breath. She stood and walked slowly toward her car where she saw Matt and Brad in the parking lot. They were stretching their leg muscles in preparation for a morning run along the river.

"Just the two I want to see."

"Oh no. I don't like the tone of your voice. Are you going to send us to the principal's office?" Matt asked.

"The three of us need to meet."

"How about Phoebe's house in a couple of hours?" Brad suggested.

***

When Matt arrived home from work he hollered, "Let's get out of here."

"In the den," Ali called out.

Matt joined Ali where she was sitting at the computer. Something in Matt's voice sounded needy. She put the computer into sleep mode.

"Where to?" Ali asked.

"The river. Better bring water. Still hot and muggy."

The couple drove to the Willoughby River where Matt parked the car near Azalea Landing. They began their walk at a leisurely pace, observing the lethargic movement of the greenish-blue water. The path was crowded with runners and joggers.

"I have some good news and some bad news," Matt began.

Bad news: Cancer. Matt had a physical last week that he'd been putting off. Good news: not terminal.

"Your health?" Ali stopped and turned to face him. She felt her rapid heartbeat and gasped for air.

"I'm fine. It's the job."

"That's a relief. What about your job?" She searched for an empty bench.

"You know how unhappy I've been since Joey Graham came on board."

Ali chastised herself for not paying attention to Matt in recent weeks. She knew he was concerned about his job, but Matt had worked for Graham Motors for over thirty years. Surely, his job was not in jeopardy.

"Since Joey came on board, I anticipated this would happen. Still, it hurts."

"Matt, please don't be so vague. What happened? What did Ellis say?"

"Basically, if I want to keep my job, I'd take a demotion, cut in pay, and train his nephew. My knee-jerk response was to tell him I had received an offer and was seriously considering it."

"What offer?"

Matt had not exactly received an offer, but Doyle Ackerman, a fellow Lions Club member and a mega dealer, had tried to recruit him to his management company.

"I was hoping Ellis would ask for details about the job offer and make a counter offer, but he didn't. Ellis's response was that I should take the offer. He said, 'Matt, sorry it has to end this way. Families, you know. Since you're going to a competitor, I would normally ask you to clean out your office immediately.' Instead, he told me to take my time, two weeks, and that I should keep it to myself for now. He said, 'You have lots of fans around here,' and he wanted to wait for the right time to tell the staff." After years of loyal service, Matt believed he was a member of the Graham "family."

Ali stopped abruptly, nearly stepping into goose droppings, and sat on a bench facing the river. "We need your income. We've earmarked all our savings for Kayla's education."

"Ellis said I could expect a generous severance." Matt picked up a twig on the ground and twirled it between his fingers. "Severance pay. Can't believe that would ever apply to me."

"You seem so calm. I would have expected you to come storming through the door screaming and yelling. Why aren't you angry?" Ali asked.

"Ellis told me about the demotion last week. I've had time to cool down."

Ali turned to face Matt. "You didn't share this with me last week? Is that what you're saying?" Ali understood how a demotion would devastate Matt, and undermine his authority at the dealership, but she couldn't understand why he hadn't told her about this life-altering change sooner. "What are you going to do?" she asked as she opened a bottle of water.

"I think Doyle will find a position for me in his organization. I'm meeting him for lunch next week." He stopped, took a deep breath, and blurted: "I've given serious consideration to buying Kitchen Bliss and I think we should go for it." His words sounded rehearsed and his voice was tentative. He scanned the river, avoiding eye contact with Ali. "We would enjoy working together, don't you think?"

Ali loved her husband but working and living together sounded like a direct route to Divorce Court citing mental anguish, pain, and suffering. The Neelys on the Food Channel can pull it off, but not Ali and Matt Lawrence. At least not Ali. Kitchen Bliss was a place where Ali thrived. She loved interacting with the customers, recommending wedding gifts, or displaying new items. She was the go-to-person without the pressure of owning the business. If she had the burden of making payroll, paying taxes, maintaining inventory—the joy of working would disappear. At the end of her workday, she removed her apron, if she remembered, and went home, leaving the major responsibility to Ellen.

"You seemed hesitant when we discussed this over dinner last week. So, I gave you some time to mull it over. I'm putting the decision in your hands, Al." They sat side-by-side facing the water.

Tubes, canoes, and kayaks packed the river. The Spirit of Willoughby paddleboat, festooned with red, white, and blue bunting, lazily floated down the river. Happy passengers filled the upper deck bouncing their sound of merriment across the water.

"I put it on hold until the book banquet was over and Janelle was out of the house. Are we sure Ellen wants to sell?"

"She's serious. I met with Brad again and this time we included Ellen to review the financials. Brad will back us with a low-interest loan to buy out Ellen. He'll take a small percentage of the profits for a few years."

"You didn't include me because...*why* didn't you include me?"

"Waiting for all the commotion to die down—book banquet, Janelle moving out. Now that both of those are out of the way—"

Ali stood up from the bench, without waiting for Matt she hustled toward the car. She didn't know she could run so fast.

"Wait up. Don't be mad."

"Is that man bothering you," a woman pushing a stroller with twins asked as Ali whizzed by. "Should I call 9-1-1?"

"I'm fine. Thanks, though." Ali waved to the concerned woman. Matt easily caught up with her. "Wait. Please."

Ali stopped running, not because of Matt, but because she felt she was having a heart attack. She hadn't run that fast since high school when Janelle chased her around the house with a pair of scissors threatening to cut her hair. She took a gulp of water from the bottle stuck in her pocket.

"I'm sorry. I should have consulted you. So what do you think?"

"Something smells bad."

"About buying the store?"

"No. Something around here."

They both examined the soles of their shoes. Ali had a big glop of goose droppings on her right foot that was working itself up the sides and oozing into her sock.

"I think I want to throw up," she groaned.

"Take off your shoe. Your sock, too."

Ali leaned against Matt while he pulled off her shoe and sock. He tossed the sock in a garbage can as he walked to a grassy area. He rubbed the shoe back and forth removing some of the disgusting smelly stuff. They walked the short distance back to their car. Matt carried one of her shoes by its shoestring while Ali limped back on one foot, sockless and shoeless. When they neared a garbage can, Ali told Matt to toss the spoiled shoe he was carrying into the garbage can.

"You may as well toss the one you're wearing, too."

"I'm keeping this one."

Matt gave her a quizzical look. "Why?"

"Think about it."

"Give me a second." Matt focused on the river meandering by.

"How can you *not* remember?"

"Oh boy. I put your engagement ring in it when I proposed." Matt's face reddened.

"When I began walking it felt like a piece of glass or a pebble. Happiest day of my life next to Kayla's birth," Ali said.

Matt leaned over to kiss Ali, but she brushed him aside.

"You don't know why I'm mad, do you?" she asked him.

"I guess I should have consulted you before talking with Brad and Ellen?"

"What else?"

"Okay. I should have told you about the job situation. Guilty on both counts."

"Please don't try to push me into a quick decision. I need time to think."

They drove home in silence.

Chapter 47

J anelle had taken the spotlight at the book banquet two days ago, but to quote Virginia, "Today is *my* fifteen minutes of fame." Since Kayla had early dismissal today, Virginia invited all three of her girls to lunch. Virginia chose a restaurant frequented by many of her friends and acquaintances—Willoughby Tea House on Magnolia Street. She had reserved the table nearest to the entrance to ensure incoming diners would see her and her luncheon companions.

Since Janelle's arrival in Willoughby, she had declined invitations from her mother to accompany her to the garden club or historical society functions. She had agreed to this family outing because she was on precarious footing and dependent on her family for a temporary place to live.

An amiable hostess led the group to their table and distributed menus. "You ladies all look so colorful and pretty. This must be a special occasion."

Indeed, the Withrow/Lawrence women were dressed for a springtime party. Virginia, striking in pink and purple, Kayla wearing tangerine and white stripes, Janelle in butterscotch yellow, and Ali in lime green.

"It's always special when I'm with my girls," Virginia replied.

A server approached their table to take drink orders and to highlight special teas of the day.

"May I see the wine list?" Janelle asked.

"I'm sorry, ma'am, we don't serve alcohol. We have lovely hot and iced teas." She handed Janelle the tea menu. "Vanilla Peach Iced Tea is featured today."

Kayla ordered for the group. "We'll have rose tea, please."

Janelle wrinkled her nose.

"It doesn't taste like roses but smells like them. It's awesome," Kayla said. "It's our favorite. Nana's and mine."

While they were reading the menus, several acquaintances of Virginia's stopped by their table and gushed over Janelle's speech at the banquet and her generous promise of a donation. In a soft-spoken voice, Janelle complimented one of the women on the smoky topaz suspended on a thick gold chain that hung on her crinkly, skinny neck, albeit she restrained from recommending a treatment for the condition of the woman's skin. The necklace was identical to one that Janelle sold at White & Co. jewelry store.

"This is so wonderful, having all my girls here," Virginia said after the women left. "A mother and grandmother couldn't ask for more joy. And everyone is getting along so well."

Ali and Janelle exchanged glances.

"The Tea House offers so many interesting items to choose from. Don't you agree, Janelle?" Virginia asked.

Janelle didn't hear her mother. She directed her attention to the table across from her where the woman with the topaz necklace sat. Janelle could hear the woman's friends gushing over the piece of jewelry. Without waiting for a reply, Virginia chatted on, stopping to acknowledge friends who passed by their table to compliment Janelle on her stellar career.

Janelle was uncharacteristically quiet. She handed the menu to Kayla. "You can order for me."

"You can order for yourself." She tossed the menu back to Janelle.

"That was rude," Virginia reprimanded.

"Sorry, I guess," Kayla said.

"I deserved it," Janelle admitted.

"You look pale, dear. Are you sick?" Virginia asked Janelle.

"I'm fine. Tired. That's all."

"Maybe the book signing was too much. All those adoring fans. 'Diligence is the mother of good luck,' dear, but I'm afraid you may have overdone it this time. You signed so many books." Their server returned to take their orders. Kayla selected Thai coconut curry bowl with shrimp and edamame. Ali said, "I think I need the Beauty Booster Salad with wild salmon."

"Excellent choices," their server said. She was a young woman with long brown hair pulled into a straight ponytail. She wore black-rimmed glasses giving her a professorial look. "Sorry...I didn't mean you needed more beauty—"

"No worries," Ali said.

Virginia ordered next. "A girl can always use a beauty booster. Make that two."

"Make it three," Janelle said.

Except for an occasional frivolous comment by Virginia, the women were somber. Kayla's issues with her aunt were multiple. Janelle was angry because Ed helped evict her and she suspected that Ali was the mastermind. Although it was difficult, so far Janelle obeyed her father's demand that she act as though the move was her idea.

Kayla broke the ice. "For a final school assignment, I have to interview three people and ask them to tell me their goals in life. Before our food arrives, let's begin. Nana, you first."

Virginia wrinkled her forehead. "Goals? I suppose I never thought much about goals like you girls do today. I took ballet lessons and thought the life of a ballerina would be exciting. But that was foolish. My goal was to marry and raise a family. Unlike what happens now—it's the reverse. Have children and then marry."

"What else, Nana?" Kayla placed her journal on the table.

"What else is there, dear?" Virginia responded. "I married, raised a family, and now I have a beautiful granddaughter." She patted Kayla on her soft cheek.

"Okay. I guess that's appropriate for your generation," Kayla noted. Her daughter's mature observation pleased Ali.

With a menacing look Kayla said, "Your turn, Aunt Janelle."

The server arrived with plates of salmon adorned with garden-fresh vegetables and baby spinach, and Kayla's curry bowl, interrupting their discussion. For once in Janelle's history of dining in restaurants, she made no complaints. With her fork, she speared a blueberry from her plate, but it skidded across the table. "At least it wasn't a pickle," she said to Ali.

After everyone began eating, Kayla said, "Your turn, I guess, Aunt Janelle." Kayla kept the journal closed.

Janelle directed her comments to Ali. The beauty pageant contestant didn't call for world peace. "I want to stay here in Willoughby. I want your life, Ali. I want a close-knit family and friends."

Ali put her fork down and gasped. "What in the world is the matter with you, Janelle?"

"Maybe it's too late. Maybe I don't deserve my family. I've treated my books as family." Janelle reached across the table, put her hand on Ali's forearm, and looked into her eyes. "You're happily married, have countless friends, and you unselfishly look after Mother and Dad. You're a terrific mother." With that last comment, Janelle glared at Kayla who lowered her head. "I'm proud of you, Ali. Proud of the life you have made in Willoughby. Proud of my Li'l Sis."

Could Janelle have undergone a personality transplant? Ali reviewed the most recent events. Janelle had delivered a semi-honest speech at the banquet, had been charming to her fans at the bookstore, had accepted Virginia's invitation today, and had been gracious and polite to her mother's friends who stopped by their table. *Now this heartfelt declaration.*

"I've been thinking about all the mean tricks I pulled on you when we were young. No wonder you hate me."

Virginia surveyed the room, hoping none of her friends could sense the intensity of the conversation. "Please, girls, not here."

"I adored you when we were young," Ali said. "As adults, frankly, Janelle you're a pain in the butt."

"Goodness gracious. No vulgarity." Virginia scanned the room again. "Remember, Alicia, virtue is its own reward."

"What about me? Don't I get an apology?" Kayla asked.

Janelle took the white starched napkin from her lap and dabbed at her eyes. "I promise to make it up to you, Kayla."

"Your promises are worthless," Kayla snapped.

"Oh dear, this is not going well," Virginia said. "Can't we let bygones be bygones, for the sake of the family?" She wiped her nose with a white lace antique handkerchief. "This is your home and we all want you here."

"Thank you, Janelle. I'm touched, but I think we need a plea for forgiveness and not a recitation of the facts." Ali was not ready to let her sister off the hook so easily.

"I'm sorry for causing discord in the family, for demeaning Ali, and for making promises to Kayla I don't keep."

"Right," Kayla said as she moved some food around her plate. "It will take time, but I'm going to try to be okay with that."

"Me too," Ali seconded.

"Now. We have that settled?" Virginia pleaded.

They nodded their heads in unison and continued eating in silence.

While chewing on baby spinach leaves, Ali contemplated her response, in case anyone asked about her goal in life. Maybe a smidgen of Janelle's former life would be nice. She still longed for exotic travel with Matt. These goals seemed trivial and not worth mentioning.

Kayla piped up. "Gee, Mom. We forgot about you. Sorry. Any goals?" She opened the journal.

"Besides having a terrific daughter?" Ali grinned at Kayla.

"Something in your future, Mom."

"Matt and I are going to buy Kitchen Bliss," Ali announced, shocked at her statement.

"What?" the threesome said.

"We still have some details to iron out." It was only yesterday that Matt approached Ali with the idea. They had not discussed the business proposition since.

Ali repeated her statement. "We're going to buy Kitchen Bliss." Ali liked the sound of the words. "That's my goal. To become a successful businesswoman—like the Spanx woman or Mrs. Fields. On a smaller scale, of course."

Virginia gave a slight smile. "You don't have any real business experience." She took a sip of tea. "But, I know you'll be successful. You've been an asset to me in my business. In fact, I couldn't do it without you, my dear Alicia."

Was that an actual compliment from my mother?

"Thank you, Mother. That means so much to me. You never say…"

"I know. You think I like your sister more than you. I don't. You're a wonderful daughter and I take you for granted. Matt had reminded me of that recently. Janelle is the way she is because of how I raised her."

"You can't take all the blame, Mother. Some of the responsibility is mine." Janelle turned to Ali. "If owning Kitchen Bliss makes you happy, go for it. Especially since—" I mean now you'll have something of substance to put in your obituary."

"Janelle, how impolite," Virginia said.

"I know what she means, Mother."

"Now maybe you'll let me have a real job. I hate babysitting during the summer," Kayla said. "I could do so much in the store. Promise you'll give me a job."

"We'll see."

"Will you give Logan a job?"

"It's a thought."

The server presented the dessert menu. "Our lemon coconut cake is popular and the crème brûlée is gluten free, in case that matters."

"Nothing for me," Janelle said.

Kayla took the initiative. "We'll have one crème brûlée and one piece of lemon coconut cake to share," Kayla said.

While they were enjoying the luscious treats, the server slipped Virginia the bill, as prearranged.

Janelle looked through her wallet hoping money would suddenly appear. "I'd be glad to. . ."

Virginia waved her hand. "No, no, my treat."

"My boss wouldn't like me doing this," the server said to Janelle. She held out a menu and a Sharpie. "Could I bother you for an autograph, ma'am?"

Janelle heaved a sigh. "I don't mind, but a word of advice. Women don't like that ma'am thing all you people around here say." She took the pen and signed the menu.

"No problem, ma'am. Whoops—I mean, I'm sorry, miss. Thank you."

"Which one of my books is your favorite?" Janelle asked.

"Oh, I haven't read any. I didn't know you're an author. But all the ladies in the restaurant are talking about you so I knew you were important."

"I suggest you read *Eye on the Sphinx*. You remind me of my character Brooks Barrington. Same lovely brown hair and glasses."

"Thank you, miss. I will," the server said before she left.

Outside the restaurant, the three generations said goodbye. Ali hugged her mother. "Thanks. You made me feel so good today."

"Perhaps it was overdue," Virginia lamented. "Remember, sisters are flowers from the same garden."

Ali hugged her mother again and then took Kayla by the hand. Virginia and Janelle went in one direction, Ali and Kayla in the other.

"That was nice, wasn't it, Mom?" Kayla said. "I still don't trust Aunt Janie completely."

"I'm hopeful," Ali said.

"It's going to be different not having her in the house. I wonder why she sort of snuck out."

"You know your aunt loves mystery," Ali replied. "Besides, your grandmother is deliriously happy to have Janelle under her roof. Better this way." Ali crossed her fingers behind her back.

"Sorry I was so upset, Mom. I thought for sure it was your idea. But I'm mad at her so I don't care."

When they arrived home, Kayla said, "I have great material for my report. Better get to it."

Ali sat at the kitchen table reviewing recent events—Matt not telling her about the demotion, quitting his job, meeting Brad and Ellen, Janelle's declaration that she wanted Ali's life, and Virginia's comments. So much to consider.

Now about Ellen. Ali was disappointed with her best friend, but she would have to give her an opportunity to defend herself. The shrill ring of her cell interrupted her thoughts. Without looking at the caller ID, Ali answered the phone.

"We have to talk. Meet me at Starbucks," Janelle said.

Before Ali met Janelle, she had somewhere else to go.

Chapter 48

Ellen stood at the checkout counter when a determined Ali walked into Kitchen Bliss.

"We need to talk. Meet me in the storeroom," Ali demanded without greeting her friend.

"Can't. I'm the only one here."

Ali returned to the front door and hung the "Be back in 15 minutes" sign. "This can't wait."

Ellen put her hands in the Kitchen Bliss apron. "Is this about my meeting with Brad and Matt?" She bit her upper lip and narrowed her eyes.

"Why didn't you tell me you were considering selling to Matt? How could you *not* tell me?"

"Matt asked me not to tell you."

"He did?" Ali felt her stomach tighten and her face redden. "Matt's another story. I'm giving you a chance to explain."

Ellen motioned to the waiting area. "Sit. Coffee? Tea?"

Ali shook her head.

"Hazelnut. Your favorite." Ellen said as she held up a cup.

"Can't humor me today. I'm mad at you and I don't want any freaking coffee."

"Okie dokie," Ellen said as she grasped the cup in both hands.

"Here's your chance and it better be good. Explain."

"I guess I don't have an explanation. My bad. My mistake. Sorry. Is that an adequate apology?" She put her hands, palms down, in front of Ali. "Go ahead, slap me."

"Be serious. Why was I excluded from a meeting that affects my life as much as Matt's?"

"You've been so overwhelmed with Janelle, her alienating you from Kayla, book banquet, the list goes on and on. Please, Ali, know that Matt and I had your best interests in mind. This was merely a preliminary meeting."

Ali shook her head. "I gave you a chance and frankly your explanation is weak. I quit." She turned the sign on the door to read "Open" and huffed out. Ali sat in her pickup with the air conditioning blowing in her face. She knew her anger at Ellen was misplaced. Sure, Ellen should have clued her into the meeting, but Matt was the culprit in this scenario. She couldn't let a lifelong friendship dissolve because of Ellen's lack of judgment. Ali wanted to keep Ellen in her life. If she hadn't promised to meet Janelle, she would have returned to the store and apologized.

Ellen watched Ali climb into her truck. She wanted to chase after her and ask for forgiveness, but two customers entered the store. Ellen greeted them and helped them find the items they requested. While they were browsing, she texted Ali: "You can't quit the store and you can't quit our friendship. I won't allow it."

Ali heard the beep on her phone signaling a text. Hoping the message meant Janelle was canceling, she read it. No such luck. She turned the air conditioning up and tried to text Ellen. After too many minutes, she was able to send "OK."

The same gut-wrenching feeling she had when she saw Janelle at the Fickle Pickle with the banquet committee members overtook her. She searched her purse for a Tums before she drove toward Starbucks.

Janelle was sitting in the corner facing the entrance wearing sunglasses and one of Ali's old straw hats. Ali motioned that she was going to place an order. She carried a venti skinny vanilla latte to the table. "Your disguise isn't working and that hat looks ridiculous on you."

"Not good on you either," Janelle said.

"That bad? Remind me to throw them all away."

"I'm going to be honest with you, Ali. I'm desperate. I took a huge advance from my publisher against my royalties, and if I don't produce, I don't know what will happen." Janelle removed her sunglasses and patted her eyes with a brown paper napkin.

The tears were for real, Ali observed.

"Janelle, I told you we can't work together. We have to admit that. What rule in life says sisters must get along? Let's promise to stay out of each other's way."

Janelle blew her nose. Two young men sitting at the next table turned around to determine the source of the honking. Her blinking eyes looked like a caution light in a school zone.

"Besides, you know that Matt and I are going to buy Kitchen Bliss. How can I write with you *and* work at the store?"

"You're superwoman, Li'l Sis. Please? Please?"

"You have several options. Borrow money from Brad. He won't turn you down. Hire a real ghostwriter, and make this book your best."

Janelle sniffed. "My last book didn't do so well, and Ken must never know about Phoebe's involvement. Never. Never. About Brad— well, he hates me. I can't blame him."

"Write the book. Promote the heck out of it."

"Listen, please," Janelle implored. She sat up straight, shoulders back. She transformed weepy and pathetic to strong and confident. "Help me out, this one time, and then I promise to change. Remember my character in—"

Ali interrupted. "Some people can never change and you're one of them." She stood up and left Janelle alone at the table in the crowded café.

***

Later in the day, Ali had called her father and asked him to meet her in the park.

"Okay. The usual place." Ed hit the record button so he could resume watching a John Wayne movie when he returned from whatever crisis was disrupting the family now. Ed had never predicted two daughters and a granddaughter could cause so much commotion. Virginia was about all he could handle.

Ed arrived before Ali. He sat on a bench facing the pond. A quacking white duck with a bright orange beak chased a dull colored mallard away from her territory. Ed pictured his two daughters constantly in battle. "So, what's the matter, Gingersnap?" He stood and embraced his daughter.

"Everything." Ali explained that Matt didn't tell her he lost his job and that he had met behind her back with Brad and Ellen to discuss buying Kitchen Bliss. "Then Janelle confessed to me—" She stopped. She didn't want anyone else besides Matt and Ellen to know about Janelle's secret, not even her dad. "Never mind about Janelle. She's the least of my worries."

Ed let her vent about Matt for a few more minutes. "I'm going to defend Matt."

Ali stiffened as she glared at her father.

"Now hear me out," he said deliberately. "You act crazed when Janelle's here. I bet Matt wanted to talk to Ellen and Brad first because, if the deal was impossible, he didn't want to disappoint you."

"Matt knows that I prefer a steady paycheck. Besides, I need time to think about this."

"He's been an excellent husband and father. I couldn't ask for a better son-in-law. Listen to what he has to say."

"You're a calming influence, Dad." Ali paused. "Even more so than chocolate."

"Glad to hear."

"Something else, Dad. Have you been talking to Mother about the way she and Janelle treat me?"

"I don't think so. Why?"

Ali relayed the surprising conversation at lunch. "Mother complimented and even thanked me."

"I don't know what's going on with you and your sister, but Janelle seems to think you can help her. For the sake of the family, Gingersnap, do what you can. Please? Your mother's so excited about the possibility of the two of you working together."

Ali returned home and went to the kitchen. A yellow sticky note on the pantry door caught her eye. "Think before eating," it read. Ali ripped off Matt's dieting advice and tossed it in the garbage can. Then she glanced at the refrigerator where a bottle of white wine was chilling. She went back and forth between the refrigerator and the pantry. Wine vs. Chocolate. Chocolate vs. Wine. Wine vs. Chocolate.

"Why not both?" Ali asked Roxie who had joined her in the kitchen. When Ali heard the garage door open, she threw the package of cookies back into the pantry, replaced the sticky note, and took her glass of wine to the sunroom.

"Let me explain," he said when he joined Ali.

"You're the second person to say that to me today."

He apologized for excluding Ali from the meeting with Brad and Ellen. "If I look at the situation from your point of view, I understand. I should have postponed the discussion until you were ready. Have I undermined your relationship with Ellen?"

"I confronted Ellen today at Kitchen Bliss."

Matt closed his eyes and shook his head back and forth. "My fault."

"Ellen texted me. We're fine."

"That's a relief. I didn't want you to accuse me of breaking up your friendship." He carried Ali's wine glass to the kitchen. "Let's talk business. Kitchen Bliss business."

Matt removed a two-inch stack of papers from a black Italian leather briefcase, a Christmas gift from Janelle several years ago. He fanned the documents across the table like a deck of cards. One by one, he explained the five-year business plan, sales projections, methods to increase revenue and customer traffic, the amount of money Brad had offered to lend, and terms of the purchase from Ellen.

"You've given this some thought." Ali's eyes glazed over as Matt continued an enthusiastic monologue detailing his plans for the purchase of Kitchen Bliss.

"Beer?" she asked.

He nodded his head.

She took the opened bottle of wine and a beer from the refrigerator.

"I never imagined Ellen would sell. However, I can't do it without you. I want you on board one hundred percent."

Ali held the stem of the wineglass between both hands and swiveled it right and left.

"No disparaging Ellen, but we have to make it our own. New name. New products. New hours. Redecorating." Matt looked at a series of notes on a tablet next to him.

"Let's keep the name. For now."

"Okay. Shake hands, partner."

"Full partner, right?" Ali asked.

"Wife, friend, lover, and now business partner." He stood from the table and approached Ali. He pulled her up facing him and gave her a lingering kiss. "I love you."

"I love you, too. I'm a lucky girl."

***

The next morning Ali made a phone call. "We need to talk," she told her sister. "Meet me at the park. Usual spot." While she drove to the park, she mulled over what her father had said the day before. The sisters met at a bench near the pond, which was becoming the family therapy couch.

"Does this mean you've changed your mind? God, please help me if you won't."

"Stop it. Stop right now or I will slap you silly. You and Phoebe have written eighteen books. Maybe overly romantic for my taste, but the plots were believable and your heroines were strong. You must have learned something from Phoebe."

Janelle scooted closer to her sister and took her by her shoulders. "I'm so stressed right now I couldn't write an e-mail."

"I don't know if I can do this but I'll give it a try."

"I promise to go to church every Sunday," Janelle vowed as she gazed at the sky and folded her hands in prayer.

"Cut the histrionics." Ali took a deep breath. "We need guidelines. You have to work hard every day, all day and night. You'll have to pitch in at the store. You did an acceptable job with the Grover twins, but your main job is to write. No troublemaking."

"What?" Janelle asked.

"Starting at eight o'clock tomorrow morning. Come to my house for a couple of days. After that, there's a small storeroom in the back of Kitchen Bliss. We'll have Dad make an office for us."

Janelle gave her sister a crushing hug.

"You better come with some outstanding ideas."

"Ideas? I'm overflowing with them. I have all Phoebe's notes from her trips to Alaska, Belize, Africa. You won't be disappointed. I need someone to organize me. I think I have AADD. And what about that x-ray? Maybe I—I mean, we can write mysteries. That's a great idea. Don't you think? Well, what *do* you think?"

"Adult Attention Deficit Disorder? Really, Janelle," Ali said. "Hmm. Let me think. Alaska. That might be fun. More men than women up there, I assume. Or, what about somewhere closer . . . D.C., New York, or—I've got it—Atlanta."

"Anything you want. Tomorrow at eight a.m. Your house."

"One more thing. Will you please meet with Kayla and apologize? Maybe I've been jealous of your relationship with her and I regret that. Your apology at the restaurant was weak. Didn't sound sincere. She deserves more. You might want to admit you never asked me if she could accompany you anywhere."

Janelle said, "Actions speak louder than words."

"Seeing is believing,"Ali said.

"Don't kick me when I'm down."

The sisters laughed as they repeated their mother's clichés.

"I'll make it up to Kayla. You'll see. Give me another chance, even though I don't deserve one. One more chance and I'll make it up to everyone. I love you, Li'l Sis."

"And I love you, Big Sis. I love you very much."

The sisters embraced and then left the park.

Chapter 49

E d zipped up his brown fleeced-lined parka, put a black and green wool knit cap on his head, and pulled it down over his ears. "Come on, Alva," he called to his new companion, a toy black and white schnauzer. "Time to bundle up." Ed wrapped his new invention around the dog—a red and green striped hoodie with Velcro closures and matching leg warmers. "This should keep you warm. Let's see what's happening on Willoughby Lane." He hooked the leash to Alva's collar and left the house. When they passed the Book in the Nook, Diane called out to them. "They're here. Come on in."

Ed and Alva entered the store. Diane was standing behind a display of books with glossy covers and a sign: *Newly Released. Local authors.* Ed picked up *Broken Bones-Broken Promises*, turned it over, and beamed at the photo of his two daughters.

"They did it!" Diane exclaimed.

"They sure did. More in the future."

Ed and Alva continued their walk on Willoughby Lane. They paused at the window of Kitchen Bliss. A banner over the door read, "Closed for Remodeling. Opening Soon Under New Ownership."

His daughter came to the door, unlocked it, and gave Ed a hug.

"Won't stay long. Hoped you might have some coffee brewing."

"Help yourself, Dad. I'm rearranging the table linen department."

"Heard from your sister?"

"She sent me a text. 'Having a great time.' They've found some new products for the store and Kayla's practicing her Italian. Mother's looking for the perfect vintage espresso maker. Don't tell Matt, though. It's a surprise."

"I wonder what your mother will say about the new product in *our* house," he said as he pointed to Alva.

"She'll get over it."

Ed poured a cup of Costa Rican coffee and wandered around the store with Alva at his heels. "How are these shelves Logan and I made working out?"

"Great. But, we need more. You better get busy."

"I'm training Logan to be my assistant. He's a natural."

"Mother did a great job of decorating the store with a combination of my contemporary ideas and her antiques."

Ed took a final sip of his coffee. "Yes, it's coming together beautifully. Better be going. See you for dinner tonight?"

"Absolutely, Dad."

Ed took a deep breath as he continued his walk on Willoughby Lane with his sartorially resplendent companion trotting by his side. "Ah, yes, Alva," he said, "peace and tranquility and happiness and harmony in your new family. At least for now."

***

Meanwhile, five thousand miles from Willoughby, GA, three generations of Withrow/Lawrence women waited for their tour guide in the lobby of a hotel in Perugina, Italy.

"I can't believe we're actually here," Kayla said. "Maybe Aunt Janie can come with us next time."

"Janelle was generous to pay for our trip," Virginia said.

Kayla pointed to Lake Cuomo on a map she and her grandmother were studying. "Next year we could rent a villa and bring Dad and Gramps."

Ali looked up from her phone. "Dad and I won't be able to leave Kitchen Bliss at the same time. Not for a while anyway."

"You've been quiet this morning, Alicia. Penny for your thoughts?" Virginia asked.

"I'm thinking about my reaction when Janelle showed me the itinerary. She wanted to make sure we arrived in time for the Eurochocolate Festival."

"She knows how much you love chocolate, dear," Virginia said.

"You might get sick of it, Mom. Look at the brochure," Kayla said.

Ali started reading the description of the largest celebration in Europe. A multitude of chocolate would be available including chocolate bars, chocolate liquor, and chocolate kebabs. In addition, chocolate sculptures, cakes, and fountains would surround the town. Chocolate Heaven!

Ali put the brochure aside and returned to her phone. She began texting.

Remember when I cried and hollered when you left for kindergarten? I watched the clock until it was time to meet you at the bus stop. I have that same feeling today. I miss you. See you soon. Love, your Li'l Sis.

The End

About the Author

Sue Horner lives in Roswell, GA, with her husband Roland Steinwart. She has a B.A. in American studies from California State University, Los Angeles. She is a member of the Atlanta Writers Club. Visit her website at: www.suehornerauthor.com or contact her at: suehorner@bellsouth.net.

95807491R00213

Made in the USA
Middletown, DE
27 October 2018